# BROM

# LOST GODS

HarperCollins
PUBLISHERS
*Since 1817*

LOST GODS. Copyright © 2016 by Gerald Brom. All rights reserved. Printed in the United States of America. No part of this book may be used or reproduced in any manner whatsoever without written permission except in the case of brief quotations embodied in critical articles and reviews. For information address HarperCollins Publishers, 195 Broadway, New York, NY 10007.

HarperCollins books may be purchased for educational, business, or sales promotional use. For information please e-mail the Special Markets Department at SPsales@harpercollins.com.

A hardcover edition of this book was published in 2016 by Harper Voyager, an imprint of HarperCollins Publishers.

FIRST HARPER VOYAGER PAPERBACK EDITION PUBLISHED 2017.

Harper Voyager and design is a trademark of HarperCollins Publishers L.L.C.

*Designed by Paula Russell Szafranski*

*All artwork copyright © 2016 by Brom*

The Library of Congress has catalogued a previous edition as follows:

Names: Brom, 1965–, author.
Title: Lost gods / Brom.
Description: First edition. | New York, NY : Harper Voyager, an Imprint of HarperCollins Publishers, [2016]
Identifiers: LCCN 2016018399| ISBN 9780062095688 (hardback) | ISBN 9780062095701 (ebook) | ISBN 9780062564894 (audio)
Subjects: | BISAC: FICTION / Occult & Supernatural. | FICTION / Fantasy / Contemporary. | GSAFD: Occult fiction. | Fantasy fiction.
Classification: LCC PS3602.R6426 L67 2016 | DDC 813/.6—dc23 LC record available at https://lccn.loc.gov/2016018399

ISBN 978-0-06-209569-5 (pbk.)

17 18 19 20 21   OV/LSC   10 9 8 7 6 5 4 3 2 1

# LOST GODS

# PROLOGUE

## MORAN ISLAND, SOUTH CAROLINA, AUGUST 1976

The rabbit pushed beneath the iron fence and into a small cemetery. It burrowed through the tangled vines and briars growing up between the cracked and fallen stones, found a patch of tall weeds, and began to nibble on the leaves.

A boy, more shadow than not, slipped silently up and took a seat on a gravestone next to the rabbit. The boy's name was Joshua, and if happened upon at just the right time of day, in just the right light, one could see he was very young, perhaps six or seven years of age, a bit thin, barefoot, and that his shirt and pants were threadbare.

"How you do, Mr. Rabbit?"

The rabbit's ears twitched.

"Good to see you again. Them weeds any good?"

Joshua looked off down the hill, through the cluster of massive oaks toward the marsh, caught the sparkle of water. "Tide must be coming in. Sure would like to take me a walk down thataway. Give about anything to feel the pluff mud between my toes just one more time." He watched the strands of Spanish moss flutter in the warm breeze as the last rays of the long summer day lit up the clouds. "That's pretty. Mighty pretty."

The rabbit looked up, nose twitching.

The boy smiled, then his face became sad. He shook his head. "Sometimes you can forget, y'know. Just for a second. That you're dead. A pretty day like today will do that." His voice turned sullen. "After all these years you'd think I wouldn't fall for it. But I get to watching the clouds, listening to them birds, and I think I can just hop up and head on home . . . see Mama . . . see my big brother." He was silent a long moment, staring at the back of his hands, at his skin, once as dark as the rich soil, now pale and wispy. "Only I can't ever leave these broken old stones." He slapped the palm of his hand against the stone; it made no sound. "But you wanna know what the worst of it is? It's the being alone."

Joshua reached for the rabbit, his hand hovering just above the animal's back. He knew he couldn't touch the living, but that fur, it looked so soft, warm, comforting. His hand passed through the animal and the rabbit kept eating without so much as a twitch.

The boy's lower lip began to tremble, followed a moment later by the sting of tears. He wiped at his eyes. "Might as well stop that, now. Crying ain't gonna help nothing. Seems I'd have figured that out by now as well."

The rabbit hopped closer to the boy, began nibbling on a large dandelion. Joshua managed a smile. "I appreciate you coming to see me, Mr. Rabbit. A spot of company is right nice."

A low moan came from somewhere off in the thicket of trees. The insects fell quiet and both the boy and the rabbit froze, their eyes wide, peering into the deep shadows. It came again, closer. The sound of pain, like a small animal caught in a snare. The rabbit stood up on its hind legs, its nose twitching.

"*Settle on down,*" the boy whispered. "*You be okay. They can't get'cha in here.*"

A figure rose up out of the tall grass. It stood just on the other side of the fence works—black smoke in the shape of a child, dissipating and solidifying. Its yellow eyes sputtered like drowning fireflies.

Joshua started to duck out of sight round the stone, to cover his eyes and ears the way he always did when *they* came around, but he saw the rabbit quivering, looking ready to bolt.

"*It's all right,*" he whispered, pushing the thought, putting all his will behind it. Sometimes, some rare times, if you tried hard enough, he knew the dead could connect with the living. "*Stay put and you'll be okay.*"

Another of *them* appeared, its pinprick eyes fixed on the rabbit.

The rabbit's breathing sped up.

There were more of *them* in the trees, made the woods look as though they were full of fireflies, but Joshua knew better. He knew what they were, what they wanted.

It spoke, the one closest to the fence. Its voice soft and sweet, almost musical. "Come play with us, Joshua. Come on out and pl-aay."

Joshua tried not to look at them, tried not to hear them. He focused on the rabbit, trying to send it soothing thoughts.

The smaller one bent down peering at the rabbit. A swirling pool of blackness formed beneath its flickering eyes, widening, and a howling wind could be heard as though from far down in the earth. The sound came closer, climbing upward, slowly turning into a hiss.

The rabbit's haunches twitched, its back legs jacked, ready to run.

"No, bunny," Joshua said, and dropped on top of it, wrapping himself around the rabbit.

The hiss turned into a shrill whistle, closer and closer, then became a scream, then many screams, the sound of children in agony. The screams burst from the thing's mouth along with a hot blast of air.

The rabbit bolted, Joshua's shadowy body doing nothing to hold it back. *"No!"* Joshua cried, as it sprang away through the briars, darting and dashing. It looked certain to escape, but Joshua knew better. The rabbit shot out the far side of the little cemetery and the moment it left the fence the smaller shape was there. It snagged the rabbit, held the thrashing animal up by its ears.

"If you come out and play, Joshua," the small shape taunted, "we'll let your bunny go. C'mon, there's lots of other little boys and girls to play with."

Joshua backed up against the gravestone, pulled his legs tight to his chest, pressed his face into his knees.

"Joshua," the larger shape called, "we know a secret. Wanna know?"

Joshua tried not to listen.

"Chet's coming home soon. You know who Chet is, don't you?"

Joshua knew.

"Chet's a daddy now," the shape said. "The waiting's over. He'll be here soon and we can't wait to peel his skin off. If you come on out, we'll let you help. What d'you say?"

Joshua remained mute.

"Your blood is on their hands." The shape's voice turned sharp, nasty. "Y'know they owe you. Owe all of us. Join us. You can help send him to the burning place. Drag him down into the ground and make him dance for the Burning Man."

Joshua shook his head, digging his fingers into his arms.

The smaller shape took a step closer to the fence, as close as it could without touching the iron. It opened its mouth and once again Joshua could hear that distant wind, the tormented cries of the children, far, far away. The shape's head fell back and the swirling hole widened. It held the rabbit over the opening.

Joshua bit his lip, clasping his hands over his ears.

The rabbit kicked and clawed, frantic, then began to scream. Joshua didn't understand what he was hearing at first, didn't even know a rabbit could scream. It sounded almost human. The shape dropped the rabbit into the gaping hole, its scream falling away, falling and falling as though to the center of the earth. The hole swirled shut, leaving them in silence. Not a single insect or frog could be heard.

The two shapes just stood there staring at Joshua with those sputtering eyes. Finally, after an agonizing space, the smaller one nudged the larger. "This ain't no fun. Let's go." The two shapes started away, heading up the hill toward the big house. "We're gonna go wait for Chet," the larger one called back. "Last chance to come along."

Joshua waited until they were out of sight, then crawled over to the fence looking for the rabbit. It lay crumpled in the grass, its eyes frozen and budging from their sockets, its lips peeled back to show all its teeth.

Joshua collapsed to his knees, put his face in his hands, and began to sob.

# PART ONE

## The Death of Chet Moran

# CHAPTER 1

Chet Moran clicked off his headlights and backed into Judge Wilson's winding driveway, just far enough that his Ford Pinto wouldn't be visible from the road. He wanted to be facing out, toward the street, ready for a quick getaway should things come to that.

He shut off the engine, got out and pushed the door quietly shut, then stood a moment in the predawn darkness, staring at the Pinto. "What a piece of shit," he said, yet he was smiling because he'd done well in the trade. Dan had really wanted his Mustang, enough to pay top dollar. Still, Chet was going to miss that car, a '65 fastback with a 302 that he'd spent the last five years restoring from scrap. But the car, like so much, was in the past now. He dug into his pocket and pulled out a ring, a thin gold wedding band. There was no diamond, but it *was* real gold. Chet flipped a clump of auburn hair from his eyes—eyes so gray and pale as to almost be silver—and looked up the long drive toward the Judge's house, hoping the ring would be enough to prove to Trish he was a changed man.

He stretched and rubbed the back of his neck, trying to work the tension from his wiry frame, trying to work up enough courage to walk up that drive. At twenty-four he'd just finished seven months in county jail for possession with intent to distribute. Trish had not visited him once.

He started up the drive, stopped, started again, stopped again, then

9

let out a long sigh. He'd received the letter from Trish about three weeks into his sentence. It was short and to the point: "Dear Chet, I'm pregnant. I'm going to have the baby. You're relieved of all responsibilities. I will always love you, but I'm all out of tries. I wish you the very best with your life. Love, Trish." He'd kept that note tucked in his pocket, reading and rereading it, but was still unsure just what she'd meant by "relieved of all responsibilities." He'd written her back at least a dozen times but hadn't received a single letter in reply.

At first he'd been angry; after all, it was his child too. But seven months gives a man plenty of time to think things over, to see things from more than one angle. How many times had he fucked up? *Too many.* That wasn't the kind of man a woman in a family way was looking for. He was going to have a child, a little boy or girl. It was a mean world out there and sitting in that cell, night after night, day after day, thinking about his child growing up without a daddy had eaten at him—to his very core. He'd left jail a different man and if selling his beloved Mustang didn't prove that, the fact that he was here, about to walk up this drive, did.

Chet sucked in a deep breath of the crisp morning air and as the first trace of dawn warmed the sky, he once more headed up the drive, the damp pine needles muffling his long stride. A sprawling brick ranch materialized out of the gloom ahead, a few bicentennial stringers still hanging along eaves. Chet slipped up to the garage and around the side, coming to a chest-high chain-link fence. A low growl greeted him.

"*Easy, Rufus,*" Chet whispered, crouching to let the old basset hound sniff his hand through the fence. The hound gave him a doleful look and wagged its tale. Chet flipped the latch and let himself into the backyard. He squatted, patting the dog and rubbing its saggy jowls. "Heard tell the Judge issued a restraining order against me. You heard anything about that?"

Rufus's eyes seemed to say, "*Nope, not me, not a thing.*"

"I guess it's pretty easy to do when you're a judge. Huh?" Chet stood up and moved on, skirting the garbage cans and a big grill, stepping through Mrs. Wilson's flower beds, careful not to trample her prize geraniums. He crept past the back porch, making his way to a set of windows at the far end of the house.

He peeked in through the screen. The window was open, the sheers fluttering in the light breeze. He made out the curve of a woman in the glow of the night-light. She lay on her side, her back to him. His pulse quickened and he almost turned around and left, but he heard his grandmother's voice, more of a feeling than any actual words, telling him to stay. This didn't surprise him, he often heard her, even though she lived hundreds of miles away. It had been his grandmother's presence comforting him on so many of those interminable nights in jail, when he felt the walls falling in on him.

"*Trish,*" he whispered.

She stirred, rolled over, tugging the cotton sheet tighter around her. It was only upon seeing her face that he truly realized just how much he'd missed her—her goofy smile, her quirky laugh—and he found himself fighting back tears.

"*Trish,*" he whispered, a little louder.

Her brow tightened and her bright green eyes half opened.

"*Trish.*"

She lifted her head, pushing long, curly strands of hair from her face. Her eyes grew wide and she gasped. She was going to scream, Chet knew it, but the fear on her face was quickly replaced by confusion and then, there, a smile. And for one moment, Chet felt all was going to go his way. Slowly, her smile faded.

"*Chet?*" She sat up, sliding over to the window. "Oh shit. What the *hell* are you doing here?"

Chet felt as though he'd been slugged in the chest.

She glanced back toward the door of her room, horrified. "If Daddy finds out you're here he's going to shoot you."

Chet shrugged.

"No, he will *really* shoot you. I don't have to tell you that." She didn't, he knew well enough that the Judge would shoot him, because Judge Wilson had looked Chet in the eye and told him that himself, told him that if he ever came near his daughter again, Chet would end up at the bottom of the Sipsey Swamp. And Chet knew the Judge would get away with it too, because the Judge had lots of friends around Walker County and could get away with just about any damn thing he pleased.

"Are you hearing me?" Trish asked, then noticed him staring at the swell of her belly beneath her nightshirt.

"It's real," Chet said.

She let out a sigh, set her hand on her swollen belly, and gave him a sad sort of smile. "It's real all right. One more month to go."

Chet had rehearsed what he wanted to say next a hundred, maybe a thousand times, but here, now, all his artful words were lost. "Trish," he blurted out. "I want you to leave with me." He felt sure she was going to laugh in his face, but she didn't. Instead a deep and profound sadness seeped into her eyes.

"Chet . . . I *can't*."

"You *can*. My car is sitting at the end of the drive. I've got things all worked out. I—"

"Chet."

"Trish, just listen—"

"No, Chet, *you* listen." The edge in her voice cut him off. "I can't *count* on you. No matter how much I want to, I *can't*."

He started to reply.

"Stop, Chet. Just stop. Do you really expect me to run off to Timbuktu and raise a child with a man who makes his living selling weed? Whose only ambition in life is fixing up his old car? Think about that, Chet."

"I have. A lot." He pulled out the crumpled letter, the one she'd sent him in jail. "Every day."

She stared at the letter.

"I'm a changed man."

She slowly shook her head. "I've heard that before."

He pulled out the ring.

Her mouth opened, but she didn't utter a sound.

"I sold my car."

Her eyes locked on his. "Your *car*? You *sold* the Mustang? But Chet, that car was everything to you."

"I said I'm a changed man. I spent every day since getting your letter thinking on who I want to be . . . on what I want. I want to be with *you* . . . and I want to be with my child. And I am willing to do *whatever* it takes to make that happen."

He saw it in her eyes, how badly she wanted to believe him.

"I've got two thousand dollars cash left over from the car. That's a good start, Trish. We can head to the coast. You've always said you wanted to see the ocean. Right? I'll get a job, a *real* job. I promise you that. I hear there's work to be had out on the trawlers, plenty of it. We can stay with my grandmother until we get on our feet."

Her eyes were distant now, as though in a dream. Her lips tightened and he saw she was trying not to cry.

"I'm not saying things are going to be perfect, but it's gotta be better than you staying here with your daddy. Y'know better than anyone that if you don't get away from that man, he'll be telling you what to do your whole life. He'll suffocate you. Trish—"

"He's making me put our baby up for adoption," she said, unable to meet his eyes.

"What?"

"Mama, she's going along with it. They even got Pastor Thomas in on it. They've already made arrangements. Some nice couple down in Tuscaloosa."

"*Adoption?*" Chet couldn't believe what he was hearing. "Is . . . is that what *you* want?"

Her eyes flared, then appeared hurt. "No it *is not*." She shook her head. "That's not what I want at all." She cradled her belly. "It's *my* baby." She wiped at her eyes. "My . . . child."

Chet pried the screen out, setting it aside, reached through the window, and squeezed Trish's shoulder. She grabbed his hand, clutching it with surprising force, and stared intensely into his eyes. "Chet. Chet, you look at me."

He did.

"Swear to me. Swear to me and Jesus Christ, that if I take that ring . . . if I agree to run off with you . . . that from this day on, you're going to fly right. You're going be a man, a father. That you're going to act like one."

He held her eyes and stated solemnly, "Trish, I love you and I swear I'll do everything I can, never to let you down again."

"If you fuck this up . . ." Her grip tightened. "I swear to God you won't have to worry about my daddy shooting you . . . because I'll do it."

He grinned so hard tears welled up in his eyes. "I won't fuck this up, baby-doll."

She stared at him another long minute before releasing his hand. "Be right back." She slid off the bed, crept to the closet, quietly dug out a bag, and began shoveling in clothes and underwear. She stepped into a gypsy skirt, pulled it up under her long T-shirt, plucked up some sandals, and headed for the window. She handed him her bag and he helped her climb down.

"We need to hurry," Trish, said. "Daddy's going fishing this morning."

"Wait," Chet said, and dropped to one knee, holding his hand out to her. "Need to do this proper." She bit her lip and placed her hand in his.

He held up the ring and she beamed at him.

"Trish, will you marry me?"

She nodded and he slid the ring on her finger, then stood up and kissed her. She hugged him, hugged him so tight he feared they might hurt the baby. Then she let go, stepped back, and looked at him. "Just remember what I said about shooting you." But she was smiling, the sweetest smile he'd ever seen.

Something pushed between them. Rufus stood, looking up, tail wagging. Chet gave the dog a pat and picked up Trish's bag. They started around the porch when a light came on inside the house. They ducked down as a big man walked through the living room in a bathrobe. It was the Judge. He disappeared into the kitchen. Chet let out a breath and they snuck around to the gate.

Trish gave Rufus a pat. "You be a good boy."

Rufus wagged his tail and gave her a look that said, "*I'm always a good boy.*"

They closed the gate and hurried down the drive toward the car, Chet watching her the whole way, charmed by the way she held her belly.

"What?" she asked.

He grinned. "You're beautiful."

She put a hand up in front of her face. "Stop looking at me. Christ, I'm as big as a blimp and don't have on a lick of makeup."

"You're a beautiful blimp."

She laughed out loud, clamped a hand over her mouth, then grabbed his hand and squeezed it. He squeezed back.

"And you gotta nice waddle," he added.

She shook her head. "Why, you're just on a roll, ain't you, honey?"

He laughed.

She spotted the car and stopped. "You really *did* sell the Mustang."

"Yeah," he said, dismally. "I really *did*."

"Well, I'm glad you did. But damn, Chet. You think you could have found an uglier car?"

He frowned and she laughed and it was music to his ears.

They got to the car and he opened her door.

She clasped his hand and pressed it to her belly. "Feel that?"

He didn't feel anything, then there, a bump, then another. "Oh, my gosh," he gasped.

She beamed at him. "Someone's glad their daddy's here."

A vehicle slowed on the road. Chet turned in time to see a truck pull into the Judge's drive, trapping them in its headlights.

"Shit," Chet said.

The truck stopped quick, sending a handful of fishing rods rattling about in the bed. Chet made out two men: Larry Wagner, his former high school PE coach, and Tom Wilson, the Judge's brother. Both men were staring at them.

Tom cut the engine and hopped out, bumping the cap off his bald head in the process. He was a big man like the Judge, thick through the gut, wearing a flannel jacket. "Trish?"

"We need to go," Trish said to Chet.

"Is that Chet?" Tom called. "Fuck, it is. Boy, you were *told* to stay away from her."

Coach got out, reached into the bed, and returned with a tire jack. He cocked back his head and smirked, like he was already reading his name in the paper—all about how he'd saved the Judge's daughter from being kidnapped by a deranged ex-con. "Go on, have yourself a seat, son. Cause you ain't going nowhere but back to jail." There was no mistaking the glee in the man's voice and Chet understood this wasn't just about the Judge's daughter, but about some unfinished business between them. Back in high school, Coach had caught Chet sharing a joint with three other boys in the bathroom. He'd lined them up, giving them each four licks with his notorious two-handed paddle—the one he'd named *Biter*—and hit them hard enough to lift their feet off the ground. When it came Chet's turn, Chet, who was all of fifteen at the time, told him to just go ahead and suspend him, because he wasn't going to take a lick from a man and not give one back. When Coach tried to hit him anyway, Chet slugged him, breaking the man's nose. Chet ran off from school that day and never came back.

Chet heard the garage door opening back at the house.

"What's going on?" someone called. It was the Judge.

Trish slid in the car. "Com'on, Chet. *Let's go!*" Chet hopped in and Tom started toward them at a run. Trish locked the door just as he grabbed hold of the handle. Chet jammed the key into the ignition and started the engine.

"*Trish!*" Tom yelled, yanking on the handle. "*Come out of there!*"

Chet hit the gas and the little car leapt forward with Tom chasing after them, shouting.

Tall pine trees lined the narrow drive and Chet wasn't sure if he could get past the truck without hitting one or not, but he was going to try. Coach, seeing this, stepped over, blocking their way, clutching the tire iron like he meant business.

Chet didn't slow down, part of him actually hoping to hit the man, wanting nothing more at that moment than to knock that smirk off that man's face for good.

"*Watch out!*" Trish cried.

There came a crack as the tire iron hit the windshield, then a thud.

Trish screamed, but Chet didn't slow, slicing past the truck, knocking off his side mirror.

Chet glanced in his rearview, saw no sign of Coach. "Fuck! Did I hit him?"

Trish was looking back. "I don't know. I don't think so."

Chet pulled out onto the highway, tires screeching, floored it, and the little Pinto shot down the road.

## CHAPTER 2

## MORAN ISLAND, SOUTH CAROLINA

A sandy one-lane road led them to a wooden, weather-beaten bridge. Chet stopped the station wagon, amazed the clunker had made it. Shortly after leaving Jasper they'd ditched the Pinto, swapping it out for an old station wagon he'd spotted behind a church. Chet had jammed a screwdriver into the ignition to get it started, and a minute later they were on their way, driving almost nonstop across Georgia and South Carolina, all the way to the coast. He'd thought for sure the Judge would've had the whole state out looking for them, but they'd stuck to the back roads and the few cops they'd passed must not have been on the lookout for an old wagon. Finally, after several wrong turns and dead ends, they found themselves staring at this bridge.

Chet allowed himself a moment to just sit and feel the late afternoon sun pour through the windshield, warming his face. He let the smell of the pluff mud take him back to his childhood as he watched the Spanish moss and marsh grass swaying in the breeze.

"We're here?" Trish asked.

Chet couldn't see the house, not through all the trees, but he knew it was the right place. His grandmother's voice called to him like a beacon, almost a song, growing steadily stronger as the distance narrowed. He nodded. "Yeah, Moran Island." He hadn't remembered it being so far from the highway, so far from everything, really. The last houses they'd passed were a few tin-roofed shanties a couple of miles back.

"I think you're right," Trish said.

"How's that?"

"No one's gonna find us way out here."

"They shouldn't. No one knows about this place, not back in Alabama, not anymore."

Trish pointed to three small scarecrows tied to the bridge post. "You wanna tell me what those are?" They were made of sticks, bones, and Spanish moss, with chicken claws tied to them with wire. A small skull sat atop one, possibly that of a possum or cat. A reddish oily substance stained the dirt and wood across both ends of the bridge.

"Like I said, she's a witch."

"You mean she's *really* a witch?"

Chet shrugged. "According to my aunt Abigail. That's why she never let me come out here. Of course she never let me play Zeppelin or the Stones either. Wouldn't put up with that *devil* music, not in her house." Chet smirked. "Crazy seems to run on all sides of my family."

"When was the last time you saw her then?"

"My grandma?"

"Yeah."

"We buried my mother here when she died, I think I was seven. That was the only time I got to meet my grandma. But I'll say this, she made a heck of an impression. So did this place. Just got into my bones, y'know. Always wanted to come back . . . wanted to stay with her. But my great-aunt, my grandfather's sister, she got custody." Chet shook his head. "I actually ran away once . . . trying to get back here."

"What?"

"Yeah, I was only eight or nine. It was before we moved to Jasper, but even back then I wanted to get away from all my aunt's Jesus preaching." Chet let out a small laugh. "Made it twenty miles on my little Schwinn before a trooper brought me back."

"So you haven't seen her since you were seven?"

"No."

"Well when was the last time you talked to her?"

Chet shrugged.

"Chet, she *does* know we're coming?"

*She knows,* he thought. *I can feel it.* But he didn't say that, because there wasn't any way to explain that even though he'd not received a single letter or phone call from his grandmother, he still felt like she'd been with him for all these years. "I think so."

"You think so?"

"It'll be all right. You'll see."

She looked at the twisted totems again. "Ah, Chet . . . I don't know."

He smiled and pulled slowly onto the narrow bridge. A wide, lazy creek flowed a good twenty feet below. Trish tightened her seat belt and winced, cupping her hand. She'd cut her palm climbing over some old barbed wire when they were stealing the wagon, leaving a nasty gash.

"We need to get that cleaned up as soon as we can," Chet said. "You'll get tetanus or something."

"Just get me across this bridge alive, then we can worry about it."

He continued forward and the whole structure creaked and shuttered, the boards popping as they crossed. They made it over and continued through the woods along the winding two-rut sandy road, passed the old rice fields and up a gentle sloping hill. Chet slowed down when they came into a clearing. Up ahead, at the top of the hill, a two-story antebellum sat among a grove of giant oaks. The house needed paint, but other than that it appeared exactly how he'd remembered it, the way it looked when his dreams took him here.

"Hey," Trish said, pointing across the field. "Is that where your mother's buried?"

Chet spotted several neglected gravestones sticking up from of the tall grass. "Yeah, that's it. I believe all my family's buried there. All the way back to when they first settled here. Late seventeen hundreds sometime." Movement caught his eye—flittering shadows within the dark woods behind the cemetery. "*Chet.*" A whisper on the wind. A sense of vertigo hit him, then dread, like a lead weight in his stomach. Chet stopped the car.

"What's wrong?" Trish touched his arm, when she did, the dread faded. "Baby, you okay?"

"Yeah . . . I'm fine. Thought I saw a ghost. That's all."

"You look like you saw a ghost." She grinned, then frowned. "You *are* kidding, right?"

Chet shrugged. "Maybe. From what I hear, there's supposed to be plenty of spooks haunting this old place."

She scanned the cemetery. "Well, wouldn't that be something? Y'know, to see a real-life ghost."

"That would be something." Chet let off the brake and headed toward the big house.

They parked in the circular drive, got out. The grounds were overgrown, but the path to the big porch had recently been trimmed back. They were about to head up the steps when Trish halted. "Look, what's that all about?" She pointed to several strings of colorful tattered yarn twisting together, weaving through the porch posts and across the steps. Tiny silver bells dangled here and there along the string. The yarn disappeared around each side of the house. "That's kinda odd."

Chet shrugged. "You're gonna find plenty of odd around here."

They stepped over the string and started up the steps. The door opened. Chet made out a thin figure behind the screen door.

"Hello, Chet," came a soft familiar voice.

"Grandma?"

She pushed the screen open and stepped out onto the porch. She looked just as he'd remembered her: an elegant woman with flowing snow-white hair cascading down her shoulders and back. She clutched a simple black cane and wore a plain white cotton dress, no jewelry or makeup, her skin, lips, and eyes all of the same paleness. A dime-size circular scar stood out prominently on her right temple. Chet remembered staring at it as a child. She'd told him then that it was a bullet hole, sounding quite proud of it. She set her silvery eyes on him, kindly eyes with a hint of sadness. Chet felt all of six years old again, wanting nothing more than to be smothered in her arms. And as though reading him, she opened her arms. "Chet, welcome home."

He embraced her and a wave of warmth coursed through him. Never had he felt so light, not even as a child. *Why,* he wondered, *why did I wait so long?*

She released him, looked past him to Trish.

"Grandma, this is Trish."

Trish stepped forward, extended her hand. "Hi, Mrs. Moran. It's good to meet you."

"Please, child, call me Lamia." Her voice still held a slight accent. Chet recalled she was originally from somewhere in Eastern Europe—Romania or Hungary maybe. Lamia's eyes fell to Trish's pregnant belly; her face lit up. "So, it seems I'll live to be a great-grandmother after all. Come here, child," she said, taking Trish's hand, pulling her forward and embracing her.

Lamia released Trish, stepped back, looking them both over. "It does my old heart such good to have you two here. Please, come inside."

She led them in and down the long central hallway, her cane thumping along with each swing of her lame leg. Despite the limp, she still held herself tall and straight, as though in defiance of her impairment. Chet glanced in each room as they passed, the rooms were mostly barren, only the occasional chair or end table, the old wall paper peeling in places, some of the plaster crumbling, laying in heaps on the floor.

They came to a bathroom and Trish stopped.

"Mrs. Moran . . ."

"Please, girl, it's Lamia."

"Lamia," Trish said, urgently. "May I?"

"Ah, of course."

Trish ducked inside.

Lamia and Chet strolled a little farther down the hall. Chet felt her eyes on him, studying him. He had so many questions, things he'd wanted to ask her for years, but here, in her presence, he found himself all but unable to speak.

"Go on," she said. "Ask."

"Huh?"

"I know you have questions."

*Yeah,* he thought, plenty, about his mother, his father, but what he most wanted to know about was the voice, her voice, the one he'd heard, or felt, over all these years. Had that been real? He just didn't know how to ask such a thing.

"You're wondering how I spoke to you." It wasn't a question.

He met her eyes. "It was *real* then . . . is real? You reaching out to me. Not just something in my head?"

"Part of me has always been with you, Chet. In your heart . . . in your blood."

"But it was more than that."

"When I say part of me has always been with you, I mean that in its true sense. My blood, our blood, it's rare and special. It binds us. It's our connection."

He wasn't sure what she was saying. "That's kinda strange, isn't it?"

She smiled at him. "Some might think it a gift. What do you think?"

"I think there were times, bad times, that if you hadn't been there, y'know, in your way. I'm not sure if I would've made it."

She smiled. "It does my heart such good to hear that." Then her smile faltered. "I only wish I could've reached your mother. Poor Cynthia. She needed me too. But they took her away from me. Chet, I want you to know I reached out for her relentlessly, but she never seemed to hear me . . . or maybe didn't want to. All I know is this gift we have, sometimes, it can let in other voices—dark voices. I think your mother heard them. I think they drove her to madness . . . to take her own life." Her voice dropped. "I felt helpless."

He saw tears sparkling in her silver eyes.

"I'm so sorry, Chet . . . sorry that I couldn't do more."

Chet wanted to say something to comfort her, but couldn't find the right words.

Trish came out of the bathroom looking relieved. Saw their faces. "Oh, sorry. Didn't mean to interrupt. Maybe I should step outside for a bit?"

"Nonsense," Lamia said, dabbing at her eyes. "I'm just being a sentimental old woman. Tell me, Trish. Would you be up for a bite to eat?"

"Oh, yes, ma'am." Trish answered.

They followed Lamia into the kitchen; it smelled of fresh baked bread. She led them to a small table set in a nook, the marsh visible from the tall bay window. The table was set for three: plates, glasses, silverware. In the center, several plump red tomatoes sat on a board next to a pitcher of lemonade and a basket covered with a cotton towel.

"You *were* expecting us?" Trish asked.

"I was."

Trish gave Chet a look.

Lamia folded back the towel, revealing a home-cooked loaf of bread. She gestured for them to sit. She picked up the pitcher of lemonade. "Try this, let me know what you think." She poured them each a glass.

Chet took a deep swig. "Wow, that's *really* good." He drained the glass.

Lamia refilled his glass, beaming. "Those lemons were grown in my atrium. Finest lemons you'll find on this coast." She sliced the bread, then the tomatoes, making them each a sandwich. "Now, try this."

They both took a bite. "Oh, yum!" Trish said and Chet's face lit up. The tomatoes were so tender they melted in his mouth, the juice running down his chin.

Lamia laughed, pulled a napkin from a holder, and handed it to Chet. "Now, tell me, have you ever tasted tomatoes so sweet?"

"No, ma'am," Chet said, wiping his face. He finished the sandwich and asked for another. Lamia talked while they ate, told them all about her garden.

When Chet finished eating, Lamia placed a hand on top of each of theirs. "It's so very nice to have someone to share a meal with." She paused. "So maybe you two will stay awhile. Yes? Make a lonely old woman happy."

Chet glanced at Trish, took a deep breath. "We were hoping you'd feel that way, because we really need a place to stay. Just for a while. Until I can get a job and get going. But I have to tell you something up front . . ."

"You're in trouble. This I already know."

"Yes, ma'am. But . . ."

"How bad?"

"I'm not sure." He told her about them running away from the Judge, didn't plan to tell her everything, but once he started it all spilled out: about Trish and him, about some of the bad things he'd done, about his jail time, finally about the two of them deciding to elope. He lowered his eyes. "I stole that car. Well, I'd like to think I traded my Pinto for it—left them my keys and a nice note. But I don't think the law's gonna see it that way. But that's not the worst of it . . . when we were trying to get away this morning—" He wasn't sure how to say it. "I think I might of hit a man."

Lamia nodded. "I'm very sorry."

"Over the years," Chet said, "I've dreamed of Moran Island. You, this place, it's in my bones somehow. Aunt Abigail made a point of burying my past, burying any connection to South Carolina. She only spoke of Moran Island in hushed whispers, so I'm pretty sure no one back in Alabama has a clue about you, about this place. That's why coming here seemed a good idea. But, me hitting that guy . . . I think that changes things. Trish's daddy, he's a judge, a real bigwig around Jasper with plenty of connections. I can't see him just letting this thing go. What I'm trying to say is if he finds us here, it might spell trouble for you too. So, I, we, understand if . . . I mean—"

Lamia squeezed his hand. "Chet, do you remember what I said to you all those years ago?"

Chet started to shake his head, then it came to him as clear as if it had happened yesterday. He'd snuck off from his aunt at his mother's funeral, hid behind the pump house, crying. Lamia found him and wiped away his tears. She led him down to the pond and they'd both gotten muddy catching frogs—and how they'd laughed about it, like a couple of imps. And something more—blood, yes, there was blood. He'd forgotten that part. "Our blood is the same," she'd said, taking a thorn, pricking her finger. She dabbed the blood on the back of his hand, made two spots. And what had she said? "Come home to me. Come home to your blood." He realized he was speaking out loud.

"There's your answer," Lamia said. "We're blood. This is your home and I'm not afraid of a little trouble. And . . . it would make an old woman very happy to have some family around."

Chet felt a wave of relief, glanced at Trish, could see she did too.

"Okay?" Lamia asked.

"Okay," Chet agreed.

"Good, then. It's settled," Lamia stated with finality. She smiled. "Now, anyone for more lemonade?"

"I got it," Trish said, starting to pick up the pitcher. She winced and let go.

Lamia narrowed her eyes. "Is it the baby?"

"Oh, no," Trish said. "It's just my hand." She showed Lamia the cut. "It's not as bad as it looks. I just need to clean it. You don't happen to have some iodine, do you?"

Lamia let out a huff. "You don't want to use that poison. Chet, go there, in the kitchen, the black box atop the icebox. Bring it to me."

Chet hopped up, found the box: it was about the size of a shoe box and made of charred wood. He brought it back and placed it on the table in front of them.

Lamia opened the chest, revealing an array of glass bottles, small tins, herbs, and roots rolled in leaves. A small bronze knife with a serpent inlaid on the handle sat strapped inside the lid. The blade looked ancient, the metal pitted and tarnished. She plucked out a bottle and held it up to the light, squinting through the murky green contents. She grunted, put it back, plucked out another, and held it up. "Ah, here." She pulled out the cork with her teeth and dabbed a drop of syrupy black goo onto the tip of her finger.

The smell filled the room and Trish wrinkled her nose.

"That's how you can tell it's working," Lamia proclaimed proudly and went to dab it on the cut.

Trish pulled back. "Wait. What *is* that?"

Lamia glanced at the goo on her finger. "What, *this*? Why it's blood honey, child. Well, it's a lot like blood honey. Only I couldn't find wild boar semen, so I used domesticated stock instead. It still seems to work. Actually, I think it works better." She looked at Trish's horrified face. "Ah, you haven't used blood honey before, have you?"

Trish shook her head.

"So much of the old ways are lost. Well, you'll see. It's a powerful potion. It doesn't taint the blood like those poisons they sell in the medicine stores." Before Trish could protest further, Lamia dabbed the foul-smelling ointment onto her wound.

Trish winced and gave Chet a helpless look.

Lamia placed one of the dried leaves over the ointment, then made a mark on the leaf, a half circle with a line through it. She closed her eyes and spoke several words that Chet thought might be in her old tongue, repeated them several times, almost a chant. She kissed her fingers and made a half-circle symbol in the air above the wound, eliciting yet another uncertain look from Trish. "There," she said, opening her eyes.

Trish stared at her palm. "What was it you said? A spell?"

"Yes. A spell to keep the dark ones away. They can enter the body through open wounds."

"So you really do practice . . . um . . ." Trish stopped.

"Witchcraft?" Lamia suggested.

Trish blushed, nodded.

"Just what has Chet been telling you?" Lamia set accusing eyes on Chet.

Chet put up his hands, smirking. "Oh no, don't look at me that way. Blame Aunt Abigail. She was the one always going on and on about what a wicked witch you are."

Lamia laughed. "And Aunt Abigail, she should know. Yes?"

Trish looked abash. "I didn't mean to insult you."

"Stop, girl. You don't insult me. I am proud to be a healer. Witchery, sorcery, whatever you wish to call it. It is an art, a craft. And one that's quickly becoming lost. But don't let my quirkiness scare you. I'm not a wicked witch, not like that green lady from Oz."

Trish grinned. "Okay, I asked for that." She glanced at her palm. "Hey, that stuff, it tingles." Her brow lightened. "Feels better though."

"Trish, tell me, if you don't mind. How has your pregnancy been?"

"Mostly okay . . . I guess."

"You guess?"

Trish's lips tightened. "Well . . . there's been some light bleeding off and on lately. The doctor didn't seem overly concerned. But he did tell me to let him know if it got any worse."

"Has it?"

"No."

"Bleeding, even late in a pregnancy, is not uncommon," Lamia said. "It could mean many things. Trish, in the old country, my mother, her mother, and her mother before, they were healers, midwives. They've passed down their ways to me. Ways to see your health, the health of the baby. If you're willing, I'd like to try a small spell . . . to check on you and your child."

"A *spell*?" Trish replied cautiously.

"Don't worry. I won't make you drink any bubbling potions. Just need a drop of your blood. Much less than these hospitals take to do their silly tests."

"Well . . . maybe," Trish said, sounding less than sure.

Lamia smiled. "Good." She unwrapped a roll of dried leaves, laid one on her plate, then opened a small tin, sprinkled a bit of gray powder atop the leaf. She picked up the knife. "Your hand."

Trish glanced at Chet.

"Don't look at me," he said.

She let out a sigh and laid her hand in Lamia's.

Lamia touched the tip of the blade to Trish's finger, the slightest jab. A drop of blood pooled and Lamia squeezed it onto the powder, watching intently as the blood soaked in. Nothing much happened that Chet could tell, other than the powder taking on a greenish hue.

Trish glanced up at Lamia. "That's it?"

Lamia held up a finger, studied the powder, she seemed tense. "There."

"What?" Trish asked, peering at the stain. The powder slowly melted away, evaporated, leaving squiggly marks on the leaves. They seemed random at first glance, but on closer inspection, Chet could see that there was a symmetry to the marks, almost like letters—strange foreign letters.

"Wow," Trish said. "What's it mean?" When Lamia's face turned stern, Trish voice became anxious. "Is it something bad?"

Lamia leaned closer, her lips moving as though reading to herself. Then a profound look of relief lit up her face. "Oh, bless the Wyrd. Bless the maiden, mother, and crone. The baby is healthy!"

Chet was struck by Lamia's absolute conviction. Whether any of this was real or not, there was no denying that Lamia believed it heart and soul. Her convictions were contagious; Trish beamed. "Oh, I'm so glad to hear that."

"Yes, yes. A very healthy soul grows in your womb. And there's more," Lamia teased. "If you wish, I can tell you if it's a little boy or little girl hiding in there."

"Oh?"

"Yes."

Trish looked at Chet. "Chet?"

Chet shrugged. "Up to you."

Trish bit her lip and nodded.

"It's a little girl."

"Are you sure?"

"Yes, I'm certain. In all my years I've never been wrong."

Trish let out a squeal. "Oh, my gosh. Oh . . . my . . . good gosh. A little *girl*!" Chet noticed that Trish was no longer looking at his grandmother like she was some sort of kook, but instead with outright admiration.

"Did you hear that, Chet? We're gonna have a little girl."

"Yeah, I caught that part." And Chet had no problem believing it either. Lamia seemed to be gifted in many ways. He wouldn't be surprised if somehow she was already connected with this child.

Lamia wiped her eyes; she was crying.

"Grandma? You okay?"

She nodded, smiled. "I'm just so happy. I've been here . . . alone . . . for so long. And now, to have my family again . . . and soon a little girl to share this joy with. So many blessings, it's a bit overwhelming, that is all."

## CHAPTER 3

Chet knew he was in a dream, yet it did nothing to lessen the horror. He was outside on Lamia's porch in the moonlight—blood upon the planks leading into the house. He could hear Trish crying—a sound of deepest anguish. He followed the trail of blood inside, up the stairs, to a room at the very end of the hall. There came the wail of a child within, as though in great pain. It was his child, his daughter, he knew with certainty. The door was locked. He pounded upon it, demanded it be open, slamming his shoulder against it, again and again. Finally the door burst open and he fell in, fell into darkness, fell and fell, the sound of his wailing child echoing all around him.

Chet awoke gasping. It took him a moment to remember where he was. He wiped the sweat from his eyes. He'd been plagued by nightmares ever since his mother had died, but this one had felt so real.

He reached for Trish; she was gone. He sat up, surprised to find the day all but over. He'd only meant to rest for a few minutes. A gentle breeze swept through the room. He climbed out of bed, went to the window, letting the air cool him. The tide was in and the last remnants of sun glistened off the marsh. Movement caught his eye. Someone—looked to be a boy—stood in the cemetery, a shadow among the shadows. Then he disappeared. Chet kept watching, hoping to see him again, thought he heard a voice, that of a young boy, so very faint. *What did he say?* Chet wondered. His skin prickled. *Run,* he thought. *He'd said, run.*

Chet caught Lamia's hearty laugh coming from below, the sound of it chasing away his unease. He headed downstairs.

Chet found them in the front room sharing a long sofa, the crimson fabric worn and faded. Trish held a glass of lemonade, Lamia a glass of wine. "What've you gals been carrying on about?"

"Your grandma's been telling me stories about her days as a midwife."

"Babies," Chet said. "I should've known." And as they continued discussing the finer points of childbearing, he made himself busy studying the paintings on the wall—most were dark and stained. The one before him was of the house, standing tall atop the hill, the lawn and garden well manicured, tiny figures working the rice fields in the background. Chet noticed an old wooden TV cabinet near the window. He saw it was plugged in, so he pulled the knob. The tiny screen fizzled on—nothing but static. "You watch a lot of TV, Grandma?"

"No, my set doesn't work."

"Yeah, noticed that." It dawned on him he hadn't seen a phone, or car. "Do you have a phone?"

"Yes. But it doesn't work either."

Chet shook his head. "How about a car?"

"Yes."

"Does it work?"

"No."

"Grandma, jeez. How do you get groceries? You're not gonna tell me you walk five miles back up the road."

"Wyrd, no. Why would I do that?"

"How do you get groceries? How do you get anything?"

"Chet, do you not remember my vegetable gardens? You should see all the canned vegetables I've stored. Sometimes I think I must be part squirrel the way I hoard such things. And anything else, I just have Jerome bring out. I pay him to take care of the yard. He's a good worker, just not worth a pinch of salt when it comes to conversation."

Chet peered out the side window, down the hill through the oaks. The moon was coming up full and bright and he could make out the tops of the cemetery stones. Chet searched for the shadowy boy he'd seen earlier. "Grandma, tell me about the ghosts."

She studied him for a moment. "So Chet, you feel them too?"

"I think so."

"He thought he saw one today," Trish put in. "Down by the cemetery when we drove in."

"And you, girl, did you see anything?"

Trish shook her head.

"And you wish to hear about them then as well?"

"I think so."

"There are a few spirits here," Lamia said. "I've seen them, heard them, but more importantly I've felt them. And I'm not alone. The local Gullah folk, they feel them too. Were there totems on the bridge when you arrived?"

"Totems?" Chet asked.

"She means them freaky dolls, Chet. The ones made of straw and bones."

"Oh, yeah," Chet said. "What're those all about?"

"Doesn't seem to matter how many times I have Jerome take those down, the locals just put them right back up."

"Why?"

"They believe the island is full of restless spirits . . . because of the bad deaths that happened here. They believe spirits can't cross running water, so they put up the totems and splash the bridge with blessed oil to keep them trapped on the island."

"The bad deaths," Chet ventured. "You're talking about Grandpa?"

Lamia gave him a long look, sighed. "Chet, why don't you have a seat?"

Chet did, next to Trish.

"What did your aunt Abigail tell you about your grandfather?"

"Not much. A lot of talk of demons, mostly. Said they'd got in his head, made him crazy. I'm really sorry to say, but she hated you. Blamed you for all of it."

Lamia shook her head sadly. "I know."

"I heard different accounts from other folks," Chet continued. "Y'know, before we moved. They said that he was mean and bad. That he killed a bunch of folks. That crazy ran in the family. And that's why mom was the way she was. After mom killed herself, it got to where we couldn't go out without people staring or saying something."

Lamia nodded, her eyes on the floor, distant.

"Is any of it true?" Chet asked. "Was he really such a bad man?"

Lamia cleared her throat. "He could be so kind at times, Chet. But as the years passed, that part of him seemed to slowly die until only the bad was left."

"Was it liquor, then? Or like they say . . . crazy?"

"Maybe it was the liquor . . . part of it anyway. Maybe it was the war, the things he saw, the things he had to do. But for me it was hard to forget that he saved my life. And it was for that I put up with so much for so long. For too long. If I'd known that the violence would eventually spill over onto my children, would lead to such hurt . . . I would've been stronger . . . at least I hope I would." She stopped, her face pained.

"Hey, Grandma," Chet said softly. "You don't need to talk about this if you don't—"

"Here is where your grandfather shot me." She touched the scar on her temple. Chet noticed a slight shake to her hand. "It's not easy to talk about the things that he did, the things that happened. Every night I ask myself what I could've done different. Would anything have changed the outcome? They haunt me . . . the voices of my children."

She took a long sip of her wine. "They were going to burn me."

"What . . . *who*?"

"At the end of the first big war, World War One, I was in a refugee camp in Hungary. I caught a man stealing from me. I accused him to the guard, but they didn't seem to care. Soon he began to tell everyone I was a witch, that he saw me poisoning a child. That child was sick, I'd only been trying to help. But later, when the child died, the camp turned on me. Feeding on each other's fears. I was a foreigner. It wasn't hard to blame me. The guards did nothing as they tied me to a post, piled wood about me, and set it to flame. It was Gavin, your grandfather, that stopped them. His squad was marching by the camp when he heard me scream. He came and kicked out the flames, began to untie me. When the guards tried to stop him, he pulled out his pistol, leveled it at them. Him, this one tall man, staring down several armed guards, his face, his eyes, almost daring them to shoot him. They backed away and he took me from the camp.

"I fell in love and we married. He brought me here, to this island. It seemed a paradise at first. The days of farming rice were long past, but Gavin started up a lumber business. We had children, first two boys, then your mother. Life was good. But the war, it caught up with your grandfather. He began to have nightmares, began to drink, and soon after, his business failed. He seemed unable to keep a job after that. He didn't like people telling him what to do and the jobs always ended with Gavin hurting someone. Then he began to transport liquor for Sid Mullins. This was back during Prohibition. He did other things for Sid as well. He never told me what, but more than once I had to boil the blood from his clothes. People . . . they were afraid of him. The few times we drove into town together you could see it, how careful they were around him, the way you'd act around a dog you know will bite.

"It was soon after my second child that his violence began to turn on me, then the children. He just couldn't control his temper. There was no standing up to him when he got like that. Then . . . then it happened. Soon after your mother was born. He came home one night, his blood up. Something had gone wrong with a shipment of booze. I don't know exactly. He was raving. He started in on our oldest boy, Billy. When I tried to stop him, his mind just left . . ." She fell silent.

Trish and Chet looked at each other, then Trish reached out, put a hand on top of Lamia's.

"I'll never forget that look in his eyes," Lamia said. "He glared at me, at the children as though we were monsters. Called us demons. Screamed it. You could see he believed it. He shot me three times, in the leg, the chest, and here." She touched the scar again. "Then he went after the boys." A tear ran down her cheek.

"Lamia," Trish said. "I think that's enough."

"He killed them . . . shot them . . . then burned them." She put her face in her hands and Trish cradled her as she began to sob.

## CHAPTER 4

Chet sat perched on the end of the bed, looking out the window into the night, waiting for Trish, hoping his grandmother and the strangeness of this house weren't all too much for her.

Trish walked into the bedroom.

He gave her a cautious smile. "How's Lamia?"

Trish pushed the door gently shut behind her. "Oh, she's fine. A little upset, a little drunk too." Trish grinned. "I helped her to bed. I think it did her a lot of good. Y'know, to be able to share what she went through."

Chet nodded.

"Poor thing. She's been living here alone ever since that horrible night. I can't image how lonely that must've been. Did you know they took your mother away from her?"

"Yeah. Aunt Abigail, Grandpa's sister, did that. Her and the rest of my grandpa's family. Don't know all the details, but I understand it got pretty ugly. Aunt Abigail went to court to prove Grandma was unfit to raise children, went so far as to try and have her committed."

"Chet, I gotta show you something." Trish opened her palm, revealing a small mark where the wound used to be.

Chet's eyes widened. "Why . . . it's all healed."

"Yeah. Isn't that something? Lamia may be a bit kooky, but she's *not* crazy. There's really something to those old ways of hers."

They were both quiet for a minute.

"I like your grandma, Chet."

"Even if she's a wicked witch?" He smirked.

"She's fascinating. She really is. The whole magic thing too. I mean, sure, the spells and witchcraft part is just ritual . . . at least I think so, but there's this whole world of herb and root medicine I never knew anything about. She showed me her atrium. And it's not just plants she's got in there; there're salamanders, frogs, snakes, bugs. She's a regular encyclopedia on mushrooms, roots, fungus, dirt—shoot, about anything to do with nature. And, Chet, the best part is she wants to pass it along, to teach someone, and by someone I mean *me*. She actually asked if I'd be interested."

"Are you?"

"Are you kidding? I thought I was gonna have to beg her, and, and—" Trish stopped. "What're you grinning about?"

"So, you want to stay then? Give it a shot?"

Trish closed her eyes, inhaled deeply, then opened them again. "I think so. At least for a while. Until after the baby."

"Yeah?"

"Yeah."

Chet got up, turned off the light. They got undressed and into bed. He lay next to her, his hand on her stomach. Trish placed her hand atop his. "Do you think they'll find us?"

"No," Chet said, trying to sound reassuring. "My aunt did a good job of leaving the past behind."

"Lamia is so excited about the baby," Trish said. "Y'know she wants us to have the child here?"

"How do you feel about that?"

"That I'd be in good hands. She's brought a lot of children into the world. And a home delivery would mean we wouldn't have to go to a hospital."

The baby kicked. Chet gasped, then laughed. "Seems like our daughter approves."

Trish fell quiet and Chet could tell there was something on her mind.

"Chet, baby, this can all be so good."

"Yeah," Chet agreed, waiting for the rest.

"I need you to do something for me."

"Okay."

"What we're doing, leaving home, leaving everything we know behind to have this child. Well . . . it's scary. Your grandma, she's a real blessing and I think we got a pretty good thing here. But, I need to know, need to hear it from you again . . . that I won't have to worry about you going back to jail. That you're done with the drugs, done selling, transporting, all of it."

Chet knew going into this that it wasn't going to be easy, that he had a lot of work ahead if he wanted to earn back her trust. They'd been together since high school. In those days he'd sold a bit of weed, but mostly to friends. Trish never seemed to mind; she'd even shared a jay with him from time to time. But somehow selling to a few friends had turned into selling all around town, then eventually to running drugs across the state line. The first time Trish had found out she'd threatened to break up unless he stopped. Said she couldn't devote herself to someone heading for prison, that she just didn't need that kind of heartache. He'd promised her never again and meant it too, but what he meant to do, and what he actually did, didn't always line up and it wasn't long before she'd caught him again. He'd sweet-talked her into a second chance, but when it happened once more, she'd given him an ultimatum, telling him that next time was strike three and they were done—that he was out of her life for good. He knew she was looking out for him and he had sworn to her, yet again, that he *was* done, only done for him meant after one last run. Two weeks later he was arrested for transporting drugs and shortly after that he'd received her letter while sitting in a county cell.

"What it comes down to," Trish said, "is I don't want our baby growing up with her daddy in jail. So I need you to swear again, but not to me this time." She pressed his hand against her belly. "But to her, to our little girl. Swear to her that her daddy is always going to be there for her."

Chet did, and he meant it, more than he'd ever meant anything in his life, having no way of knowing that by morning, he'd be dead.

## CHAPTER 5

Chet awoke sometime after midnight. No dreams this time, but the dread felt like a weight upon his chest. He sat up, his skin clammy, his breath labored as though there wasn't enough air in the room. He got up, slipped on his shirt, pants, and shoes and found his way downstairs in the dark. He headed for the kitchen, poured himself a glass of lemonade, and went out onto the porch, careful not to let the screen door slam.

He leaned against a post, watching the sea fog seep into the lowlands, the big moon setting the mist aglow. He could just hear the distant waves breaking as the fireflies danced. He'd never seen so many fireflies. A calm began to steal over him and he closed his eyes. A vision came to him, as vivid as a real memory. It was of him, Trish, Lamia, and a little girl with dark curls playing on the beach. He caught himself smiling.

Chet opened his eyes. There—on the walkway—stood a boy.

Chet almost dropped the glass.

The boy appeared to be around five or six years old, white hair and dark eyes, jeans, but no shirt or shoes, a Mason jar full of flickering yellow lights in the crook of his arm. "Boo."

Chet stared at him, trying to make sense of what a kid was doing way out here by himself, especially at this time of night. "Hey . . . do your folks know where you're at?"

The kid smiled, held up the jar. "Come look what I caught."

"Where do you live?"

"With the Burning Man. He wants to meet you."

"Burning man?" Chet started down the steps; his hand bumped the strings and the little bells chimed. The boy's face creased as though in pain. He fell back a step, glaring at Chet.

"Hey," Chet said. "Don't be scared. What's your name?"

"I hate them bells," the kid said and took off, darting around the hedge and out of sight.

"Wait," Chet called, following after the boy. Chet came to the end of the walk, looked about the circular drive then down the dirt road. He squinted, thought he saw someone running near the cemetery, but the fog was thick that way.

"Hey, mister," someone called. Chet started, spun round to find another boy. This kid also had white hair and dark eyes, but was a bit older, wearing a loose button-up shirt and baggy pants with suspenders.

"You seen my kid brother?" The boy looked worried.

"Um . . . yeah. I think so."

"He ain't suppose to be out here, y'know."

"Well, I'm pretty sure he headed that way." Chet pointed down toward the cemetery.

"Mister . . . would you mind too much coming with me . . . to help me find him?" The kid dropped his eyes as though embarrassed. "Please. I don't like being out here in the dark by myself. Don't know if you heard or not, but there's suppose to be all sorts of spooks trapped on this island."

"Sure . . . okay. Let me go see if I can rustle up a flashlight." Chet started back in.

"Need to hurry," the kid said, starting down the road. "He might fall in the creek, or off the seawall. Davy, he can't swim so well."

"Yeah, okay," Chet said and followed, realizing they really didn't need a flashlight, not with the moon so bright.

"What's your name?"

"Billy."

"Well, Billy, I'm Chet."

"I know," the boy said.

"Y'know?"

"You're Lamia's grandson, ain't you?"

"I am," Chet said, trying to figure out how the kid would know that.

They passed the cemetery, the fog growing thicker, dimming the moon's glow. As they entered the trees the shadows began to blend together. "Damn," Chet said. "Have you ever seen so many fireflies?" The bugs appeared to be following them.

"Those ain't fireflies."

There was a guttural, husky pitch in the boy's voice that hadn't been there before. Chet glanced over and noticed patches of marred skin across the boy's face and neck, as though the boy might've suffered burns years back. Chet couldn't understand how he'd missed them earlier. He took a harder look, surprised at how gaunt and malnourished the kid appeared, how dark the shadows were under his eyes. Chet wondered what sort of home life this kid might have. If maybe the boy's parents were the sort to put money toward drink before feeding their kids.

"Not fireflies? What are they then?"

"Souls. The souls of all the trapped children."

A chill slid up Chet's spine. Someone had been filling this kid up with stories, and Chet could tell by the way the boy said it that he believed them. Chet let out a weak laugh. "Souls, huh? Where'd you hear that?"

"I know it 'cause I seen them."

"Oh . . ."

"If you want, I can show you where some of them died."

Chet imagined the boy was referring to the murders committed by his grandfather, could only imagine at the local folktales circulating about.

"I can even show you where me and my little brother died."

A moan came from deeper in the woods. Something moved toward them. Chet felt his hair stand on end, fell back a step, then stopped, an annoyed smirk on his face. "You can come on out, Davy," he called.

A shape stepped out from behind a tree, walking out of the shadows toward them. It was the younger boy. He wore a sheepish grin.

Chet shook his head, let out a long sigh. "All right, you guys got me."

They both snickered.

"Wanna play a game?" Davy asked.

"Nope. I'm all done playing games," Chet said, trying to keep the irritation out of his voice. "I'm tired. Going to bed." He turned, started back, and realized he wasn't sure which way back was. The fog was now so thick he couldn't see past the nearest trees. The fireflies caught his attention, jigging about as though agitated. He'd never seen fireflies do that before. He started to point them out to the boys, when a moan, little more than a whisper, echoed about him. More moans followed, louder; the sounds seemed to be emanating from beneath him, from under the ground. They sounded dreadful, as though someone or something was in great pain. Chet felt a twinge of real fear grip his stomach. Something poked Chet from behind. He wheeled and found Davy smirking at him.

"C'mon, Chet. Let's play awhile." The kid, his face, something was wrong with his face. "We made a game up all on our own. Wanna know the name?" Davy's grin grew, his lips peeling back, revealing black, broken teeth, far too many teeth. "It's called Kill Chet."

Chet's eyes widened. This wasn't the boy he'd seen before; this boy looked starved. Burn scars began to crisscross his bare skin, spreading, darkening. The boy's eyes receded, shrinking into their sockets. An odor hit Chet, the smell of burning meat. *"What the hell?"* Chet shouted and spun away, colliding with Billy. Billy grabbed him, clinging to his waist. Chet tried to shove him away, but the boy's blackened, scabby skin slid off, sticking to Chet's hands like melting cheese, exposing raw sinew and putrefied meat.

Billy laughed, his eyes now sputtering yellow sparks. His head snapped forward, striking at Chet. The mouth with too many teeth sank into Chet's arm.

"Hey! *HEY!*" Chet screamed as sharp, burning pain shot up his arm. Chet shoved the boy again, stumbling and thrashing until he tore free.

Chet ran, not caring where he was going so long as it was away from the two boys. Branches and briars grabbed and slashed his flesh and clothes as he barreled through the trees and underbrush. He lost first one shoe, then another. He ran and ran, trying to get back to the house, ran until his breath burned in his throat and lungs, until his feet were cut and bleeding.

Chet thought he heard crashing waves and stopped, tried to quiet his panting to listen. He did hear waves—just ahead. *Dammit. Wrong way.* He turned creeping along, trying to get his bearing. When he felt sure he was heading away from the surf he again began to run. The sound of the breakers disappeared and just as he felt he was almost to the house, again the sound of the surf. *Shit!*

"*Let's plaaaay,*" echoed the boys' voices.

Were they in front of him? Behind? Chet couldn't tell. His heart drummed in his ears. "Grandma," he whispered, trying to reach out to her. Never had he more wanted to hear her reassuring voice. *Grandma, please hear me.*

Two sets of fireflies bounced toward him in the fog. Dark shapes formed around them. It was them, the boys, only now they were nothing more than molten black flesh. He could see smoke rising off their bodies. They extended their hands to him and began to laugh.

Chet bolted, running heedless of obstacles. His shoulder hit a tree, spinning him, and he struck his head on a branch, hard, knocking him off his feet. He tried to stand, reeled, dropping to his hands. He touched his head, felt wetness, saw blood on his hand.

They appeared again, walking slowly toward him, all their teeth exposed in a face-tearing grimace. "*Chet,*" they said, their voices low, almost a growl.

"Children," came a firm, strong voice. Lamia appeared out of the mist behind the ghouls. Their faces changed when they saw her, shifted. Even scabbed and twisted, Chet could read their joy.

"Mama!" they both exclaimed and ran to her. She bent, gathering them in her arms. They hugged her, pressing their blackened, blistered faces into her chest.

"*Grandma?*" Chet called.

Lamia looked at Chet. "Chet, I'm sorry. Did they scare you?"

"What . . . no . . . they're . . . *monsters.*" He could barely get the words out.

She released the children. "Boys, stay back. You're scaring him." She spoke to them calmly, sweetly.

"We just want to play," they groaned.

*This isn't real,* Chet told himself, struggling to one knee. *No way this is real.* Yet his horror, his desperate need to escape this madness, that *was* real and he tried to stand, stumbled, landing back on his hands.

Lamia came to him, kneeling down, draping her arms about him.

"Now, there, dear. It's all okay. Don't fear them. They cannot help what they've become." She touched Chet's face and he felt all of six years old again. Lamia was warmth and love, the moon and stars, his safe harbor, and all he wanted was to curl up in her arms. "Kindness is the only way to alleviate their suffering," she whispered.

A sharp sting along his throat, something warm and wet, gushed down his neck. Chet saw a knife in Lamia's hand, the one with the serpent on the handle from her box—it was now covered in blood.

She gazed at him with doting eyes and the silvery specks within her irises began to pulse, then slowly spin, and Chet felt himself spinning along with them.

Chet tried to raise his hand, but his arm felt impossibly heavy. Everything was dimming, growing darker and darker. He closed his eyes, and began to drift.

## CHAPTER 6

Chet opened his eyes and tried to focus, but everything was cast in a silvery light. He climbed to his feet, feeling weightless, unsteady, as though he were drifting. He clasped his head, struggling to maintain his balance. His surroundings were hazy, distorted, and drained of color. Even the crashing waves sounded muted.

He heard lapping, like that of an animal drinking. He turned toward the sound and made out a hunched shape. He blinked, a bit more detail came into the world, and he saw it wasn't an animal, but a woman. She was on all fours straddling a body, that of a man. Chet blinked again and his vision cleared, only he wished it hadn't, wished he could unsee what he was seeing. Lamia, except not, her limbs too thin and too long, her bones pushing at her ashen flesh as though they might tear through, her spine a row of spikes beneath her gown. She was hunched over, grunting and slurping as she licked and sucked at the man's neck.

"Grandma?"

Slowly, she lifted her head, looked at him, her face now elongated and goatlike. Blood dripped down her chin, neck, and chest in gooey strands, matting her long white hair. She set eyes on him, small silvery eyes with black slits down their middles, eyes that pulsed. She smiled. "Chet, I thought all was lost, but you . . . *you* have saved me. I love you, child. I'll always love you."

Chet glanced at the body, at the face of the man his grandmother now straddled. Saw his own face, his own blank eyes staring back at him, and somewhere deep down understanding began to dawn. He put his hand to his mouth. "Oh, no. Oh, *no . . . no . . . no!*"

"Go play, Chet. Go play with your brothers and sisters." Lamia gestured to the fireflies around them. Chet saw that they weren't fireflies after all, but eyes. He blinked and saw more—faces behind the eyes, faces of children, hundreds of them, from toddlers to four- and five- and six-year-olds. And all of them, every single one, stared at Lamia, their faces tormented with longing. Never had Chet seen such desperate plaintive need.

"*Mommy, Mother, Mama,*" they murmured. The words garbled, in many variations, many languages, but regardless, what they were saying was clear: they were calling for their mother. They pushed closer, and closer, hands outstretched, reaching for Lamia.

Davy and Billy moved forward, snarling and baring their teeth. The children's faces turned from longing to fear. They backed away, keeping plenty of distance between them and the two ghoulish creatures, but never so far as to lose Lamia from their sight—all those eyes, those desperate eyes, staring and staring.

*This can't be. Can't be,* Chet thought. "Grandma!" he cried. "*Grandma!*" he screamed, almost wailed. "*Help me! You gotta help me. Make it stop. Please, oh God, please make this stop!*"

Davy and Billy laughed but Lamia took no notice, returning to the body, *his* body, returned to feasting on *his* blood. The sounds of her chewing and sucking echoing in his head, making him want to claw out his own eardrums.

Chet started toward her, his hands out, reaching. "Grandma. *Please.*" And he realized how like the others he must look, must sound.

Billy and Davy set eyes on him, showing him their teeth as they stepped toward him.

Chet stopped, tried to back away, found his feet sliding as though on ice.

As the demons moved from Lamia, several of the children rushed forward, swirling around her, clutching at her, sliding their fingers across her face, through her hair as they sang her name. Lamia hissed and batted at them the way one would a mosquito.

Davy and Billy spun about, leaping after the children. The children screamed and dashed away. But Davy caught one, a girl of no more than three, clamping his teeth into her arm. She shrieked as he shook her savagely back and forth, tearing her arm from her shoulder. No blood, or gore, just wispy, stringy tendrils. Screaming, she stumbled away, disappearing into the misty woods.

And as Davy devoured the girl's arm, a thought hit Chet, chilling his heart. *Trish. Oh my God, Trish!* He had to get to her before these monsters did—tell her to get out of here *now*. He stumbled back, trying to flee, felt as though he was sliding, unable to get any real traction—floating, drifting into the mist, into the trees.

"Don't go too far," Davy called. "The Burning Man still wants to see you." The two ghouls burst out laughing, the sound of it grating, biting into Chet's head.

Chet pushed through the children. Their bodies were soft and yielding, cold, none of them paying him any heed, all of them vying for a view of Lamia. With focus and effort Chet gradually managed to gain some control of his movement. *God, what's she gonna do to Trish?* He pushed through the trees, searching for the house, fighting the urge to shout for her. He was about to turn around, try another direction, when he came upon the sandy drive. He headed up the road, managing to move faster, more of a pushing effort than running, almost gliding, almost like ice skating.

Chet stopped at the edge of the field. A light breeze blew the thinning mist about, giving him glimpses of the house at the top of the hill. A light was on. *Is Trish awake? Did she hear me? Did she hear any of it? God, please.*

Lamia came into view, no longer hobbling, but strolling up the hill on the far side of the field. The demons walked at her side, snapping at any children who dared come too close.

Chet ducked down in the reeds.

Lamia entered the house and as soon as the door shut, the demons turned on the children, chasing them back into the woods.

Chet waited until the demons were out of sight, then he headed up the hill. He approached the house, sticking to the bushes, praying he could get to Trish before Lamia hurt her. He dashed up the porch steps and collided with something solid, something hard enough to knock him down. There came a jingle, followed by a blast of pain in his head. He clasped his hands over his ears until it ceased. He looked at the porch: there was nothing—no wall, no fence. He noticed the multicolored string, the bells, reached for them and again bumped something firm, the air darkening, a numbing chill traveling up his arm. One of the little bells jingled, followed again by the blinding pain in his head. "Fuck!"

"We hear you, Chet." It was one of them, the demons, but it sounded far away, a voice on the wind. "Time to meet the Burning Man."

*The burning man? Who's the burning man?* But Chet thought he knew and it struck him that there might be worse things than death, far worse things. He pushed to his feet and darted around the house, searching for a way across or over or under the string. He found none; the string wound all the way around. He stopped under Trish's window. The room was dark. "*Trish!*" he cried. "*TRISH!*" he screamed as loud as he could.

"Better find a hiding place, Chet," called one of the demons in that maddening singsong voice, closer now.

Chet searched the ground for a stick, a stone, something to hit the window with. He found a rock and grabbed for it. His hand passed right through. "Oh, for fuck's sake."

"Che-et, ready or not, here we *come.*"

He looked at his hands, squeezed them together. They felt solid. He tried again, concentrating, and again, his hand passed through, but this time it moved, just a nudge, but he *had* moved it. He tried once more. *Focus. Just focus.* It was in his hand, he could feel the weight of it.

"Che-et, where *are* you?"

The rock slid through his palm, hit the ground with a thud. "Dammit!"

"Che-et." The voice sounded right around the corner of the house.

Chet dashed back down the hill, searching for a place to hide, sliding behind the trunk of a great oak. He pressed his back against the tree and gritted his teeth, trying to calm himself. *There's gotta be a way.*

"We *smell* you, Chet."

*Fuck you,* Chet thought, wondering how much longer he could play this game.

Something touched Chet's arm. He started, almost cried out.

A young black boy in tattered clothes, no more than five or six years old, hunkered in the weeds behind him. Only he wasn't really a boy, but a wispy play on shadows, much like the children who followed Lamia. Chet started to flee, but there was something in the boy's eyes, the urgency, the fear, that Chet knew must mirror his own.

The boy put a finger to his lips, waved Chet to him, turned, and crawled away into the tall grass.

Chet hesitated.

"Olly, olly, in come free," one of the demon ghouls called out.

Chet glanced past the tree, saw Davy wandering around the house. Chet bit his lip and followed the child, catching up with him a moment later. "*Where we going?*" he whispered.

The child slapped his hand over his mouth, shook his head, wagging a finger frantically at Chet.

Chet got it, put his fingers to his own lips, and nodded.

The child pointed ahead to the gravestones poking up from the grass, then leaned forward, putting his lips near Chet's ear, and spoke in the softest whisper. "*Safe there.*"

The boy glanced anxiously about, then headed quickly away. Just as he passed an oak, Billy jumped out, catching him by the arm and slamming him into the ground. "Got'cha!" Billy cried, leaping atop the boy and shoving his face into the dirt. Claws sprouted from Billy's fingers and he raked them down the child's back, shredding his wispy shirt and flesh. The boy let out a piercing scream.

Chet leapt up, every instinct screaming at him to flee, escape while he could, but he charged instead. At the last moment he thought of the rock he'd tried to pick up, wondering if he'd pass right through this monster. He didn't pass though. He slammed into Billy, knocking him off the child.

Billy tumbled, then sat up fast, wide wild eyes on Chet. Even on that twisted, burned husk of a face, there was no hiding the shock, surprise, and something else—perhaps a touch of fear.

The child didn't waste a second, scrambling away and leaping into the cemetery.

Chet made to follow, but Billy jumped up, blocking his way. Whatever

Chet thought he'd read on Billy's face was gone, replaced by pure malice.

"Gonna peel your skin, Chet. Nice and slow. And when I'm done, I'm gonna do it again. That's the nice thing about being dead. The suffering never ends."

Chet balled his hands into fists. He was tired of running, tired of being scared. Whatever this was about, it needed to be over. "Well c'mon, you little fucker!" Chet cried. "Just c'mon!"

Billy slowly raised his hands—they were mostly hands again—and held them to either side of his head, palms out, fingers splayed. He jabbed a thumb in each ear and began to wiggle his fingers.

"What," Chet said. "What the h—" He didn't finish. Something hit him from behind, knocking him to the ground. It was Davy. Both of them fell upon him, wrestling him onto his back, pinning his arms. Their small shapes were inexplicably heavy and he found himself staring up into their sputtering yellow eyes.

Davy held up his hand, rubbing his fingers together. They began to smolder, spark, then his whole hand burst into flame. He lowered it until it was just inches from Chet's face. "It hurts when you burn," Davy said. "Hurts worse than anything."

"Know how we know?" Billy asked. "Because your grandpa, he cooked us to a crisp."

Davy pressed his fingertip against Chet's cheek. There came a sizzle, followed by searing pain as Davy ran his finger down Chet's face and neck. Chet flailed, struggling to twist free. Davy clasped Chet's shoulder, his fingers burning into Chet's flesh like a branding iron. Chet screamed through his clenched teeth.

"*ENOUGH!*" A voice boomed across the field, gusting across Chet, knocking the flame out.

Billy and Davy tumbled off Chet and onto all fours, searching the shadows, all the play gone from their faces.

"Leave him be." The voice was heavy with authority and seemed to come from everywhere.

"Go away!" Billy snarled.

A bent man, with skin as black as the night, strolled from the shadows. Long dark robes, dirty and tattered, hung down his lean frame and a thin golden band crowned his bald head. His brilliant blue eyes came to rest on Chet. "This is Gavin's grandson?"

"Y'know it is," Billy spat. "We caught him, so that makes him ours. You can have what's left of him after we're done."

The man shook his head. "You are done."

"And what if I say we ain't?"

"I have no patience for your games, Billy. Not tonight." He raised a fist above his head and opened his hand. Chet made out a symbol in his palm. It rose and began to glow, floating in the air in front of him, the soft blue light rolling like smoke toward the two boys.

The boys raised their hands, shielding their eyes, and fell back snarling.

"Your God's done forsaken you, angel man," Billy hissed. "You're dying, we smell it. Soon enough it's gonna be you on your knees crying, begging *us* for mercy."

The man's face betrayed nothing.

The demons stalked back and forth along the edge of the smoky light, growling, hissing, their hungry, angry eyes on Chet.

"He's ours," Davy snarled. "Just you remember that."

## CHAPTER 7

*A*ngel? Chet wondered at that. The man appeared to be no more than forty. High cheekbones protruded from a gaunt face, his skin unlike any flesh Chet had ever seen before, so black it was almost blue. And now, beneath the glow, he appeared haggard, emaciated, his eyes sunken. It was the look of someone slowly starving to death.

The man set his piercing gaze upon Chet, and Chet felt as though every deed of his short life was being scrutinized. Slowly, the man's eyes softened. "Stand."

Chet stood, wincing from the burns along his neck as he did. "What's going on?" Chet asked. "Who are you?"

"Show me your palms," the man said, his voice urgent.

"What?"

"Do as I say. Time is short."

Chet held out his hands and glanced from his palms to the man's eyes, not liking what he saw. "What? What now?"

The man slowly shook his head. "Why must despair be my only friend?"

"What?" Chet stared at his palms, then raised them closer to his face, noticing strange markings on his right palm.

The man waved a hand and the marks momentarily glowed an angry red, forming a primitive horned beast head like a brand. "Lucifer has claimed you."

"Lucifer?" Chet's chest tightened.

"You have been marked a murderer and left to the mercy of the demons . . . of which mercy there is *none*.

"*Murderer?* What are you talking about? I'm no *murderer*. I've never—" He stopped. "Oh, no. Oh . . . dear God . . . *Coach*." Chet's knees felt weak. *I killed him. Good God, I killed him.* "Jesus . . . forgive me," Chet said, all but moaned.

"*You are wasting your breath,*" the man said. "*Jesus does not hear the damned.*"

Chet stared at him. *Damned?* An hour ago he might've scoffed at the notion of having his soul weighed, even challenged the very existence of God and Satan, for that matter. But he was seeing things differently now. Now all he could think of was a childhood full of Sunday morning sermons warning him of unrelenting flame and torment.

"This will make things difficult." The man sounded utterly defeated.

"Make what difficult?" Chet asked.

The man didn't answer, just pressed his hand against his brow and shut his eyes tight as though trying to block everything out. The sigil fluttered, dimmed, and the demons took a cautious step forward.

"Make *what* difficult?"

Still, the man didn't respond.

Chet felt his temper getting the better of him. "Hey . . . I'm talking to you."

Nothing from the man.

"Hey," Chet said again, raising his voice. "Hey." He stepped forward, clutched the man's shoulder, and gave him a shake. "Talk to me, goddamnit!"

The man's eyes flashed opened; he looked from the hand on his shoulder to Chet, glared at him. Chet released him, but held his eyes.

"You dare?" the man said. "Dare to touch an angel, an emissary of God?" But he didn't sound angry, he sounded intrigued. "You are bold, Chet. That I give you . . . and perhaps a bit foolish." He seemed to weigh this. "And maybe that is just what is needed." A thin smile graced his lips. "Perhaps there *is* hope. Yes, I am wont to believe so. Because a chance, no matter how slim, is still better than no chance."

"Who are you?" Chet demanded.

The man gazed upward, his lips moving silently—a prayer, or maybe a curse. A light lit in his eyes. "I am Senoy. Gabriel's sword. I serve Heaven and righteousness." The angel straightened, drew himself up to his full height, seemed to grow taller. The sigil brightened and an aura bloomed around him, forming great, ghostly wings. The demons fell back, shielding their eyes, but not Chet. The light felt of all things good and he basked in its radiance, felt an overwhelming desire to enter its glow. Then as quick as it had appeared, the aura faded. Chet reached for the glow, but it was gone.

The angel slumped. "I serve the one true God," he gasped weakly. "And this"—he made a dismissive wave to the land around them—"from sea to sea . . . was once my ward to watch over." His voice fell to a labored whisper. "Until it was *stolen* from me." Senoy set his eyes on Chet. "Hear me, Chet. And hear me well if you want to save your dear Trish."

"Trish?" Chet bristled. "What do you know about—"

"Silence," Senoy snapped. "We do not have long." The sigil flared, gleaming off the boys' scaly, scabby skin. "See them, Chet. See them true. And Lamia as well. Know them for what they are . . . profane and ungodly creatures all. It was my charge to rid this land of them . . . but, as you can see, I have . . . *failed*. And there is but one reason, one only." He tore open his cloak, revealing a large deep wound above his heart. "Gavin Moran." His voice filled with venom. "*Your* grandfather killed me. Stole everything from me."

Chet couldn't look away from the gory gouge in the man's chest.

"It was Gavin that brought these demons here." The angel's voice rose with each word. "Him that murdered his own children, traded their souls—his own children's souls—for Lucifer's favor. Him that brought ruin to all." His words turned into a hacking cough. He grabbed Chet, his cold, hard fingers digging into his arm. "He stole my key, trapping me. Then left me here, imprisoned upon this island to rot."

Chet stared at the angel, shaking his head, trying to make sense of any of this.

"Do you want Trish to live? Do you?"

"Yes."

"Are you sure?"

"Yes . . . yes, of course. Fuck. Of course I do. But—"

"Then you must go down and find him, find Gavin, take the key, and return it to me."

*Down?* Chet's head reeled. *What does he mean by down?* But he thought he knew.

"The key is the heart of my divinity, the cornerstone of my will, strength, and purpose. With it I can unlock my shackles, can call down Heaven and bring this evil to an end. Do you understand? I must have the key if I am to stop her . . . to stop Lamia. To set us all free."

Chet didn't understand, not any of it.

Senoy stole a furtive glance at Davy and Billy, then slipped his hand beneath his cloak, withdrawing a leather pouch. He shoved it into Chet's hand. "Here." It felt heavy and something clanked inside. The angel swooned. The sigil flickered, dimmed, and he clutched Chet's arm for support.

Davy and Billy snorted. "Soon, angel man. Soon."

Chet started to open the pouch.

"No, not here," Senoy said sharply, glancing at the demons. "They must not see. Now, into the cemetery." He pushed Chet toward the fence. "It is consecrated ground."

Chet slipped over the low fence.

"Aww, Chet. Where you going?" Davy asked. "We wanna play some more."

Strain lined Senoy's face; Chet felt sure he would collapse at any moment. The glowing sigil fluttered like a dying candle and the demons moved yet closer.

"Go now," Senoy said. "Go down and find Gavin. Make great haste as Trish does not have long."

"What'd you mean?"

"Keep your mark hidden," Senoy said, speaking faster as the sigil continued to dim. "Satan's hounds will be sniffing after you."

"What'd you mean Trish doesn't have much time?"

The sigil sputtered and went out, leaving a faint glowing vapor around the angel.

Davy and Billy crept closer and closer.

"When you find Gavin," Senoy said, "no matter what he seems to you, no matter what he says, remember this one thing . . . he traded the souls of his own children for Lucifer's favor. Show him mercy and it is your Trish that will suffer, your unborn child that will lose her soul."

"Gavin, huh?" Davy said, and shared a surprised look with Billy. "What kind of mischief are you up to, angel man?"

Senoy looked deep into Chet's eyes. "Go, Chet. Go with God's might on your side." And with that the angel turned and slipped away.

"Wait," Chet called as a thousand confused questions raced through his mind. *Wait. Oh, please wait.*

Billy and Davy watched the angel disappear into the trees.

"Wanna get after him?" Davy asked

"Naw," Billy said. "He ain't going nowhere." The two demons moved up to the iron gate and stared at Chet.

"You better run fast," Billy said. "Because the Burning Man, he's gonna be after you. Gonna drag you to Hell to *burn* with the other sinners."

# PART TWO

Erebus

## CHAPTER 8

Chet walked past a few markers, glancing at the names until he found a small, simple stone in the very back of the cemetery. The inscription read, GAVIN MORAN, BORN 1900, DIED 1932, and nothing more. Chet read the name over and over. "*Why?*" he whispered. "*Why?*" He sat his foot against it, tried to push it over, but his foot pushed through it, causing him to slide to the ground. He sat there on his knees staring at the name. *Goddamn, you. God . . . damn you.*

A light flickered on up at the house, on the second floor, catching Chet's attention.

"You think that's Trish up there?" Billy asked.

"I think so," Davy put in, his voice turning guttural. "She'll be getting her turn soon. We can burn her up nice and slow, then do it again, and again."

Chet balled his hands into fist, stepped closer to the fence.

"Don't you be letting them get under your skin, Mr. Chet," Joshua warned. "They trying to play you, trying to get you to step out."

Billy and Davy began circling the small cemetery, shifting between demon and boy, snarls and giggles. They began to howl, screech, the sound eating into Chet's head. He covered his ears, unable to bear it. "Where is it?" Chet growled. "Josh, the door, the way down. Where is it?"

"Door? There's no door. Not like you're thinking, anyhow."

"Then what?"

"You have to sink." Joshua pointed down. "The earth claims the dead. Going down's easy. Just close your eyes and let go of the ground."

"Huh?"

"Watch here." Joshua closed his eyes, sank into the earth, just slipped away. Chet stepped over to where Joshua had been standing, knelt down, laid his hand on the ground. He took one last glance up at the house, at Trish's window, then closed his eyes and—*let go*. He didn't have to will it, or force it; the earth indeed seemed eager to claim him. He felt himself sliding through it, tugging him down as though hungry for him.

A moment later he stopped sinking and opened his eyes. A light fog shifted about him, giving off a dim gray glow, illuminating a cramped earthen cavern.

Joshua stood in front of him, a small smile. "See there, Mr. Chet. Weren't so hard."

Chet touched the wall. It wavered as though a mirage, yet he couldn't push through it. He saw only one way out, a hole on one side of the cavern. Chet stepped over and peered down, found only darkness. "What's down there?"

Joshua shrugged. "Don't rightly know."

"So you've never gone any farther?"

"No, sir. Scared to. Sometimes I come down here when Davy and Billy get mean. But I don't care to stay long on account of some of the things I hear coming up from that hole. Besides, Senoy, he said I wasn't supposed to go down there, that I'm supposed to go to Heaven." Joshua's face brightened. "That as soon as he gets his key back he's going to fix things. That angels gonna come and take me home and that I'll get to see my mama again." Joshua beamed.

Chet touched the ceiling. "Joshua, how d'you get back up? Up to the graveyard?"

"Why, I can see my bones up above. Like little twinkling stars."

Chet saw only darkness.

"Going back up's a lot harder though. I have to stare at them bones, have to really put my mind to it, but when I do, I go back up." Joshua shrugged. "Don't know the why or how of it. When I asked Senoy, he said a soul comes home to its bones."

Chet wondered where his bones would end up. Would anyone ever know he was dead? Would Trish even know? And his aunt? A sudden stab of guilt struck him. *She warned me. Flat out told me that Lamia was a witch, a devil. Spent her whole life trying to steer me away from Moran Island. Insisted I attend church with her every Sunday, all trying to save me from this.* "Dammit," Chet whispered, thinking of how he had repaid her with nothing but disrespect and resentment, leaving her the first chance he got. *I never went back. Not once. Not even to just check on her.* Chet wondered just how much his aunt really knew about what happened that night, about her brother's role in this madness. "Joshua, did you know my grandpa?"

"Yes, sir. Well, I never spoke with him or nothing, but my mama, she cooked for Mr. Gavin and Mrs. Lamia."

"What did she think of him?"

"She told me to steer well clear of the man, to steer well clear of all the Morans. Said there were some unsavory goings-on in that house."

"Was she there? That night he lost his mind?"

"No, she weren't, but I was."

"You?"

"Yes, sir. That was a bad night. That was the night Mr. Gavin killed me."

Chet couldn't hide his shock. "Joshua. Why—?"

"I got burned up right along with his boys, Davy and Billy. I was out back when I heard all the shouting and screaming, then the gunshots. I ran and hid in the play fort. Well, Davy and Billy did too. Mr. Gavin came after them. Set the fort to fire. It weren't a good way to die, Mr. Chet."

Chet stared at the boy, trying to make sense of what he was hearing.

"It's my own fault," Joshua said. "I liked to sneak up there sometimes after the boys were called in and play for a while. Mama warned me . . . told me to stay away. But I had a bad habit of not listening. Well . . . I sure picked the wrong evening that time."

Chet shook his head, looked down the hole. *Bastard's down there. Somewhere. Waiting.*

## CHAPTER 9

Chet stood in the small chamber, the silence bearing down upon him. He was alone, Joshua having returned to the above.

"What now?" he asked the walls, his words dying the minute they left his mouth, not even an echo. *Where am I even going?* He realized the angel had given him nothing, no hints, no details. *No . . . not nothing.* He tugged the pouch around, untied it, and turned it up. Dozens of pennies spilled out. He picked one up, examined it. It was old, they were all old, most with Indian heads, the copper turning green. "Pennies?" he said, feeling certain now that he'd been sent on an errand by a madman.

There was something else in the pouch. He withdrew a knife in a simple but elegant sheath. The knife was nearly a foot long overall, the bronze hilt covered in scales and a round white stone set in the pommel. He slid the blade from the sheath and found the ore was bright gold, almost white, without the slightest scratch or sign of wear.

He ran his hand around the inside of the pouch hoping to find a note, something, anything to give him some guidance, or at least a clue to what he was supposed to do. He found nothing. "That's it? Pennies and a knife? I'm supposed to brave the horrors of Hell with pennies and a knife?" He tried to laugh, but the sound came out more like a groan.

He gathered up the knife and coins, putting them back in the pouch, and crouched next to the hole, staring into the blackness. The blackness stared back, cold and empty, not a sound, not a glimmer, nothing, and it was that utter nothingness that most unnerved him. He slid first one leg into the hole, then the other, but that was as far as he got. "*I can't,*" he whispered. "*Can't.*" It was his own face that came to him, staring at him with dead eyes while Lamia—hunched over him like a beast, like a vampire—slurped up his blood. The weight of it hit him and a sob racked his body. "*I'm dead. I'm fucking dead!*" The words tore from his throat. He held out his palm, looked at the mark. "Dead and *damned.*" Fear clutched his heart. *But it was an accident. I never . . . never meant to kill him.* Only he knew that wasn't true. He *had,* in that one moment of rage, meant to kill Coach. *Eternal damnation for a moment's rage? God, how can that be fair? How can any of this be fair?* He closed his hand and looked upward. Trish and his child were up there *alone,* with *them.* He'd promised her, swore he'd always be there. He clenched his hand into a fist. "I'm sorry, Trish. So fucking sorry." He wiped angrily at his eyes. "I *am* coming back. I swear it." He faced the hole again, gritted his teeth, clenching them so hard his jaw hurt, slung the pouch over his shoulder, and slipped into the hole.

Chet slid, clawing at the blackness, finding nothing to grab hold of, nothing to slow his descent; it was as though the darkness was dragging him down. Finally the shaft began to level and he drifted to a stop. He groped about, realized he was in a tunnel, and began to crawl, almost swim, feeling his way forward as the blackness gathered weight around him, pressing in on him, threatening to smother him. He shoved his fist against his teeth. "*Keep it together,*" he whispered. "*Just keep it together.*" He heard it then, or felt it—a distant thumping, moving toward him. He fumbled for the pouch, snatching the knife out and yanking it from its sheath. To his surprise the blade gave off a faint glow, just enough to see he was in a tiny cavern with smoky black walls. He glanced wildly about, saw no one, nothing, only a chamber honeycombed with passages, some leading upward, some down. He had no idea which one he'd come from. *How am I ever gonna find my way back?* He forced the thought away. *Keep moving,* he told himself, glancing from tunnel to tunnel. *Which way? Which one? Down,* he thought, and it was the only thing he felt sure of.

The tunnel split, branched off again and again. Chet took any path that headed downward or appeared larger than the one he was currently in. Down, down he went, sliding, drifting, and again that swimming feeling, as though he were liquid seeping into the earth. Time meant nothing and after what could've been a few hours, a few days, even a week, the tunnel began to broaden and he could walk upright.

He didn't hear the thumping again, but as time crept along he almost wished he would, would hear something, someone, so that he'd know he wasn't trapped in some endless maze within his own crazed mind.

Pockets of gray fog began to pool here and there, giving off a slight glow. Soon the trail became less of a tunnel and more of a series of large caverns, the walls trembling, wobbling, forming and reforming like drifting smoke. Boulders and stones floated in clumps, melting into one another and shifting to and fro in an ever changing maze of walls and alleys. On and on he walked, only not really, as he was all but weightless, pushing more with his mind than his feet.

Chet heard sobbing. He stopped, peered into the shadows, and saw a man.

The man, maybe in his sixties, was dressed in an old forties-style suit. He sat on the ground, hugging his legs, weeping, his head nodding up and down.

"Hey," Chet called. "Hey there."

The man didn't appear to hear him.

Chet took a step closer, realized the man was barely there, just a wispy form.

"Mister. You okay?"

The man's head jerked up. He set terrified eyes on Chet. "Stay away from me!" he cried. "*Stay away!*" The man was obviously shouting, screaming, yet his voice sounded muffled and far away, his lips out of synch with the words. "*All of you stay away from me!*"

"Okay," Chet said, stepping back.

The man struggled to his feet and pointed a long bony finger at Chet. "*I'm not going!*" he shouted, then turned and ran, disappearing down the dark corridor.

When the man didn't return, Chet continued on. The fog grew denser, and brighter, and Chet put away the knife. He was still trying to make sense of the man when a woman walked out from the shadows, startling him.

She appeared to be in her mid-twenties, her simple knee-length dress disheveled, her hair in disarray. There was no color to her, not her dress, hair, or flesh. "Have you seen my baby?" she asked, her desperate eyes searching his. Chet fell back a step and she grabbed his arm. "Have you? Have you seen her?" Her voice, like that of the man, was distant and full of echoes.

"Baby?" Chet shook his head. "No, I haven't seen any babies."

Pain creased her features. "You have to help me find her." Her grip tightened.

"Sorry, lady. I can't help you right now." He tried to pull away but she wouldn't let go.

"She's my baby. My little girl. Please."

"I can't."

She tugged Chet, trying to pull him along with her.

"Let go," Chet said, giving her a shove. She tumbled to the ground.

"Shit, ma'am. Sorry." He reached to help her up. "Here—"

She cringed, let out a cry, and scrambled away on her hands and knees. Chet watched her crawl along the path, sobbing, peering into every alleyway and shadowy corner, calling for her baby.

"*I hate this place,*" he whispered.

Chet continued, coming upon two men and a woman ahead—also shades of gray like the lady. When they noticed him they stopped and waited for him to catch up.

"Do you know the way?" one of the men asked, a thin fellow, with a shaggy beard and thick spectacles.

Chet shook his head. "To where?"

They glanced at each other. "We don't really know," the bearded man said.

"We think we're dead," the woman put in—she was elderly, short, and heavyset. Her words were also muted, out of synch and with that distant echo to them. It seemed everyone's were.

"We're hoping there's a path," the bearded man said. "To the afterlife. You know anything about that?"

"No," Chet said. "But I got a feeling we should be heading down."

"Yeah, we got that same feeling," the bearded man said. He gave Chet an apprehensive look. "Just hope we're not heading for, y'know—"

"Don't you start with that again," the woman said, her face grim. "There'll be answers ahead. Have to be." She headed away.

They followed the woman and it wasn't long before they began to run into others. At first people seemed glad to find other souls, their faces full of hope that someone would have answers, but as more and more people joined the line, it became evident that there were no answers, not among the dead. And the line grew, first dozens, then hundreds, the procession stringing out through the floating boulders and stones, disappearing into the foggy gloom, everyone and everything dull shades of gray. Many souls appeared scared, confused, mumbling, sobbing, but most wore a grim mask, the face of people on a sinking ship, marching quietly, clinging to some small bit of hope that answers, good answers, lay ahead.

As the crowd grew, Chet began to hear other languages mixed in with English. People sat and lay about the path and between the stones. Many appeared to be fading, almost invisible on first glance, not moving, just staring heavenward or blankly out into space.

Chet felt something above him, like a weight bearing down. He looked up into the swirling grayness and saw nothing. Slowly, an immense shadow materialized, taking shape and blotting out everything above. Long, stringy tentacles of black smoke dangled from beneath the mass as it drifted, like some enormous jellyfish, right toward him. The tentacles swept along the ground, stirring up large clouds of gray dust.

Souls began to scream and Chet saw that every person touched by the tentacles became part of them. Those stuck flailed and shrieked as they were slowly absorbed.

Souls floundered as they tried to run, sliding about in that painful slow-motion dance of nightmares. Chet fell as others crawled over him, clawing to escape. A tentacle slid right above him, taking the woman on top of him away. Her eyes lit up, actually began to glow as she was absorbed into the smoky appendage.

The creature drifted on, disappearing into the mist, yet still Chet could see those eyes in the gloom, hundreds of glowing eyes staring back at him. He lay there, shaking, until the eyes were finally gone, until the last screams faded.

"*What was that?*" Chet cried. "*What the fuck was that?*" He scrambled, trying to propel himself down the slope as fast as he could. But his efforts were fruitless, and soon, like those around him, he gave up and just continued his slow descent, sparing furtive glances toward the clouds and wondering what other horrors might await.

A murmur arose ahead. Chet tried to peer over the crowd to see what was going on, but it wasn't until the path made a hard bend that he understood. One side of the trail opened to reveal a steep ravine shrouded in thick, rolling clouds. The clouds broke for a moment and Chet caught a glimpse of a wide dark river and something else: a spark, or flickering flame, on the far side of the river. Chet squinted. *Torches. Those are torches.*

## CHAPTER 10

Trish's knees buckled and she stumbled, almost fell on the steps. A hand, a big hand, caught her. The hand belonged to Jerome, Lamia's handyman. He put an arm around her and helped her onto the porch.

"Sit her on the couch," Lamia said, holding the screen door open. Jerome guided Trish into the sitting room and over to the couch.

"Here, now, child," Lamia said. "You just sit while I fetch some tea."

Lamia left Trish staring out the window, out across the bay. Trish could see the sun glistening off the distant waves. *The day's got no right to be so beautiful,* she thought, *not with Chet lying cold in the atrium.* She'd never have believed it, not if she hadn't seen him. Lamia had tried to soften the blow, laying him out on the bench and surrounding him with white camellias, but nothing could've prepared Trish. She shook her head. *No. It's not possible.* Lamia had told her she'd heard a cry early this morning and sent Jerome out to investigate. The big man had found Chet at the bottom of the seawall. Lamia thought Chet must've gone for a walk, hadn't seen the cliff in the fog.

The bay blurred as the tears returned. A sob grew, doubling her over as it wrenched its way up from her guts. She let out a wail, slapped the sofa, again, then again. "*No!*" she shouted. "*No!*" She fell over onto her side, spent, clutching her belly as she sobbed. "*Oh, God, Chet. You can't be dead. You can't. You just can't.*"

Lamia walked back in the room carrying a tray, set it on the coffee table.

Trish realized then that Lamia was walking without her cane. "Lamia, your cane. You shouldn't be—"

"Don't you worry. I have my good days and bad days. Here now, this will make you feel better." She handed Trish a cup of warm tea. "It has a touch of dandelion and poppy. Might make you a bit drowsy. I like to have a cup in the evenings to help me sleep."

Sleep, that sounded good to Trish. She took a sip. It numbed her tongue and she noticed a slight bitter taste beneath the sweet. The warmth spread through her body and she felt lighter, and lighter, until she felt she could just drift away. The room appeared to sway and she found it hard to keep her eyes open.

She looked at Jerome; he still stood by the door, hadn't moved or spoken. *Lamia's right,* Trish thought, *he's sure not one for words.* And a thought struck her. *What's Jerome doing here? And so early? Lamia doesn't have a phone. So strange.* She tried to ask Lamia, but found it hard to speak.

Lamia took her hand. "There, there, darling. Don't you worry about anything. I'll take care of you."

Trish closed her eyes and drifted away.

## CHAPTER 11

Chet followed the throng of souls as they plodded along the riverbank. He could see nothing of the far shore, no sign of the flickering flame through the dense rolling fog. He came to a low-lying embankment and left the line, walking out onto a slim sandbar in hopes of catching a glimpse of the far shore, all the while scanning the sky, watching for any sign of the shadowy jellyfish creature.

A few dozen souls shared the shore, their eyes distant, lost, staring into the depths. Chet heard a low melodic sound, almost a chant, coming from the river. He stepped closer, right to the edge, found only the dark, churning water. He caught movement, noticed shapes swirling deep below—wispy and writhing, like bones tangled in gossamer. The shapes drifted toward him and he saw faces, just a few—sad and tormented. Then more and more, a multitude, all twisted into tortured masks. The chant rose, individual voices distinguishing themselves, calling to him, beckoning him, begging him to help them.

Chet gasped and backed away.

A man walked past, face full of anguish. He pushed right out into the water, his ghostly form mingling with the black water, deeper and deeper, sinking up to his waist.

"Hey," Chet called. "I don't think you should—"

The water began to churn about the man and still he pressed on. Arms and hands—bony, sickly, and all but translucent—rose from the waves, grabbing, clawing, pulling him under. The man didn't resist, just sank beneath the surface.

"Oh, jeez," Chet gasped.

A long moment with just the surging water, then the man broke the surface several yards out. He let out a horrible wail, flailing, eyes full of terror and pain. Long fingers clawed his flesh, his hair, digging into his eyes, his mouth, stifling his cries, tugging him down until he disappeared beneath the black waters.

Chet scrambled back to the ledge. He made the top of the bank and stood there, chest heaving, watching the river, sure those tormented faces would be clawing their way up the bank after him. He fell back in line, continuing his trek. The trail followed the shoreline and Chet kept a keen eye on the river, staying well away from the ledge.

About a mile farther along the crowd began to slow and bunch up. Chet tried to peer over and around the others, but could see nothing beyond the fog, found himself caught in the crowd with no choice but to shuffle along.

The crowd pressed through a row of large boulders, stopping and going periodically. It became evident that something was allowing the souls through in groups. The crowd halted again. As Chet waited he heard a squall from somewhere nearby. It was hard to pinpoint, as all sound was muffled and full of echoes and it took him a moment to realize it was coming from near his feet. There, among a cluster of rocks, he spotted a small shadow. "Oh, Lord."

It was a baby, not more than a year old, naked, a boy. The first thought that came to Chet was of the woman far back in the tunnels, the one searching for her child. Could this be her child? He didn't think so. Hadn't she been searching for a little girl?

The baby met Chet's eyes and reached out to him.

Chet looked around, hoping to find the baby's mother or father—someone to help. A few souls gave the child anxious, pitying glances, then looked quickly away. It dawned on Chet that the child probably didn't have a mother or father, not down here, that it was on its own. *God, what's gonna happen to it?*

The crowd began to amble forward again. The baby waved his arms at Chet.

"I can't help you . . . I just can't," Chet said, more to himself, hating feeling so helpless, hating that death was so unfair, so merciless. He gritted his teeth and began to move away. After a few steps, he glanced back, expecting to see the baby crying at the crowd again, but the child was still staring at him, his look of hope replaced with confusion, then fear as Chet walked on. It was obvious the child had no one, but what hit home, what cut Chet to the core was the fact that this child had no way of understanding what had happened to it, what *was* happening to it.

"*Keep going,*" Chet said under his breath. "*Keep going.*" He thought of Trish, of his unborn child, her tiny kicks against his hand, how much that little life was counting on him. Chet stopped and turned, staring at the infant. *He's got no one.* "Fuck," Chet said and pushed his way back to the child, scooping him up. The child grabbed him, his tiny hands clutching tightly to his shirt. Chet glanced about, hoping someone might step forward and claim the child. But other than a few worried, furtive looks, he found only an endless line of dazed, shell-shocked faces.

"*How did you get here?*" Chet whispered. "*Did you crawl all this way alone?*" The child stopped sniffling, leaned his head on Chet's chest, began to suck his thumb. "Oh, you're just what I don't need," Chet said with a sigh as the crowd began to surge forward again.

Bits of stonework began to appear along the path, turning into a crumbling wall. The wall led to a rampart and then a tower—a crude, ancient-looking structure. The tower was the entrance to a great bridge, the span of which disappeared into the gloomy mist. The massive doors were shut, barring any from crossing. People formed lines, making their way down the wide stone steps along either side of the tower to the landing below. Chet joined one of the lines.

A wide barge drifted toward the landing from out of the mist. A lone cloaked figure manned the wheel, cranking it along two thick cords of rope strung out across the river. A hood fell across the figure's face, obscuring all but its hard-set mouth. The ferry bumped against the dock.

The ferryman didn't look up, didn't say a word, just stood next to the wheel, waiting.

The souls began murmuring anxiously among themselves, but no one boarded.

"Where does the ferry go?" a man called out.

When the ferryman didn't answer, others began to call out. Soon they were talking over one another, all demanding answers, in several different languages. The ferryman continued to stare at the black river.

A man boarded, just walked right onto the barge and took a spot next to the railing. The crowd quieted, all watching. When nothing happened, a few more boarded, then a few more until a line formed.

Chet followed the crowd, the infant making a small whimpering sound as they boarded. *"It'll be okay,"* Chet whispered, but inwardly he shared the child's unease.

The ferry quickly filled, at least a hundred souls. When no more could board, the ferryman began to crank the big wheel, tugging the craft slowly away from the landing and out into the river.

Chet clung tightly to the rail as the craft bumped along the slow-moving current. Low moans echoed up from the waters. The tormented faces were there, following in the wake, staring up at him from the depths. Chet suppressed a shudder and clutched the baby tighter.

As the shore disappeared into the mist behind them Chet noticed a young woman in a flannel shirt, with short-cropped hair, staring at the baby. She met his eyes then pushed toward him through the crowd. As she approached Chet saw she carried an infant on each hip, both clinging tightly to her shirt.

"Are those yours?" Chet asked, then saw they weren't, as neither child shared her Hispanic features. He hadn't noticed at first, as everyone was ghostly pale down here.

She spoke. It sounded like Spanish to him.

"You don't speak English?"

"English, no," she said, shaking her head.

He pointed at the infants, then back at the shore.

She nodded, looking sad.

A man bumped into Chet. He was carrying another man on his back whose arms and legs were twisted and bent, emaciated like those of a quadriplegic. Chet noticed then that most of the souls appeared elderly, hunched and crippled, and thought again how unfair death could be that one should have to carry their ailments even into death.

The mist continued to thicken, becoming so dense Chet could barely make out the souls nearest him. It settled around them, on them, dusting them in a powdery whiteness. The mist felt as if it were crawling over his flesh, into his flesh. That sensation of floating, that he might drift away at any moment, dissipated. He felt the press of the planks beneath his feet, the weight of the child in his arms. Slowly he began to feel more and more substantial, as did the child, as did those around him. He squeezed his own arm, then that of the child's, and there was no doubt that he was touching flesh—cold, clammy, and fish-belly white, but solid, real flesh.

There came cries and gasps all around. Cold water splashed against his ankles and he noticed with some alarm that the barge was taking on water, settling in the river from the weight of all the souls.

The tang of sulfur hit him. He sucked in a breath. Realized he could smell again, really smell, and could feel his cold, wet clothes against his skin. Colors deepened as the world around him came into sharp focus. His ears popped and he could clearly hear the murmurs of joy and relief as they swept the crowd. It was almost as though they were *alive* again. People grinned, some laughed. Souls looked heavenward as though granted a reprieve, a second chance. Hope began to show on their faces.

But something else, something so obvious, Chet didn't even notice at first. The old people, they were gone. *No,* he thought, *not gone.* He looked again: they were the same people, most now in their prime. And the man, the one with the bent, emaciated limbs, he was a teenager now, standing on his own feet and staring at his hands as he clasped and unclasped them.

"None of this makes any sense," the woman with the two infants said.

"Oh, you *do* speak English?"

She looked at Chet confused. "No. I don't."

"Huh? You're speaking English now."

"No, we're speaking Spanish."

Chet glanced from face to face, listening to those nearest him. He could understand everyone, not perfectly—there was an odd, barely perceptible echo at times—but somehow they all seemed to be speaking the same language.

The child in Chet's arms reached for one of the children the woman carried, a little girl, patting her hand. The little girl laughed and the woman managed a weak smile. "Did you find the child along the way?" she asked.

"Yeah, not too far from the landing."

The woman hefted the two infants. "I found these two in the tunnels."

Chet nodded.

"Did you see any others?" the woman asked.

"Other babies? No."

"I did. Several. Just sitting by themselves, y'know. I couldn't . . ." Her voice choked up. "Couldn't do anything . . . just couldn't carry any more."

Chet's mouth tightened and he nodded. They held each other's eye a moment longer, not speaking, yet somehow sharing something on a deeper level. Seeing her, holding those children, caring so for them, made him feel that at least some humanity survived in this cold world of death.

She blinked back tears and looked out into the thick mist. It was as though they were floating aimlessly in a cloud. "My name's Ana," she said.

"Chet."

Anxious murmurs rolled through the crowd as ominous gray shapes loomed out of the mist ahead.

"Do you think were heading for a good place?" Ana asked.

Chet didn't, but he didn't say so, just shrugged.

A stone embankment, much like the one they'd left, materialized and a moment later the barge thumped up against a landing. Torches lined the embankment, casting hazy shadows into the gloom. A bell tolled nearby and they heard the sound of heavy boots clumping toward them. Everyone fell quiet.

The landing lay level with the river. The only way off the landing was a flight of stairs leading up into the gloom, and down these came around a dozen shadowy figures. The figures stopped at the bottom of the steps and appeared to be waiting for them. Chet saw they were armed with spears, clubs, and even swords.

The ferryman stepped over and unlatched the rope strung across the rail, then returned to the wheel without a word.

"What do we do?" someone asked.

The ferryman didn't answer, but Chet caught sight of his eyes beneath the hood. They were set on the armed men, glaring. Never had Chet seen such contempt and hatred on anyone's face.

Souls glanced from one to another, unsure. Slowly, one by one, they began to disembark, stepping cautiously up onto the wet flagstone. Chet and Ana disembarked with the rest, following the crowd toward the armed men because there was nowhere else to go.

The guards formed a line and lowered their spears, blocking the stairs. They were large men, wearing ragged lumpy coats and blazers from different periods and styles, all various shades of green—some looked to be dyed, others painted. Most wore hoods or hats, Stetsons and bowlers, also green, and baggy pants stuffed into boots. Their faces were covered with deep ritual scarring. Veins and knotted muscles rippled like taunt wires just beneath their leathery hide, the gray flesh riddled with pocks and bumps. But it was their weapons that held Chet's attention. Most carried spears, but several held clubs with spikes and long hooks on their ends— hooks large enough to fit around a man's neck.

"Can you tell us what this is about?" a man in the very front asked. He wore a business suit, sported a nice haircut, an important person's haircut, the sort a lawyer or politician would wear.

The guards didn't answer, just stared at them with hard, dispassionate looks.

"Can you at least tell us where we're at?" the man in the suit persisted.

"Heaven," a huge barrel of a man said as he tromped down the stairs. He wore a dark green overcoat with loose leather pants stuffed into pointed cowboy boots. "Doesn't it look like Heaven to you?" He raked his fat fingers through his thin yellowy hair and waited, staring at them with bleary eyes. "No?" He pushed aside the hem of his coat so that everyone could see the big knife and what appeared to be a flintlock pistol jammed into his belt. "My name's Dirk Robertson, I'm the law here in Styga." Chet noted a tin star pinned to the man's breast pocket. "So let's just get one thing straight right now. What I say goes." He waited, his eyes daring anyone to challenge his assertion. "Here's the deal. You owe a toll. It's the law . . . been the law for an eon. You can either pay, or swim back. That's up to you. But no one goes up these steps until they've paid."

"What's Styga?" It was the man in the suit again, a desperate, almost frantic edge creeping into his voice. "Can you at least tell us that?"

Dirk ignored him, giving instructions to one of the guards.

"Hey," the man called, his voice cracking. Chet wanted to tell him to cool it, that Dirk didn't look like someone you wanted to push. "Hey, sir? Sir?" The man reached out, actually tapping Dirk's arm. Dirk grabbed the man, yanked him out of the line, and slammed him to the stones, then drove his boot into his side, sending the man tumbling toward the river. Dirk took a sword from one of the guards, stepped over, and with a solid overhand swing, brought the blade down on the back of the man's neck, twice, separating his head from his body on the second strike.

The crowd let out a collective gasp. No one moved, not even a whisper. Everyone was staring at the man's head lying on the stones, gulping as his eyes rolled about.

"You think because you're dead you got nothing left to lose?" Dirk shouted. "Well think again, because death isn't that simple . . . not down here." He placed the tip of the sword against the side of the man's head. The man's eyes darted desperately about, as though seeking escape. Dirk leaned his weight onto the weapon, driving the blade into the man's skull. Chet wanted to look away but couldn't. Dirk twisted the sword and there came a loud crack as the man's skull split open. The man let out a long wail and Chet saw silvery smoke slithering from the wound, drifting slowly upward.

The man's eyes stilled, his mouth fell slack. Above him the silvery smoke gathered, forming into the vague semblance of a human body. A face materialized and Chet realized it was that of the man. He appeared confused, then his eyes grew wide, darting about as though hearing something terrible the rest of them could not. His wispy limbs flailed and his mouth opened into a scream, but no sound came out. His mouth opened wider, then wider, tearing completely in half, then reforming, only to tear in half again, and again. He continued drifting upward, higher and higher, twisting, writhing, slowly disappearing into the mist above.

Many in the crowd were openly weeping. Chet clutched the child tightly to his chest, clinched his eyes shut, trying to push the image of the man's horrified face from his mind. "*Hold it together,*" Chet hissed through his teeth. "*If you want to get back to Trish, you gotta hold it together.*"

"Some think of purgatory as some kind of second chance," Dirk said. "Well I'm here to tell you it's not. It's your *last* chance. Y'know, you can hear them sometimes, the dead dead, lost souls like this numbfuck up there in the clouds. Don't know what's happening to them, but it doesn't sound like they're having much fun." He walked casually back to the line, returning the sword to the guard as though nothing had happened. "My job is to take the toll," Dirk called out. "Not to help you find your way through the great fucking beyond. If you want to give us trouble you'll end up in the river or like this man. So the sooner you shut up and do what you're told, the sooner you can be on your way to find peace, redemption, penance, mommy, or whatever other shit your famished soul may be starving for." He pulled a lighter and hand-rolled cigarette from his inside jacket pocket, lit it, and took a long drag. "Now, if you want to speed things along, we're looking for copper, as in pennies. You got pennies then you can head right on up. Gold will do, most anything made of metal, good boots, jackets, knives, hell, guns if you got them. If you don't have anything you pay with flesh."

*Pennies?* Chet thought, remembering the pouch.

"Can't take it with you, they say?" Dirk continued. "Shows what anyone upstairs knows. If you're buried or cremated with it, it usually shows up here. Now search your pockets, see what you can find."

People began to explore their pockets. Many seemed surprised to find that they did indeed have coins, rings, watches; a few even had wallets and purses.

Chet slid his hand into his own pockets and for the first time realized he had on his jean jacket. He'd certainly not been wearing it when he died. Other than that he had on what he usually wore—worn-out cords, boots, and a T-shirt. He glanced about, saw that many appeared to be in their Sunday finest, what Chet guessed to be the clothes they were buried in, their faces covered in funeral makeup, but they were in the minority; most instead were in normal day-to-day clothes, even a few with no clothes at all. Chet found no coins in his pockets, just an old lighter. He clutched the pouch full of pennies, suddenly very grateful to Senoy.

Two of the guards lifted their spears, waving a few souls forward. When the souls didn't move, the guards tugged them along, keeping weapons ready while other guards patted them down, asking what they had for payment.

"*No!*" a woman cried. "That's my wedding band." They paid her no heed, pocketing the ring, then rifling beneath her skirt, tearing open her blouse, their rough gray hands searching where they pleased.

The woman burst into tears.

"Save your tears, woman," a guard said, shoving her along. "You'll need them later."

She stumbled up the stairs clutching her blouse, looking dazed, lost, disappearing into the gloom. The guards patted down another soul, then another, taking whatever they wanted, then sending them up the stairs.

*Can't lose the knife,* Chet thought, searching for another way off the landing, but finding nothing but slick black walls disappearing into the mist above.

"He's got nothing," a guard called, pulling aside a nude man.

Dirk nodded toward a block set against the wall. A man stood behind it holding a large cleaver. When the nude man saw this he began to struggle. "*No!*" he cried.

"No?" Dirk asked, walking over. "You pay. Everyone pays. If you don't have coin, you pay with a pound of flesh. Now, it's up to you, flesh or the river?"

The man just kept shaking his head.

Dirk nodded and the guards yanked him over. The cleaver rose, fell, chopping the man's hand clean off. Chet flinched, anticipating the blood, the terrible scream that was sure to follow. But there was no blood, nor scream. The man's face contorted in pain, but only for a moment. He looked more confused than injured. They released him and he just stood there holding his stump.

Several baskets lined the wall, most empty, others full of jackets, shoes, boots, and gloves. The guard threw the severed hand into the basket full of gloves and it was then that Chet understood they weren't gloves. *Oh, fuck.*

The guards pushed the man on his way and he stumbled wordlessly up the steps, clutching his wrist. Anxious murmurs rolled through the crowd, growing in volume.

"Settle down!" Dirk yelled. "Nothing's free. Not in life . . . not in death. You crossed, now it's time to pay. No copper, no gold, then you pay in flesh. It's the law."

Chet found himself caught in the press of souls; it was almost his turn. He knew he had to think of something quick, or he'd lose the knife, wondered if he could slip it through in his boot.

"No way!" a woman cried. It was Ana.

"Lady," Dirk said, reaching for one of the infants, "do them a favor. Do us all a favor. Let the river have them. It'll save you, them, us, all a lot of grief."

"Keep your hands off them!" Ana snapped, pulling the babies back and glaring at him.

"Calm down, lady. Nobody wants your little monkeys. I'm just trying to tell you the river is truly the best thing."

She shook her head.

He shrugged. "Your call, but you'll have to pay . . . for you and for them. No one passes for free." He held out his hand.

She stared at his palm.

"Do you have coin? Pennies? Gold?"

Ana didn't reply.

The man sighed. "Then it'll cost a pound of flesh. A pound for each of—"

Ana bolted, just took off, ducking past the big man, heading for the stairs with a baby clutched beneath each arm.

The guards sprang after her, one of them catching her arm with a hook, yanking her off her feet. The second grabbed hold of an infant, trying to wrestle it from her grasp. She wouldn't let go and he drove his boot, hard, into her ribs. Ana let out a cry, but held tight to the child, kicking and screaming.

"*Stop it!*" Chet cried, pushing forward. "*I can pay for them!*" No one heard him over the shouting and screaming. "Get out of my way," he growled, trying not to drop the baby as he shoved his way to the front.

A guard brought his club down onto Ana, driving the spikes into her stomach. She let out a dreadful scream.

"*Stop it!*" Chet shouted, rushing up. A guard hit him in the back of the head, sent him sprawling. Chet slammed down onto the stone, losing hold of the child. The infant tumbled, ending up on his back at the edge of the river. The baby squalled and tried to sit up, rolling even closer to the ledge. Chet scrambled for the infant and something hit him from behind. He looked down and found a spear blade protruding from the middle of his chest. Chet gasped, coughed, tried to rise.

"Stay down!" a guard yelled, giving the spear a hard shove, pinning Chet to the stone. Chet clutched the blade, grunting through clenched teeth. The pain was a numbing chill, so cold it burned.

"Toss him in the fucking river," Dirk said.

The guard yanked the blade free and Chet gasped as a fresh wave of pain shot through him. He coughed violently, the pain doubling him over, saw the large wound in his chest, marveled that he was still alive—whatever that might mean down here. Two guards snatched him up, the pouch falling from his shoulder when they did, hitting the stone with a clank.

"Wait," Dirk called, stooping to pick up the pouch. The big man untied the cord, removed the knife, giving the hilt a curious look. He slid the blade partially out from the sheaf and his face lit up with surprise. His brow furrowed and slowly his surprise turned to concern, then to what looked like fear. "How—" He shoved it back in the pouch, slapped the flap closed, tying the cord tight, and set hard, suspicious eyes on Chet. "Where did you get this?"

Chet didn't answer, couldn't—the pain overwhelming.

"Who sent you?" Dirk demanded.

Chet could only shake his head.

Dirk slammed his big fist into Chet's chest, directly into the wound, knocking Chet back to the stones. The pain made Chet's vision blur.

"I'm not playing games. Who sent you?"

"I . . . I . . . ." Chet started, trying to get the words out, when another round of violent coughs racked his frame.

Dirk's eyes narrowed. "Who the hell are you?"

All three infants were wailing now, their cries echoing up and down the landing.

Dirk stuffed the pouch into the front of his belt, walked over, and grabbed an infant—the one Chet had carried—up by the leg, dangled it over the river.

"*No!*" Ana screamed.

Chet clutched his chest, trying to sit up.

"Tell me who sent you or this little tyke goes for a swim."

"An angel . . . I was sent here by an—"

"*What madness is this?*" someone shouted from the top of the stairs.

All heads turned as three women tromped down the steps onto the landing. They wore black robes, their faces hidden beneath hoods, their cloaks billowing out behind them as they headed for Dirk. Chet saw they wore swords beneath their cloaks.

The one in the lead tossed back her hood, revealing dark eyes set in a pale, narrow face. Her quick movements and the forward thrust of her birdlike figure gave Chet the impression of a raven in search of prey. When she got closer, Chet noticed a black jewel set into the middle of her forehead. Her severe eyes took in the scene. When they landed on the baby in Dirk's hand the jewel in her forehead blazed crimson.

"Ah, hell," Dirk muttered, lowering the child. "Here's some shit I don't need today."

The woman stormed up to Dirk, her lithe figure half that of the huge man. She held out her hands—waited.

Dirk let out a long sigh and placed the wailing baby in her arms.

The other two women went to Ana, shoving the guards out of the way. They helped Ana to her feet, glaring at the guards, daring them to do something.

The woman with the jewel whispered to the baby and the baby stopped crying, looking at her the way it would its own mother. She nodded toward one of her companions and the woman came forward, taking the child.

The woman with the jewel locked eyes with Dirk.

"Glad to see you're out making everyone's day brighter, Mary," the big man said.

"If it were in my power," Mary said, "I'd strike you down where you stand for this."

"Then it's a good thing for me," he said, smiling wanly, "that it's *not* within your power."

"There are consequences for breaking the law."

"I've broken no laws," Dirk replied. "Those that cross must pay."

"Those bearing infants are granted safe passage," she shot back. "It has always been so."

Dirk shrugged.

"You bring shame to Charon."

"Don't lecture me on your bullshit. The Defenders rule this post now," Dirk said. "And we don't bend knee to the unjust laws of dead and bygone gods. Now, I suggest you take your precious infants and be gone, before I forget my manners and things turn unpleasant."

She appeared ready to strike him. "The last I checked, the Red Lady was very much alive and full of vengeance. Do you really wish to tempt her ire?"

Dirk struggled to hold her eyes. "The old ways are dying along with the old gods." His tone changed, the challenge gone; what was left sounded like a man pleading truth. "That's all. You know it's true. We all have to do what we have to do."

"Lines are forming, toad. Choose your side wisely, because thugs and thieves hiding behind banners will be the first to taste the flame." She turned away, stepped over to Chet. "Are you able to stand?"

Chet realized that the pain was slowly dissipating, that injuries were indeed different here. He got to his knees, taking a moment as the pain continued to subside. Mary put a hand under his arm, helping him to his feet. Chet swayed slightly, looked again at the wound in his chest, and tried to understand how he was alive at all.

"It'll get better with time," she said, leading him toward the women.

Dirk stepped in front of them. "The woman, the babies. They're free to go. But this man, he stays. We have unfinished business."

"I say your business is done," Mary stated flatly.

"Don't press me," Dirk replied, his tone hard, almost desperate. "There's no way he's leaving." He nodded to the guards and they readied their weapons. Dirk touched the hilt of his pistol in warning. "Mary, just take the infants and leave and we'll all live to see another day."

"It's no longer between us," she said, nodding toward the stairs.

At the top of the stone steps was a creature, some sort of big cat with sleek red fur and large feathered wings. Only it wasn't a cat, not from the shoulders up anyway—the creature had the neck and head of a woman. *Why, that's a . . .* it took a moment for the name to come to Chet. *A sphinx,* he thought.

The sphinx stood statue-like, easily twice as tall as any of the souls. Her green eyes locked on Dirk and her tail began flicking back and forth.

Dirk opened his mouth as though to speak but only a long wheeze escaped. The guards all lowered their weapons and stepped well back from the women.

Dirk's hand left his pistol. He too backed away, one step, another, bumping into Chet, seeming unaware of anything other than the piercing stare of the sphinx.

Chet saw his chance, slipping Senoy's pouch from Dirk's belt and moving quickly away from the huge man.

Dirk touched his belt, a slow, distracted movement. He frowned, glanced down, noticed the pouch gone, and saw Chet walking away. "Hey!" He took a step after Chet.

A low growl came from the landing. Despite the deadening fog, this sound rumbled, resonated; Chet felt it right to his core.

Dirk froze.

"Leave now," Mary said, addressing those souls still remaining on the landing. They hesitated, staring at the sphinx, but one left, followed by a few more, then the rest, tromping quickly past Dirk and his men.

Mary gave Dirk one last dark look. "Watch your deeds, toad. The Red Lady's wrath is unforgiving." She spun away, her cloak twirling, and headed up the stairs. The women fell in behind her, escorting Ana and the babies. Chet started after them.

"Hey," Dirk hissed.

Chet glanced back.

"Leave the pouch or you'll be sorry."

Chet kept going, quickly following the others up the stone stairs.

## CHAPTER 12

Chet made the top of the stairs before he stopped and examined the wound in his chest. The meat around the injury was gray and leathery and a fair amount of blackish liquid oozed from the edges. It still throbbed, but the pain continued to recede. He touched the gash; it felt more like clay than flesh. He wondered just what he was made of, noticed a speck of ivory deeper in the wound and realized it must be bone, part of his rib cage. He grimaced. *I'm still walking. That's something.*

The women gathered around the sphinx on the far side of the wide square. Chet approached, captivated by the creature. She was beautiful and dreadful in equal measures. Her face, though human, was still catlike, regal and fierce, framed by two thick braids and tousles of long red hair forming a great mane that spilled down her shoulders and ran the length of her back. Two large horns curved out from an ornate copper headdress of curling spikes. A wide, layered necklace of spiked copper plates draped across her chest. Her emerald eyes seemed disinterested in those around her, staring intently downriver. Chet followed her gaze, saw only the ghostly outlines of ramshackle shacks and docks.

A handful of shadowy souls shuffled past along the cobblestone street; the ones that noticed the sphinx kept well away. Chet hesitated, unsure if coming any closer was a good idea.

Mary noticed him, beckoned him over, and he found the full weight of her intense gaze upon him. The gem in her forehead glowed faintly as she looked him up and down. "What's your name?"

"Chet."

"Chet." She said the word slowly, as though tasting it. Her face softened a degree and the gem briefly glowed a pale green. "That was a brave thing you and Ana did."

Chet shrugged.

"It's not easy," Mary added. "Coming over. It is a daunting enough task to find one's own way, much less to take on the burden of others.

"I'm Mary." She touched her forehead. "This is Sister Elaine and Sister Nora. And this," she gestured to the sphinx, "is Sekhmet, the Eye of Ra, the guardian of the gods. Known by most as the Red Lady."

The sphinx made no acknowledgment, only continued her vigil.

A grinding sound approached. Four more women wearing black robes materialized out of the mist, pulling a cart with a wood cage on the back. One of them ran ahead, breathless. "Were you in time?" She pushed several strands of long dark hair from her face, tucking them beneath her cap, and her eyes alighted on the three infants. A relieved smile spread across her face. "Thank God's good grace we heard them when we did."

"No, thank Chet and Ana's good grace," Mary said, introducing the woman as Isabel.

"Was it Dirk again?"

Mary nodded.

Isabel spat on the ground. "Does he think we're stupid? That we can't see through his bullshit?"

"I don't believe he cares."

"We can't allow this," Isabel said.

"He's broken no laws," Mary replied, the frustration obvious on her face.

"If he's throwing children into the river, he has."

"There's no law forbidding such. None other than that of common humanity."

Isabel squinted across the square. "It's *him*! That man. The one that's been following us."

A figure in a wide-brim hat and cloak leaned against the wall near the top of the stairs. The man kept his eyes hidden beneath the brim.

"It is indeed," Mary said.

"Another fucking Green Coat spy," Isabel spat. "They're everywhere these days."

Dirk came up the stairs with a few guards, walked over to the man, and they began conversing.

Isabel slid back her cloak, clutching the hilt of a long sword. "What are we waiting for? Let's send them all for a swim."

Mary glanced up to the Red Lady, but the sphinx's face remained stone. "Not today," Mary said.

"Then when?" Isabel asked. "If we wait until the last temple is burned, the last god is driven away, it'll be too late."

"Not today," Mary repeated.

Isabel's jaw tightened, obviously struggling not to say more.

The women pulled up with the cart. Chet thought the cage full of blankets at first, noticed the blankets moving, and realized there were babies among the linens, some sleeping, others quietly watching the souls march by.

The infant in Ana's arms began to whimper, then cry.

"Here," Mary said. "May I?" Ana handed the child over. Mary cuddled the baby, the gemstone in her forehead turning soft green as she whispered to it. The infant stopped squirming, fixated on the stone, and began to coo. After a moment Mary strolled over and sat the child in the cart with the others.

"What's going happen to them?" Ana asked.

"We're taking them to Lethe. These fortunate few will be spared endlessly wandering Erebus, or worse, drowning in the river of torment." Mary looked sadly at the infants. "But there are always others."

"Lethe? What is Lethe?"

"Ana, what is it that you seek?"

Ana took a moment. "I'm not seeking anything."

"We're all seeking something. It's why we're here." Mary nodded toward the other women. "The sisters gather the lost infants, shepherd them to a better place. For many, this act of selflessness brings purpose to their existence . . . helps them to heal, but more importantly, helps them find what they need."

Ana's brow furrowed.

"Ana," Mary said. "The sisterhood is always in need of courageous hearts. Join us. Redemption need not be a path walked alone."

"Redemption," Ana said, almost spat. "There's no redemption for me."

"You aren't the first to say that," Mary countered. "Once you have a taste of this place, if your heart doesn't find what it needs . . . seek us out."

Chet cleared his throat. "Could I ask you something?"

Mary turned to him.

"Hell, this is gonna sound stupid . . . but any chance you've heard of a man named Gavin Moran?" Chet waited, searching for some sign of recognition among the women's faces, found none.

Mary smiled. "Purgatory is a big place, Chet."

Chet sighed. "I thought it might be."

"Is he your father?"

"Grandfather."

"If your grandfather's soul indeed resides in purgatory, then you need but find a bloodseeker."

"A bloodseeker, huh?"

"A true bloodseeker, not one of the hucksters on the riverfront. They're all working for the Green Coats now. They will steal what they can, giving only lies in return."

"Yeah, head to Old City," Isabel put in. "The Green Coats don't have much hold there . . . not yet anyway. Some of the ancient ones are still there and their sight is strong. It's not far. At the top of Calvary Hill, what some call the Place of the Crosses. Just head up the path here until you get to the main square. You can see Calvary Hill from there if the fog's not too bad. A whole hillside full of crosses. There's one in every little dipshit town down here. Souls, trying to get right with Jesus by doing awful things to themselves. Someone needs to tell them there's no shortcut to redemption."

Mary nodded. "Once you reach Calvary Hill, look for an archway topped with ravens. Pass through and look for signs bearing the eye with the red teardrop." She took a step closer to Chet, spoke low. "And, Chet, keep your mark well hidden."

Chet tensed, instinctively clutching his hand shut.

"Your mark is hidden from most." She touched the jewel on her forehead. "I have my own sight. It's my gift, sometimes my curse, to see into people. But just know there will always be those who see, those who would trade your head for the bounty."

"Bounty?"

"Lucifer's minions pay well for damned souls. And though it is forbidden to trade with demons, to even talk with demons, there are plenty, as you have seen, who pay little heed to the edicts of the underworld."

Chet glanced at the souls stumbling past. He felt as though everyone was watching him, as though they could all could see the mark.

"The cities are safest," Mary said. "Demons won't enter, but the soul hunters, they can be anywhere. Your best chance is to find your clan, your family, your grandfather. Blood looks after its own."

*If only that were true,* Chet thought bitterly.

One of the infants pulled itself up on the bars, reached for Ana. "It's as though God overlooked them," Ana said.

Mary sighed. "Yes, but which god? All have hopes that the afterlife will somehow be an orderly place. Death is madness and chaos—a hundred gods fighting over the dead. Sense, reason, fairness . . . they're all foreigners here."

A cry echoed from somewhere down the bank. It sounded like a baby. The Red Lady looked over, then started away.

Isabel and the rest of the sisters followed. Mary held back a moment, clasping Ana's hand. "Ana, when you're ready, seek us out." She released Ana, striding quickly away after her companions.

## CHAPTER 13

Chet watched the robed women disappear into the mist, then glanced back toward the stairs. Dirk and the man in the wide-brim hat were still watching him.

"We need to get out of here," Chet said.

Ana followed his eyes, nodded. They started walking in the direction of the town. "Are you going to try and find one of those bloodseekers?" Ana asked.

"Yeah, guess so. How about you? Think you have any family down here?"

"God, I hope not."

"Might be good to at least see."

"My family would spit in my face . . . and I wouldn't blame them a bit."

He glanced over. Her mouth was set, grim. He didn't press.

"When I did it," she said, "took all those pills . . . I thought I was escaping." She shook her head. "Didn't know there'd be all this . . . y'know . . . all this shit after. Thought death was the end. And fuck you hallelujah if the shit doesn't just keep going and going."

They continued walking, neither talking, watching souls shuffle by with despondent, sorrowful faces. Chet kept glancing behind, expecting to find Dirk and the man in the wide-brim hat following, but saw no sign of them.

"Hey," someone said. Chet felt a tap on his shoulder, turned to find a teenager. It took him a moment to recognize him from the barge. He was the one who looked to have had paralysis before the change. He fell in with them. "What was she like?"

Chet gave him a questioning look.

"The lion woman. The sphinx. Holy shit, I can't believe you got that close. I mean she was just as real as we are. I still can't believe it. Can't believe any of this. Keep thinking I'm going to wake up, y'know. It's so cool."

Chet and Ana stared at the kid as though he'd lost his mind.

"Hey, I'm not crazy." The kid laughed. "I'm just free. Free from that chair." He darted away, hopped up onto a boulder, and leapt into the air—practically bounced back to them. "Oh, man, feels so good to be able to move."

"What's wrong with you?" Ana asked.

"Me?"

"Can't you see you're dead? We're all dead. That this place sucks?"

The kid looked around. "I don't know. It's all overwhelming, terrible, yet . . . *fascinating* too. Y'know."

"You were in a wheelchair?" Chet asked.

The kid nodded. "Fifteen years. I was paralyzed, a quadriplegic. It was worse than this . . . I mean to say I'd rather be here right now than back in that chair." He lowered his voice as though talking to himself. "Rather be anywhere than back in that chair."

Chet hoped the kid still felt that way once the weight of this place really sank in.

"Hey, I'm Johnny by the way." The kid stuck out his hand.

Chet took it. "Chet. And this is Ana."

"Man," Johnny said. "Thought you were a goner back there. I mean when he stabbed you. But even with that big hole in your chest you're still going. Can't say the same for the poor guy with the cracked skull. Gets you wondering, too—what happens to *dead* dead?"

"Probably just go someplace else where there's even worse shit," Ana said.

The stone road became more and more populated as they continued, souls of all races coming and going, many barefoot, some nude, and several with missing hands and limbs, most of the traffic moving toward town.

It quickly became apparent which souls had been here awhile—the older inhabitants' skin, hair, and eyes were all turning gray like wood left in the weather, as though they were becoming one with the dirt and stone around them. They wore an assortment of dress, and even that seemed to be fading to gray, from rags to finery, styles from all down the ages, from biblical to modern times. Chet saw horned helmets, top hats, turbans, baseball caps, sandals, tennis shoes, combat boots, jeans, fatigues, robes, tunics, and cloaks, in endless variations and combinations. But it was more than their dress, it was their manner, the older inhabitants going about their business with purposeful intent, not hiding their annoyance of the slow-moving, confused newcomers. Many carried weapons: swords, knives, spears, clubs. A few even wore bits of chain mail and armor.

The tents and mud-brick shacks gave way to taller structures, some two- and three-story stone buildings—empty, hollow-looking places with crumbling facades, the top floors collapsed or vacant, their windows dark. Scripture, names, and proclamations were scratched here and there along the walls in chalk and charcoal. Over and over they saw the words DO NOT FEED THE GODS and FREEDOM written in tall red letters.

Stalls began to appear in front of many of these buildings. Chet stepped up, peering into one of the shops, and found ragged clothing, shoes, and a few shoddy-looking clubs hanging along the wall. The shopkeeper didn't even bother to look up, just sat staring at the dirt floor.

They kept moving and soon the road emptied into a large circular plaza paved with massive flagstones. Hundreds of souls, carts, and wagons were milling about or crossing through, along with the occasional group of patrolling Green Coats. An enormous statue lay toppled in the center of the plaza, surrounded by the shattered remains of dozens of smaller statues—life-size dancing figures. The central figure lay on its side, its head broken off at the neck, the androgynous face contorted, its mouth open as though wailing, its eyes smashed away. Someone had stuffed its mouth with the arms and legs of the shattered dancers.

"That must've really been something in its day," Johnny said. "Must've stood, what, two hundred feet tall?"

Chet spotted a post topped with signs jutting from the rubble next to the giant head. He started forward, stopped as a wagon rumbled past. Six souls were harnessed to the front of the wagon, their skin charred, their eyes gone. A dwarfish man sat atop the wagon, driving them with a rein and whip. Two guards wearing green jackets sat next to him, holding some sort of muskets. The wagon bed was full of arms, legs, and hands.

"What do you think of that, Johnny?" Ana asked; her tone bitter. "Was that *fascinating?*"

Johnny didn't answer, just stared after the wagon.

Chet and Ana made their way to the base of the statue. A moment later Johnny caught up, caught Chet by the arm. "Careful." He pointed at a broken statue Chet had just set his foot on. The statue was missing both legs, an arm, and most of its torso. It opened its eyes, opened its mouth. No words, no sound, just a blank stare.

Chet stepped back and really looked at the statues, realized that many of them weren't statues at all, but souls, broken, twisted souls, gray as the stone—lying motionless, their eyes listless and unblinking.

The three of them moved to the front of the giant head. Someone had splashed the broken arms and legs hanging from the enormous mouth with red paint, had written along the cheek in that same paint, DO NOT FEED THE GODS.

"What d'you think that means?" Johnny asked.

"It sure doesn't mean anything good," Ana replied.

Chet turned his attention to the signage. The post was topped with a soggy banner reading, CITY STYGA. Below that several arrow-shaped signs pointed in different directions: River Styx, Caravans, Temple Lethe, Calvary Hill, Old City, River Road. One sign held his eye, a black arrow below the others and pointing back down river. The four red letters read: HELL. Chet suppressed a shudder, surprised at the power those four letters now held. He glanced downriver, knowing that if he went that way Hell *would* claim him. That there would really be demons, creatures from his worst nightmares waiting to torment him, to bite, burn, and tear his flesh from his bones over and over. He found himself clutching his hand, keeping the brand hidden.

"Calvary Hill must be that way," Ana said, pointing up the main avenue.

Chet nodded. He could just make out the misty outline of a hill in the distance.

"What's there?" Johnny asked.

"Supposed to be someone that can help you find family," Chet said. "They're called bloodseekers."

"Bloodseekers," Johnny repeated, then said it again as though liking the sound of the word. "Y'know, that could be interesting." He cut his eyes to Ana. "Could be like a quest." He laughed. "Quest for the bloodseekers of Styga. Sounds like a grand adventure. Count me in."

"Quest?" Ana said. "What's it going to take for you to understand that this isn't some adventure from one of your storybooks?"

"Know what?" He gave her a wicked grin. "Peter Pan once said, 'Death is a mighty big adventure.' I'm going with that."

## CHAPTER 14

Larry Wagner, better known to many around Jasper, Alabama, as simply "Coach," trudged up the main thoroughfare of Styga in the direction of Calvary Hill. He didn't know where he was heading, didn't care. He was just following the other aimless souls, following the broad ruts running along the flagstone and wondering just how many millions of feet it had taken over how many eons to carve such profound grooves into the hard stone.

The avenue narrowed, pressing the drifting crowd together, making the going slow. There were more stalls along this way and soon calls from shopkeepers began to break the monotonous sound of shuffling feet.

He caught the rumble of far-off thunder and a flake drifted past, another, then many. *It's snowing,* Coach thought, looking upward. The fog had lifted a degree, revealing dense, dark clouds overhead. He caught a flake, saw that it wasn't snow, but ash. The falling ash increased as he walked, swirling down the avenue and pooling along gutters and walls.

Coach looked at his hands, at the pale grayish flesh. *I'm dead . . . fucking dead.* He shook his head, still trying to understand how one minute he was heading out for a nice day of fishing, the next looking down at his own cracked skull. *And that piece of trash, Chet, that little fuckup, just driving away.* What Coach wanted, wanted more than anything at this moment, was to get his cold, dead hands on Chet. He clenched them into fists as the events played and replayed themselves in his mind, the way his old high school football days often did—the day the Bear himself showed up scouting players, and that pass, him in the all clear, the ball hitting him right on the numbers and bouncing away, just bouncing away along with any shot at college ball. How many times had he replayed that in his mind, a thousand? More like a hundred thousand. If *only* he'd caught that ball. Now it was the kid, Chet. *If only I'd moved a little faster, timed it a little better. I'd've gotten that fucker. Would've put that tire jack right through the driver's window. Then it'd be that boy with his head cracked open, that boy walking around this hell. Not me. Not me!*

An arm slipped around his, startling him.

"Don't be afraid," came a breathless voice. "I am here to help you."

A woman, smelling of incense and draped in gypsy scarves, walked beside him. She gave him an alluring look. "I am Madeline, queen of the bloodseekers. Let me help you find what you need." She tugged him, trying to steer him toward a small checkered tent bearing the mark of an eye with a red teardrop. A beefy man in a green jacket stood beside the tent, watching them intently. Coach didn't like the woman's overdone makeup, the ridiculous-looking eye painted upon her forehead, but more than that, he wanted nothing more to do with these green jacket men, not after his ordeal back at the landing. He pulled away.

"Just a pence," she called after him, a note of desperation in her voice. "That's all and I can bring you home to your loved ones."

Coach didn't look back, just kept shuffling along. He heard music drifting down the avenue and came upon a man playing a fiddle—a somber, mesmerizing tune. Coach closed his eyes, trying to float away with the song, trying for one moment to forget he was dead. Someone touched his arm and he opened his eyes to find a small wisp of a woman, with a streak of red paint smeared down the middle of her face, staring up at him. She wore a tattered gray cloak, her large dark eyes shadowed beneath the hood. "Your mother is waiting for you."

"Leave me alone," he said and tried to pull away. Her grip tightened and then . . . he *saw* her, his mother, just a glimpse.

"Your mother is waiting for you," she repeated.

"What do you know about my mom?" he asked, shaken.

She nodded toward a stall covered in gray tarps. "Sit with me and I will tell you all I can."

He hesitated.

"I am not with the Green Coats. Pay me what you can." She seemed sincere.

Larry had lost the few coins he'd crossed over with to the Green Coats at the dock; all he had left was his brass whistle. He pulled it out of his pocket.

She looked at it, smiled. "It will be enough." She turned, headed into the stall.

Coach sucked in a chest full of air and followed.

## CHAPTER 15

Chet, Ana, and Johnny headed up Styga's main thoroughfare. As they made their way along the avenue, Chet noticed that the shops here offered shoes and clothes, as along the river road, but of better condition and quality. Weapons as well, not only clubs, but steel swords and knives, even chain mail. There were also stalls offering potions, crosses, and totems, signs and banners touting bloodseekers, readings, cobblers, offerings of work for coin, or guided passage. There were many more of which he couldn't readily discern the meaning, such as "Bone Spice" with a picture of a cigarette, "Moore Mine—Five fleshies for forty turns of Eye," and the more ominous ones he could understand only too well, like "Coin for Flesh." He also noted the occasional Green Coat standing about here and there, eyeing everyone who passed.

"There's no eating places," Johnny said.

"How can you be hungry?" Ana asked.

"That's just it. I'm not. Are you?"

Chet and Ana shook their heads.

"That's my point. Do we need to eat? Or drink? I'm not thirsty either, but that sure looks like a saloon over there." He pointed to a sign above a green door reading "Drown Your Sorrows." Had a picture of a bottle with the word "Lethe" written on it. Another just across the street also had a bottle with the word "Lethe." It was simply called "Forget." A man who looked half out of his mind stumbled out with a bottle in his hand. He leaned against the wall and slid down onto his rump next to a few other souls with similarly muddled expressions.

"They're drunk," Ana said.

"Or high," Johnny said, nodding to a group of souls standing in front of a stall inhaling smoke from long, curved pipes.

Chet noticed plenty of the shopkeepers smoking as well, mostly from long reeds or hand-rolled cigarettes. The smoke didn't smell like tobacco; it had a sour bite that stung his nose.

Something bumped into Chet's leg.

"Watch it, jackass," came a sharp voice. It was a kid, no more than six years old. There was a gang of them, maybe a dozen altogether, none looking older than ten years of age, several with cigarettes hanging out of their mouths. They all glared at Chet.

"Hey . . . sorry," Chet said.

"Sorry yourself, cocksucker," the kid shot back.

"Well, don't you have a nasty little mouth," Ana said.

The kid gave her the bird, a look on his face daring Ana to do something. That's when Chet noticed every one of them was carrying a knife or sharpened stick.

"C'mon," Chet said. "Let's go." They left the kids and their glares behind, continuing up the avenue.

A woman, smelling of incense and draped in gypsy scarves, fell in step with Ana. She gave Ana what Chet guessed was supposed to be an alluring look, one of mystical prowess, but the overdone makeup and large eye painted upon her forehead created a more comical effect. "I am Madeline, queen of the bloodseekers." She placed a hand upon Ana's arm, trying to steer her toward a checkered tent. "Allow me to reunite you with your loved ones."

"My loved ones don't want a damn thing to do with me," Ana said bitterly, her eyes daring the woman to say more.

The woman backed off, searching the crowd for more amiable prey.

The shop next to the checkered tent had a small selection of weapons on display. It occurred to Chet that the three of them might stand a better chance if they were armed, that at the very least it might make them less of a target. He weighed the pouch, wondering what, if anything, the pennies could buy. He stepped up to the counter; the shopkeeper was haggling with a woman over a pair of boots. A girl in her teens—she might've been the shopkeeper's daughter, judging by their similar sharp noses—walked over to him.

"How much for the club?"

The girl picked it up. "Well, this is a really good one. See, no rust on the spikes. It's four fleshies."

"Fleshies?"

"You're still wet, aren't you. Fleshies . . . ka coins. See?" She pulled a brown leathery coin from her pocket, held it up. "You got any of these?"

Chet shook his head and she instantly lost interest, looking beyond him for the next customer.

Chet pulled out a handful of pennies. "Can I pay with these?"

The girl's eyes grew wide. "Why . . . why, you could buy all the weapons on this street with those." The shopkeeper suddenly appeared, pushing the girl aside. "Sir, you don't want this old club." He reached under the counter, brought out four steel swords. "Take your pick. Why I'll even throw in a helmet. A shirt of mail perhaps?"

Chet caught sight of a Green Coat moving rapidly toward them, a spiked club in his hand.

"Sir." It was the shopkeeper talking to Chet. "Here, how about two swords then. Two—"

The Green Coat stepped up behind them, blocking them in. He leveled the club at Chet and Ana. "You two. Stay right where you're at." He peered down the avenue, pursed his lips, and whistled loud and sharp.

Chet caught sight of a man—the one in the wide-brim hat from the docks, scanning the crowd far down the avenue. The Green Coat whistled again; this time the man saw them. Chet realized there were at least a dozen Green Coats with the man, all carrying weapons, all looking at him.

Ana saw them too, and made to slip past the Green Coat guarding them. He cut her off, jabbing the club into her stomach, knocking her down.

Johnny came out of nowhere and hit the guard, catching him completely by surprise. He smashed a fist right into his neck, followed by two more driving punches to the side of his head, then a knee into the man's abdomen. The guard doubled over.

The armed men were shouting and shoving their way toward them through the throng of souls.

Chet grabbed Ana, pulling her to her feet, helping her away. Johnny snatched the club away from the fallen guard, giving him a solid kick to the stomach before following Chet into the crowd.

Chet hooked a right at the first intersection, a left up an alley, followed by one quick turn after another, sprinting down the winding streets and lanes. The streets branched off, spiderwebbing in all directions, and Chet quickly lost any sense of where the main avenue might lie. The three of them came out into a small square and stopped.

"Smell that?" Ana asked.

A thick haze filled the square; the air was dense, sticky, a smell akin to burning tires. Chet saw no other new souls here, only a handful of gray, weathered men in rags, pushing carts or carrying bundles. He glanced back the way they'd come, heard no sign of the Green Coats.

Souls began to notice them, giving them grim, ominous looks.

"We should keep moving," Ana said.

"That way seems to lead uphill," Johnny put in.

They crossed the square, making their way along a narrow street lined with workshops and warehouses, doing their best to avoid the potholes, refuse, and the oily, mucky water snaking its way along the gutter. Smoke and steam drifted from grates and pipes jutting from the walls and roofs, staining the shop fronts black with soot and grease.

"Y'know," Johnny said, "that was the first real fight I've ever been in. Felt good to be able to do something about an asshole like that. You have to take a lot of shit when you're stuck in a wheelchair. People staring, saying whatever asinine thing they want to you." He slapped the club into his palm. "Felt good."

A blast of hot air blew from an open door. Chet saw men, their skin burnt and blackened, hammering ore in front of a furnace, several others pumping a huge bellows, sending heat and sparks rolling across the cobblestones. In another shop they saw bones of all sizes and shapes, some massive, like elephant or dinosaur bones, stacked in heaps. Souls cranked gears and belts, spinning a tall saw blade, while others pushed the large bones through the blade, cutting them into planks, stacking them like lumber.

Ana stopped, pointed, but didn't need to. Chet saw them right away: severed heads, dozens of them, hanging along the side of the building ahead. As they approached, Chet noticed a sign hanging beneath them reading THIEVES. He peered through the bars lining the narrow windows where he could see workers unloading cords of wood from a wagon, only he realized it wasn't wood but arms and legs, even a few torsos, but mostly baskets of hands, like he'd seen down on the landing. Farther in, among the smoke, workers chopped them into chunks, dumping them into huge steaming kettles. Chet caught sight of three armed men in green jackets standing inside, watching over the workers.

"Shouldn't be down here," a voice came from above. Chet looked up at the severed heads. Most of them appeared dried up, mummified, but several were watching them.

"You lost?" one of them said, the one with long stringy hair and a thin mustache.

"Looking for Calvary Hill," Johnny replied, and Chet wished he hadn't. Didn't think it was a good idea to tell anyone where they were going.

"Tell you what," the head said, lowering his voice. "You cut me down off here and I'll take you right there. Take you wherever you want. What d'you say?"

"You touch him and your head will end up right next to him," the next head over said, a woman with black curly hair. "You don't want to be messing in Green Coat business."

"Why don't you keep your nose out of this," the man retorted.

"Just keep heading the way you're going," the woman continued. "To Mirror Square. You'll know it when you come to it. Take the first alley on the left, the widest one. Follow that. It'll weave all over the damn place, but eventually it comes out just below Calvary. Won't take long to start seeing all them fools and their crosses."

"You listen to her and you'll end up getting cut up and eaten. I'm telling you, you need a guide. You need—"

"Hey," a stern voice called. "What do you want?"

Chet turned to see a man in a green jacket, holding a spiked club, standing in the doorway.

"You got business here?"

Chet shook his head. "No. No business."

The guard eyed them suspiciously. "Then you best be off. Hadn't you?"

They moved on, heading quickly up the street. Chet glanced back when they were about a block away. The guard still stood there, watching them.

CHAPTER 16

_____

Ana fought an overwhelming sense of claustrophobia as the alley
continued to narrow, as the rickety buildings loomed over them, leaning
inward as though they might topple at any moment, as the fog grew denser.
They skirted heaps of gray bricks and bones of structures that had long
since fallen beneath the weight of time. The sky darkened as the ash continued to drift downward, adding to the sense of being slowly buried. She
wondered where the ash was coming from. Was it volcanic? Or something
worse? She recalled the black sign with the red letters spelling HELL.

A few souls huddled together in a shadowy alley. Ana was unsure if they
were men or women, as they weren't much more than rags and bones—
their withered flesh crumbling like old tree stumps, hard to distinguish
from the rubble as the ash piled up upon them. Most stared at the wall,
or nothing at all, but a few followed her with their eyes. _Hungry eyes,_ she
thought.

She glanced back the way they'd come. It had been a long time since
they'd seen a shop or anyone other than these withering souls.

"Fuck," Chet said, and Ana followed his eyes to a few souls hunched
over some rags; they appeared to be eating them. Ana was trying to convince herself the rags weren't what she knew they must be, when Johnny
stepped closer and the souls glanced up. She then clearly saw that it was
a man, his head, torso, and one remaining arm riddled with gaping bite
marks. She was prepared for that, or at least she thought she was until the

man, the thing they were eating, looked at her with miserable pleading eyes, his mouth opening and closing silently.

"Oh, God," she gasped.

Johnny slapped his club against the ground. "Get away from him!" he yelled and the souls slid back, snarling like dogs, dragging what was left of the man into the alley with them. Johnny took a step after them and Ana grabbed his arm. "No."

Dozens of faces stared back at them from the gloom, then more and more. She saw heaps of souls tangled together. There came a rustling as slowly, the souls began to stir, writhing like maggots in rotting flesh as they pulled themselves from beneath the moldering rags, bones, and clumps of human hair.

"Let's go," Ana said, and when Johnny just stood there staring, she grabbed him. "Now."

They moved on, Ana keeping a sharp eye on the alleys as they passed, and here and there she saw them, those hungry faces watching them from the shadows. A shudder ran down her body. *I hate this place. Fucking hate this place.*

"Hey . . . there," Johnny said. "That's has to be it."

They came to the edge of the small plaza and stopped. Six standing stones, seven or eight feet tall, ringed the plaza, each tiled in broken bits of mirrors. A handful of souls sat in front of the stones, staring into the glass, their eyes glazed and distant. A woman was sobbing as she leaned against the base of a stone, touching her reflection with her fingertips.

Johnny walked up to one of the stones, peered into the glass, fell back a step, obviously surprised. He turned his head from side to side, studied his reflection. "That's really strange."

Ana walked up, looked at his reflection, noticed nothing out of the ordinary. Then her own reflection caught her eye. She let out a gasp. It was her, but not.

"Ana, how old do you think I am?" Johnny asked.

"I don't know. Seventeen. Eighteen maybe?"

"I was thirty-eight when I killed myself."

She looked at him again.

"I'm like I was . . . *before* . . . the accident." He touched the glass. "After the accident, I avoided mirrors. Hated what I saw there." He pointed at his reflection. "When I thought of myself . . . *this* is who I saw. The kid, the one who could run and jump. Not the twisted, shriveled thing I became. I think there's something to that. Remember all the old people on the barge? They changed too."

Ana looked again at her own reflection. *He's right. It's me, but a younger me, before all the hard lines and shadows, before all the bad.* She started to turn away when something else caught her eye: the background of the glass. It wasn't reflecting the gray walls of the square, but . . . she leaned closer, stared, as it slowly came into focus. "Oh." Her breath left her.

"Hey," Johnny said. "It's . . . why that's my old bedroom."

Ana nodded. It was her living room she was seeing, the one in San Juan. But before the fire. It was so vivid. *God, the colors.*

Johnny turned away from his reflection. "I hated that place. It was a prison. I never want to see it again."

Ana put her hand on the glass. *God, please . . . one more chance.*

"We need to go," Chet said. Ana heard him, but didn't.

Chet sat a hand on her shoulder. "Ana." His words were soft, but stern. "Ana." He tried to tug her away and she shoved his arm, her eyes never leaving the glass. "Wait . . . just a little longer."

He wrapped his arms around her, lifted her, dragging her from the mirror.

"Stop it!" she cried. "Fuck, let me go!"

He turned her toward the sobbing woman and pointed.

The sobbing woman began scratching at the glass as though she might be able to claw her way in, began to wail. Ana glanced around at the others, the souls sitting in front of the mirrors, all lost in the reflections.

"It's okay," she said. "You can let go. I get it."

He let her go, but still kept an arm around her, leading her away. She fought not to look back, wanting one more glimpse of a time, of a place, when things had been so good.

## CHAPTER 17

They met no other souls as the narrow lane slowly wound through the crumbling buildings, nothing but shadows staring at them from the windows and doors. Chet dug through some rubble, found two shafts of bone, and handed one to Ana. The club felt solid and she was glad to have something in her hand.

After a bit the thick mist turned into a light drizzle; a drop of water hit Ana, another, then another. "You have to be kidding me," she said. "Rain, down here?"

They marched along to the sound of water dribbling from overhangs and gutters. The rain mixed with the ash, melting, turning into muck, the stones becoming dark and slick. Soon they were soaked.

"Johnny," Ana said. "You said you killed yourself. Well . . . but . . . weren't you a quadriplegic?"

"Hard to figure, huh?" He gave her that big grin of his.

"It's not my business. I just—"

"I spent most of the last fifteen years trying to answer that question. Just how does a man, who can't move anything but his mouth, eyes, and a few fingers, kill himself? Well, one way is to chew off your own tongue and bleed to death. Thought about that one a lot, just couldn't do it. You can *not* eat. But that wasn't an option, not while my mom was looking after me. Not unless I wanted a feeding tube crammed down my throat. My answer arrived one day in the form of a powered wheelchair."

"Wheelchair?"

"Yes, ma'am. Bright red. Damn thing could hit six miles per hour. Only needed one finger to operate. Well, that I had.

"Mom liked to get me outside as much as she could. Felt the sunshine was good for me. Our house backed up to my uncle's property. He had a little catfish pond. Mom used to wheel me over there to watch my cousins fish. I can tell you, there's not much more exciting than watching other people fish." He laughed, but Ana didn't hear any humor in it.

"Well, she brought me over in my brand-new, used power chair. I asked her if she wouldn't mind getting me a soda. The minute she was out of sight, I maneuvered that vehicle up onto the dock, pushed that stick forward, and off I went. Flew off the end going full speed and *sp-lash*!" He punctuated the sound by slapping the end of his club into a puddle. "I was strapped into that hunk of metal, so down I sank. Right to the bottom. The sunlight was so pretty from down there . . . you should've seen it." His grin faded. "Of course I was long gone by the time they dragged me out. I did hang around a bit. Y'know how it is. Watched them pull me out. Might've stayed awhile, but it was hard to watch my mom. She was so broken up."

Ana nodded. "I'm sorry, Johnny. I shouldn't have pried."

"No, it's fine. Really. I mean it was best for everyone. I did it as much for my mom as for me. That's the thing, the way she cared for me . . . she was just as much a prisoner to that chair as I was. I just hope to God she's getting on with her life now."

Ana reached over, touched his arm. "I'm sorry anyway, about you . . . and your mother."

He smiled. "I don't know what this place holds. But for now, I'm just trying to enjoy being free from that chair. If there's a way to have a life down here, any kind of life, I'm going to find it."

They continued on, the sound of their shuffling feet accompanied by rain dripping from the desolate buildings.

"How about you, Ana?" Johnny asked. "How'd you go?"

Ana started to answer, hesitated.

"Don't feel like you need to say if you don't want to."

Ana took a deep breath. "Overdosed."

"Drugs?"

"No. Yes. But not like you think. They were prescription . . . pain pills. I took two bottles of them."

"You killed yourself?"

"Yeah, Johnny, that's what they call it when you take two bottles of pills."

He was quiet.

"Sorry," she said. "Hard to talk about. I . . . just . . . I screwed up. Screwed up so bad." She choked up, unable to continue.

"Hey," Johnny said, putting an arm around her. "Don't be so hard—"

"No!" She shrugged his arm off. "Don't comfort me. Don't you dare. I should be burning in Hell for what I did."

Both Chet and Johnny looked at her surprised, concerned, and it was their concern that did it, that brought on her tears.

"I killed him." She stopped walking. "I killed my little baby boy."

They both looked at her in horror and she knew she deserved it, deserved their scorn, their disgust. She turned away.

"I set the place on fire. It was my fucking smoking. How many times had Juan told me not to smoke in bed? Y'know, and I'd get all pissed off at him. Tell him he wasn't my father. And look, look what happened." She let out a sob. "I woke up coughing, choking. The carpet was burning, the curtains. It was like they were made of gasoline. Smoke already so thick I couldn't see the door. I heard him, can't stop hearing him. My little baby boy . . . coughing, crying. He was over by the curtains." Ana let out another sob. "I tried to get to him, swear to God I did. Couldn't breathe. Smoke burning my eyes. I kept trying to find him. Trying, and trying. I was on my knees by then, crawling around and around. At some point I passed out."

She sat down on the curb, crying and staring at her feet.

Johnny sat down beside her.

"If God had any mercy he would've let me die with my baby. But I didn't . . . no . . . woke up in the hospital. The inside of my lungs were burned pretty bad. My parents came and took me home. No one said anything, y'know. Not to me . . . not the things they should've. I might've kept going. But when I heard they were sending Juan home from Vietnam on

117

bereavement leave . . . well . . . well, how could I face him? How do you ever look a man in the eye after killing his only son? Can you answer me that one?"

Johnny shook his head.

"That's when I took all the pills. Just wanted an end. Wanted to stop hearing my baby crying in my head. Now here I am. I guess this is my punishment . . . my Hell. To have to live with what I did for all eternity."

She buried her face in her hands. Johnny put his arm around her again. This time she didn't push him away. After a moment she touched his hand, held it, and for the first time since the fire, felt some comfort.

A clack, it sounded like it came from down the alley behind them.

"We should keep going," Chet said in a hushed voice.

They heard another clack, they couldn't tell from where. Johnny stood up, pulled Ana to her feet, and the three of them got moving, keeping a sharp eye on all the dark windows and doors as they plodded up the narrow street.

CHAPTER 18

———————

Tony watched the Green Coats, or the Defenders of Free Souls, as they liked to call themselves, spill into the square. Tony hung on the wall next to Brenda, Brenda who'd been telling him to shut up for the last month. Or was it the last year? He wasn't sure anymore; time felt so foggy these days. He feared it wouldn't be much longer before he was like the other hanging heads, the ones who had lost their minds and were crumbling to dust. Brenda, stupid big-mouthed Brenda, had sent those three fresh souls on their way before he could talk them into taking him with them. *Never gonna get a chance like that again,* he thought. *Never.*

"Macy," called the man in the wide-brim hat. He didn't have a tin star, but it was obvious he was in charge.

The door opened and Macy rushed out. "Carlos," he said, almost choking on the name, stiffening as he glanced anxiously at the armed guards. "I know we're behind. The copper . . . it overheated again. But . . . we did manage to save most of the ka."

Carlos tugged at his mustache, not looking the least bit pleased. "We're looking for three souls. Two men, one with red hair, and a Latino woman. You seen them?"

Tony perked up.

"Yeah," Macy replied, sounding relieved. "As a matter of fact I did. They were heading up the street."

"Did you talk to them? Hear anything?"

Macy shook his head.

"I did," Tony volunteered and almost wished he hadn't as Carlos set hard eyes on him.

"And?"

Tony suddenly found it hard to speak, searching for just the right tack, knowing if he played this right he just might get down. "Well . . . well, see. I was hoping maybe we could strike a deal? I'll tell you where they're heading and you cut me down off here."

Carlos's face didn't change.

Tony swallowed hard. "Mister, all I'm asking for is a chance. I'll ride with you. Fight with you . . . whatever you want. Just cut me down from here."

"Okay," Carlos said.

"Okay? It's a deal then?"

Carlos nodded.

"All right, sir. I can see you're a man of his word." Tony hesitated, knew he was playing a dangerous game. "They were asking how to get to Calvary Hill."

Carlos exchanged a look with the big man next to him. "Must be looking for a seeker."

"Then we know just where to find them," the big man said.

Carlos nodded and the lot of them headed off.

"Hey," Tony called. "Hey, man. C'mon. *C'mon!*"

"You're a fool," Brenda said. "A thickheaded fool."

"We had a deal!" Tony cried after them. The men kept going, disappearing up the alley into the fog.

"*Please!*" Tony shouted, his voice breaking down into sobs. "*Please!*"

## CHAPTER 19

We're lost," Ana said.

"No, it's this way," Chet said, not wanting to admit she might be right. The road had spilt so many times he had no idea if they were still on the right path. They stopped at an intersection, the narrow avenues forking off in three directions.

"Which way?" Johnny asked.

Chet shook his head, finally giving in. "I don't know."

A scraping sound drifted up one of the avenues, growing steadily louder. A moment later, two men came around the bend dragging a cross made up of beams bound together with frayed rope.

"Anyone care to take a guess where they're going?" Johnny asked.

As they drew near, Chet noticed the barbs tied tightly round their chests. The barbs dug deep into their skin, peeling back the flesh, all the way to the bone in some places. They grunted in obvious pain as they dragged the heavy cross.

"Calvary Hill?" Chet called out to them. "You know the way?"

They looked up, somewhat surprised. One of them managed a smile. "You seek salvation, brother?"

Chet nodded. "Of sorts."

"Well, you're on the right path," the man grunted. "Calvary Hill is just there, that way." He nodded to the avenue they'd been following.

"Thanks," Chet said and started away.

"Suffering is Jesus's language, brother."

"Yeah?" Chet replied. "Seems everyone speaks it down here."

The man frowned. "You're new here, I can see that. You haven't seen his words upon the old wall, have you?"

Chet shook his head.

"Well, you need to. It'll open your eyes. 'Rebirth to all thee who suffer in my name—Jesus Christ O Mighty,' it says in letters ten feet tall. Jesus put them there himself. Put them there for *us*. For *you*, brother!" His voice grew more severe and demanding with each word, his eyes bearing into Chet. "Come join us. Save yourself!"

Chet had always considered himself a Christian, just not a very good one. He'd stopped going to church as soon as he was old enough to get away from Aunt Abigail. He'd never felt the need to have someone preaching at him and he certainly didn't right now. Chet smiled at the man and moved on, the three of them leaving the cross-bearers behind as they made their way up the hill. A few blocks later they overtook another man, who carried a large hammer in one hand and a sling full of spikes over his shoulder. He nodded at them, touching the brim of his straw hat as they passed.

"I do believe we have arrived," Johnny said.

The lane ended abruptly in an open field, a park of sorts surrounded by a low wall, the field disappearing up a steep slope into the mist. Upon the hill, not hundreds, but thousands of crosses of all shapes and sizes.

Moans, groans, chants, drifted here and there and it took Chet a moment to see that the figures hanging from many of the crosses were not statutes or effigies, but actual souls—men and women, some tied up but most with large spikes driven through their hands, feet, and torsos. Souls also lay about on the ground around the crosses, some in heaps, looking like bags of bones.

"Think they did that to themselves?" Johnny asked.

Chet and Ana both nodded.

The man carrying the hammer and spikes caught up with them. "Pick a cross. There's plenty unoccupied. For two coins I stake you. For three I'll throw in a crown of thorns. Hell, I can even make a package deal for the three of you. What d'you say?"

"Gosh, that's a tempting offer," Johnny replied.

"I'm the best. None better. You won't be pulling loose. That's for sure. Got my word on it."

They kept walking.

"Look here, I hate to see a good soul denied the kingdom of Jesus. Tell you what, I'll do it for one. How does that sound? You won't find a better deal than that. What d'ya say?"

"Fuck off," Ana snapped.

The man shrugged, spotted a woman wandering up the hill looking at the crosses, and headed after her.

"I don't know, Ana," Johnny said. "That package deal was sounding pretty good to me."

She shook her head. "This place is so fucked."

They continued on, passing a cluster of souls flogging one another—thanking Jesus with every blow. A man held up his severed legs to them as they passed. A woman sat in the middle of the walking path, nails and spikes driven into every part of her body. She caught them staring and smiled. "I'm going to Heaven."

"Over there," Chet said, pointing to an arch with six ravens carved into the stone.

They passed beneath the arch and stopped. Wide stairs descended before them, weaving down the hill, disappearing into the foggy valley below. Terraces and balconies branched off on either side of the stairs, leading to structures, some looking like temples, others like large mausoleums. Elegant buildings with delicate architecture all in ruins—columns toppled, arches broken, walls collapsed and blackened from fire.

"This can't be it," Johnny said.

Chet saw a man and a woman digging through the rubble of a collapsed temple, piling planks into a cart. "Hello. Hey. Excuse me."

Neither looked up.

"Hey," Chet said, raising his voice. "Just got a question."

The couple looked up, startled. The woman's eyes narrowed. "What d'you want?" The man dropped the plank he'd been carrying and set his hand on the hilt of his knife.

"Whoa," Chet said, putting his hands up. "We don't want any trouble. Just looking for the bloodseekers."

"They're gone," the man said. "The Defenders, again. Drove 'em all off."

"Them Green Coat bastards is taking over," the woman added. "I think when the Red Lady finds out what they've done here, she's going to be out for blood. And from what I hear, her wrath can be murderous, as in *apocalyptic*. But between us, I wouldn't mind seeing them so-called Defenders taken down a notch or two, or even three or four."

"Yeah," the man said. "A lot of folks believe things is gonna be better without the ancients meddling in our business. But I'll take a few crazy gods any day over these Green Coat assholes."

"So there's no more bloodseekers . . . *anywhere*?" Chet asked.

"There's that spider lady," the woman said. "She's still here. Take more than those Green Coats to scare her off."

The man shook his head. "Well, wouldn't be advising anyone to go near her. She's a frightful creature. Folks gone in there that ain't never come back out."

"You don't know beans, Bernard." She looked at Chet. "Don't pay him no mind, he's always exaggerating. That's her temple down there. See?" She pointed. "You can just see it. The one with the green dome."

Chet thanked her and the three of them continued down the steps.

"Ana, look at that sky," Johnny said. "The colors. Have you ever seen anything like that?"

Chet looked skyward, they all did, watching the coppery clouds churned together as light fluttered deep within. Chet noticed torches glittering far below in the mist leading out onto a valley, mountains beyond, and beyond that, far, far in the distance, a hint of fiery clouds. There was no denying the beauty.

"You guys ever think that maybe none of this is even real?" Johnny asked. "That maybe it's all part of some hallucination I'm having while waiting to drown?"

"Well if it is," Ana said, "I wish you'd just hurry up and drown so I can be done with it."

"Seems to be getting darker," Johnny said. "Wonder if they have night here."

They found a path leading to the temple and followed a winding terrace strewn with broken furniture, smashed vases, and soggy, ash-covered tapestries. The terrace led to a red door set into an arch, framed by two narrow windows. Over the door, written in red dripping letters, was DO NOT FEED THE GODS.

Chet walked up, tried to peer in through a window. All was dark. He stepped to the door, noticed it was busted, that someone had done a hasty job to repair it. He knocked. Waited. Nothing.

"Looks like we might be too late," Ana said.

Chet knocked again. Louder.

"Try it," Johnny said.

Chet did. The door slid inward a few inches. He gave the door a shove, it slid in farther, and suddenly Chet found a spear pointed at his neck.

"State your business," someone growled from within the shadows. "Quick."

"Uh, the . . . spider. I'm looking for the seeker, the bloodseeker."

The owner of the voice stepped forward, a dwarfish figure with a bristling beard and fierce eyes. "She's not here. Now leave."

"I need to see her . . . to help me find someone. I can pay."

The man pressed the blade. "I won't tell you again. Be gone."

"We were sent by the sisters," Ana said. "Do you know who I mean?"

"I don't care if Jesus sent—"

"Otis," a silky voice called behind him. "Send him to us."

Otis grimaced, shook his head. "If you're with the Green Coats, you won't make it out of here with your head."

"I'm not."

"Leave the club."

Chet sat his club on the ground.

The dwarf gestured down the hall.

Chet walked in. Johnny and Ana started to follow but the dwarf jabbed the spear at them. "No one invited you."

Johnny started to protest, but Chet shook his head. Johnny let out a sigh, stepped back. "Fine, but we're right here, little man. So you better watch yourself."

The dwarf shoved the door shut and braced it with a plank.

Chet made out a tunnel disappearing into darkness. He hesitated.

"What's the matter?" the dwarf smirked. "Change your mind?"

Chet drew in a breath and headed into the passage. The dim, dirty light fell behind, leaving him in complete darkness. He realized he was alone, that the dwarf hadn't followed. He took small careful steps on the uneven floor, feeling sure he would step off into a bottomless void at any moment. He stumbled, catching himself on the wall, his hand landing in something stringy and sticky. He snatched his hand free and forced himself to press on. Soon the echoes of his footsteps deepened and though he couldn't see the walls, he could tell he'd entered a large chamber. The tang of cinnamon and mint met his nose; it seemed to be masking a deeper smell, that of rot and decay.

He stopped.

Something was breathing, a soft, rasping sound. It moved around him, closer and closer. Chet fought the urge to turn and bolt.

"Are you scared, little fly?" A woman's voice, soft and silky.

"I need your help."

Six tiny orbs appeared before him. They blinked.

"Come closer that we may better see you."

Chet stepped closer.

"Not much to look at." She sounded disappointed. "Another sad soul, with another sad story."

An emerald glow appeared above the orbs. A stone, or gem, placed into some sort of delicate wickerwork. It brightened just enough for Chet to see that the orbs were eyes set in the forehead of a pale oval face—tiny eyes, no bigger than peas. Her face was feminine, beautiful in spite of its strangeness. There were two more eyes, very human in shape, set in the middle of her face, and a larger, seventh eye centered between the six in her forehead. It remained closed.

"So the sisters sent you to us?"

Chet nodded.

"And does the Red Lady still watch over them?"

He nodded again.

A pale, delicate hand, set upon an arm as thin as a pipe, rose and tapped a stone with one long, spindly finger. The stone began to glow. Another hand rose, another, and another, six in all. Each tapped a stone, each stone bloomed to life, bathing the creature in their soft emerald glow. The stones were set into a throne of woven, silky webbing that fanned outward, into the darkness. Chet wasn't sure if it was a trick of the light, but the webbing appeared to move, squirm, like a nest of worms, forming and reforming into intricate patterns. Her hands settled gracefully upon her chest, cradling one another.

"You saw her? The Red Lady? Actually saw her here in Styga?"

"Yeah. No mistake there."

Her face grew pensive. Her small, dark lips, little more than a splotch, pursed tightly together. "And yet she does nothing." She wrung her tiny bone white hands together.

The stones continued to brighten, revealing an ornate headdress with two small curling horns jutting from each side and bits of jewelry and beads woven into its silky fabric. She had no legs, but six arms sprouting from a torso that was wrapped in layers of black webbing and adorned in feathers, jewelry, and beads, the lacy webbing covering her from her wrists to just below her tiny chin. Her cinched waist, a waist Chet could have wrapped his thumb and forefinger around, and broad abdomen gave the overall impression of a corseted Victorian lady in all her finery.

"As you can see . . . we have had visitors," she said bitterly. "They were very ill-mannered."

Chet glanced around; the chamber was in shambles, broken pottery, furniture, the pieces of what looked like a giant loom. He noticed small arms, legs, and heads, had a moment of shock and revulsion, then realized that they belonged to dolls—silk dolls, torn and shredded, lying about like mutilated children.

"What is your name?"

"Chet."

"Just Chet?"

"Chet Moran."

"Do you know my name?"

He shook his head and saw her disappointment.

"I am Yevabog." She waited, searching his face for some sign of recognition. "Have you heard that name?" It was almost a plea.

Again he shook his head.

"Never? Not in all your time on the earth above?"

He shrugged.

Her face darkened. "It is a hard thing to be forgotten." She was quiet for a long moment. "It is what they want . . . these godless men. They burn the temples and still the Red Lady does nothing." She waved a thin arm at the wreckage. "They fouled my sanctuary. It was a warning, they said. Leave, they said. Leave or burn." Her eyes drifted upward to the ceiling. "I cannot leave." Her voice cracked. "I love them, my husbands . . . each and every one. They are my heart . . . my soul."

Chet followed her eyes and his breath caught in his chest. Hanging above him, figures wrapped in silky webbing, like cocoons, perhaps as many as twenty.

"If I leave, there will be none to protect them. They will burn along with everything else and then . . . and then I *will* truly be forgotten." She trailed off, her two human eyes sad and distant. She closed them, closed all her eyes.

Chet waited for several minutes for her to speak, to open her eyes, to do something.

"Ma'am . . ."

She didn't seem to hear him.

He spoke up. "Ma'am . . . *Ma'am*?"

Her eyes slowly opened, looking at him as though for the first time.

"I'm sorry about all this," Chet said. "And I hate to bother you at such a time, but . . . see, you're my only shot at this point. So . . . I was hoping maybe you could help me out? Help me find my grandfather?"

She continued to stare at him.

Chet swallowed. "I can pay." He untied the pouch, removed a handful of pennies, held them out to her.

She gazed at the coins, sighed. "In better times, on earth above, they would bring me songs and dance, harvest and the flesh of their beasts. They gave of themselves, of their blood. Sometimes offering even their own children. Asking nothing more in return than my blessing. Is that not so, Ivan?" Her eyes drifted up to the wrapped bodies.

A moan from above startled Chet. He realized one of the bodies was squirming.

"They loved me. All of them and I . . . I loved them. But I have so few now." Her eyes settled on Chet. "You are fresh dead. Yet unsoiled by the grime of death." Her middle eye opened, fixed on him unblinking, a pulsing green glow; he couldn't look away.

She leaned toward him, extended a hand, slowly touching his cheek with the backside of her fingers—the lightest caress. "Your flesh still soft. Pliable." A chill rolled down his spine. He knew he should run, yet he didn't.

She slid forward until her face was inches from his, her lips near his ear. He felt her breath on his neck. "I have much to offer." She was in his head, his heart, like a sweet song. He felt calm, he felt loved.

"Come into my arms."

But it was no longer the spider he saw in his mind, in his heart, he saw Lamia—Lamia crouched over his body, drinking his blood. *No,* he thought. "No." He jerked back, pulling away from her grasp. "*No.*"

Her hand hung there, her fingers drooping like a withering flower. Her arm drifted back to her breast. She cradled it as though it were injured. Her middle eye closed. She appeared confused, staring at Chet, the stare turning into a glare, the confusion into anger. Her dark lips peeled back, revealing tiny sharp teeth. All six of her hands clenched into small fists. "I shall not seek. Not for you . . . not for any soul . . . never again. I am *done.*" Her voice became shrill. "*Done. Done. Done with it all!*"

The fire left her, just went out. She sagged, fell back into her throne. A great sigh, almost a moan, escaped her lips. "How sad I have become. How utterly pathetic. There was a time when the earth was my playing field, when men and women lined up to be mine, would have cut out their own eyes for a chance at my attentions. Now, none even know my name. Not on earth above, not in death below. What is left when I cannot seduce even a common oaf . . ." Her voice faded. "Let them burn my temple down around me, for I am done . . . all done." Her eyes fell shut.

Chet waited, waited as long as he could stand it, glancing anxiously about, shifting from foot to foot. "Ma'am?"

She didn't respond.

"Ma'am, please."

No answer.

"Ma'am, I don't know where else to go. I'll beg you if that's what you want. I'll give you my blood . . . my flesh. Just tell me what you want."

Still she didn't answer, didn't move, not a breath. He continued to wait, the minutes sliding slowly by, until finally it struck him that maybe she'd expired, had just let go. He slipped up closer, leaned over, peering into her face. *She's dead,* he thought, felt sure of it. He reached out then, touched her, the slightest poke on her arm.

A flash of movement. A sharp sting.

"*Oww, fuck!*" Chet cried, stumbling back, clasping his neck.

She glared at him, holding up a finger, a dab of his black oily blood staining her pointed nail.

"What'd you do that for?" Chet mumbled as his vision blurred. His knees grew weak and he sat down hard.

"You dare touch me, you lowly sod of a man?" she muttered. "Touch a god. Do you know the penalty for such? I may be forgotten, but I am still a god, not some lowly seeker peddling tricks for a pittance. Now leave. Leave me before I suck out every last drop of your soul." She licked his blood from her fingernail.

Chet grabbed hold of an overturned table and tried to pull himself up, but slid back down.

She watched him, amused, then slowly her face changed. She licked her lips as though tasting something bitter. Her brow furrowed as she stared at her fingernail. "That cannot be." She licked the nail again and a spark came into her eyes, a slight glow. She leaned forward. "Who is your mother, Chet Moran?"

"My mother?"

She waited.

"Cynthia."

"Cynthia. No . . . that is not right. Your grandmother. What is her name?"

"Lamia."

"Lamia?" She tapped her lips, considering. "Yes, Lamia, one of the lil-iths. There were her sisters, Eisheth, Igrath, the others . . . I do not recall all their names, but Lamia I remember. She was fierce, that one, a demon to be reckoned with." She gave Chet a curious look. "How is it you should have Lamia's blood?" She seemed to be asking herself, then her eyes grew even larger. "Tell me, is she . . . is Lamia, still on earth above?"

Chet nodded.

Yevabog fell quiet, lost in thought. "Lamia, the firebrand. Who else? Who else would have the will, the tenacity, the spirit." She smiled. "So, at least one ancient still roams earth above. Still defies the One Gods. She is a wonder."

"She's a *murderer*. She killed me. And I think she killed hundreds of others, hundreds of children."

"Thousands."

"What?"

"She has slain thousands . . . maybe tens of thousands."

"And you call her a wonder?"

"She is a lilith." Yevabog said this as though it excused everything.

"She's evil. A demon. You said so yourself."

"Who is to say what is evil? The Christ god tried to bend her to his will. Bend all the liliths. Have them serve men . . . bear their children." Yevabog smiled. "The liliths, they turned that around. Oh, by the stars did they." Yevabog gleamed. "Using their blood not to breed for men, but to *feed* on them. It gives one heart." The spider god smiled. "And now, to hear she still lives, still walks earth above . . . a bright light in this twilight of the ancients." Yevabog studied Chet. "Yet, somehow your spirit escaped her spell." Her voice changed yet again, almost playful. "Why, Chet Moran, blood child of Lamia, you are a riddle. A delicious curiosity. Come closer."

Chet stayed where he was.

"Come, do not be afraid."

Chet didn't move.

"Do you wish to find your grandfather? Come, I shall show you."

Chet glanced up at the bodies hanging in their cocoons above. Every instinct told him to leave. Instead, he pulled himself up on unsteady feet and stumbled forward. He knew he was a fool, but he also knew he had no other options. She took his right hand in two of hers, pulled him close. With a third hand she clasped his wrist. With a fourth, she danced her fingers across one of the glowing gems on the throne. A small compartment rolled open, revealing dozens of vials and pins of various shapes, colors, and sizes. She plucked out a vial and held it up, examining its dark contents.

"Show me your mark."

*She knows,* he thought. *Of course she does.* He opened his hand.

"A penny, now."

He pulled out a penny, gave it to her.

She examined the coin, tasted it, appeared pleased. "Copper binds the spell, binds all spells." She placed the penny on top of the mark, then pulled the cork, and held the vial over Chet's palm. "We must blind Lucifer. Doors can open both ways when one seeks."

She tilted the vial; a single drop fell onto the coin. There came a sizzle, then searing pain shot up Chet's arm as the penny melted into the mark. She held his wrist tight. He gritted his teeth, surprised by her strength. The mark lit up, angry red, then both the mark and the pain receded.

Yevabog set a hand atop his, pressing their palms together, closed all of her eyes. The green stones dimmed. Her hand grew warm. Her eye, the one in the center of her forehead, opened. Again it drew him in—deeper and deeper. He felt her many hands upon him, her fingers crawling up his arms, along his neck, his face, then through his hair, probing, prodding. Felt as though they were in his head, four little spiders crawling around in his mind.

"Think of her. Of Lamia."

"No," he said, only he wasn't speaking, but talking to her from within. "My grandfather. Need to find my—"

"It is the price," she hissed. "Show her to me and I will give you your grandfather."

Chet did as he was bid, feeling powerless to do otherwise. His mind drifted to his first memory of Lamia: him as a child, the two of them catching frogs. Just a glimpse. The spiders, the ones in his head, seized on it, and it was as if they were plucking his memories like strings on a harp. Images flashed by: Lamia inviting Trish and him into her home, Lamia feeding them, Lamia laughing, Lamia drinking from his corpse.

Yevabog grunted and the spiders clawed deeper. Another vision appeared. It felt real, as though it were happening now: Lamia standing over Trish. Trish staring at the wall, her eyes glazed as though drugged. "*No,*" he said, from within. "No," he growled. "*NO!*"

The spider god released him. The vision disappeared.

Chet gasped, fell back, feeling drained.

Yevabog too, her head down, all eyes closed.

"That was real?" Chet asked. "That last. That's happening right now? Right?"

She let out a long breath, nodded. "Yes. We touched her." She opened her eyes.

"What was she doing to Trish?"

"Trish is your wife?"

"Yes."

"Is she with child?"

"Yes."

"Your child."

"What? Of course."

"A daughter then."

Chet wondered how she knew that.

"Lamia is an ancient demon, one of the first to plague mankind. But she is unique even among demons in that she feeds only on her own blood. Do you understand what that means?"

Chet shook his head.

"She breeds with men, passes her blood onto her offspring, the blood mixes, and it is this concoction that she needs."

"Feeds on them? What . . . her *own* children?"

"Or grandchildren, great-grandchildren even.

"So my mother . . . she was one of these . . . *liliths*?"

"No, the lilith is the soul, the demon that worms from body to body. But both you and your mother carried the lilith's blood. Your mother should have been her next vessel; something must have happened. Yes?"

"Vessel? What do you mean?"

"A lilith's soul is a slippery thing . . . it worms its way from one body to the next. Do you see? Her immortality is dependent on claiming a new vessel before she dies, and that vessel must be female and only of her own bloodline in order for her soul to bond. She breeds to produce children, sons and daughters, not only to feed off, but in the case of her daughters, to also possess as future vessels. And so the cycle goes, on and on through the centuries, passing her blood down the line, then reclaiming it over and over."

"*Feeds off her own children,*" Chet whispered, trying hard to understand such a thing, trying hard not to. *She knew,* he thought. He thought of Lamia's voice in her head, how she'd called him home to her. He gritted his teeth, recalling the joy on her face when she'd found out Trish was having a girl.

"She will raise your daughter, feeding off her blood, preparing her. When she feels the girl is ready, she will take her body . . . will cast out her soul."

Chet thought of the children, all their sad eyes, the longing. "There were children, ghosts, hundreds of them following her. Were . . . were those all *her* children?"

Yevabog nodded.

"But . . . there are so many."

"I am sorry, Chet Moran." For the first time he saw sympathy in Yevabog's eyes. "Once she takes your daughter, your little girl will be one more desperate soul following the lilith until the end of days."

Chet's mind reeled, struggling to make sense of any of this, thought of how he'd started hearing Lamia in his head shortly after she'd marked him with blood at his mother's funeral. Wondered if his mother had heard those voices too, if that was what had driven her mad. He kept seeing Lamia's face from the vision, the way she was leering at Trish. *I will stop her,* he thought. *Whatever it takes to get that key to Senoy.*

"I would never have believed it possible," Yevabog said somewhat absently. "An ancient still roaming the above. Somehow she has found a way to hide from Gabriel and his wolves."

Chet looked into Yevabog's eyes. "Gabriel's wolves? Did you mean angels?"

"Angels to some, brutal assassins to others. They are the ones who hunted the ancients down. Murdering us or banishing us to the underworld."

Chet felt a surge of hope. If the angel was indeed real, indeed Lamia's enemy, then there was truly a chance to stop her. "I need to find my grandfather. You promised."

"Yes. We will find your grandfather. Just . . . just give me a moment." She dropped a hand to the drawer, plucking out a red vial. Pulled the cork and took a small swig. She sat dead still for a long minute, appeared to be preparing herself. "Okay . . . your hand." Again, she sat her palm atop his. Her middle eye opened. "See him. See your grandfather. Call his name."

"Gavin Moran."

"Seek. Let yourself go."

*Gavin,* he thought, letting his mind drift. *Gavin.* The spiders returned, only this time they sought with him, calling to Gavin.

A dark shape formed out of shadows. Just a silhouette of a tall man standing on a cliff, but Chet knew it was him. Felt it. *Gavin,* he called from within. Dim details emerged—a fitted long coat fluttering in the wind, a porkpie hat with a flat, battered brim, knee-high boots, a bandolier slung across his chest, and guns, big guns, hanging from his hips.

The man held something—a sword. There, on the ground before him, a woman, her hands bound. The man's boot, Gavin's boot, was planted against her back. Decapitated bodies lay around him, dozens of them, red blood pooling about his feet. The vision came in and out of focus. Suddenly Chet could actually smell the blood, hear the moans—the woman wailing. Gavin, his face like stone, raised his sword, then hesitated and turned as though looking for someone. His dark, brooding eyes stared directly at Chet, directly into him. Chet shuddered. The eyes were cold, dead, devoid of any humanity.

There came a scream, from far, far away. It sounded like Ana. Drumming. Someone hammering on a door. The spiders, the ones in his head, were all hissing, and the hissing grew into a shrill shriek. The vision evaporated.

He was falling.

Chet hit hard stone. He blinked and the chamber came into focus— several men wearing green jackets and bowler hats rushed in carry torches, clubs, and spears.

Yevabog grabbed a vial and threw it at the lead figure, a huge man carrying a spear. He ducked and the vial flew past, smashing into the wall, sizzling upon the stone, sending up a plume of green smoke.

The man charged Yevabog, thrusting his spear into her chest. She screamed, clawing at the weapon. The man drove the spear all the way through her and into the throne, pinning her like an insect to a board.

Chet grabbed his pouch, digging for the knife. Something hit him, knocking him facedown. A boot slammed into his back, pinning him. The huge man, the one who'd just driven his spear through the spider god, reached down, tearing the pouch from his grasp.

Another figure entered the chamber—the man with the wide-brim hat. The big guard handed him the pouch. He took it, and looked at Chet. "It's time me and you had a talk."

# CHAPTER 20

Gavin Moran stood on the ledge, the black waters of the River Lethe swirling far below. A woman knelt before him, her hands bound behind her back. She looked up at him, her eyes wet, her thick eye shadow running down her cheeks. *"Mercy,"* she whispered. "Mercy . . . I beg of you."

She looked no more than fourteen, but Gavin knew that meant nothing, she could be a thousand years old. She was one of Lord Horkos's creations, creatures of divine beauty whose veins actually ran with warm red blood—a testament to Horkos's sorcery. Judging by her simple gossamer dress and long loose hair, Gavin guessed her to be a temple servant. Her small hands and delicate fingers probably prepared Lord Horkos's clothes, maybe played a flute or harp. In a world of gray withered skin, her soft, pale flesh appeared as though bathed in milk—flesh now smeared in mud and blood.

"Mercy." Her voice broke into a sob.

Gavin heard the words, just another sound, no different than the river swirling around the rocks below. It had to be done, so it would be done. He brought the sword up, then down. Her head fell from her shoulders; her body toppled over, lifeless. He watched the red blood spurt from her neck.

He stepped over to her head, her eyes still staring at him, still pleading, and felt nothing. He nudged her head with his boot toe, sending it bounding down the boulders and into the river below, and felt nothing. He

137

looked at the pile of bodies, at least twenty now, all dead by his hand, and felt nothing.

A screech drew Gavin's attention—a ropey, slightly stooped man, one of the longtime rangers, was tussling with a woman. And even though she'd been stripped of her clothes and jewelry, her painted eyes and blue tattoos showed she ranked high in Lord Horkos's court, possibly even a priestess. Her hands and arms were bound, yet still she kicked and screamed, cursing them all.

"Move, you witch," Ansel barked as he struggled to drag her over.

Gavin stepped to her. She met his eyes and it was as though his glare sapped away the last of her will. "No," she moaned.

Gavin dragged her up to the ledge, pinning her beneath his boot. He raised his sword, then hesitated—someone was calling him, calling from far away—yet, *near*, as though inside his head. The very air appeared to blur. He blinked, fell back a step, lowered the sword, and shut his eyes. He heard his name again, closer. A vision bloomed, slowly coming into focus. The face of a young man with red hair and eyes so pale they were almost silver, peering at him, squinting as though trying to see into the dark. There was something familiar about the face. A scream, but this too from far away. The vision faded.

Gavin opened his eyes.

"You okay?" Ansel asked, giving him a look.

Gavin steadied himself.

"Been a long couple of days," Ansel added. "Don't think these folks here will mind a bit if we take a little break."

Gavin looked at the sword in his hand, all the blood, the stack of bodies as though for the first time. He heard the wails, saw the tears, looked in the eyes of those waiting their turn for his sword, saw their terror and . . . *felt it*.

He clenched his eyes shut. *You don't care.* A voice, a desperate voice, his voice. *You are dead and the dead do not care.* He gritted his teeth and thought of dirt—mounds of it being shoveled atop of him, deeper and deeper, farther and farther away from the screams, the ones lurking within, waiting for their chance, waiting to remind him of what he did. *Dirt.* He clenched his eyes tighter, sucked in a breath through his teeth.

*I am dead. I am dirt in the ground and dirt does not care . . . does not feel.*

He opened his eyes. The woman was still there beneath his boot, quivering. Only she wasn't a woman, she was nothing. "Nothing," he said and brought the blade up, then down.

The woman jerked away, causing Gavin to miss his mark. The blade bit into her shoulder. She screamed. Blood gushed. He struck again, then again. His face was stone—no anger, no sorrow. It was a chore that needed doing, nothing more. On the fourth blow her head came free, hit the dirt, rolled to his boot. Gavin Moran nudged the head off the ledge, and watched it fall into the river below.

"Dirt," Gavin said. "Dirt feels nothing."

## CHAPTER 21

The man removed his wide-brim hat, revealing ponderous eyebrows and wavy black hair greased back from his forehead. He opened Chet's pouch, pulled out the knife, held it up to the torchlight, tugging at his handlebar mustache as he examined it.

Chet made an effort to sit up and the guards kicked him back down, pinning him beneath their boots. He felt a spear tip against the back of his neck.

"There will be a price, Carlos," Yevabog said, her voice strained.

"Yeah. There's always a price," the man with the handlebar mustache answered, not even bothering to look at her. "And it seems your debts have finally come due."

The wall still sizzled from the broken vial, green smoke drifting about the octagonal chamber. There were six guards in the chamber other than Carlos and the big guard, and they glanced about with wide, nervous eyes.

Carlos walked over to the big guard, held out the knife so the man could get a good look at it. "What d'you think, Troy? This come from Hell?"

Troy was broad-shouldered and thick through the chest, the sleeves of his green dinner jacket cut off at the shoulders to show his muscular arms. Troy shook his head. "Looks to be older. Perhaps before the angels fell."

Carlos slid out the blade and both their eyes grew wide.

"That's god gold," Troy said. "Has to be."

Carlos took the knife and pressed it against a marble stand. The blade sawed through the marble as though it were paper. "I believe you're right. So how, then, did some lowly soul bring it across from the other side?"

They both looked at Chet.

"Someone had to have given—" Carlos started.

"I give you fair warning," Yevabog hissed, her voice rising. "Leave . . . leave now." She coughed and spat blood. A moan came from above and all eyes went to the hanging bodies. Several of the cocoons squirmed as though the torchlight hurt them.

"See them," Carlos said, speaking to his men and pointing up at the cocoons. "This is why we fight. To put an end to such evil." Carlos walked over to Yevabog, held the blade in front of her eyes. "The time of gods feeding on souls has come to an end."

"You godless souls know nothing of the bonds of gods and men," she spat. "The tangle of love and worship. But soon"—her eyes cut to the guards—"you will know the suffering incurred by those who trespass." Her eyes flared; her middle eye opened and glowed. "I set curse upon any who take hand in the spilling of my blood. Their ka shall rot and their ba shall never find a home."

The guards exchanged anxious looks, sparing glances toward the door.

Carlos shook his head and laughed, then without warning, slashed the knife through one of her arms. The limb fell away, tumbled to the stones.

Yevabog let out a cry.

Carlos bent, retrieved the arm, and held it before Yevabog's face. "Where's your curse, monster? Come, smite me. Set me to flame." He waited. "Your sorcery's all dried up. Sure as shit. Because you, like so many of your kind, are *forgotten*."

He held the arm out to the men. "See there, she's nothing but an empty shell . . . a husk, another lost god like the rest of them." He tossed the arm away as though a piece of trash.

Yevabog let out a moan, a guttural, forlorn sound, as though Carlos's words cut as deep as the spear now pinning her to her throne. Her chin dropped to her chest, eyes squeezed shut.

Carlos pushed back his long coat and hooked a thumb into his fist-size belt buckle—a large brass scorpion—and stared at Chet. "Let's start this off with an easy one. Tell me your name."

Chet just glared up at him.

Carlos frowned. "You think this is a game?" He nodded at one of the guards. "Fetch the boy." The guard ran back up the corridor.

Troy bent down, setting a knee onto Chet's back, grabbed Chet's wrist, and looked at his palm.

"Shit, he's marked," Carlos said, stunned.

"Sure is," Troy said. "How do you think he pulled that one off?"

"You got a lot of explaining to do," Carlos said to Chet. A moment later the guard returned, along with another guard, dragging Johnny between them. Johnny had a gash across his face and one arm was severed below the elbow.

Carlos set the knife against Johnny's neck and looked at Chet. "Now, I asked you a question."

"Chet. My name's Chet."

"Now we're getting somewhere. Chet, if you answer my questions straight, then you and your friends just might leave this place with your heads still on. You got that?"

Chet nodded.

"Now tell me. How did a damned soul escape Lucifer's hounds? How'd you come by this knife? How is it that the Red Lady and her witches just happened to show up at the same time you crossed the river? Why is it you're here, conspiring with Yeva? What's going on, Chet? Huh? Talk to me."

"Conspiring . . . *what*?" Chet said. "I'm *not* conspiring with anyone."

Carlos gave him a look of grave disappointment, then nodded to the guards. The two guards threw Johnny to the ground, onto his stomach, set their knees into his back, and pressed his face against the stone floor. Carlos knelt next to Johnny, setting the point of the blade against the back of his head. Johnny's eyes found Chet's; he looked terrified.

"Wait. *WAIT!*" Chet shouted. "You've got things all mixed up. It's not like you think. I got nothing to do with the Red Lady. I'm just trying to find my grandfather. That's *all*!"

Carlos shook his head sadly. "I don't like games, Chet." He slowly pressed the point of the knife into Johnny's flesh. Johnny let out a scream, kicking, fighting to twist free.

"*Stop it!*" Chet cried, struggling against the guards. "*STOP!*"

The blade sank deep into Johnny's skull. Carlos gave the knife a sharp twist. There came a crack and Johnny stopped screaming, his eyes bulging, his mouth gasping.

The room fell silent; even the guards appeared shocked. Chet stopped struggling, just stared.

Carlos slid the knife free and tendrils of wispy, silvery vapors drifted up from the large wound in Johnny's skull, forming into a wavy version of the boy. Johnny's smoky form hovered above them, staring down at his body, his face confused. He glanced about, eyes fearful, as though something was coming for him, something terrible.

Carlos waved his hand through the vapors, sending Johnny's form swirling away into the haze, but as Johnny's form melted, Chet saw, clearly saw, the boy was screaming.

"*Fuck,*" Chet whispered, unable to stop staring at Johnny's split skull. "*Fuck!*"

"Chet, now that you know I'm serious, are you ready to give this another try?" Carlos nodded at two of the guards. "Bring the girl." The two guards left the chamber. "Y'know," Carlos continued, "no one really knows where the soul goes once it's lost it's ka. Not even the gods. Isn't that so, Yeva-*bog*?"

The god made no response.

"Doesn't seem to be a very pleasant place, I'll say that," Carlos added.

They brought Ana in, shoved her to the stones. "Johnny," she gasped. "Oh . . . dear, God." She stared at his body, then up at the guards, her eyes brimming with hate and tears.

Chet tensed and the guards pressed down on him.

"Bind her," Carlos said, and the guards tied her wrists to a stone pillar.

Carlos squatted before Ana. "Chet, one of the wonders of being dead is your body, your ka, can take a lot of punishment before giving up its ghost." Carlos waved the knife back and forth between Ana's eyes. "Might be fun to find out just how much of your girlfriend's hide I can cut away before she gives up hers." He touched the tip of the knife to Ana's face and with a flick, cut open her cheek. Ana let out a small cry.

"It was the angel," Chet said. "The angel gave me the knife."

"An angel?" Carlos repeated, then laughed. "Chet, you're still playing games." He slid the knife along the side of Ana's head, clipping off an ear.

Ana cried out.

"*Fucker!*" Chet shouted, twisting, trying to shove up from the stone. One of the guards drove his spear into his chest. Chet let out a yell. It was then that he saw Yevabog struggling to reach the drawer, pulling against the spear, trying to get her fingers on one of the vials.

"Chet, we can play this out all day long if you want." He jabbed the knife into Ana's chest, twisted. Ana let out another scream. He pulled it out, stuck her again, then again, then again. Ana's screams echoed round and round the small chamber.

Yevabog gripped the throne with three of her hands, pulling herself against the spear blade, actually tearing open her own flesh, inch by inch, closer and closer to the drawer. A small grunt of pain escaped her lips as she wrenched herself the final inch.

"Watch out!" Troy shouted. He leapt up off Chet, moving fast for a big man, but not fast enough.

Yevabog's fingers closed around a large vial. She slung it upon the stone floor in front of the big guard. The vial exploded, spattering fluid, dousing Troy and the two guards nearest him. The fluid instantly lit up into bright yellow flame. The guards howled as they tried to slap out the burning potion, but the flame stuck to their touch and spread.

The potion spattered Chet's leg, searing his flesh, and hit Carlos across his chest and face. Carlos yelled, the knife falling from his grasp. It clattered to the floor as he smacked the sticky flame.

Chet dove for the knife, snatched it up, rolled to his feet, and rushed Carlos.

Carlos reached into his jacket, came out with a revolver. There came a deafening blast and Chet felt the bullet punch through his side, spinning him, almost knocking him off his feet. Still he came, slashing the knife before the man could fire again, catching Carlos at the shoulder, taking off his entire arm. Carlos let out a howl.

A guard charged Chet, swinging a thick, short sword. Chet met the blade, his knife slicing right through the heavy steel and into the guard's chest, cutting the man open, slicing him nearly in two. The guard toppled to the floor in a screaming heap.

Troy and several other guards were now entirely engulfed in flame, crashing over the broken furniture and into the walls, setting everything they touched on fire. Chet caught sight of Carlos fleeing the burning room.

"*Chet!*" Ana screamed, still bound to the pillar, flames all around her. Chet rushed to her and cut her free, yanking her to her feet. They started for the door. Chet stopped, searching for the pouch, the coins, but found only the scabbard. He snatched it up, then saw Yevabog, her throne ablaze, the flames crawling down toward her. Yet she just hung there, making no effort to escape.

"What are you doing, Chet?" Ana yelled.

Chet dashed back into the thick smoke, made his way around the flames, to the throne. He shoved his knife into his belt, grabbed hold of the spear, and wrenched it free. Yevabog let out a moan and fell forward. Chet caught her and tried to pull her away, but she snagged hold of the throne and held fast.

"No," she cried, staring upward. "No. I cannot leave my husbands."

The heat and smoke grew unbearable.

"*Let go!*" Chet yelled, yanking her loose and dragging her away, stumbling half-blind through the burning smoke, searching for the door.

He heard Ana screaming for him, someone grabbed his arm, tugged him along, leading them out of the chamber and down the long corridor. They fell into a heap out on the terrace. Chet coughed, trying to clear his eyes, his knife out and ready, but he saw no sign of Carlos or any other guards, only the brutalized body of the dwarf.

"What were you thinking?" Ana shouted.

Yevabog's hair and dress still burned. Chet grabbed one of the soggy tapestries and threw it on the creature, smacking and smothering the flames.

Ana watched him as though he were out of his mind.

Chet pulled the tapestry off Yevabog. She lay quivering, curled up like a dying insect. "She knows where Gavin is."

## CHAPTER 22

Gavin turned away from the blood, the bodies, toward the river, wedged the toe of his boot beneath a large stone, and flipped it over the ledge. The stone plummeted end over end, dropping into the lazy river more than two hundred feet below. The splash echoed up the ravine. It seemed to call his name. A smile touched his thin, tight lips.

He saw the kid's face again, couldn't shake it, especially those pale gray eyes. They'd been so like his children's eyes. He tugged a small bottle out from his coat, pulled the cork, and lifted it to his lips, taking a long swig and grimacing at the bitter taste. The contents of the bottle were derived from the River Lethe below, not the thin stuff they sold in the sob joints, but a concentrated inky sauce brewed by the monks of Fallen Faith. It was supposed to make you forget for a while—the good, the bad, all of it. It had been a long time since he'd had a swig, but the vision, the kid, the one with the red hair . . . "Goddamnit," he said and took another sip, drank deep, not caring about the risks as the sauce numbed his mouth. Too much and you forgot for good: forgot your name, how to button your pants, became one of the mindless dead wandering the streets until someone finally cut you up and ate you.

The numbness spread into his head and the rocky landscape blurred, yet his memories wouldn't let go, they never let go. *How long ago was it?* he wondered. *Forty years? Fifty? Then why does it seem like yesterday?* He held the bottle up and locked eyes with the grinning skull on the label. "How many years does it take for a man to forget murdering his own children? Huh? How long before he won't hear their dying screams no more?" He took another swig, draining the bottle, then chucked it, watching it tumble all the way down to the river. He stared into the dark waters. "One step," he said. "That's how long." He slid his other foot up until both his boot toes hung over the edge. "*Go on,*" Gavin whispered. "*Just one more step.*"

"Hey, Gavin," Ansel called. "That's rot rock, man. Gonna fall in the river and take you with it."

*Be a real shame if that happened,* Gavin thought, feeling dizzy. He rocked on his boot heels, felt the stone cracking.

"Gavin, you hearing me?"

The clang of arms. The sound of men making their way up the bluff, shouting to one another, voices full of bravado. The sound of men who had just fought and won a battle that they didn't think they could.

"Hey, Gavin," Ansel called. "You're gonna wanna see this."

Gavin turned. A man rode up the hill astride a dirty white horse. It was Colonel Turner Ashby. He rode straight in the saddle, one hand thrust beneath the lapel of his jacket—that of a Confederate cavalry officer—the very one he'd crossed over in. A long dark beard, a mountain man's beard, framed a critical, but agreeable face. A cart followed behind him, not any cart, but one of Horkos's carts, gilded in gold. And strapped upright onto a bench sat none other than Lord Horkos himself, legs severed at the knees, arms at the elbows, one eye torn out, and his mouth a mutilated gash.

"He did it," Ansel said, and you could hear the weight of the thing in the man's voice. "The son of a bitch did it. A *god,* we've taken a *god,* Gavin. Can you believe it?"

Gavin stepped away from the ledge.

The Colonel held a spear with a gold blade, so light it almost glowed. He was smiling, and Gavin thought never did a man more earn the right to smile.

The Colonel's ragged crew of men, which he'd dubbed Ashby's Rangers—a throwback to his days commanding a group of partisans in the Confederate army—surrounded him, following him up the hill. Many of them were wearing the spoils of victory, donned in the armor and carrying the finely crafted weapons of the lord's guard. A few even wore the fancy feathered headdresses of the dancers, cutting up, laughing so hard they could barely walk, drunk on the spirit of conquest. But every one of them wore a red scarf or kerchief around his neck to clearly identify himself as the Colonel's rangers. Behind them were men leading horses—more than a dozen fine beasts. And Gavin nodded, knowing the difference these mounts would make in the trials ahead.

The Colonel pulled on the reins and hopped from his horse onto the cart to stand next to the god. "I made each of you a promise," he cried in a commanding voice. "Today . . . today, I make good on that promise." He raised the spear high for all to see. "Here it is. Here it is. *Here . . . it . . . is!*"

The men cheered, clapping and banging their weapons against their shields and armor. Gavin guessed there to be at least two hundred men now. But it wasn't long ago that Ashby's Rangers amounted to little more than a handful of souls wandering the Barrens. All following the Colonel as he dealt out his vigilante style of justice: hunting down soul traders, bandits, even demons—anything that preyed on souls. He even robbed from the gods themselves, making swift, stealthy raids on their caravans and temples, freeing slaves whenever he could. Back then, most had considered the Colonel a ranting idealist and his crusaders fanatics, but of late the Colonel's talk of a new age for souls was catching on like fire. Gavin had heard speculation that it was due to a new godless breed of souls entering purgatory, but Gavin thought it was simply that souls had had enough, that they just needed someone to bring them together, and the Colonel appeared to be that someone.

*And now this,* Gavin thought, looking at the mutilated god. *This changes everything.* He walked toward the crowd, part of him envying those who had been there for the ambush, had witnessed the god fall. His detail had been assigned the rear assault, to round up any trying to escape back to the city of Lethe.

"A god," the Colonel continued. "Together, we have slain a *god!*"

Another round of cheers. The Colonel whacked Lord Horkos with the hilt of the spear. The god's face twitched and Gavin knew that somewhere in that lump of mutilated flesh, the god was trying to scream. Only the Colonel had made sure it had no mouth left to scream with, no hands to weave spells with, no legs to run away with, his useless body now nothing more than a prison for his spirit.

"It's only the beginning," the Colonel continued. "For as word spreads, more will flock to our banner. Our ranks will swell. Why even today, we welcome over fifty new souls into our fold." He gestured toward a cluster of dirty, battered souls—Horkos's slaves—souls with bewildered but elated looks upon their faces, all now wearing the red scarves. "Fifty souls no longer in bondage. Fifty souls ready to put an end to this reign of tyranny forever. A band of rangers brought down Horkos . . . imagine what an army can do."

Stomping. Cheering.

"Here and this day, I now make you another promise," the Colonel cried. "Soon, very soon, souls will no longer kneel to the gods. No longer toil beneath their tyranny. One by one, they shall fall and soon it is not us that will quake before the gods, but the gods that shall quake before *us*!"

They shouted his name, some even dropping to one knee before him, and Gavin wondered why men seemed to always need someone to bow down to. Wondered how long before the Colonel became a god in his own right.

"The winds of limbo blow in our favor," the Colonel called. "Mother Eye has turned full circle and the Gathering draws near, the gods will be on the roads—*vulnerable*. The Defenders of Free Souls from Styga are even now on their way to join us. Together we'll hunt down the gods . . . slay them one by one. Who will join me on this hunt?"

The cheers intensified; the bloodlust was upon them like a fever. Gavin could see it in their eyes. Their colonel was no longer a ranting idealist, but a god killer; they were all god killers. Gavin wouldn't guess at where this would end, but of one thing he was certain: there would be more blood, much more blood.

## CHAPTER 23

Where're you going?" Ana asked.

Chet stopped, realizing he had no idea. He'd been bent solely on getting away from Carlos, running down one twisting avenue and stairway after another. He glanced up and down the narrow stone steps; the temples were lost behind them in the mist, but a few torches fluttered in the valley far below.

"Can we hold up for a minute?" Ana asked, sitting down on the steps. "Just a minute."

Chet rolled Yevabog from his shoulder. He'd wrapped her in a tapestry, carrying her across his back like a sack of seed. He laid her upon the steps, wincing as he took a seat next to Ana, wondering how many more holes his body could take and still go on. He examined the burns on his leg, grateful that the searing pain was at last receding.

"Johnny," Ana said.

Chet met her eyes, saw the deep pain.

"He's gone. I mean really gone. Right?"

Chet shrugged, trying not to think of the terror in the boy's face as his soul drifted away, grateful Ana had at least been spared that.

"*Yes,*" Yevabog said, little more than a whisper. It was the first she'd spoken since leaving the flame. "His ba has been released. There is nothing left to bind him to this world."

"He was happy here," Ana said. "Actually having a good time. The place was just one big Neverland to him. I mean, shit. Why did it have to be him? Why couldn't it have been me? I'd be glad to go."

"No," Yevabog said. "Not that way. For your ba to float away unfettered . . . down here in the underworld. Never wish that." She tugged the tapestry tightly around her as though trying to hug herself. "My husbands," she said, a slight quiver in her voice. "They are adrift now. Their souls lost to the winds of chaos. Maybe if I had burned with them, maybe I could have guided them . . . I will never know." She stared upward, her eyes distant.

They sat silently for a long spell. Chet didn't know if souls needed sleep, but he certainly felt weary to his core, felt he could sit here and never move again.

"Lethe," Yevabog said. "We go to Lethe."

Ana and Chet looked at her.

"You will take me there. And in return I will take you to your grandfather."

"He's there?"

Yevabog nodded. "Near."

"What is Lethe?" Ana asked.

"A city. A river. A path to oblivion."

"Oblivion?"

Yevabog nodded. "Souls who drown in her sweet waters disappear forever." She said it longingly.

"But we saw faces in the river," Ana said. "Such pain . . . horror."

"That was Styx. Each river sings it own song: Styx is the river of hatred; Phlegethon, the river of fire; Cocytus, the river of wailing. There are many others, but Lethe is the river of oblivion . . . the only path to a true end."

"A true end," Ana said, speaking the words as though referencing some holy grail.

"All roads lead to Lethe," Yevabog said. "Souls, denizens of the underworld, sometimes even gods. When they are done, have given up, or are just tired, they make their pilgrimage to Lethe's tranquil waters." She paused. "My heart has died with my loves. There is nothing left for me, not even revenge. When a god no longer cares for revenge, their time is indeed done." All emotion fell from her voice. "I am done."

Ana nodded and whispered, "*Yeah . . . me too.*"

"Lethe," Chet said. "How do we—"

"The Green Coats will be watching the river roads," Yevabog said, her breath shallow, as though all this talk was taking a toll. Chet noticed there was a lot of blood on the tapestry. "Our only chance is across the barrens . . . but we cannot cross alone . . . too dangerous." She paused, gathering her strength. "The stockyards are below. If we are lucky, a caravan will be gathering. That is our best hope."

## CHAPTER 24

$C$oach approached an arch bearing the crumbling bust of a great stag. He could see the wagons gathering within, felt sure this must be one of the caravans that the bloodseeker, Gerda, had been referring to.

He joined the long line of souls at the entrance and as he stood waiting to enter, his thoughts returned to the bloodseeker. She'd cut him as they'd sat cross-legged beneath the tarps, taking a sliver of his flesh, tasting it and then pressing her palm against his cheek, telling him to close his eyes and reach for his mother. They'd drifted together through his memories, until he saw her, his mother lying at the feet of some giant statue, her eyes glazed and half-closed. This wasn't a memory; he'd never seen that statue before. He called to her, again and again, and slowly her eyes cleared and she looked about her as though waking from a deep sleep. She heard him, he was certain, because, as the vision faded, she spoke his name. "She's in the temple at Lethe," Gerda had said. Telling him he could walk up the river road to Lethe, along with the masses, but the quickest path was by caravan. It was an easy decision; the sooner he found his mother the better.

A man bumped Coach as he walked by. Coach looked, then looked again, not believing what he was seeing. It was *Chet! Chet, right there in front of him!* "Hey," Coach growled, grabbing the man by the arm, but when the man turned Coach could clearly see it wasn't Chet. "Oh . . . sorry," Coach said, letting go. "Sorry." *Christ,* he thought, *what's wrong with me? Why in the fuck would Chet be down here?* This wasn't the first time he'd thought he seen the boy either. He could've sworn he'd seen him in the crowds of Styga, then hanging from one of those crosses on the hill. He rubbed his eyes. He knew why he was seeing the boy: because next to finding his mother, there wasn't anything he wanted more than to get his hands on that little cocksucker.

*Shiner,* that's what the kids had started calling Coach back at Walker High, right after Chet had broken his nose, giving him that black eye. And it had stuck too, for a while. He could deal with the kids, they were all shits anyway, but when David Jenkins, the fat-ass economics teacher, had slapped him on the back and called him that in the teacher's lounge, in front of half the faculty no less, that had been too much. After class that day, Coach had paid David a visit, walking into the economics room and shutting the door behind him. When David looked up from grading papers and saw the look in Coach's eyes, he did *not* call him Shiner. Matter of fact, once their little meeting and the things Coach had made abundantly clear to David got around, none of the faculty ever call him that again.

"Four fleshies."

"Huh?" Coach realized it was his turn.

"The fare is four fleshies," the gatekeeper, a brawny man with a long red beard, said.

Coach patted his pockets one more time, but it was all gone—the handful of change, his whistle. "I'm a hard worker. I can—"

"No coin?"

Coach shook his head.

The man frowned, glanced over his shoulder. "Beck, we got any more work-for-passage slots?"

"Hell, yeah. Seet needs at least two more shovelers."

"We got a slot. But it's crappy work. You have—"

"I'll take it."

"Suit yourself." The gatekeeper handed him a yellow tag tied to a strap. "Wear this where it can be seen. Follow Beck, he'll take you to the line."

Coach hung the tag around his neck and followed. *I'm on my way, Mom,* he thought, his mind turning to all the things he wanted to tell her, needed to tell her, hoping to God, that in the end, she'd see fit to forgive him for what he'd done to her.

## CHAPTER 25

The clouds above them began to lighten, dousing the stone buildings in a reddish glow. Chet and Ana stood within the shadows of an alley
watching souls as they pulled carts and carried bundles and baskets pur-
posely up and down a broad avenue. Most of the souls here were dressed in
dingy work clothes and heavy boots. A brick wall, blackened with grime,
lined the far side of the avenue. It was too high to see over, but Chet could
hear sounds of laboring coming from the other side.

Ana waited for a large wagon to pass, then stepped out. "No sign of
them," she said and headed down the street. Chet followed, shifting the
bundle on his back. Yevabog moaned, the first sound from her in hours.
They followed the road to an archway topped with a crumbling bust of a
great stag that led into a muddy yard. Wagons and carts were lined up in
rows within—souls running about, packing and loading.

"You think this is it?" Ana asked.

Chet nodded.

Several souls and a few carts lined up outside the arch, waiting their
turn to enter. A brawny man with a long red beard stood next to a small
guard shack, manning the gate. "Have your coin ready," he yelled. "We're
leaving in two shakes."

A small man with an anxious, puggish face, dressed in crimson and gold
silk—much like a jester's outfit—rode up in an ornate cart drawn by two white
horses. The cart was also crimson and gold, painted like a circus wagon.

"It's about time," the gatekeeper called, holding up the line as he waved the man through. The horses clomped forward then stopped at the arch; they appeared spooked.

"Get on now!" the gatekeeper yelled. "The whole caravan is waiting for you!"

"Don't you yell at me, Samson," the man in the cart growled. "Stupid beasts got a mind of their own." Chet noticed just how strange the horses were, one of them in particular, its snout short, stumpy, the other thin to the point of emaciation. Neither one had any fur, just a pale, blotchy hide.

Two guards armed with swords and draped in matching crimson cloaks leaned against the gate, sharing a cigarette. They watched the proceedings with bored, bemused expressions. Chet approached. "This caravan going to Lethe?"

One of the guards, the younger, slender one, rolled his eyes and nodded. "Yes. Yes," he said in a highly annoyed tone. "All roads lead to Lethe."

The second guard, a heavyset man with a bulbous nose, shook his head. "Don't mind him, he's a jerk to everyone. The Barrens of Styga border Lucifer's kingdom. Lethe is the next real city along the trade route. So unless you're wanting to visit Satan, you're going to be going through Lethe."

"I'm not a jerk to everyone," the younger guard corrected. "I'm very selective." Then added to Chet. "Getting out of Styga isn't a bad idea. Nothing good left, not since the Green Coats took over."

The older guard nodded. "If you got coin, just pay the gatekeeper. If not, there might be a few work-for-passage spots left. You can always try the Smith Caravan just down the way. But don't believe they're heading out for a day or two."

Chet thanked the guards and headed to the back of the line with Ana.

"Chet," Ana said. "I don't have any coin. Do you?"

"No. Carlos took everything."

"Stop. *Stop!*" the gatekeeper shouted at the little jester man. "You're stuck." The horses had managed to wedge the cart against the gate post, blocking the entire line. One of the horses reared, fighting the bridle.

"Watch it!" the gatekeeper shouted.

The jester man got the horses back under control, but they remained skittish, snorting and stomping.

"Dammit, Joseph!" the gatekeeper cried. "You injure one of those horses and Veles will cook us both alive."

Chet felt Yevabog tense against his back.

"*Veles,*" she hissed.

"What?"

"*Leave,*" Yevabog whispered. "*Find another caravan.*"

"But," Chet said, "they're leaving now. We don't have—"

"*Veles . . . he is a monster.*"

"What's she saying?" Ana asked.

"That this is a bad choice."

"The guard said there was another caravan," Ana said, stepping out, peering down the avenue. "I think I see it. Let's just—" Ana pulled back, tugging Chet with her. "It's them—the Green Coats. They're down at the other gate." Chet and Ana started away, stopped. "Shit," Chet said, seeing more Green Coats coming from the other direction. The men were poking their heads into every doorway and window, stopping souls, searching carts, asking questions. Chet and Ana took cover against the gate, behind the line of souls, searching for an escape, finding the arch to be their only way off the avenue. "We gotta get in," Chet said.

"The wheel's jammed against the gate," the gatekeeper barked. The horses whinnied and stamped, tugging on the reins. "You're going to have to unhitch them and back it up. Now get to it."

The little man hopped down wearing a thunderous scowl and started unhooking the horses.

"Hey, you two!" the gatekeeper shouted at the guards. "How about pulling your thumbs out your assholes and helping out!" The two guards exchanged a frown, but headed over.

The jester man unhitched the horses and led them to the gate, tying them to a post behind the gatehouse, then returned.

"We're going to have to lift this side and push it back," the gatekeeper said.

All four men lined up along one side of the wagon. The moment everyone's attention was on the wagon, Chet nudged Ana, pushing her along, the two of them slipping behind the little gatehouse. "*When they lift the wagon,*" Chet whispered, "*we go.*"

Ana nodded.

"Just follow—" Chet didn't finish, cut off by a loud stern voice.

"Hail, there." It was Carlos, addressing the gatekeeper.

Chet and Ana ducked down out of sight. Chet only got a peek at Carlos but realized he had his arm back, and was pretty sure the burns, the ones on the man's face, were gone.

"We're on the lookout for two criminals," Carlos continued.

The gatekeeper and the guards either didn't hear or didn't care, all their attention on moving the cart.

"Were looking for a man with red hair and a Latino woman. Traveling together. They—"

"For fuck sake," the gatekeeper said. "Can't you see we're busy?"

"We're here on Defender business. It's urgent."

"Do I look like I give a shit?"

"You don't." Carlos's tone turned hard. "We will just check around for ourselves."

The gatekeeper let go of the wagon and faced Carlos. "The hell you will. This is Veles's caravan and he don't care much for you Green Coat fuckups. So bugger off."

Chet stared at the wagons just inside the yard, all the souls going to and fro. *So close,* he thought, knowing if they could get around the arch they could disappear among the chaos.

The men continued to argue, their voices heating up. Chet snuck a peek; everyone's attention was on the gatekeeper and Carlos. It looked like things were about to come to blows. *Now,* Chet thought. *Now.* He bit his lip and slipped up alongside the horses, keeping the animals between him and the guards. The horse closest eyed him, stamping its hooves. "*Easy, there,*" Chet whispered, patting it along its neck.

He untied the beast, grabbing hold of its bridle, then nodded to Ana. She looked at him as though he were crazy, but joined him. Chet had spent a summer cleaning the stables for his neighbor's two horses—had even been allowed to ride them on occasion—and always felt he had a way with them, but he wasn't feeling any connection with this strange beast.

He tugged the horse, unsure if it would come along or not. Surprisingly, the horse followed, seemed eager to escape the clamor. Chet maneuvered it along, using it for cover, as they headed through the archway and into the yard.

They reached the first wagon and Chet was about to let himself breathe again when the horse collided with a man coming rapidly around the wagon—only, Chet saw, it wasn't a man, but some kind of creature. It reminded Chet of a goblin or gargoyle with its gray, stony hide and beakish, reptilian face, its hindquarters similar to those of a goat. A single horn protruded from the back of its flat head and a crest of stringy hair ran down its spine, all the way to its stubby tail.

"Sorry," Chet said, trying to move past the creature.

The goblin man grabbed hold of the reins, setting its small black eyes on Chet. "Who are you?" the creature demanded, its words clipped, as though hard to form.

Chet stole a glance back to the gate and to his horror saw the little jester man staring at them with a puzzled expression.

"Let go," Chet said. "*Now!*"

The goblin man's eyes narrowed. "Who are you?"

The jester man began shouting and pointing at them.

"Ah, fuck," Chet said as every eye fell on them: the gateman, guards, Carlos and all his men.

Chet punched the goblin man, stepping into the punch, driving his fist hard between the creature's tiny eyes. It was like hitting a rock, but the goblin man crumbled all the same.

Chet threw Yevabog up on the horse, grabbed a handful of mane, and pulled himself after her. "Come on," he yelled, reaching for Ana. She took his hand and he tugged her up, seating her behind him.

The horse kicked and spun, braying more like a donkey than a horse. Chet tugged sharply on the reins, trying to get the beast under control.

They came for them, *all* of them.

Chet could see open terrain out past the wagons. "*Giddy-up!*" he shouted, driving his heels into the horse's sides. "*YAH! YAH!*"

The horse bucked and kicked, spun around a few more times, and then—to Chet's utter horror—took off at a full gallop back *toward* the gate.

Ana screamed, clinging to Chet's waist.

"*WHOA!*" Chet cried, yanking the reins, fighting not to be tossed.

The gatekeeper came out of the arch waving his arms, the guards right behind him. The horse veered sharply, its legs tangling, and crashed headlong into the arch.

# CHAPTER 26

Chet shook his head, unsure where he was. Pain shot up his leg and drummed in his skull. He blinked, saw Carlos peering down at him.

"Hello, Chet."

"*Crap in a hat!*" someone yelled. "Crap in a hat. Crap in a hat." It was the little jester man. "What're we going to do?" He sounded on the verge of tears.

The horse lay among the toppled stones, its head crushed beneath the rocks. It wasn't moving. Ana sat against the wall, staring at the horse. Yevabog, still wrapped in the silk rag, lay next to her.

Chet tried to get up but couldn't, both of his legs pinned beneath the horse.

"Grab him," the gatekeeper said. "*He* can explain to Veles what happened to his horse."

The two guards started forward, but Carlos stepped in their way. "No worries, fellows. We'll take care of him."

"The hell you will," the gatekeeper said. "He has to answer to Veles. 'Cause if he don't, then we will."

Carlos waved his men, his Defenders, forward, close to twenty of them. "Sorry, but he's coming with us."

"And I'm telling you he's not," the gatekeeper said, drawing his sword.

Chet, seeing where this was going, struggled to reach his knife, but it was wedged beneath him.

"We don't want any trouble," Carlos said. "But this man is a wanted by the Defenders of Free Souls."

"Fuck the Green Coats," the gatekeeper spat. "This ground belongs to Veles and you're trespassing. Now get out!"

When Carlos didn't, the two guards drew their swords and stood next to the gatekeeper.

"Don't throw your lives away for a god," Carlos said.

The gatekeeper and two guards tightened ranks.

*Hell, they mean to do it,* Chet thought as he strained to get his hand on his knife. *Three men against twenty.*

Carlos nodded and his crew spread out, slowly surrounding the guards.

"My Vindo. My poor Vindo," came a deep, resonate voice. All heads turned. There, standing upright upon its hind legs like a man, was a stag of grand proportions with magnificent antlers jutting out from its thick mane and a golden corona glowing dimly behind his great head. The mane—dark green, the color of forest moss—flowed down its neck, back, across its deep chest. It raised a hand and made a circle in the air—a slow, elegant gesture—and that's when Chet noticed that its hands were human, the fingers long and graceful.

Carlos lowered his sword; his men followed suit. "I'm sorry for your loss, Veles. It was a beautiful animal."

The stag's golden eyes found Carlos. It cocked its head. "A Green Coat. What is a Green Coat doing in my yard?"

"My apologies, Lord Veles. No disrespect intended." Carlos's words were polite, but Chet could hear the disdain beneath them, as though it hurt to speak that way. "We're only here to capture these criminals. We'll see to it that—"

"No disrespect? Hmm . . . yet you do not bow? You and your men barge into my yard, and no one bows."

Carlos grimaced; Chet could see the man wrestling with his temper.

"Oh," Veles said. "I forgot. Green Coats do not bow to gods. Do they? For they have no need of gods. Well, Green Coat man, when souls have no need of gods, then gods have no need of them. Now be gone while I still allow it."

"*Veles,*" Carlos began, the words terse, almost a growl. "I'm marshal here. I've been given authority to—"

"Authority?" Veles said, his voice low, dangerous. "Now you claim *authority* . . . over a *god*? You, little insect, should leave while you still have your ba."

Carlos's mouth tightened; he met the god's eyes, held them. "No. Not without the criminals."

No one spoke, moved, not so much as twitched.

The two figures, the towering stag and the soul, stared at one another and to Chet's surprise it was Veles who blinked, his face softening. "You are playing a game. I like games. These two"—he gestured to Chet and Ana—"owe me a debt. Therefore I, Veles, claim them as my own, as my slaves, to be punished as I see fit. Now, Carlos, what will you do? Will you take them? Would you dare try to steal from a god?" Veles smiled. "It appears to be your move, godless man."

All eyes shifted to Carlos, who didn't appear in any mood to play games. He sucked in a deep breath. "We're not leaving without the criminals."

The Defenders exchanged quick nervous glances.

Veles raised his hand, his lips moving, the softest whisper, his elegant fingers dancing across the air as though playing an instrument. The great stag's golden corona brightened slightly and the air crackled, feeling suddenly warm. Several of the Defenders fell back a step; two turned and fled.

"Hold your ground," Carlos commanded. "You're free men."

Veles blew along his fingertips. Chet noticed smoke drifting off two of the guards, then a third, a fourth. One of them cried out, his hair suddenly bursting into blue flame. They all turned then, turned and fled. All except Carlos, who stood alone glaring at Veles.

Veles smiled. "It appears these men do not wish to throw away their ba for you. Godless men lack conviction. True loyalty lies only in devotion."

"A new day's dawning," Carlos muttered. "Mark my words, god. Soon, very soon, we'll no longer be your little playthings." He spun, stormed away.

Veles watched Carlos go, the mirth fading from the god's face.

Heavy boots ran up, the goblin man leading a band of souls wearing the crimson tunics and bearing spears and swords. They halted, taking in the scene, mouths agape.

"Should we give chase, my Lord?" one of the guards asked.

Veles didn't answer, his eyes on the horse, eyes full of bitterness.

The guards exchanged looks, shifting stiffly from foot to foot.

"My Lord?"

Veles let out a great sigh, a sorrowful sound. "Why must everything I love come to an end." His eyes drifted to Chet, slowly turned grave. Chet found himself wishing he'd gone with Carlos.

"And can you give me one reason why I should not crush your skull?"

Chet opened his mouth, trying to think of something to say, anything.

"Because he belongs to me," came a weak voice. Pale hands and spidery limbs slid out from the tangled silk. Yevabog pushed herself up on trembling arms, the exertion plain on her face. "They serve me."

Veles's face changed to one of confusion, then displeasure. "Dark omens abound. I am fearful for what lies ahead on this journey." He stepped over, towering above her. For a moment Chet felt sure he meant to crush her beneath his hooves like some pesky insect. Instead he stooped, lifting her up by the nape of the neck. She hung lifeless, no fight left in her.

Veles turned, started away, stopped. "The slaves, they are yours, Seet," he said, addressing the goblin man. "Do with them as you please. Only"—he looked at his horse again—"do not kill them. I want them for the games." Veles continued away then, Yevabog dangling from his hand like a soggy rag.

Chet met Seet's small, dark eyes.

Seet's lips peeled up in a smile, revealing dozens of tiny sharp teeth.

# PART THREE

## The Games

## CHAPTER 27

Hard hands took hold of Chet and dragged him out from under the horse. His knife tumbled from his belt, landing in the dirt. Chet made to grab for it but then something slammed against the side of his head, knocking him back, and everything went blurry.

Seet swam into focus, standing over him, staring at him with soulless eyes. He held a lash, the hilt of which was a large bludgeon. "Hell just got much worse for you," Seet said, his words difficult to understand, coming out clipped and half-formed.

The guards grabbed Chet and yanked him to his feet, pinning his arms tightly behind him.

Seet bent and snatched up the knife, giving it a curious look before slipping it into his own belt. Then, without warning, he hit Chet again, smacking the bludgeon across Chet's temple and leaving Chet's head ringing. He raised the lash. "This is Agony," the goblin man said before driving the weapon into Chet's ribs, doubling him over. "Agony is your new very good friend." He struck Chet again, then again. "Take them to the line," Seet barked at the guards. "Hook them up to Priscilla. Let them get a taste of Hell."

Several guards half-carried, half-dragged Chet away. "Not sure how you done it," one of the guards said, "but I'll be damned if you haven't managed to piss off just about everyone you shouldn't."

They escorted Chet and Ana up the line of wagons, most of them rickety contraptions made of bone and patchwork cloth, but several brightly painted and ornate, festive as though they belonged in a carnival.

Souls ran up and down the line, shouting orders. Chet's head still reeled, but he found he could at least walk on his own. Something bellowed next to him, startling him. The guards laughed. It was a tiger, of sorts, a hairless, cadaverous creature with dark, hollowed eyes. They passed cages on wheels. Beneath the tarps he caught glimpses of ordinary house cats and dogs, a few goats, as well as strange beasts looking from another time and place, some staring back at him with painfully human faces.

Chet felt a rumble through the ground, noticed a large statue made of black ore at the head of the wagon train. As they approached he could see it was in the shape of a massive woman, at least twenty feet tall. She was thick and squat through the legs and waist, a power lifter's build. Her face was fixed in an expression of perpetual rage. A great furnace burned within her chest, smoke billowing from the tall crown atop her head while spark and flame danced from her slanted eyes and cruel mouth. A wide yoke sat atop her shoulders, with chains running to a boxcar stacked with what appeared to be chunks of coal. Two men, with rags tied across their mouths and noses, shoveled the coal into a grate in the back of the iron woman.

The statue let out a deep, low groan and stomped its feet. Chet and Ana halted, staring at the thing horrified.

"Meet Priscilla," the guard said, prodding them forward. "She's one of the biggest golems in these realms. And you're going to find out only too soon that she's got a temper to match her size."

The guards led Chet and Ana up to the coal car. "More fodder for Priscilla!" the guard shouted above the rumble.

A squat, shirtless man gave Chet and Ana a pitying look. "Sure, okay. Just a sec." The man snatched up two metal rings, hopped down. "Chin up," he said, clamping the steel collars in place around their necks.

"Hitch them up right there," he said, pointing to a rail jutting out from the side of the coal car. The guards pushed two other collared souls over and hooked a short length of chain to Chet's and Ana's collars.

Thick oily ropes and chains ran from the coal car to the wagons behind them. Between them, several lines of souls—around fifty or sixty—hitched up like a team of mules. All wearing iron collars, their skin scarred and dark with soot and grime, many missing hands and arms, their faces laden with misery.

A whistle blew and the man next to Chet nudged him. "Down."

"What?"

The man wore a tunic and sandals, both worn and stained. He had high, prominent cheekbones and sharp, clear eyes. He was lean but muscular, a boxer's build. His gray skin was spotted with scars, but most appeared to be ritualistic, swirling across his strong African features. He crouched down behind the rail, shielding his face with his arms. Several of the other slaves did the same. Guards and workers all moved quickly away from the golem.

Chet had no idea what was going on but followed the man's lead, grabbing Ana, tugging her down next to him.

Another whistle blew, this one from just ahead; there came a loud blast followed by a roar. A bright flash of flame bloomed, enveloping them in a cloud of hot steam and smoke. Sparks and flaming cinders rained upon them, stinging and searing their flesh.

The golem let out a great moan, lifted a foot, and leaned into the yoke. The chains pulled taunt, sending a shudder through the whole line. The coal car jerked forward, almost knocking Chet down.

"Up! Up!" Seet shouted. "*PULL!*" he cried, lashing the nearest souls. The souls stood, the ones in the harness pulling, those next to the coal cart pushing against the rails.

A fresh gust of steam billowed from the golem's stack and she took another step, then another, inching the caravan forward, building momentum.

A wave of shouts and cheers went down the line.

The golem picked up pace, her powerful strides moving the wagons along at a rapid clip. The smaller wagons and carts started forward, falling in line with the big train.

A sharp slash of pain struck Chet, followed by another and another. "Push, horsekiller!" Seet cried and lashed him yet again. "Push!"

## CHAPTER 28

Trish opened her eyes. She was in a small, dark room with tall ceilings. She sat up, trying to understand how she'd gotten here. A thin slice of daylight peeked through purple velvet curtains. Ornate flower designs, looking much too much like faces, ran up the faded wallpaper. There was no furniture other than the bed.

She slid her feet onto the floor, then it hit her. "Chet." For one moment she tried to convince herself that seeing his cold body in the atrium had been a dream, but she knew it wasn't. "Oh, God. Chet." She clutched the bedpost as the tears came again, tears spilling onto her bare skin. She looked down and realized she was nude. *Where are my clothes?*

She stood up, swooned, waited for the dizzy spell to pass, then walked over to what appeared to be a closet door. She opened it to find a small windowless bathroom with only a toilet and sink. A white nightgown hung from a hook. She took it and slipped it on, then went to the other door, the wood planks creaking beneath her bare feet as she crossed the room. The door was locked. "What the hell?"

She knocked on the door. "Hello? Lamia? Hey, anyone there?"

Nothing.

She banged again, this time louder, and heard footsteps coming down the hall. A key entered the lock, there was a click, and the door opened. Lamia peered in.

"Lamia, why am I locked in here?"

"Oh, child. I'm so sorry, you were in such a state. I was fearful you'd wander off."

"Where are my clothes?"

"Are you hungry, dear?"

"What? No. I just want my clothes."

"Now, don't get upset. Here, why don't you go back to bed while I fix you something to eat." She started to close the door, but Trish set her hand against it.

"I don't want to go back to bed." Trish tried to push the door open, but Lamia held it. "What're you doing?"

"You're not well. You really should go back to bed."

"Lamia, I appreciate you looking out for me, but I'm okay. Truly." Lamia still held the door.

"Lamia, let me by." This time Trish gave the door a solid shove, pushing past the old woman and into the hall. Her throat was parched; she headed down the hall to the kitchen and poured herself a glass of water from the faucet. She could see the atrium from the kitchen window, thought of Chet lying out there alone.

She took a long sip and closed her eyes, the cool water doing her good. When she opened them, Lamia was there, in the reflection of the window. Trish started, almost dropped the glass. She turned. "You startled me."

"I'm sorry, dear. Just want to keep an eye on you. You're not well."

Trish wished the old woman would stop saying that. "Lamia, I want to go out in the atrium. I need to see Chet again."

"But he's not there."

"Oh. Where is he?"

"We buried him this morning."

Trish stared at Lamia. *Buried* him? *Buried* him? What do you mean? Where?"

"Down there next to his mother."

"You buried him without me?" Trish's hand began to shake and she had to set the glass down. "You had *no* right. You had no—"

"Be quiet, child," Lamia snapped, her sharp tone catching Trish by surprise. "You've been in a state for two days. Ranting and going in and out of consciousness. Someone had to take care of things. The boy needed to be put in the ground."

*Two days,* Trish thought, trying to make sense of that.

"We couldn't take him anywhere else without stirring up trouble. Your father would've found out, come for you. Then what would've happened to your baby? Tell me."

Trish knew what would happen. The child would be taken from her and put up for adoption. She'd never even get to see her little girl's face. "Lamia, I'm sorry. I just . . . I just wanted to see Chet one more time."

Lamia's tone softened. "Perhaps I was rash. We're all a bit overwhelmed." She laid a hand on Trish's shoulder. "We'll go visit the grave tomorrow . . . when it's light."

Trish glanced out the window. The sun was only just starting to set. "If you don't mind, I'd like to see him now. I'll go get my shoes." She walked from the kitchen, headed up the stairs to the room she and Chet had last shared. She entered, stopped—everything was gone. Even the bed had been stripped. It was as though they'd never been there. *What's going on?*

Lamia waited at the bottom of the stairs in front of the main entranceway, a cup of tea in her hand.

"Lamia, where are my things?"

"You sound upset. Don't be upset, you'll stress the baby."

"*Where* are my things?"

"Here now, why don't you have some tea and go lie down. A rest will do you good."

"I'm leaving."

"The car is gone, dear."

"Move out of the way."

Lamia just stood there staring at her, her head cocked at an odd angle.

"I'm asking you one more time . . . *get* out of my way."

"You don't want to go out there. There are things that will *hurt* you out there."

*She's crazy,* Trish thought, and tried to shove her aside.

The old woman grabbed Trish's wrist, twisting, forcing her down to her knees.

"Stop it!" Trish cried. "You're hurting me!"

"I'm trying to help you."

Trish struck out, punching Lamia in the chest, knocking the tea from her hand, the cup shattering on the floor.

Lamia slapped her, twice, and twisted her wrist even harder, until Trish felt sure the bones would snap. Trish cried out, struggling, but the old woman's grip was unrelenting. She half-led, half-dragged Trish down the hall.

She shoved Trish back into the little room and slammed the door. There came a click. Trish grabbed the knob; it was locked. She slapped and kicked the door. "Let me out!" Trish shouted. "Let me out *right* now!"

"We have to do what's best for the baby."

Trish went to the window, threw the heavy dusty drapes aside, and let out a gasp. The entire window was boarded up. She gave one of the slats a tug. It didn't budge. She set a foot against the sill and pulled with all her strength. A sudden sharp pain stabbed at her stomach. She doubled over, clutching her belly, and slid to the floor. She began to cry, gently rocking back and forth, holding her stomach. "*Oh, little one,*" she whispered. "*You hang in there. Just hang in there.*"

## CHAPTER 29

The sky cast all in its ruddy amber gloom. A light ash fell, blowing along the ravines and fissures as thin wisps of low-lying clouds swirled around them. Cliffs and peaks spiraled above like crumbling Gothic cathedrals, looking ready to topple down upon them at any moment. The city was now hours behind, the only structures the occasional clusters of standing stones.

A burst of steam escaped the golem's stack as she clumped along, her chains clanging with every footfall. She let out one of her long moans, a forlorn sound that echoed across the desolate landscape.

The guards had spread out, weapons in hand, keeping watchful eyes on the surrounding crags and peaks. Chet noticed bones among the rocks, all sizes and shapes, human and animal, some huge, like dinosaur bones. Only a few at first, but more and more until the entire valley looked to be full of them. He wondered how long before his bones would be among them, before Trish and his child were forever lost. His eyes dropped to his feet, watching the chain hanging from his neck swing back and forth with every grinding step. *What chance is there now? What fucking chance?* He heard Seet yelling ahead, looked up, saw the hilt of Senoy's knife jutting from the creature's belt. *What was it Senoy had said? Something about a chance, no matter how slim, is still better than no chance. Yes,* Chet thought, clinging to the angel's words. *I made a promise, swore to my little girl that I'd always be there for her.* He looked at the chain again; it appeared ancient.

**177**

He grabbed it, twisted the links against the stock pin, the rust crumbling away, revealing several thin spots. *There's always a chance.*

A shrill whistle blew, and grew steadily in volume.

"Down!" the man next to Chet shouted. They all ducked, and a moment later a large blast billowed from the golem, sending sizzling cinders again raining about. Souls cried out, slapping the embers off their skin.

Seet came up the line, cursing and flogging everyone back to their feet.

"It is important to pay attention to Priscilla," the man next to Chet said.

Chet nodded.

"My name is Ado."

"Chet. And this is Ana."

Ana was staring out into the valley, at an immense skull, half-buried in the black dirt, easily thirty stories tall. It had human features, but with thousands of jagged teeth. "Is that what's out there?" she asked. "Monsters like that?"

"There are plenty of monsters out there," Ado said. "But not like that. That belongs to one of the ancient titans. They were all slain long before the first angel fell."

Chet noticed several carts and dozens of figures milling around the skull, sawing the giant bones into planks, loading them on carts.

"See them," Ado said. "They come all the way out here, risking their ba, to gather that bone. It is good bone for building, but that is not why they go to such trouble. It is because they believe it is full of magic and will bring them luck."

"Just bones, rocks, and dirt forever," Ana said.

"Not forever," Ado replied. "The nether regions are vast. I have seen a lot, but that is still just a little. I have heard tell that there are realms not unlike earth. Gardens of great beauty created by the ancients such as Asphodel Meadows and the Elysium Fields. I still hold hope that I will see them one day, before they are gone altogether. And there are other beings, creatures who came *before*. Some that are alive in their way. Some whose flesh even runs with blood like Seet. Have you noticed how difficult it is to understand him? That is because he is a Trow, one of the few remaining underworld races, and cannot speak true Babel as we do."

"Before what?" Ana asked.

"Before?"

"You said those who came *before*."

"Ah, before the One Gods, before the angels fell. Before—"

Seet fell in step with Chet, staring at him with his cold reptilian eyes. Chet kept his own eyes forward.

"Every step you walk," Seet said, "takes you closer to the games . . . to horror and torment." Seet let out a snort and continued on.

"I am sorry, Chet," Ado said. "Seet takes pleasure in our misery. As I said, he is one of the before creatures. They feel the dead are a plague upon their land . . . and perhaps we are."

Chet tried not to think about where they were headed, these games, but instead of escape. He glanced at the rusting chain again, at the pins holding it to the cart, and felt sure, when the moment was right, he could tear it loose. He just need that moment.

"From where do you hail, Chet?"

"What?"

"Where is it you come from?"

"Alabama, mostly."

"Alabama? Hmm, is that from the new world? The Americas?"

Chet nodded.

"I come from Africa, the Kingdom of Nri. It is there that I first served the great goddess, Oya. My whole life was dedicated to her. And then, when the angels drove her beneath, I took my own life so that I might follow, that I would have the honor of serving her too, in death."

Neither Chet nor Ana seemed to know what to say to that.

Ado looked to Ana. "And you, Ana. Are you from the Americas?"

"Yeah, Puerto Rico."

"It seems many of the souls arriving in Styga come from the Americas. I believe the doors from earth above must be aligned somehow to the cities along the River Styx. But this is just a guess, one of many ponderings on the workings of this realm. My great goddess, Oya, she said I spend too much time contemplating things that do not matter. Trying to find logic in a world with none." He laughed. "She said chaos is the only truth down here."

The valley of bones fell behind and the clouds settle in, turning the landscape gray. A light drizzle began to fall.

"Is there no sun, Ado?" Ana asked. "Something besides these damn clouds?"

Ado looked up. "Mother Eye. She and her children are above. When the clouds are thin you will see her watching over all. When she sleeps . . . the world goes dark."

"An eye, huh? Why not?" Ana shook her head. "And those?" She pointed to what appeared to be a row of jagged mountain peaks, only they jabbed downward from the clouds.

"It is the same above as below. On a clear day one can see the land above us, and even after being here hundreds of years, it is still a fearful sight. Many of the mountain peaks touch, like giant teeth, connecting the realms. I have spoken to those who have climbed up one mountain and then down another."

"So we're in a giant mouth full of jagged teeth with an eyeball glaring at us," Ana said. "That's just wonderful."

"Some say that we are in a great cavern beneath the earth above," Ado continued. "I do not believe that. The earth above could never hold all of the nether realms. They are far too vast. Great Oya, she said that the netherworlds are infinite. I like that. It gives one hope that somewhere out there, perhaps just beyond the next hill, lies a place of peace and tranquility."

Ado continued talking, seemed to be full of stories about his goddess, about his travels. Chet came to enjoy hearing the man talk, found his deep voice soothing, but as the miles dragged on even Ado ran out of things to say. The rain continued to fall, turning the dirt underfoot to mud, the slippery muck sucking at their feet, making the going difficult. They trudged along to the drum of the golem's heavy footsteps, punctuated with the occasional blast of steam and ash. Chet found himself fighting to keep his mind off Trish, away from hopelessness and despair. "Ado," Chet asked, hoping to get the man talking again, "how'd you end up here? I mean as Veles's slave."

Ado started to answer, hesitated, struggling to find the right words. "Because I am a thief," he blurted out. "And not a very good one. I tried to steal from Veles." He met Chet's eyes. "And I would do it again. I would do anything for her. For my goddess, Oya." He was quiet a minute. "My soul belongs to her. She is my moon and stars. But like so many of the ancients, she is fading. A hard truth to face, but I must, as there are jackals everywhere . . . these godless souls, demons, and even other gods . . . watching, waiting their chance to devour her. And that is why I stole from Veles . . . for her . . . to help her."

"I'm sorry, Ado," Chet said and sighed, wishing he'd just kept to himself.

"Yes, I am sorry as well. Sorry that I am not a better thief. I can only hope—"

Seet was there again, walking in step with Chet along with two guards. The two guards stared at Chet as though he were a circus freak. "So that's really him?" one asked.

"Yes," Seet replied. "The horsekiller."

"Seems Veles would've skinned him alive," the guard said.

"He is saving him for the games. Him and the girl."

The guards nodded, giving Chet and Ana a look of deep pity.

Seet held up the lash to Chet. "Agony just wishes to say hello." The goblin struck again and again. Chet raised an arm, trying to ward off the blows. The lash tore open his sleeve, biting into his flesh.

"*Stop it!*" Ana cried. "Stop it!"

Seet did stop, his cold eyes fixing on Ana. "Are you his guard dog?"

Ana didn't answer.

He leaned in close, tapping her forehead with the hilt of the lash. "Agony thinks you are a bad dog." Seet struck Ana across the face with the bludgeon.

She let out a cry.

Seet snapped the lash across her back, then struck her again, but this time Chet caught a handful of the lash—held it. The goblin man tried to yank it free. "Let go," he snarled.

Chet didn't.

"Let go." Seet's cold facade cracked and Chet saw the mounting fury. Seet yanked, tugged, and suddenly Chet did let go, sending the creature tumbling back. Seet fell, landing with a wet splat in the thick mud.

The guards laughed.

Seet's black eyes flared. He started to his feet when a whistle blew ahead. The golem came to a stop and men began shouting.

"What now?" one of the guards said as they rushed away.

Seet snatched his lash out of the mud and scrambled to his feet, glowering at Chet. "That will cost you much flesh," he said before running off toward the clamor.

Chet grabbed the chain, shoved one of the worn links over the pin, and gave it a twist. It held. He twisted harder.

Ado put a hand on his. "Chet, no. Not here."

"I'm getting out."

"There is nowhere to go. It is a maze of caves and cliffs. There are things that will eat you whole out there. You will have no chance unarmed and alone."

"Not going to be unarmed," Chet muttered under his breath. "Gonna get my fucking knife back." He gave the chain another twist, felt it give, and checked for guards—they were all up ahead. He noticed a man, one of the ones shoveling coal, staring intently down at him from the cart. His face was black with soot and partially wrapped in a rag, but Chet thought there was something familiar about his eyes.

Seet was yelling again—heading back.

Chet bore down on the chain link, gritting his teeth as it bit into his fingers—still it held.

Seet led four guards their way. They dashed up to the first row of slaves and began unlocking their pins. Seet unlatched the two rows of slaves in front of them, then, to Chet's surprise, he unlatched Chet's row. Chet found himself being led up the line by heavily armed guards. They passed the golem and Chet saw the problem. One of the lone carts had slid into a ditch, one wheel now hanging over the steep ledge, the runoff threatening to drag it away. A length of rope ran from its rear axle, and a handful of guards were struggling to pull it from the muck.

"There!" Seet shouted. "Grab the rope! Pull!"

The slaves fell in, snatching hold.

Chet hesitated, his eyes darting to Seet, the belt, the knife.

"Move it!" a guard yelled, jabbing Chet with his spear. Chet fell in behind Ana and Ado. He grabbed hold of the rope and dug in his heels, pulling along with the rest of the slaves, but his eyes stayed on Seet.

## CHAPTER 30

*It can't be,* Coach thought as they unlatched the man, sure that this twisted place was playing tricks with his mind again. He watched the guards lead the man away. *That gait, that hair, his build. No, that's Chet all right.* Coach drove the shovel into the coal, twisting, grinding, clutching the handle so hard his hands hurt. *"That's him,"* he hissed, his breath coming faster and faster.

"You okay?" Jorge, the man next to him on the coal cart, asked.

"Never been better," Coach said coldly, hopping to the ground and heading away.

"Hey," Jorge called. "Where you going?"

Coach shouldered the shovel, getting a good tight grip on the handle with both hands. "Going to even some shit up."

## CHAPTER 31

Mother Eye began to dim, turning the rocky landscape the color of a bruise. A cloud blossomed along the ridge—riders, trailing a plume of gray dust. Hands dropped to weapons, hard eyes all on the approaching riders. The Colonel halted the procession.

Gavin tugged the reins, pulling the wagon to a stop, and checked the cargo. Lord Horkos's one bloody eye stared back, and behind him the twelve prisoners—souls unwilling to denounce their god—stumbled to a halt.

Four horses approached bearing seven men wearing green coats, three of them riding double. The Colonel's forward scout signaled the all clear, but the Colonel waited until he could see their faces before lowering his musket. "It's them all right," he said, then yelled to his ragtag troops. "Fall out. Rest your feet while you can."

The rangers dropped their weapons and gear, and collapsed upon the rocks and boulders, weary from a full day's march.

The Colonel dismounted, walked up to the cart, and stood next to Gavin.

The lead rider galloped ahead, a man in a long overcoat, his face covered against the dust. Even so, Gavin knew exactly who it was. The Colonel leaned toward Gavin. "Let's not have any trouble, Gavin. We have to work with them."

Carlos rode up, his eyes falling on Lord Horkos's mutilated body. He

185

yanked down his kerchief, revealing a broad smile, the smile of a man whose number had just come up on a roulette wheel. He leapt from the saddle, dashed up to the Colonel, clasping the man on both shoulders. "You've *done* it! A god, Colonel. You've taken down a god." He let the Colonel loose and climbed onto the cart, sneering at the god. "What are you now?" he said. "*Nothing!*" He jabbed his thumb into the god's remaining eye, grinding it back and forth. The god's face distorted with pain, and blood bubbled about the gag. Carlos laughed.

The remaining riders rode up, their mounts looking to have been pushed too hard. Gavin knew the horses to be common soul-shifts, could tell by their eyes—still human, haunted, only too aware of their plight.

The six men dismounted, looking bushed and glad to be out of the saddle, Carlos's select crew—big, muscular men with faces covered in ritual scars. But their size hadn't come naturally. You could tell by the clusters of lumps and knots growing on their skin that these men had gorged themselves on ka. Along with swords, three of them carried muskets, one even a revolver.

They called themselves the Defenders, as in the Defenders of Free Souls, but Gavin thought fancy coats and grandiose names did little to hide what they really were—a gang of thugs, much like the crime syndicates he'd run liquor for during Prohibition. The Defenders had started out as common bandits and soul thieves, gaining turf in Styga over the years, taking over ka coin production with their own brand of protection racketeering and extortion. Then they threw in with the Colonel and suddenly they were freedom fighters, using the Colonel's revolution as justification to try to take over all of Styga.

*Defenders*, Gavin spat in the dirt and glanced at the Colonel, searching for some trace of disdain, some sign that it pained him to deal with this vileness, but found none. *There was a time, old man, not so long ago, when you would've shot their sort dead on sight.* Gavin's lips tightened. *All's good in the name of the grand crusade. Right, Colonel?*

Carlos hopped down from the wagon and strolled to the Colonel's horse, where the spear, the one the men were now calling God Slayer, was harnessed to the saddle. He laid a hand on the spear, almost a caress. He looked to the Colonel. "So, how d'you feel about Lord Kashaol now?"

"To be honest, there at the end, when the only thing between me and Horkos was the spear, I felt sure I was gonna die a fool. But, as you can well see, Lord Kashaol did right by us."

*Lord Kashaol,* Gavin thought, hardly believing the Colonel had just referred to a demon, a servant of Satan, by its proper title. An act the Colonel himself had warned many a man was akin to allegiance. *Can you really be so blind? Or do you choose to be?* Gavin, recalling all the demons they'd tracked and killed together, felt sure it was the latter. *You're playing with fire, Colonel.*

"Wish you could've seen it," the Colonel went on. "Musket balls and arrows bouncing off his hide, but the God Slayer, it did its work. Sure as hell it did. Like a hot knife through butter. Most of his guard turned and fled after that. Them that stayed, well, they didn't have much fight left in 'em. It was pretty much a clean rout."

"Damn sorry to have missed it," Carlos said. "But there'll be plenty of glory to share in the days ahead."

"You sound sure."

"I should, because there's much afoot." He hooked a thumb into his big brass belt buckle and led the Colonel around the wagon, out away from his troops, a swagger, almost a strut in his stride. "Heard back from Lord Kashaol. He's promised us twenty muskets in exchange for Horkos's head."

"Twenty!" the Colonel repeated. "Why . . . do you know what that means?"

Carlos's cocky smile showed he did.

"And with the God Slayer . . . we'll have the means to defeat Veles."

"Yes, sir, we sure will. And Veles is on his way to the Gathering even as we speak. Out in the barrens, easy pickin's. And there's more. Lord Kashaol's emissary gave me some details on the weapon he promised. The one for the Red Lady."

The Colonel looked at him like a child waiting to open birthday presents.

"It's some sort of handheld canon, like a blunderbuss perhaps. Designed to deliver a load of shot made from that same god-slaying metal. If we can get close enough it'll tear her to bits."

"How soon?"

"Soon. In time to take her before she gets to Lethe."

The Colonel nodded, a man hearing exactly what he most wants to hear. Gavin was disturbed not only by the Colonel's trust of Carlos, but of a demon lord. This was the Red Lady, the warrior goddess, whose sworn duty was to protect not only the gods, but the entire realm of the ancients. She'd kept the demons at bay for ages. Gavin had heard she'd once crushed an entire battalion of demons that had dared to enter her territory. And here was the Colonel, willing to go head-to-head with her on the word of Kashaol.

"The other gods will either still be at the Gathering, or on the road," Carlos said. "By the time they find out, it'll be too late for her, for all of them."

"And where's she now, the Red Lady?" the Colonel asked. "Did you find her?"

"Yeah. Wasn't hard. She's a creature of habit. We caught up with her in Styga. When I left, her and her witches were still rounding up children. So it'll be at least another night or two before she heads out. I got a man on her. He'll let us know."

"So you still think we should go after Veles first? Huh?"

"Yes, I do. Once he's gone, the road to Lethe will be ours. The Red Lady will be alone. That will give us the best chance."

The Colonel nodded agreeably.

"It's all lining up," Carlos said. "Why, if I were a religious man, I'd venture to say God's on our side."

The Colonel laughed at that, his eyes distant, a man already envisioning glory. "And nothing's changed with Kashaol? No new demands? No funny business?"

"Colonel, we've been around this. Y'know as well as I do that the One Gods would never let a demon rule over the river realms. That's why Lord Kashaol came to us. Because he needs a go-between. Someone to gather the damned for him."

"I understand the situation," the Colonel spat. "Just seems there'd be some other way."

"Well, you let me know if you find one," Carlos said, then let out a long sigh. "Look, Colonel, dark is coming on. We need to be heading out."

"You mean *now*?" the Colonel asked. "You don't want to be riding through the canyons at night."

"There's just no time to lose."

"Something's got you spooked."

Carlos tugged at his mustache. "A bit. When we caught up with the Red Lady, a man was there with her."

The Colonel waited.

"The thing is . . . he'd just come across, his flesh still moist and lily white."

"You're suggesting the Red Lady came there to meet him. Someone from the *other* side?"

"Sure looked that way to me. And there's more to it. We tracked him to the temples. Caught up with him meeting with Yevabog."

The Colonel looked unsure.

"Yevabog. She's an ancient god . . . a real small-time player. But . . . she's still one of them."

The Colonel frowned.

"We thought we had him, but things got out of hand. Him and Yevabog, they got the best of us, got away, and you aren't going to believe where they went."

Again the Colonel waited.

"Veles."

"No."

"Yeah. Veles took them in. The best we could tell they all left for the Gathering together."

"That's odd. You think perhaps they're conspiring?"

"Something's going on."

"Yeah, but—"

"Wait, now, another thing. Two things. That man, or kid rather, he was young. And, well, he's damned. Seen the mark myself and I'd sure like to know how he escaped from topside before the demons caught him."

The Colonel nodded.

"The other, he had a knife. Dirk said he brought it over with him, and get this . . . it was white gold, just like the God Slayer. Cut stone like butter."

"He has a demon weapon?"

"Uh-huh."

"But . . . that don't make any sense."

"No, it doesn't. When we pressed him he said he got it from an angel. Figure that."

"What sort of man was he?" the Colonel asked.

"That's what I want to know."

"Well, what'd he look like?"

"Lean, not much taller than you. Shaggy head of red hair. Young, like I said, early twenties. Oh, and the palest damn eyes you ever saw."

Gavin turned, then looked at Carlos, finding it hard to believe what he was hearing, wondered if it could be the same boy from his vision. Seemed unlikely, yet something in him felt sure there was a connection.

"Said his name was Chet. Didn't get a last name. If we're lucky, he'll still be with Veles when we take him. We'll sure get some answers then."

The Colonel nodded, his face troubled.

"Well," Carlos said, "the last thing I feel like doing is putting my sore ass back in a saddle, but it's best we be on our way."

"You'll need fresh mounts," the Colonel said, somewhat distractedly, and called for horses to be brought round. "One more thing I'll need you to do for me. The prisoners there. Need you to take 'em into the canyon and leave 'em."

Carlos raised his thick eyebrows.

"It's ugly business, I know. But we can't risk word getting back. Not now, not with everything at stake."

"Colonel, don't worry about them. I'll see to it they don't tell anyone . . . *anything*."

"No," the Colonel said, looking levelly at Carlos. "Don't kill 'em. I'll not have that. Just leave 'em in the canyon. Our business will be done by the time they make it out."

Carlos shrugged.

"Do *not* kill them. Are we clear on that?"

"Yeah, we're clear, Colonel."

"Good. There'll be killing enough before all's said and done and we need to remember, that it's these souls we're fighting for."

A man brought the horses around. Soul-shifts crafted by Lord Horkos himself, magnificent beasts with sleek black coats and long legs.

Carlos and his men each picked one and started saddling them up.

"Ansel," the Colonel called. "Load up the prisoners." He stepped toward the front of the wagon, next to Gavin. "Gavin, I want you and Ansel to go with 'em."

Carlos turned around. "Colonel, I appreciate that offer. But I got my own men."

"Things get tight, you'll be glad to have their guns along."

Carlos started to say more, but the Colonel cut him off. "I want the extra guns along, Carlos. This thing's just too important." He didn't say it was an order, but you could tell by the way he said it, it was.

Carlos grimaced, a man not used to taking orders. He set eyes on Gavin, making no effort to hide his contempt.

Carlos walked away to saddle up his horse. The Colonel leaned closer to Gavin. "No need to pretend. I got a pretty good idea how you must feel toward me right about now. Colluding with demons and these lowlifes. I might be foolish, Gavin, but I'm not a fool. We need their help. It's the only way. And in the end, if we play our cards right, then you mark my words, this land will be free of god and demon alike."

Gavin didn't say anything.

"Look here," the Colonel continued. "I know the sort of man Carlos is. But sometimes the spirit of revolution can change a man. I've seen it happen. I'm holding out hope that's gonna be the case with Carlos. But for now, I'm wanting you to keep an eye on him. Anything that don't seem right, I need to hear about it. Can I count on you for that?"

Gavin nodded.

"Good. And Gavin . . . you be careful."

## CHAPTER 32

H old up," Carlos called.

Gavin tugged the reins, pulling the wagon to a halt.

A howl echoed from somewhere behind them. They'd been heading down the canyon trail going on two hours now, and he guessed by the dim purple glow peeking over the steep ledges that they might have another hour, tops, before everything was pitch black.

Carlos rode back down the line, pulled up to the wagon, and dismounted. "Hugo, Steve, Justin, here, get the prisoners down. Line them up and put them on the ground."

The three men dismounted and unloaded the prisoners from the back of the wagon. The prisoners were still strung together, their hands tied behind their backs. The rest of the Defenders stayed in their saddles, keeping sharp eyes on the surrounding caves and crevasses.

The prisoners glanced fearfully about at the deepening shadows.

"Check them, Hugo," Carlos said. "Bound to be a few."

Hugo, unlike the other Defenders, wasn't bulked up on ka. He was lean, clean-shaven, wiry, and had a cocky swagger to his stride. His wore a dark green jean jacket, stovepipe pants, and pointed boots. His Stetson sat low on his head, keeping his eyes in shadow, his long dark hair out of his face. But the thing Gavin took note of was the gun hanging low on his hip—a real revolver—a rarity among the dead.

Hugo walked down the line, kicking the prisoners in the back of the knees and shoving them to the ground. "On your belly!" he shouted. "Face in the dirt. Anyone caught looking up will lose their eyes." He grabbed each prisoner by their right wrist, checking their palms until he came to a woman who wouldn't open her hand.

"Let loose," Hugo said and punched her twice in the back of the head. Still, she refused.

He slipped out his knife. "Last chance."

"No," she pleaded, then screamed as he sliced off her fingers. He held her palm up. "Got one." He dragged her over, shoving her up against the wagon wheel. "Sit tight, little miss. We're not done with you."

She crumbled there, clutching her mutilated hand, sobbing.

By the time Hugo was finished, they had two more. "Hell must be bursting at the seams," he said. "Swear there's more of the damned escaping every day."

Carlos dismounted, pulled his saber, and walked up to them. "Thought the gods would protect you? Huh?" He stuck the blade under the woman's chin. "Gods don't give a shit about you. About any of you."

"Don't send me back," she pleaded. "You got no idea . . . no idea. Listen to me . . . it's like being smothered, buried beneath all the earth, burning while you're slowly crushed to death . . . only there is no death, no end . . . never." She was bawling now. "Send my ba into chaos, anything you want, but for the love of Jesus, please, *please,* don't send me back to Hell."

"It's a little late for Jesus," Carlos said, and swung the blade, slicing her head clean off. Before it hit the dirt he'd decapitated the two souls next to her. The woman's head tumbled up against a rock, her eyes wide with disbelief.

Gavin's hand dropped to his gun. He felt a hand on his wrist. *"Nuh-uh,"* Ansel whispered. *"We ain't after soul hunters. Not today we ain't."*

Gavin ground his teeth. There was plenty of bad that he understood, souls did cruel things to one another, but a soul willing to hand over another to Hell, to endless torment for a few bullets or a spot of copper— that was beyond him.

She began to wail.

"You need to shut up," Carlos said.

"Don't take me back!" she screamed. *"No! No! No!"*

Carlos picked her up by the hair and whacked her twice against the stone, turning her face into pulp, her wail into a low moan.

Gavin's grip tightened on his revolver.

*"Hear me, Gavin,"* Ansel whispered. *"You do this and everything the Colonel's worked for is lost."*

Hugo held out a sack and Carlos tossed the head inside, then picked up the other two, shoving them in with her. Hugo threw the sack into the back of the wagon behind Gavin.

*"Just you remember where you'd be if the Colonel hadn't found you when he did,"* Ansel added.

Slowly, Gavin's hand fell away from his gun.

"There a problem?" Carlos asked, eyeing Gavin.

"No problem," Ansel replied. "We were just discussing how pretty your little outfits are. How that green brings out the color of your eyes and all."

Carlos's face soured. His men glanced back and forth between their boss and Ansel, their hands near their weapons.

Carlos shook his head. "Looks like the Colonel sent along a couple of clowns. Isn't that just grand." Carlos returned to the souls on the ground. "Hugo, toss me your ax."

Hugo slid the weapon from his belt and handed it to his boss. Carlos hefted it, and brought it down on the first soul's ankle, cutting his foot clean off. The soul's howl was quickly joined by the rest, as one by one, Carlos cut the right foot off each one.

"There, that should slow them down," Carlos said. "Untie them and let's go."

Carlos mounted up, rode over next to the wagon, and set eyes on Gavin and Ansel. "Either of you got a problem with my way of soldiering, you just let me know. Hear me?" He stared at them—waited.

Gavin didn't even bother to look over.

"Problem?" Ansel said. "Why, can't recall the last time I seen such smart soldiering. By golly if it were me in charge of medals I'd pin one on you right now."

"That smartass mouth of yours is going to say the wrong thing one day," Carlos said and spat. He turned away, spoke to the souls. "I'm not putting coin on any of you making it out of here, not even making it through the night, but if any of you do, you spread the word . . . those who serve gods are traitors and will be treated as such.

"All right, boys," Carlos called. "Let's move out." He kicked his mount and rode on.

## CHAPTER 33

The rain picked up, the runoff swelling, and the wagon slid farther over the ledge.

"Pull!" Seet shouted at the slaves. "Pull!" The wagon continued to slide. "All of you!" Seet cried, shoving the remaining guards forward. "Now!"

The guards dropped their spears and grabbed hold of the rope, pulling, fighting for purchase. Chet saw his chance, didn't think he'd ever get a better one—Seet had his back to him, the knife, it was right there shoved in his belt.

Chet let go of the rope and made it one step for Seet before a blood-curdling cry came from behind him. He spun about in time to see a man coming at him with a shovel raised over his head. The man brought the shovel down and Chet dodged to one side, sending the man crashing into Ana and Ado, knocking them and several other slaves off their feet. The cart teetered on the brink.

The man leapt back up, his eyes wide, wild, manic, and swung again, catching Chet in the shoulder, knocking him into a tumble.

"Son of a cunt!" the man screamed and Chet felt sure he knew that voice. The man brought the shovel high overhead and down for Chet's skull with all his weight behind it. Chet rolled and the shovel plowed deep into the mud next to his head. Chet kicked out, driving his boot into the man's gut, knocking him back. The man crashed into the line again, knocking over two guards. The cart lurched forward, yanking the rope from their hands.

There came a loud pop as one of the wheels snapped and the cart toppled over the ledge, sending slaves and guards alike diving out of the way as the rope whipped along after it.

The man tried for his feet, slid in the mud, and several guards rushed in, wrestling him to the ground.

Chet stood up, getting his first clear look at the soul, and there, beneath the soot and mud, was the man he'd hit with his car. *"Coach?"*

"HIM!" Coach screamed, still struggling to get at Chet. *"That fucker right there! He killed me!"*

Seet stomped over to Coach. "What madness is this?"

"He killed me!" Coach yelled at the goblin man. "Him! He's a *murderer*! *A goddamn murderer!*"

Understanding dawned on Seet's face and for a moment he actually appeared amused. "Pick him up."

The guards lifted Coach, held him.

"You are mine now," Seet said, striking him hard across the face with the bludgeon end of the lash. "You go to the games with the horsekiller. You can kill him there, kill him all you want."

# CHAPTER 34

Chet glanced over at Coach's battered face, at the collar now strapped about his neck. Coach hadn't spoken a word since Seet chained them together.

The whistle blew, steam billowed. Chet and most of the slaves ducked. Coach didn't. He hardly flinched as Priscilla blew her stack, raining cinders down around them.

The caravan once again moved out, rolling along to the drum of the golem's heavy footsteps. They passed the remains of the cart, nothing but a splintered heap, the caravan steering well clear of the treacherous ledge.

Chet glanced at Coach again. The man's head hung low, staring at his shuffling feet. Chet thought he might be crying, but it was hard to tell in the drizzle.

"I didn't mean to kill you," Chet said.

Coach didn't reply, just kept staring at the mud.

"It was an accident. I swear. Things . . . things just got out of control. Maybe if—"

"Fuck you," Coach said, said it without any emotion, just cold, dead words.

"Okay," Chet sighed. "Sure. Why not? Why not? Go right ahead. I'm already about as *fucked* as I can be." Chet's eyes fell to the chain swinging back and forth before him. He grabbed it, gave it a hard yank. This one was solid; there'd be no breaking loose.

199

They marched on in silence, Chet forcing his thoughts away from what lay ahead, trying to think of Trish, her warm, sweet smile. For a horrible minute he couldn't remember what she looked like; she seemed so far away as to not be real, as though she'd *never* been real. He closed his eyes and it was the patter of the rain that brought her to him: a summer night and him helping her sneak out of her bedroom after her father had once again forbid her from seeing him, the deep soothing purr of the 302 as they sped down that lonely highway in his Mustang, her singing along to Zeppelin while the wind tousled her long curly hair, feeling like they were the only two people in the world. A summer shower had sprung up and they'd pulled over and just sat there holding hands, mesmerized by the distant lightning as rain pattered on the windshield. He remembered how, at that moment, there was nothing else he needed or wanted in the whole world.

Chet heard a deep bong and opened his eyes. The rain had stopped and somewhere up ahead, a great bell tolled.

A tall archway lined with torches emerged out of the mist ahead and a cheer went down the line. As they drew near, Chet saw hundreds of eyes carved into the arch's facade. The eyes followed them as they marched through. Chet shivered, feeling as though they were all, every one, on him alone.

They passed into a great courtyard occupied by several groups of wagons, each flying its own banner. Guards stood sentry near each encampment, wearing the colors of their camp, some in ornate armor, others in road-worn leathers. The air was alive with music—drums, flutes, guitars. Souls in all manner of garb hurried about, along with creatures Chet found it hard to believe he was seeing: cyclopes, horned men and women, a man with black-feathered wings.

A group of gossamer-clad girls, with skin so white it glowed, skipped out of the way as four heavily armed centaurs galloped past—fearsome-looking creatures brandishing spiked clubs. A smell struck Chet, almost stopping him in his tracks—flowers, a gold vase full of lush white flowers. Chet inhaled deeply. *Life,* he thought. *It smells of life.* And a wave of longing threatened to overwhelm him, not for his life, but for life itself.

The caravan pulled around, forming a circle. The great golem came to stop with a loud groan and sat down. Workers and slaves began unloading the carts and wagons.

"Where are they?" a woman shouted, running up to Seet. "Where are our ring-bearers?"

"They are here," Seet snapped.

"Well, hurry. They won't allow Veles entry, not without his offerings."

Seet shouted at the guards. "Get the slaves! Need sixteen! Quick, now!"

"No, just twelve. There are only twelve gods this year."

"Twelve?" Seet frowned. "Every year, there are less." He shook his head and yelled to bring twelve.

The guards began unlocking chains, rounding up slaves.

Seet walked over to the row with Chet, Coach, Ana, and Ado. He fixed his cold eyes on Chet. "Enjoy yourself, horsekiller." He unlatched the post. Nodded to the guard. "Take them."

The guard pulled all of them from the line and led them away, herding them out from the yard through another arch. Jagged keeps and spiraling ramparts towered above them, spanning massive craggy boulders, the ornate structures adorned with uncountable stern-faced demons and dancing beasts. The buildings leaned at odd and precarious angles, as though the whole city were sinking into the ground.

Ahead, a giant contorted face was carved into a rock wall, a gate set in its gaping tormented mouth. Two minotaurs, thick-chested beasts armed with axes, stood on each side. They looked the slaves over with dark, dispassionate eyes.

"These are Lord Veles's offerings," the guard said.

The minotaur nodded and took the slaves, driving them down a short flight of steps and into a damp underground passageway. Drums echoed up the tunnel, growing louder as they were rushed along. The passage opened into a large chamber full of cages and cells.

Dozens of gnomish creatures—none taller than Chet's waist—rushed up to meet them as they entered. Spots covered the creatures' rust-colored skin, their tiny black eyes hid beneath long, oily hair; stumpy tails jutted out from robes made of hide and what appeared to be human hair. Their features varied widely, some with snouts full of sharp teeth, others actual beaks; a few even had talons instead of fingers. They reminded Chet somewhat of Seet, only much smaller and without the horn. Yet, there was something distinctly feminine about these and he realized that they must be female goblins or gargoyles. He tried to remember the word Ado had used—*Trow*.

The Trow women herded the slaves into a line, gabbing away in some guttural tongue that was closer to barking than speaking. They yanked and tore the slaves' clothes from them, hurriedly stripping them down. More Trow women came up carrying buckets and splashed the slaves with lumpy grease that smelled of burnt meat, then doused them in brown powder that turned bright red on contact.

Chet coughed and spat, wiping the oily mess from his eyes and nose. Someone grabbed his arm with strong, knobby fingers that felt like tree roots. An iron ring was clamped around his wrist and crimped into place with large pliers.

The minotaurs shoved Chet and the other slaves onward toward the far end of the chamber, out through an arch, and into a long hall lined with stalls.

More Trow waited here, these ones larger, like Seet, most with one, two, or three horns growing from their skulls. They wore spiked leather vests and carried pitchforks. Rows of slaves were lined up within the stalls behind them.

The first stall was stacked with banged-up helmets and shields. Each slave was handed a helmet as they passed, some receiving a shield as well. A helmet ringed with horns was thrust into Chet's arms.

The Trow drove them down the hall, putting them randomly into the stalls with other slaves. Chet lost track of Ana and Ado in the shuffle. Fearful eyes met his as he was led to a stall at the end of the hall and pushed in with about a dozen other slaves. They were lined up in front of a round, plated door, glancing about, a few clutching themselves and shaking.

The drums gained tempo. Stomping came from above, gaining intensity, causing dust to fall from the ceiling.

The slaves stood staring at the round doors, silent, like men waiting for a bomb to fall.

A horn blew from outside and the large gears rattled to life, lifting the plated doors, rolling them slowly upward.

Firelight greeted the slaves.

"*Out!*" the goblin men yelled, jabbing them along with their pitchforks.

The slaves spilled from the stalls and into an arena about the size of a soccer field. Several large fire pits blackened the field, each surrounded by dozens of standing stones. Twenty-foot-high walls spiked with blades ringed them in and stone balconies, full of spectators, spiraled upward into the mist above.

The spectators jeered as the slaves entered.

The Trow herded the slaves around the perimeter, stationing them between the fire pits in clumps of about ten souls each.

Chet searched for Ana and Ado, couldn't find them, but saw Coach just behind him. Coach seemed in a state of confusion, just staring at the dirt.

Trow pushed a few carts of weapons around, mostly rusty and bent swords and spears, handing them out at random. The slaves on either side of Chet both received weapons, but Chet did not.

"Helmets on!" the goblin men shouted, jabbing at anyone moving too slowly.

Chet slipped his on and tugged the strap in place to secure it on his head. All the helmets had faceplates, and between the helmets and red paint, Chet found it impossible to tell one soul from another and gave up on finding Ana and Ado.

The flames flared, then simmered down. The drums stopped. The crowd fell quiet as a tall set of red doors swung inward. The spectators leaned forward, many standing, all watching the dark opening.

Chet swallowed, tried to focus on breathing, on remaining calm, tried not to imagine what horrors were heading their way.

There was movement in the shadows, and then—*monsters.*

A cheer went up from the crowd as the monsters entered the arena.

Chet fell back a step.

Twelve creatures paraded around the field. They all walked on two legs and appeared to be somewhat human, but that was where the similarities ended. Animal and human characteristics meshed together into every manner of monstrosity. But as they marched, Chet began to see reason to the madness, that they appeared more enhanced than deformed, as though a hand had crafted them to maximize their lethality. Many were even majestic in their own unique and deadly way, sleek and brilliantly colored, some hulking, with rippling muscles and bulging veins, others sinewy, lithe, and agile, looking fast and dangerous. One creature even had four arms. Chet saw razor-sharp bones protruding from forearms, elbows, and knees like blades, deadly horns, hooves, claws, and beaks. They wore no armor, but many had thick hides, feathers, fur, or scales. They carried all manner of weapons: swords, axes, tridents, and maces.

The monsters circled once, then stopped in front of a row of ornate balconies. Atop the balconies, figures reclined beneath colorful canopies in high-back chairs, surrounded by servants and guards. Chet assumed these to be lords, gods perhaps. He counted twelve altogether. He noticed Veles's banner, saw the god being attended to by his servants.

A figure stood up in the center balcony—a woman, tall and gaunt, with bone-white skin, her black gossamer robes so thin they floated about her like smoke. Bones and bronze scales fanned out from her headdress like a peacock tail and her long black hair—tied in braids—twisted down her shoulders like snakes. A veil of web shrouded her features, but Chet could still make out the silver specks of her eyes.

She moved to the rail holding a scepter of copper and bone across her chest, and made a slight nod.

A servant stepped forward carrying a large bronze bell, and rang it sharply. "Queen Hel shall speak."

The crowd fell silent.

"Welcome, champions," Queen Hel said, her words ringing with an odd echo. She set her eyes upon the monsters, calling out names. With each name, one of the monsters raised its weapon to her. When she called out Veles, a lithe creature with a gymnast's build—appearing mostly human except for horns and scales—bowed and Chet realized that these monsters must represent the gods.

She raised her scepter. "Watchers may enter."

Three cloaked figures walked purposefully to a tiered stone platform in the center of the field. A large bronze coffer sat at the base of the platform. They set one palm atop the coffer, tapped their chests above their hearts, then ascended the steps to the uppermost stone, each facing out in a different direction. One by one they pushed back their hoods, revealing bare heads and deeply scared faces, with pockets of black flesh instead of eyes. They pulled pouches from their cloaks and untied them, releasing nine small orbs. The orbs floated upward, stationing themselves above their heads. Chet saw that they were eyes, three eyes for each Watcher.

"Let all hear the laws of play." They spoke as one, their voices soaring over the crowd. "The first contender to gather and drop six rings into the coffer wins the trial. Rings may be gathered by any means."

*Rings?* Chet glanced around looking for the rings, noticed several slaves looking at the band around their wrist, and a sudden and terrible understanding hit him. "Aww, fuck."

"There shall be three trials," the Watchers continued. "The victor of first trial is to be awarded one copper ring. The victor of second trial is to be awarded two copper rings. The victor of third trial shall be proclaimed Grand Victor and awarded six copper rings."

Their floating eyes turned toward the gods.

"Are these rules and honors understood by all lords?"

Each of the gods nodded.

"Are these rules and honors understood by all champions?"

Each monster nodded.

"Champions, to your posts."

The monsters strolled to the center and stood beneath the pole flying their lord's banner, their eyes scanning the slaves.

*Don't even have a goddamn sword,* Chet thought.

"Ring-bearers," the Watchers continued. "Those of you that survive a trial still in possession of your ring shall advance to the next trial. And further, any that survives all three trials still in possession of their ring shall be awarded their freedom."

*Freedom?* Chet clutched the ring on his wrist, wondered if any souls ever survived.

The large red doors rumbled shut with a resounding thud.

"Champions," the three Watchers called as one. "Prepare yourselves."

The champions hefted their weapons. One, a lean, muscular woman with black shiny scales, had no weapons, just long, powerful talons and jagged shark-like teeth. She had her small pale eyes locked on Chet's group.

The Trow hastily left through the stall doors, bolting them shut. The ring-bearers began backing away, falling out of line. The man next to Chet collapsed to his knees, hands clutched together in prayer. Someone else was crying, sobbing. A man began hacking into his own wrist with his sword, cutting off his hand to remove his ring.

Chet started backing away, then spotted Coach sitting in the dirt holding his helmet and sword in his lap, staring at the ground.

"*Get up,*" Chet hissed. "*Get your ass up.*"

Coach didn't move, didn't even look up.

"Champions, are you ready?" the Watchers shouted, raising their hands. The monsters nodded and shook their weapons. Souls broke away and began to run toward the walls, some even throwing down their weapons.

Chet kicked Coach, knocking him over. "Move it, jackass."

"*Fuck off!*" Coach shouted.

"Get up!" Chet yelled. "You *do not* wanna die down here. You hear me? *Now get up!*"

A light came into Coach's eyes and he glared at Chet. "I'm already dead," he snarled. "Because some asshole killed me. Remember? *Remember!*" Coach snatched hold of his sword and lunged at Chet, swinging wildly for Chet's leg. Chet jumped back and stumbled, falling to one knee.

"May the bravest and boldest win!" the Watchers cried, dropping their hands in unison.

A horn blew a long, loud blast and the fire pits erupted, sending pillars of flame swirling skyward. Drums thundered and a roar came from the stands as the champions charged toward the slaves.

Coach stared in terror at the monsters, as though seeing them for the first time. Chet ran, heading toward the wall with all the other ringbearers. A woman stumbled and fell in front of Chet, tripping him. He landed next to a fire pit. Before he could gain his feet several other souls also collided in their panic, falling atop him, pinning him to the ground. The flames flared and searing heat shot up Chet's leg. He cried out, clawing and kicking, trying to free himself.

A wild scream—it was the demon woman, the one with the black scales. She was upon them, tearing into the slaves above Chet with her long claws, their screams mixing with hers as she ripped their limbs from their bodies.

Chet kicked free from the pile, gained his feet, and escaped into the smoke. Souls dashed in all directions amid the screams and smoke, running around and into Chet. Chet spotted a sword in the dirt and snatched it up. The tip was broken, but Chet was glad to have something in his hand.

"Stand together!" a voice cried. "Stand or perish!" Chet couldn't miss that voice; it was Ado. The wiry man stood with five other souls among a cluster of standing stones, swords and spears on guard. Chet dashed over to them.

"Ado, it's me!"

Chet caught the man's smile through the cage of his helmet. "Do you feel alive, Chet?"

"What?"

"Steady!" Ado cried to the souls behind him. "Stand true. It's your only chance."

Chet caught glimpses through the rolling smoke of the monsters as they chased down souls, of mutilated bodies writhing in the dirt. He noticed another group of slaves holding together, putting up a defense as a group. The monsters left them alone, going instead after isolated individuals or those fleeing or putting up no defense. Chet understood then what Ado was doing, that the game wasn't to defeat these monsters, but to avoid looking weak, easy.

A man without a helmet ran toward them. It was Coach, his eyes wide with horror, three deep gashes across his chest. A shriek came from behind him and the demon lady leapt from the smoke, clutching a handful of rings in one hand. She spotted Coach and started after him.

"*Over here!*" Chet shouted at Coach. Coach dashed to them, joining their ranks.

"Show her steel and teeth!" Ado cried. "Growl at the bitch!"

They did, shouting, growling, and brandishing their blades. Chet joined in, howling, slashing the air. Coach too, screaming at the monster as though he'd lost his mind.

The demon lady stopped, looking unsure, snarled, but she *didn't* attack. A man ran out from the smoke, his eyes on something behind him, and almost collided with the demon. She pounced, knocking the soul down and cutting off his arm with one stroke. She snatched up the arm, tugging the ring free. A huge shadow burst from the smoke behind her, driving into her, knocking her to the dirt.

This monster, easily the size of a grizzly bear, planted a huge foot atop her, pinning her to the ground. She shrieked and writhed, and dug her claws into its leg. It hefted its ax and hacked into her back, cutting off her scream. The huge monster pried the rings from her hand, held them up. It had five rings, needed but one more. It caught sight of Chet, Ado, Coach, and the other men. It let out a grunt and charged, appearing not the least intimidated by their show.

One of the ring-bearers broke and ran, then another.

The monster barreled down upon them.

"Stand!" Ado shouted, stepping forward to meet the attack. The beast plowed into them, knocking Ado and his blade aside with a wide sweep of its ax. Chet ducked, tried to dive from its path. The ax caught him and sliced through his arm, flipping him into the air. Chet had no idea which way was up until he slammed into the dirt. The monster stomped down upon his leg. There came a horrible snap followed by blinding pain.

Chet screamed.

The monster raised its ax as a horn blew, the sound blasting across the arena. The monster stopped, ax still raised, and jerked its head around, looking over its shoulder toward the center.

A tall, hulking beast with bluish skin spiked with horns and tusks jutting from a fearsome grin stood at the coffer, sword held above its head, a triumphant look upon its face.

The bear-sized beast slowly lowered its ax, spat, then slapped its rings into the dirt. It muttered a curse, then lifted its foot off Chet and just walked away.

Pain rolled over Chet, engulfed him. He yelled through clenched teeth.

Someone grabbed him. "Chet."

Even through the pain, Chet had no problem recognizing Ado's big grin.

"Chet. You did it. You still have your ring!"

CHAPTER 35

_____

H ere, careful," Ado said, helping Chet off the stretcher. Two goblin men rolled Chet off, then turned and headed away.

Chet tried to sit up, and abruptly realized his left arm was missing,
simply gone from the shoulder down. *Oh no,* he thought. *Oh, no.*

Ado helped him into a sitting position, propped him against the wall.
They were back in the underground chambers.

"You made it, Chet."

Chet looked at the twisted and broken mass that was left of his leg. *I'm
done for. Fucked. So fucked.* But his despair went far deeper, his grief not
for his leg, or for what might happen to him now, but for Trish and the
baby.

A woman's scream rose above the other moans and cries. Chet scanned
the room. "Where's Ana?"

Ado shrugged. "I have not seen her."

The wounded and maimed lay everywhere. Souls sat in the dirt or stood
staring blankly at the wall or ground. Chet searched every face, looking for
Ana, but it was hard to distinguish one soul from another due to the oily
red powder.

"Perhaps she is among those who lost their rings," Ado said. He stood
and walked over to the iron bars separating their chamber from the next.

The souls in the adjoining chamber appeared in an even worse state—
the maimed, the burned, the crushed. Farther back, Chet saw piles of

severed arms, legs, next to those—bodies. Their heads were crushed, or missing altogether. *The dead dead,* Chet thought. He couldn't see their faces and could only hope that Ana wasn't among them.

Trow moved through the chamber gathering weapons and helmets, stacking them in carts along the far wall, as more and more bodies were brought in.

Ado returned, sat next to Chet. "No sign of her."

Another wave of slaves shuffled in. A Trow woman checked their wrists, sending those who still wore rings into the chamber with him and Ado, the rest into the other. Chet scanned their shell-shocked faces. He didn't see Ana, but he did see Coach. Coach still had his ring and came stumbling in, collapsing on a bench near the far wall.

"Here, you," someone barked—an older Trow woman, with shaggy gray hair, a cluster of whiskers sprouting from her chin, and what looked like a cigar jutting out from the corner of her mouth. But, unlike the sour-smelling cigarettes Chet had encountered so far, this one smelled pleasant, almost like cinnamon. She prodded Chet's leg.

Chet gritted his teeth against the pain.

She looked at the stump where his arm used to be and shook her head. "Bad time." She tapped the ring around his wrist—smiled. "You keep ring. Good." She held up four fingers to the Trow woman beside her.

The younger woman dug four brown coins out of a large satchel, handed them to Chet, then moved on to Ado. The old Trow woman prodded a large gash across Ado's chest, held up one finger. The other woman handed a single coin to Ado and then headed on to the next soul.

Chet looked at the coins. "They pay us?"

"Pay? No. They're to heal you. Eat." Ado placed his coin into his mouth, began to chew.

"Eat the coins?" Chet held one of the coins up and pinched it; it was like hard leather. "These are supposed to heal me?"

"Yes."

Chet put one in his mouth, began to chew. It dissolved, almost evaporated within his mouth, leaving behind a bitter powdery taste.

"Nothing's happening."

"Wait."

A tingling sensation, almost an itch, started around his injuries, then the pain began to recede. Chet quickly ate the remaining coins.

Music drifted down through the trapdoors above, a whimsical tune. Someone or something began to sing, a hearty male voice.

Chet set his head back and closed his eyes, listening to the song as the pain continued to ebb away.

"I wish Queen Oya could hear," Ado said. "She was never much on the tournaments, but she dearly loved the performances. I fear there will be no more . . . not for her." He sighed. "Maybe if I am bold and brave the gods will smile upon me and I will win my freedom . . . return once more to Oya's side."

Chet opened his eyes. "You'd go back to being a slave?"

"No, not a slave. I was never her slave. I was her servant."

"There's a difference?"

"Yes," Ado said, and Chet could tell by his tone that he'd been insulted. "Most of these condemned souls around us, they are bandits, thieves, flesh merchants. Those who have insulted the gods. I am here because I committed a crime, an offense against Veles." His tone softened. "I serve Oya because my heart is hollow without her. If you serve a god . . . and let them into your heart, that life, that magic, it makes one whole. Chet, do you not feel it? Around you now, even in this pit? The spirit in the air? That is the gods' doing. Gods take and they give; some take more than others. But one thing is certain: what little life there is in this world of death, is their doing."

"Seems to me—" Chet stopped midsentence. "Whoa, that's weird." He could see his arm, the one that had been severed, a ghostly, smoky shape. "What's going on?"

"What do you mean?"

"Look . . . my arm." The shape slowly became opaque. Chet realized he could feel it, warmth, then a prickly, crawling sensation, like worms beneath his flesh, same as when he came over on the barge.

"Yes, it is the ka."

"What the hell is ka?"

"There is ka and there is ba. Ba is you, your true self. Ka is just the clay from which you are made here in the netherworld, the vessel that holds your ba."

"Uh-huh."

"Your ba lives here." He knocked on his skull. "Your skull its cage. When the cage is broken, the ba escapes. Did you not see the ghosts?"

"Huh?"

"In the arena. Those whose skulls were crushed, or smashed. Their ba, it escaped, drifted away."

Chet thought of Johnny, of the apparition that had floated upward from his skull. "So what happens to your ba then?"

Ado shrugged. "Most believe your unanchored ba is claimed by the winds of chaos . . . battered about for an eternity." Ado looked upward. "I do know there are times . . . when the clouds are low and the winds blow just right . . . that you can see them churning above in a tangled mass, sometimes even hear them, their moans and cries. It is not a comforting sound."

"So this ka, these coins . . . they're made from what? Not from other souls?"

Ado nodded.

Chet's face wrinkled in disgust.

Ado grinned. "Yes, there are those who like to pretend we are not all ghouls. The coins, I guess, just make the act of eating one another more palatable. There are plenty out there, souls, demons, other things, that have no quarrel with eating ka straight from the bone. Some that even prefer it."

Chet's thoughts turned to the carts of limbs and hands back in Styga, then his severed arm began to take on weight. It was numb, but he found he could curl his fingers. *There's still a chance,* he thought, trying to temper his excitement. *Trish, there's still a chance, baby.*

"See there. Your ba is forming the ka you consumed into you. If your spirit is strong you don't even need ka, your ba will heal itself. But it would take time, possibly years. And likewise, those of weak spirit, or those who have given up, their ka will rot and wither."

Chet rapped his knuckles against the wall. His flesh was still somewhat translucent, but felt solid. He prodded his thigh. It too felt whole. He braced himself against the wall and pushed up on his good leg. Gingerly, he placed his weight on his injured leg. No pain. He took a light step, then another. "The coins work fast."

"Faster for some than others. Your spirit is strong, Chet."

Trow entered carrying two bodies in on one stretcher. One of the bodies was decapitated, the other that of a young woman. "Oh, no," Chet said, limping over to the bars. "Ana," he called. *"Ana!"*

She looked up and a wave of relief passed through Chet. The goblin men dumped her onto the floor. Chet saw her hand was missing, her ring gone. She managed to get to one foot, the other appearing to be broken at the ankle, and hobbled over to the bars.

Chet reached through, grabbed her shoulder.

"You need some coins," Chet said. He looked for the old Trow woman, found her assisting a soul over near the door. "Be right back."

Chet stepped over and around several souls, walked up to the Trow woman, putting a hand on her arm.

She looked at him. "Yah?"

"The lady there." Chet pointed at Ana. "She needs some coins."

The Trow woman looked over, shook her head. "No ring, no coin."

"Just one. Can we get just one?"

"No, no," she said, glancing toward the big minotaur near the door. "No ring, no coin."

The minotaur eyed Chet.

"No make trouble," she said and pushed Chet's hand away. Chet felt something slide into his palm. It was round.

She winked.

*"Thank you,"* he whispered and headed back to Ana.

"Here, take this," Chet said. "Eat it. But don't let them see." He slipped the coin through the bars into her hand.

"What is it?"

"Just eat it."

"Is it medicine?"

"Yes, that's exactly what it is."

Ana slipped the coin into her mouth, chewed, and swallowed.

"It might take a minute," Chet said, "but it should—"

Seet walked into Ana's chamber accompanied by three guards. They spread out and began searching the slaves, checking their collars for Veles's mark.

"There is one," Seet said, pointing at a man missing an arm.

One of the guards pulled the man away from the wall, checked his collar, gave him a shove toward Seet. "Looks like he can still walk."

"Good," Seet said. "Hook him back up to Priscilla."

Several other guards, bearing the insignia of their gods, entered the chamber and began rounding up their wounded.

"Hey, missed this one?" a guard said, standing over a man with two crushed legs.

"No," Seet said. "He is not worth the coin. Leave."

"You no leave," the Trow woman said to the guard. "You must take."

Seet said something sharp to her in their own tongue and the Trow woman let loose on him with a tirade of guttural barks and grunts, jabbing at him with one fat finger. Seet stood there flinching at every word until finally the woman stormed away.

"I'm guessing we're not going to be leaving this fellow," the guard said.

Seet let out a snort of disgust. "Take him."

"Where to?" the guard asked.

"I do not care," Seet said. "Toss him in a ditch."

The guard shrugged, grabbed the man by his one remaining arm, and dragged him out of the chamber like a bag of trash.

Seet and his guards found six more of Veles's slaves, tied them in line. Seet spotted Ana, then Chet through the bars. He walked over. "How do you like the game, horsekiller? Are you having fun?" He leaned up close to the bars. "Today was hard . . . tomorrow, much fewer slaves. Glad I am not you."

Chet just stared at him.

Seet set his dark eyes on Ana. "Your guard dog does not look too good." He hitched a rope to her collar, yanked her to her feet. "Up, dog." Ana winced, but thanks to the ka, managed to stand on her injured ankle. Her hand had only partially reformed and now hung like a hook—she needed another coin.

Seet headed away, yanking Ana along. Chet could see the pain on her face as she limped after him. Seet glanced back at Chet. "Do not worry, horsekiller. I take good care of your dog."

CHAPTER 36

A roar came from above them, through the trapdoors. Chet thought
it sounded like a tiger. The roar was accompanied by galloping hooves, the
braying of a donkey, birds singing, and dogs howling together as though in
chorus, all punctuated with cheers, laughter, and applause.

"That must be Veles," Ado said. "He once had the greatest collection of
animals in the known netherworld . . . a show that could rival earth above.
He even had a few real flesh-and-blood animals." Ado sighed. "It was a
different time then. The creatures he has now are mostly soul-shifts. Just
more ka sorcery. Though I believe he does have a few actual animal souls."

"Animal souls?" Chet mused, wondering why the thought hadn't
crossed his mind until now. "So you're saying animals *do* have souls?"

"Of course they do."

"Well, where are they all at?"

"Oya spoke that they have their own place, but sometimes they stray
or are brought into our realm. Sometimes on account of sorcery, other
times just happenstance . . . a soul gets lost, wanders down a path it was
not meant to go. It is a wonder to see what the gods can create with ka, but
there is something special about the real thing. Knowing you look into the
eye of an innocent, not some poor soul twisted into a beast."

"So those monsters, the champions, they're just souls like us?"

"They were once. Before the gods gorged them on ka. To the gods,
ka is like clay . . . the more skilled the hand, the more clever the creation.

That's the heart of this contest, not just prowess, but also beauty and sometimes absurdity. The gods love to show off."

Another burst of cheers from above.

"Real or ka," Ado said, "I would still love to see Veles's show again."

"I would love to see it burn."

Ado laughed. "And you just might one day, my friend. The tide is turning against him, against all the gods. And yet they choose to keep their heads in the sand. All their pomp and pageantry, pretending nothing has changed, but they only fool themselves. There was a time when a hundred gods came to the Gathering. And I too, was here, serving my great goddess." Ado's eyes drifted off. "The air was alive with the smells of living plants and animals. So many gods . . . so much magic and splendor . . . it was as earth itself."

Dogs bayed above; Chet realized they were actually carrying a tune.

"Did you see his face?" Ado continued. "Veles's face? The strain beneath his smile. The cost of his vanity is almost more than he can bear. He must contribute copper and slaves. Copper he doesn't have. Then there is the cost to create a champion . . . the ka, and though forbidden, it is well known that many of the gods use god-blood." Ado fell silent, then after a long moment he said, "It was this . . . the god-blood which I was trying to steal. It is great magic, coveted, rare. I know that it is the one thing that can heal a god. That is why I tried to steal it for Oya. I had heard Veles had god-blood in abundance. So I felt it no great crime to take from him. Now I see that even Veles is struggling in this new age."

Whistles and applause from above.

"Does hardship keep Veles from putting on a good show?" Ado smiled. "No, he would go on no matter the cost." He let out a long sigh. "These ancient gods, they are different than the One Gods. Regardless of their flaws, they have heart, a lust for life, and will do whatever it costs to keep life alive, even in the very pits of death. And it is that which I admire."

"That's all good and well," Chet said. "Won't matter much come tomorrow. Not once we're in the arena again."

"Tomorrow is an opportunity," Ado said, standing up. "A step closer to our freedom. Come." He headed off toward the back of the chamber.

Curious, Chet stood and followed Ado to a stack of busted weapons. He passed Coach on the way and the man followed him with his eyes, his face unreadable. Ado picked through the pile until he found two broken shafts of equal length, about the length of a sword, and handed one to Chet.

Chet cut his eyes to the minotaurs guarding the main door. "You think we can bust out?"

"No, there is no chance of that. I have a better idea. My friend, you and I, we are going to *win* our freedom. I have had the privilege to serve in Oya's guard both in life and in death. I was never a great warrior, but over the centuries I have picked up more than a few tricks. You do not have time to master the art of swordplay, but you do have time enough to learn a few key defensive moves. Maybe enough to make the difference."

"I'm game."

"A couple of things to remember: Tomorrow there will be fewer slaves, but also fewer champions, for champions who cannot walk from the arena on their own are not allowed to return. Those champions left, they shall be fierce. Slaves willing to just give up their rings will be gone. Those left, they wish to win their freedom. They will be fighters. So there will be more to it than just staying ahead of the sheep. We will have to fight. But we need not fight to win, only to escape slaughter. Understand?"

"I guess."

"Stand there. Hold your staff by its end. See, like this, like a sword. There. Okay, weapon up. No, more like this. Now come at me."

Chet did and was surprised at how easily Ado slid past his attack. He demonstrated several more times, then had Chet try.

"No," Ado said. "Remember, you will never match their force. If you are rigid they will break you, but if you are fluid, you will flow past their assault. Now watch me." Ado showed Chet the move again, but slowly. "Now try again."

Chet tried again and again, each time a little better.

"Good. You catch on quickly, Chet."

Chet didn't know about that, but he did feel he was getting the principle at least. They went around and around, Ado showing him several variations, how an attacker's foot-play forecast his intentions. Ado replayed the moves over and over until Chet could read most of his attacks.

At some point, Coach had moved closer. Chet noticed him leaning against a pillar, watching them.

"Here, now try this." Ado showed Chet a few basic feints. "Good weapon play is the art of deception. Mislead your attacker, make them commit where you want, and you take the advantage."

They practiced, going back and forth. Ado seemed genuinely pleased with Chet's progress.

"Remember, you need not defeat them, only dodge, escape, evade, and survive. Survive and you win your freedom."

Chet caught sight of Coach walking toward him carrying a broken staff. Chet turned, faced the man with his own weapon ready. "Stay the fuck away from me."

Coach halted, lowering his staff. "I don't wanna die down here."

Chet kept his staff level.

Coach frowned. "I'd like to practice with you guys."

Ado looked to Chet.

Chet started to tell Coach to fuck off again, but there was something in the man's eyes, desperation perhaps. He certainly saw no anger, or hostility, not toward them.

"My mom's in Lethe," Coach said. "I just wanna see her. Y'know, one more time."

"Three is a good defensive number," Ado said.

Chet sighed and slowly lowered his stick. "Hell . . . fine."

Ado smiled. "Good." He lined them up, going over the basics again, drilling both of them, then positioned them facing each other.

"Okay," Ado said. "Coach, I want you to try and tap Chet. Ready?"

They both nodded. "Go."

Coach swung low, switched to high, swung past Chet's block, catching Chet against the shoulder—hard.

"Ah . . . fuck," Chet cried. "That wasn't a tap, asshole. He said tap."
Coach was grinning.

"Tomorrow," Ado said, "they will hit much harder. Now . . . your turn,
Chet."

Chet tightened his grip. "Hell yeah, it is."

Coach's grin fell away and he got ready, sliding into one of the stances
Ado had showed them. This time it was Chet who landed a blow, a sharp
stinging strike to the neck. And this went on, back and forth, each trying
to outdo the other, Ado egging them on, showing them how to avoid, or
block each attack, how to read what their opponent was trying to do. After
a bit he switched to defensive formations and patterns that the three of
them could use to foil an aggressive opponent.

They continued sparring, drill after drill. Chet took to it, glad to have
something to focus on. Soon he came to read Coach's attacks and as the
moves became instinctual, it became harder and harder for Coach to tag
him. Several other slaves gathered around to watch, but most kept to
themselves, their eyes distant and shell-shocked.

After many hours, Ado raised his hand. "Enough for now. We should
rest." Chet noticed there was no longer any light coming through the overhead grate.

They found a spot away from the others and took a seat against the
wall, Coach sitting down next to Ado. For a long time they just sat there
listening to water dripping from one of the overhead grates. It was Coach
who finally broke the silence. "Ado, you ever been to Lethe?"

"Yes."

"I was told it's where souls go to end it. This life or whatever this is.
That true?"

"It is."

Something was obviously bothering Coach. "My mother, she's supposed
to be there. That's what the woman, that bloodseeker back in Styga, said."

Ado nodded. "Many souls make the journey to Lethe."

"I . . . I just hope I'm not too late . . . just want the chance to tell her
I'm sorry." His voice grew husky with emotion. "It was my fault she died."

Chet glanced at Coach. The man's eyes were distant, his brow knotted.

"I was only ten years old when it happened, but I should've done something. Anything. But I . . . *didn't*." He cleared his throat. "He beat her. My dad. You wouldn't of guessed he was the type looking at him. Skinny guy, glasses, worked down at Sears in billing. Didn't even drink. But every now and again, something would just set him off. Little stuff, weird stuff. That was the worst of it, you just never knew.

"It was my birthday . . . just the three of us there, sitting around the kitchen table. Mom had baked me a cake. Spent most of the afternoon decorating it. She used the icing to make a football on top. It said, '*Larry is a winner.*'

"It was the candles that did it. They were purple and he wanted to know why she'd put purple candles on a boy's cake. She told him they were the only ones on hand. His eyes started twitching then, the way they'd get when something was bothering him. He shook his head, said, you can't put girl candles on a boy's cake. She laughed, said it'd be all right, that nobody would ever know but us. He told her, no, it's not all right to put sissy candles on his son's cake. I said I didn't mind. Asked him if I could please just blow out the candles.

"I could see Mom's hands shaking. She asked him then, asked real nice for him not to make a fuss, not on my birthday. He slapped her . . . hard enough to knock her out of her chair.

"Mom didn't say anything else, just got up holding the side of her face and went into the bedroom.

"Dad sat there staring at the candles with those twitchy eyes. I was too scared to move, too scared to do anything but watch the candles melt all over my cake.

"After a bit he got up and went back to the bedroom." Coach was quiet a minute. "He was yelling at her at first. She was crying. Then I could hear every blow . . . *every* blow. She started screaming, begging him to stop. I remember staring at the phone, it was right there in the kitchen. Mom had put the police and fire number below it, told me to call them in case of an emergency. I kept trying to make myself pick up that phone. But I . . . *didn't*. I was scared. Scared he'd beat me.

"After a while she stopped screaming . . . I could still hear the sound of his fist hitting her body. Just whap, whap, whap, whap. God, when will I ever stop hearing that?"

"*I'm sorry,*" Ado whispered.

Coach looked at Ado. "I don't care what happens to me down here. Not so long as I get a chance to tell her I'm sorry . . . sorry for being such a coward."

"Get some rest," Ado said, lying down on the dirt. "If you want to see your mother again, you will need some rest."

Chet lay down next to Ado and closed his eyes, trying to find sleep, but found himself staring at the ceiling. "Do we sleep?"

"If you are lucky," Ado said. "Real sleep is a thing to treasure. For when you sleep . . . you dream of *life*."

Water continued dripping from the grate, a steady, *twack, twack, twack,* and all Chet could hear was the sound of Coach's dad beating a dead body. He forced his mind away, replaying all the moves Ado had shown him. Slowly his thoughts turned to Trish, her eyes, her smile, the feel of his unborn daughter kicking against his hand. *I have to stay alive. Have to.*

## CHAPTER 37

Carlos and his Defenders rode up to the base of a towering figure and came to a halt, all staring up at the giant statue—a two-headed woman with six breasts sagging atop her swollen belly and three pairs of arms, each ending in giant hooves. One of her heads smiled perpetually heavenward while the other frowned down upon them. She was cast from iron, the ore pitted and streaked red with rust.

Carlos nodded to Hugo. "Light her up."

The statue's belly formed a cage, a cage large enough to hold dozens of souls. The belly was supported by a large oven. The men rounded up chunks of old bone, shoved them into the oven, and set them to blaze. A few minutes later green smoke began to rise, spewing from the statue's mouths and eyes.

Carlos was glad Mother Eye was full open; even after all these years, he didn't care for meeting with demons in the dark. "Keep watch," he said. "They'll be coming from the south." He tugged a silver lighter from his breast pocket, followed by a cigarette, cupping his hands around the flame as he lit it. He inhaled deeply, letting the sour-smelling bone-spice seep its way deep inside him. He closed his eyes as the rush hit him. It reminded him of cocaine the way it pumped him up, made him feel alive, ready for anything, even a band of demons from Hell itself. Carlos felt there were really just two kinds of souls in purgatory: those that drank Lethe and those that smoked the bone-spice. The ones that drank Lethe, they were the walking dead, pathetic rueful souls who wanted little more than to pass on from this world for good. Those that smoked the bone-spice, though, they wanted to live—to make something of this life after death. Carlos had already wasted one life and had no intention of wasting another.

"Must've been a hell of a sight," Ansel said.

Carlos realized he was talking to him. "What's that?"

"The iron lady there, she belonged to Lord Osiris. Still does I guess, but looks like she ain't been visited in a long spell. She's called Osiris's Mother and they say that in his glory days Osiris used to burn a hundred souls in her belly at a time. Not slaves neither, but his worshippers. Supposed to be some great honor to be chosen. They believed their ashes would rise up to earth above and they'd be reborn."

Carlos tried to image a hundred souls crammed into the iron giant, screaming and squirming against the blistering metal as they cooked. *And to go willingly,* he thought. *God, what would it be like to wield such power? To lord over a kingdom, to bend souls to my will, to cook them in an oven if it pleased me. Now, that . . . that would be worth getting out of bed for.*

"Purgatory's gonna be a better place once all these gods is gone," Ansel said. "Yes, sir."

*For some,* Carlos thought. *Those with a plan. What fools like this man don't understand is that there'll always be someone lording over them. If not a god, then a man.* And Carlos intended to be that man, because he'd spent his whole life being told what to do—the nuns as a child, with their endless rules and sharp rulers, his brief stint in the military, then all those years in prison—and he was done with it. *Always someone waiting to beat you down. Well, if there's one thing I've learned, it's if you don't wish to be beaten, then you'd better be the one holding the whip.*

"There, boss," Hugo said, pointing to a figure on the near ridge. The figure signaled and seven horsemen trotted out from the canyon, followed by a black wagon.

Carlos scanned his men, his Defenders, hard men, some of his best. Most had been with him since his early soul-hunting days. Yet they too appeared on edge. Demons had a way of doing that to you. He glanced over at the Colonel's two men. Ansel appeared nervous as well, but not the other one, the one with the cold eyes—he appeared almost bored.

Carlos dismounted and waited beside the wagon. He spotted Gar, Lord Kashaol's warden, riding in the lead and relaxed somewhat. The two of them went back more than a decade now, starting out with a bit of soul trading, building into so much more. Gar wasn't one of the Fallen, but close. Carlos still didn't fully understand demon hierarchy. He did know that there were as many types of demons as there were bones in purgatory, that the Fallen, the original angels cast out by God, were on top, lording over the vast realms of Hell in various factions and kingdoms. All part of a tenuous alliance held together by Lucifer himself.

Gar rode up, pulled his mount to a halt. The hell horse stomped and snorted as molten flame dripped from its eyes and muzzle. Hell horses weren't soul-shifts, but demons, stupid and dangerous, known to eat souls if given the chance.

Six demons rode behind Gar. They appeared to be lower-caste, beastly creatures with long, snoutish faces and burning yellow eyes. Gar, by contrast, appeared almost human, and Carlos could see he was anxious, glancing around furtively, that he didn't like being so far out. The two of them usually met much closer to Hell's border when Carlos brought souls in.

"Relax, Gar," Carlos called. "The Red Lady's nowhere near."

"Easy for you to say," he retorted. "It is not you that she hunts."

"She cannot smell you from Styga. Saw her there just yesterday."

Gar appeared to relax a degree. His eyes flashed to the tarp in the back of the wagon. "Is that what I hope it is?"

Carlos flipped the tarp down, revealing Horkos.

Gar stared in amazement. "You have done it?" Gar guided his mount closer to the wagon, reached down, and grabbed hold of Horkos by the hair, tugging him up for the other demons to see. They let loose a savage howl that set Carlos's teeth on edge.

Horkos's one eye bulged at the sight of the demons. It was clear he saw his fate. Carlos wondered what the demons would do with the god. Gar had only said Horkos would be going to a place of no return, which was exactly what Carlos wanted to hear, as gods had a way of coming back.

"Lord Kashaol's plan comes together," Gar said, speaking like a man finding his faith.

Carlos nodded. It had been Kashaol, through his emissary, who had asked him, "Why be a soul hunter, when you can be a lord?" It was Kashaol who'd instructed Carlos on how to lead the Colonel down the road of temptation by offering him that which he most wanted, had explained to Carlos how if you wanted to rob your fellow man blind, just tell him you're doing it for the betterment of all. Everything had changed after that, joining the Colonel's revolution creating the perfect guise for Carlos to seize power and take over the docks, then most of Styga, and all in the good name of freedom.

"Now," Gar said, dismounting, "I have something for *you*." He led Carlos over to the black wagon. A stack of crates sat in the back. He lifted the lid off one, revealing several muskets. He pulled one out and handed it to Carlos.

Carlos ran his hand along the barrel. "The ore . . . why, it's flawless."

"Forged in Hell's flame. These will not explode in your face like those made in Styga." He patted one of the smaller crates. "Powder here, balls there. Enough to fight a war."

"Indeed," Carlos said. "Tell me, Gar. Any news on the cannon?"

"It is a marvel."

"It's done?"

"Yes, Lord Kashaol's weapons smith is gathering bits and pieces of broken weapons from the Fallen to create shot for it. They are not easy to come by, but Kashaol is going to extraordinary measures. It will be ready in a few days and Lord Kashaol intends to deliver it in person."

Carlos's thick brows rose in surprise. "In person?"

"Yes, he wishes to meet you. To better know the soul in which he is placing so much trust."

Until now, all Carlos's dealings with Lord Kashaol had been through Gar. Carlos didn't know whether to be pleased or fearful. Lords of Hell didn't come wandering into the river realms without good cause.

"Tell Lord Kashaol it would be my pleasure to meet with him. And, oh, I got a little extra something for him." Carlos turned, looked at the Colonel's two men sitting on the wagon bench; the sack of heads lay directly behind the stoned-faced man. It took him a second to recall his name. "Gavin, toss me that sack."

The man stared at him.

"I said toss it here."

The man just continued to stare at him with those dead eyes.

"You hard of hearing or plain stupid?" Carlos knew Gar was watching, felt his face heating up. "I'm not going to tell you again."

Gavin spat in the dirt.

Carlos went for his gun, then saw that Gavin already had his out. *Christ, didn't even see him move.*

Defenders and demons alike tugged out their weapons.

"Whoa! Whoa, now!" Ansel yelled. "Everybody just put their dicks back in their pants. Here. Here's your godforsaken heads, you soul-trading lowlife." He hefted the sack and tossed it on the ground in front of Carlos.

Another moment went by with everyone watching one another, all except Gavin, who kept his eyes locked on Carlos.

"Put it away, Gavin," Ansel said. "C'mon now."

Carlos sucked in a deep breath, struggling to keep his anger in check. *Later,* he told himself, *deal with him later.* He pushed his gun back into its holster, stooped, picked up the sack, and walked Gar over to the black wagon. "He's one of the Colonel's men," Carlos said to Gar. "They lack for discipline."

The demon nodded. "They hate those who hunt the damned."

*Yeah,* Carlos thought as he untied the sack, *they sure do.* He often wondered why souls would even allow the damned among them, much less feel a need to harbor them. Didn't they understand that these were men and women who'd committed grave sins of one kind or another? To Carlos, the damned were no different than the horrible men he'd served prison time with.

Carlos held the sack open for Gar to see the three heads inside. "A small token of things to come."

Gar peered in and his face lit up. "Ah, Lord Kashaol will be pleased." He took the sack.

"Once the Red Lady is out of the way, there won't be anyplace left for them to hide."

Gar glanced back at Gavin, spoke low to Carlos. "I tell you something, that man . . . he is damned. I smell his mark."

This didn't surprise Carlos. There were a handful of damned among the Rangers, even a few among his Defenders. Hell's borders were vast and porous. Carlos knew the only reason he himself didn't wear the mark was that he'd never believed, not in any of it. He'd always thought religion was for suckers, had often joked that the only church he belonged to was the Church of Carlos.

"Those guns that man carries," Gar continued. "Those are Hell forged. He did not trade or bargain for those . . . he *killed* for them . . . killed a high-caste demon. Bring that man's head to Lord Kashaol, and he will reward you well."

Carlos nodded. "It would be my pleasure."

## CHAPTER 38

"He's still following us," Isabel said.

Mary nodded. "I know." The man had been trailing them ever since they'd left Styga. He had done an admirable job of staying hidden, but out here in the Barrens, among the bones, it wasn't so easy to remain unseen.

Mary surveyed the line of carts, nine all together, forty-six sisters, and even armed as they were with swords and spears, it wasn't easy sheltering infants and children, not out where so many unnamed things stalked the hills and ravines hungry for their flesh. But the Red Lady walked with them, as she had been doing for decades. Mary knew no sane soul would dare challenge them so long as she was their escort, and that was what made her most uneasy about their follower.

"Keep everyone moving along," Mary said. "I'm staying here. I think it's time to have a talk with our trail mate."

Isabel started to protest, but Mary cut her off. "It's better if it's just me; one less might go unnoticed."

When the carts entered a cluster of boulders, Mary slipped out of line and into the shadows of the leaning stones, drew her sword, and waited. She didn't have to wait long before she felt him, sensing him through the jewel in her forehead—*contempt, hatred, arrogance.* It was that last, she knew, that would be his undoing. Men had a tendency to underestimate her because she was a woman, a mistake that had cost many dearly.

She waited until he passed—creeping by without any idea she was there—then slipped out, moving quickly and quietly up on him from behind. He turned at the last moment and she cut his neck from his shoulders, watching dispassionately as both his body and head thumped to the dirt.

She squatted next to his head and looked into his wide, horrified eyes. "You have a choice. Answer my questions true and I will grant you oblivion. Answer false and I leave you here for the unnamed."

He blinked back tears.

"Are you with the Green Coats?" she asked.

"No."

Mary sensed his lie, or rather her jewel did; she felt its heat. "You're lying. Should I leave now?"

"I'm not one of them . . . not one of the Defenders. I swear it. They made me follow you. Said they'd throw me in the river if I didn't."

More lies. Mary stood up, started away.

"Wait. Wait. *Please!*"

She continued.

"Okay, *yes*!" he cried. "I'm with the Defenders."

She returned. "Why are you following us?"

"Supposed to keep tabs on your whereabouts."

There was more, she sensed it. "And?"

"And?"

She waited.

"To tell them if you took another road, anything other than Lethe."

"And why would they need to know that?"

"Don't know. They didn't tell me why, didn't tell me anything. Truly."

He was speaking the truth.

"Where are they?"

"Ahead . . . somewhere along the road to Lethe."

"How many?"

"I don't know," he was crying. "I've told you all I know about them."

And she could tell he had. She turned, started away.

"Wait. Wait. You promised."

"And you lied," she said without looking back.

"No. Don't leave me," he cried. "*No!*"

She continued, moving quickly, the man's cries fading as she headed over the rise. She caught up with Isabel and the Red Lady shortly thereafter.

"It is time to find a new path. Something is going on. I don't know what. But I don't like it. Let us take the road to Osiris's Mother."

"You mean through the canyons?" Isabel asked, sounding concerned.

"Yes. I think we should."

## CHAPTER 39

The plated doors rolled upward and the goblin men marched the slaves out into the arena to the beat of the drums, spreading them out along the perimeter of the field. Chet, Coach, and Ado stood together, surveying the field. Chet guessed there to be around sixty souls left, about half the number of yesterday.

"It will be a different game today," Ado said. "Different strategy. We need to avoid the larger groups this time, as they will only draw the champions." He scanned the field. "The smoke is denser . . . there, near the gates. When the horn blows we will go there, and use the pits, smoke, and stones to stay clear of the champions."

Chet nodded, noticing that most of the remaining ring-bearers appeared alert and held their weapons like they meant to use them.

The tall red door slowly opened and the champions marched out. Like yesterday, they paraded around the arena once, hailing the crowd and the gods, then took their stations in the center of the arena beneath their banners. There were nine today, three fewer than yesterday.

Chet tightened the strap on his helmet. There were many more weapons to go around and he'd managed to claim a decent sword.

The three Watchers entered, took their places atop the stone platform.

Ado sucked in a deep breath. "Feel that?"

"What?"

"Life. It is in the air. A gift from the gods." Ado appeared to actually be enjoying himself, his face not full of dread like so many of the others, but of vitality. "Savor the feeling; it is as close to life as you will get in the netherworld."

Chet shook his head, wished he could share his friend's enthusiasm, but there was nothing about the moment he wished to savor.

"Watch that one," Ado said, nodding toward a tall, hulking champion with thick tusks jutting from its grim mouth and bluish skin spiked with horns and bony plates—the winner from yesterday.

"His name is Mortem. He is Queen Hel's champion, has been for the last twelve Gatherings and has won Grand Victor every time. They say he is undefeatable. They also say that Hel feeds him god milk from her own tit. Either way, he is a formidable force—even the other champions fear him. His method is to slash and hack, destroying all in his path and picking up the pieces. And there, the man next to him, that is Kwan, Veles's latest creation."

Kwan had retained most of his humanity, appearing Asian to Chet, perhaps Chinese, with strong high cheekbones and a hawkish gaze. Brown scales ran down his back and blades of bone extended from his forearms. He appeared spry, even now bouncing on his toes like a spring ready to launch.

"He is small and untried," Ado said. "But it is not all about size. Some are quick, others strong. Each god designs and crafts its champions with different strategies in mind. It is part of the game. Mortem plays on savagery, relying on intimidation, a true berserker." Ado said this as though he admired the monster.

The Trow fled the field as the red doors once again closed with a heavy thud.

Chet drew in a deep breath. "Here we go."

Coach appeared vigilant, his face hard and resolute.

"Are all champions ready?" the Watchers shouted, holding up their hands.

The monsters nodded.

Ring-bearers began spreading out, others forming clumps and clusters, weapons and shields ready. Ado began to drift toward the gates where the smoke was thickest; Chet and Coach followed.

"May the bravest and boldest win!" the Watchers cried, dropping their hands. A horn blew and, like the day before, the fire pits erupted and the drums thundered, sending the crowd to their feet.

The champions hurled themselves toward the ring-bearers.

Ado, Chet, and Coach dashed into the smoke and for the moment, Ado's strategy seemed to work; the three of them went unnoticed while the champions charged into the larger clumps of ring-bearers.

Mortem roared, his teeth bared as he smashed into a cluster of slaves. They broke and ran, the slower ones hacked and mangled beneath the ferocity of his ax. The impacts of his blows sounded like gunshots as his blade chopped through steel and bone alike.

Screams and cries resounded from all sides of the arena. Souls ran past and around the three of them. Chet spotted a creature chasing two souls their way. It bounded along on its knuckles like an ape, long, cruel claws curving out from each hand.

Ado, Chet, and Coach dashed around the fire pit, keeping the flame between them and the monster. It ran past, snagging one of the slaves by the ankle and flipping her. It hooked its claw in her ring and tore it loose, tearing off her hand. The creature held up the ring and started hooting when a big shadow rushed up through the smoke, leaping across the pit and through the flame, slamming into the monkey beast. It was Mortem. He landed atop the monkey beast, crushing it beneath his bulk, driving his ax into the back of the creature's skull.

The crowd let out a roar.

Mortem grabbed the ring, but even in death, the monkey creature held on. Chet didn't wait around to see what happened next, the three of them dashing away, disappearing into the smoke.

They slid up behind one of the larger standing stones, trying to survey the field. Chet spotted Veles's champion, Kwan, in action, leaping almost thirty feet to catch a soul, taking him down with a quick, precise slash of his sword, slicing the ring off at the wrist, then up and after another— leaping and darting about like a gazelle.

The wind shifted, exposing Chet, Ado, Coach, and two other souls.

"Oh, fuck," Chet said, seeing Mortem not fifty feet away, his eyes on them.

Chet started to run, but Ado grabbed him. "We cannot outrun him. We have to stand. Together; we feint together."

Every ounce of Chet wanted to flee, but he nodded. Coach too, his face grim, his eyes wide, almost fierce.

"Be fluid," Ado said.

Mortem came for them. One of the slaves ran. Mortem caught him in three strides, slashing a broad stroke, cutting off the slave's arm and slicing through most of his abdomen. He snatched up the ring. He now had five, needed but one more. His eyes landed on Chet.

"Form up!" Ado cried, urging them into the defensive formation he'd shown them.

The creature bellowed, snorted, raised his ax, and came at a full run.

"Steady!" Ado called, widening his stance, sword pulled back as though prepared to hit a homer. Chet and Coach followed suit, giving every indication that they meant to meet the attack head-on. Chet steeled himself and Coach howled, sounding more animal than human.

Mortem leapt for them, ax coming around in a wide sweep with his full formidable weight behind it. Chet and Coach slid back at the last second, in separate directions, just as Ado had shown them, giving the monster a moment's hesitation on where to land his blow. Ado feinted, drawing Mortem's aim, then slid down. Mortem's blade met only air, sending the giant stumbling past, off balance. He tumbled and fell.

The crowd roared.

The monster rolled up, shaking his head as though trying to understand what had happened.

The crowd was on its feet as Chet, Coach, and Ado ran.

Chet caught sight of something flying toward him. Mortem's ax struck him in the side of his chest, cutting deep into his ribs, knocking him off his feet and into the dirt. Chet tried to get up, tried to move through the pain. Suddenly Mortem was there, upon him, slamming him back to the ground beneath his huge sandaled foot. Chet let loose a cry as Mortem grabbed the ax and yanked the weapon free of his flesh, raising it above his head.

Ado slid up from behind, low and fast, brought his sword around in a full hard swing, catching Mortem in the back of his ankle. The blade bit deep, cutting almost all the way through.

Mortem let out a howl and leapt for Ado. He made it one step before his wounded ankle collapsed beneath his weight, sending him to the ground. He let out another howl, more of rage than pain, and tried to grab Ado, but Ado was already away.

Cheers erupted from the far side of the arena. A figure was running toward the center of the field. It was Kwan, six rings in his hand.

"*No!*" Mortem shouted. He tried again to gain his feet, and fell.

A champion, a large bearish brute, made to intercept Kwan. Veles's champion spun, effortlessly dodging past the monster, leapt up to the coffer, and slammed six rings into the chest.

The horn blew and the arena erupted in cheers, spectators on their feet, stomping, clapping, and shouting.

Mortem stared, face stunned, confused, as though not able to comprehend what he was seeing. He let loose a choking moan and sat down hard.

Kwan walked around the arena one time, holding his sword high to the cheering crowd. He bowed low to the gods. The red doors opened and those champions that could began to leave the field.

Coach slid down next to Chet, helped him to sit up and take his helmet off. "We made it, Chet. We fucking made it!"

Chet grinned through the pain. "We made it."

Ado walked up.

"Ado," Coach cried. "We did it!"

Ado's face was grim. "Maybe."

"Maybe?"

Ado watched as Mortem tried to stand, the crowd too, all waiting, watching the injured giant. "They want to know if he will return tomorrow to restore his honor."

The giant pushed himself up onto one knee.

"Champions must make it from the arena on their own," Ado said. "Or they may not return."

Mortem stood up on one leg, trying to keep his balance, trying to keep his weight off his mangled ankle. He tried to hop, lost his balance, lurched, and fell hard.

Jeers and laughter came from the crowd.

Mortem stayed upon his hands and knees for a long moment, just staring into the dirt. Chet wondered if the giant had given up.

Someone shouted at him from the stands to crawl like a lizard. Several others picked it up, all shouting, "Crawl, lizard, crawl!"

Mortem's mouth tightened around his tusks. He looked at the crowd, met them with hard, proud eyes, and pushed himself up again. Then he placed his weight on his broken ankle, his face contorting with pain as he fought not to cry out. This time he did not try to hop, but took a step, walking on his broken ankle, his foot twisted sideways. Chet could barely stand to watch. One step, then another, and another.

The crowd fell silent, all eyes locked on the giant as he moved closer and closer to the door with each awkward, painful step. And as he neared, as he pressed through what was obviously extricating pain, the crowd began to shout encouragement, to cheer. And, as he took those final few steps, lurching forward, grabbing hold of the door, the crowd exploded in applause and shouts.

Mortem clutched the door, his whole body shaking. He looked back at Ado, just a look, but there was no misreading his meaning.

"I am afraid tomorrow will be my last day," Ado said.

# CHAPTER 40

The old Trow woman set two ka coins in Chet's hand and moved along. Chet placed them in his mouth, trying to block out the moans and cries of those around him as he chewed and swallowed. He leaned back against the chamber wall and waited for the pain to subside.

Coach and Ado sat beside him. Ado had not spoken since leaving the arena.

"He's not gonna waste time trying to find you," Coach said.

Ado didn't answer.

"Think about it. How's he gonna find you? We're all painted the same color and wearing faceplates. With the smoke and confusion, he's just gonna be after the rings."

"He will find me," Ado said. "It is a matter of honor with that one."

"Still, he has to—"

"Dead meat," came a harsh voice. Seet stared at them through the bars with his soulless reptilian eyes. "That is what they are calling you, dark man. There are no bets on you keeping your ba. Only bets on how long for Mortem to crush your skull. My coin says you do not have a chance in Hell. What do you think?"

"I think you should fuck off," Chet said.

Seet's thin lips peeled upward into some horrible parody of a smile.

One of Veles's guards walked up with three slaves in tow. "This is all of them."

"Good," Seet said, heading away, then to Chet. "Tomorrow, I will find a seat up close. I want to see your ba when it flies off."

Ado stared at his hands, his face that of a man who had already accepted his fate.

"Seet seems to think we don't have a chance in Hell," Chet said. "Well, I happen to think we do . . . so long as we stand together." He pushed to his feet, mindful of the big wound slowly healing in his side, went to the pile of busted weapons, found the broken staffs they'd been practicing with, and brought them back. He gave one to Coach and held the other out to Ado. "You said you had a few more tricks to show us."

Ado looked at the staff, then past Chet to the chamber door. A hulking hooded figure stood just outside, conversing with the two minotaur guards. The figure's size left little doubt to who it was. After a moment, the figure slipped something into the guards' hands and they let him through.

Mortem had to stoop to enter. He pushed back his hood, revealing the bony plates of his face, and scanned the room until his eyes lit on Ado. His mouth tightened around his tusks and he headed over. Chet noticed he walked without so much as a limp now.

Ado took one of the staffs from Chet. "You two should go."

"No," Chet said. "Can't do that."

Coach stood up, standing with them.

Mortem stopped several feet away, observing the staffs in their hands. "I'm unarmed." He opened the cloak showing he wore no weapons. "I'm not here to fight. But to talk . . . to commend your skills and bravery."

Neither Ado, Coach, nor Chet lowered his guard.

"And to offer you a chance." He looked at each of them in turn. "I hate to kill brave men. But tomorrow I will win at any cost. So, I've come to offer you this deal. Should you be in my path . . . *submit*. Bare your ring for me to take and I'll spare you. Should you resist . . . I'll *crush* you. I'll send your ba to Mother Eye."

He set his eyes on Ado, spoke low. "It is you that I'll come for first.

I have to. Honor demands it." He tapped his broad belt; row after row of notches lined the dark leather. "A notch for every soul. In twelve games I have slain more souls than any other champion in the history of the arena. Don't be a fool. Remember my offer and save your ba."

Ado said nothing.

Mortem pulled his hood back up and left the chamber.

Chet looked at Ado.

Ado met his eye, tapped his sword. "A chance in Hell then."

# CHAPTER 41

$T$rish awoke with a start. She had no idea how long she'd been asleep. It was dark now, the dim glow of moonlight seeping through the window slats.

She felt sure Lamia had drugged her, but thought the effects were wearing off, her head clearer now. She slid off the bed, went over to the window, and peered through the boards. The moon was bright and she could see across the yard, toward the marsh. She spotted the graveyard at the bottom of the hill, thought of Chet lying all alone beneath the ground, and fought back the tears. *Stop it. You can cry later. Chet's gone. He's not coming back. If you want out of this you're gonna have to get yourself out.*

She tested the slats, tugging each board, searching for a loose one. They were all solid, but she found a nail that had gone in sideways and began working it back and forth until finally it came free. She used it to scrape the wood around another nail, digging away the wood one tiny splinter at a time. It was slow work, but after about an hour, she'd loosened another nail. She was hungry, thirsty, and her fingers were sore, but she felt encouraged, sure that, given enough time, she could work all the nails loose from the board.

Footsteps came down the hall. Trish tugged the drape over and shoved the nails beneath the mattress. The door opened and Lamia entered carrying a tray. She hit the switch with her elbow and a single lightbulb hummed to life above them.

Lamia looked the room over with a keen eye. "Good evening, Trish. I trust you slept well?"

Trish didn't say a word, just stared at her.

"Our little baby needs nourishment. I've fixed up a plate of herbs and vegetables all fresh from my garden." She lifted the napkin off the plate, revealing a steaming plate of vegetables.

The smells caused Trish's stomach to rumble. She had no idea how long it had been since she'd last eaten; it felt like days.

"Lamia, I understand you're upset about Chet. We're all upset . . . not ourselves. But you can't keep me here like this . . . like a prisoner. This isn't good for anyone."

"Trish, dear, you don't understand. I'm not holding you captive . . . I'm *protecting* you. Protecting the baby. You need to stop being so selfish and think of your child. Now . . . eat up."

Trish shook her head. "No, I'm not eating any more of your poison."

"Poison? No, girl, I would never allow you to eat anything that might harm our child."

*Our child*, Trish thought. *She thinks the child belongs to her too.*

Lamia took a pinch of greens and put it in her mouth. "See, no poison here."

Trish stayed put. "I'm not eating anything from you."

"Come out on the porch with me," Lamia said. "I want to show you something."

Lamia took the plate and left the room, heading down the hall. Trish stared at the open door, after a moment stood up, walked down the hall, and found Lamia out on the porch.

"Let me show you why you must remain in this house."

Trish looked out across the estate, at the light fog drifting along the low country. *She's trying to trick me.* She scanned the bushes, looking for Lamia's worker, Jerome, wondering if at eight months pregnant, she could outrun the man.

"They'll be here in just a moment." Lamia set the plate down on a small table between the rockers. "Keep your eyes along the edge of the trees . . . there, among the marsh fog."

"Who will be here?"

"My children."

They waited several minutes, but nothing happened. Trish glanced at Lamia, hating the half smile on her face, the smile of a queen overlooking her kingdom. Trish peered down the drive toward the road, trying to remember how far back the last house was. She felt it was about two miles, maybe three. Could she walk that far in her condition? She thought she could, thought she could do about anything she had to in order to escape this crazy woman. She took a step toward the edge of the porch.

"Here they come."

Trish saw nothing but fireflies and moved closer toward the steps, gauging the distance around Lamia. It was then she noticed something odd: the fireflies, they appeared to all be moving up the hill, toward the house. But even odder: they were in pairs. *Like eyes,* she thought.

They drifted closer and the fog began to swirl about them, slowly forming into ghostly figures. Trish gasped, not believing what she was seeing. "Children," she said. "Those are children."

"Yes, I told you. They're my children."

They began to call, a plaintive chorus. Trish's skin prickled; the sound was so desperate, so forlorn.

"*Mommy, mother,*" they murmured. They were calling for her, for Lamia. They pushed closer, and closer, hands outstretched.

Lamia smiled, positively glowed. "My children, I love you all."

They walked up to the porch, stopping at the steps, staring up at Lamia with eyes full of longing. The despair in their voices brought tears to Trish's eyes.

Lamia laughed. "Are they not wonderful? How they love me, with their very souls."

One of the children, a girl, not more than two years old, bumped the string along the porch steps and the bells jangled lightly. All the children fell back, hands clamped to their ears, pain on their faces.

"What's wrong?"

"It's just the bells. They cannot cross. It keeps them out of the house. Keeps the demons at bay. Keeps you safe."

"Demons?"

"Billy, Davy," Lamia called. "It's okay, come out so this nice lady can see you."

The children's eyes grew wide. Trish followed their fearful looks to a large oak at the end of the porch. Two boys came around from its trunk and strolled over to the steps. The children all backed away.

The boys wore sweet smiles, but their eyes, there was something about their eyes.

"Show the nice lady one of your tricks. Go on, don't be so shy."

The two boys exchanged a sly smile, then looked up at Trish. Their smiles grew, and grew, stretching across their faces, up past their ears, revealing row upon row of tiny jagged teeth. Their eyes shrank into their sockets, until they were just floating in pools of blackness.

"They smell your unborn child."

Trish backed away.

"Okay, don't scare the lady. Go now. Go play."

The demons spun around, leaping after the children.

The children screamed and fled in all directions. The demons cut one off from the rest, a little boy, circling him like jackals, laughing and snarling. The boy tried to get past and the larger demon caught him by the arm, spinning him to the ground. The smaller demon dove in, sinking its jagged teeth into the child's stomach, tearing into him.

The little boy screamed and Trish did too, turning away, burying her face in her hands. "Stop them. Oh, please, make them stop."

"So, child," Lamia said. "Do you still wish to leave?"

CHAPTER 42

 

Trish crept down the dark hallway, feeling along the wall with her hand. Tears streamed down her face, but she made no sound as she slipped across the living room to the door. She quietly let herself out onto the porch and into the night. In the moonlight she noticed the blood running down the front of her nightgown. It was coming from between her legs. She let out a slight cry, headed down the steps, careful not to step on the string. She walked out into the yard and stopped, glancing up and down the long drive, her eyes wide and fearful. Laughter—it came from all around her. She spun about. The two boys stood before her, smiling. Their smiles grew into something wrong, something grotesque—far too many teeth. She turned to flee but they leapt upon her, tearing into her flesh, into her throat. She screamed.

Chet sat up gasping, Trish's scream still echoing in his head. *It was a dream, just a dream,* he tried to convince himself, hoping against hope it was not some sort of vision, like the one Yevabog had shown him. It took him a moment to remember where he was, that he was dead. He didn't even remember lying down, only that he, Coach, and Ado had sparred for most of the night, Ado making them go over and over the moves until they were all exhausted. Chet saw Ado sitting alone beneath the grate, staring upward, his eyes distant. Coach lay next to Chet, still sleeping. Somewhere a bell tolled. Chet let out a sigh, wondered if any of them would still be around come tomorrow.

Footsteps approached. The sound of keys and the door swung inward. The Trow entered, beckoning the ring-bearers to their feet. They were different this day—no pushing and prodding, almost respectful. They led them down the hall, through the round doors, and out onto the field, where they were met with rhythmic clapping instead of jeers and taunts. Chet glanced down the line of remaining ring-bearers and thought he understood: they were no longer common slaves, but souls who'd managed to survive two rounds in the arena with the champions.

The Trow spread them out around the arena. Chet, Coach, and Ado stood together.

Today, four women dressed in golden robes brought the weapons around. They handed the three of them each a helmet, shield, and sword. These weren't the broken rusted implements of the previous battles, but solid polished steel, the edges of the swords razor sharp.

"They want us to be able to bite back," Ado said. "They want a good show."

Chet set his shield aside—it would only slow him down—and strapped on his helmet. It was padded and fit snugly.

"You will need to stay well clear of me today," Ado said and showed them his helmet. Chet didn't understand; it looked like all the other helmets. Ado tapped one of the horns.

"Oh, shit," Chet said. The horns on Ado's helmet were dark brown, almost black. All the other helmets had red horns.

"I have been marked, my friends."

"Yeah, well that's bullshit," Coach said and started after the weapon girls.

Ado grabbed his arm. "No. It will not matter. Look." He nodded toward the stadium. Almost all eyes were on Ado. Mortem wouldn't need colored horns to find the man.

Ado slid his helmet on and buckled the strap. "Chet, Coach, hear me. Stay clear. It is me that he is after. Do not throw away your one chance at freedom."

Chet met and held his eye. "Our best chance is together."

"It's our only chance," Coach added.

Ado looked away.

The tall red doors opened and for the third time in as many days, the champions paraded onto the field to the ovation of the crowd. Only six champions remained.

*Six champs and twenty slaves,* Chet thought. *Is that even a chance in Hell?*

"Not enough rings to go around," Ado said. "That's why they call it the champion's trial, as it is as much about them beating each other as gathering the rings. It was always the most exciting match to see."

The champions took up their stations around the center platform. Mortem move into the spot directly in line with Ado.

The Watchers entered, took their places.

Mortem's eyes fixed on Ado.

The red doors closed with a deep thud, a sound of finality.

The Watchers raised their hands as one.

The stadium quieted.

"The third trial," they announced. "The champion's trial. Today we find out which champion will bring glory and honor to their god."

"I will say it again," Ado said to them. "Do not throw away your chance at freedom."

"Yep, got that the first time," Chet said, trying to sound brave.

"I am telling you," Ado growled. "Do not be a fool."

"I know a fool that saved me yesterday when he should've run."

Ado shook his head. "You are a good friend, a stubborn friend, but maybe not a very smart one." He managed a laugh, but Chet caught the underlining despair.

"Are the champions ready?" the Watchers shouted.

The champions nodded.

"Okay," Ado said, speaking quick. "If you are going to stand with me, here is what must be done. We cannot face him head-on. Our only chance is to lose him in the smoke." He pointed to a cluster of nearby stones circling a fire pit. "We have to beat him to those stones."

Chet and Coach nodded.

Mortem leaned into his stance like a sprinter awaiting the gun, his mouth twisting into a snarl around his tusks.

"Get ready," Ado said to Chet and Coach, setting his hands on their backs.

Chet took a few steps toward the stones.

"It has been an honor to fight with both of you," Ado said. "It is in the hands of the gods now."

"No," Chet said. "It's in our hands."

Ado grinned. "Yes, our hands."

"May the bravest and boldest win!" the Watchers cried, dropping their arms. The horn blew, the fire pits erupted, and the drums thundered. The arena filled with the cries of the spectators.

"*Go!*" Ado shouted, giving them both a shove-off.

Chet ran for the stones, ran for all he was worth, knowing how fast Mortem was, knowing it would take every ounce of speed to beat him into the smoke.

The crowd roared, all up and on their feet.

Chet made the stones, glanced back, saw Coach right behind him but not Ado. He halted, Coach bumping into him. "*Move!*" Coach shouted. Chet didn't, couldn't. Ado wasn't with them, because he was running, actually charging *toward* Mortem.

"*Oh, no!*" Chet cried, realizing that Ado had tricked them. Chet started back for his friend, but Coach grabbed him, trying to pull him into the smoke. "Chet, *no*! There's nothing you can do!"

"*Let go!*" Chet yelled, shoving Coach away and leaving him behind as he ran as hard as he could for Ado.

Ado met Mortem's attack head-on, feinting at the last second, bringing the sword low, going for Mortem's ankle. Mortem sidestepped the cut, bringing his ax over and down, catching Ado across the shoulder, severing the smaller man's arm and driving him into the dirt. Ado attempted to gain his feet, but Mortem was upon him. He brought his great ax up high and Chet screamed Ado's name as Mortem's blade fell, two hard strikes, smashing Ado's helmet, crushing his skull.

The crowd roared.

"*No!*" Chet cried, stumbling to a stop, overcome, as though he himself had received the blows. He dropped to his knees. "*No! No!*"

"Another notch for the gods!" Mortem shouted, and chopped Ado's hand off. He scooped up the ring, held it high for all to see.

A wild cry came from the smoke. Chet spotted a reptilian woman carrying a scimitar. She was chasing a soul and it took Chet a moment to realize it was Coach. The woman held two rings and Mortem must have seen them, for he charged toward her. The reptilian woman was so intent on Coach she didn't see Mortem. He blindsided her, coming out of the smoke and catching her in the midsection with his ax, nearly splitting her in to halves. He tore away her rings, then leapt after Coach.

Coach kept running, but there was nothing but open arena before him.

"Halt!" the giant yelled. "Halt and I will spare you."

Coach saw then just who it was chasing him, and stumbled to a stop, his face one of utter despair and resignation. He dropped to one knee, offering up his ring.

*No*, Chet thought. *No, you stupid fuck!*

Mortem caught up to Coach, kicked him to the dirt, but instead of cutting off his ring as promised, he stomped his heel into Coach's head, twice, a savage grin upon his face as he crushed the man's skull. Chet found himself frozen by the monster's viciousness.

"And *another* notch for the gods!" Mortem bellowed as he hacked off Coach's ring.

Chet got to his feet and ran for the nearest cover, for the center platform where the Watchers stood. He didn't look back, not until he made it, and when he did, he saw Mortem heading straight for him. Chet glanced wildly about, searching for escape, some advantage, found nothing but screams and the clang of arms coming from all directions. Chet's sword suddenly felt small in his hand, but he had no intention of making the same mistake as Coach. He slid into one of the defensive stances Ado had shown him and leveled his blade at the charging monster.

A wild cheer rose from the crowd. Veles's champion, Kwan, stood over a burly, brutish beast, his sword planted deep into its neck. The creature lay on its back, clutching its throat with one hand, three rings with the other. Kwan seized the rings, tearing them from the beast's grasp. The monster made a feeble grab for Kwan, but the agile fighter was already away, sprinting for the center—a total of six rings now in hand.

"*No!*" Mortem snarled, shifting course, moving to intercept Kwan.

The crowd, all on their feet, began stomping as the two champions raced toward one another.

Kwan spotted Mortem and began to dart back and forth, keeping Mortem off balance. At the last possible moment Kwan made as if to strike, but tucked and tumbled instead and Mortem completely missed his opponent. Kwan rolled past and up onto his feet, dashing for the coffer.

"Yes!" Chet shouted, almost forgetting he was on the field and not in the stands. There was now nothing between Kwan and the coffer and Chet began to believe he just might make it out with his ring—with his freedom.

Mortem roared and flung his ax—a powerful overhand throw. The ax hurled end over end and Kwan must've sensed it, for he glanced back. When he did the ax caught him on the side of the head, lodging in his skull. Kwan hit the ground and all six rings flew from his hand, bounced and rolled along the dirt, smacking up against the platform not five feet from Chet.

Mortem let loose a triumphant shout.

Chet started to flee, saw champions rushing in from all directions, and his eyes darted back to the rings. *The rings,* he thought. *Just throw them the fucking rings!* He dove for the rings, snatching them up from the dirt.

"*Here!*" came a thunderous cry. Mortem started toward him with his hand out. "Hand them here, now and I'll spare you!"

"*Not today, motherfucker!*" Chet shouted.

Mortem's face twisted into a knot of rage and he broke into a run.

Chet spun away, heading around the platform, toward the other champions.

"*Drop them!*" Mortem shouted, his footfalls thundering after Chet. "*DROP THEM!*" The footfalls gained rapidly, closer, *closer.* Mortem roared, right behind him, and Chet did a trick, not a move that Ado had showed him, but a simple schoolyard stunt. He dropped—just fell like a rock, leaving his pursuer no room to react.

Mortem's foot caught Chet's side, tripping the giant, sending him tumbling. The impact also flipped Chet and he landed not two feet from the coffer. It was then that he spotted Ado's body still lying mangled in the dirt, that his friend's sacrifice, that Mortem's wanton brutality, hit him like a kick to the chest. His rage, his utter hatred for this monster before him, overcame his fear, his panic. Chet knew he was done, but even if it was his last act, he intended to see to it that Mortem did not, would not, get these rings. He stood, stepped to the coffer, and held the rings out over the open chest.

Mortem rolled to one knee, looked from the rings to Chet. Chet locked eyes with the giant, a wicked grin, a crazy grin, spreading across Chet's face.

Mortem's brows cinched together. "What are you doing?"

Two other champions ran up, stopping when they saw Chet, their faces unsure.

The crowd fell quiet.

"You can't do that," Mortem spat. "It's forbidden."

"For Ado," Chet said and dropped one ring. It hit bottom—the loud metallic clang echoing all the way to the top of towering stands.

"*Stop!*" Mortem cried, getting to his feet.

Chet dropped another ring, another.

"*You will stop!*" Mortem screamed and charged.

Chet slammed the remaining rings into the bronze chest.

The horn blew.

Mortem halted, looking up at the Watchers, his eyes blazing with fury. The drums petered out. Every soul in the stands stared on with shocked, surprised expressions. And then, only then, did Chet wonder at what he had just done.

## CHAPTER 43

B<sub>y</sub> . . . the . . . *gods*," Mortem growled, "you *will* pay for such insult." He reached for Chet, but Chet leapt back, sword on guard.

"Cease," three voices called in unison. The Watchers held up their hands.

Mortem set hard eyes on them. "Cease?"

"He has placed the rings."

"He's a ring-bearer. A ring-bearer cannot place the rings."

"He has placed the rings."

"I'll not stand for this!" Mortem cried. He took several long strides past the platform and stood before the gods. "Hel, my queen. What do you say to this madness?"

Hel, like all the gods, was out of her chair and at the edge of her balcony, her veil pulled aside, her face as surprised as the others. Gradually, her expression darkened and she exchanged sharp words with the two guards in her booth, then pointed angrily at Chet. The guards left in a hurry, leaving through a door in the back of the chamber. Hel gave Chet one more dark look and followed after them.

*Christ,* Chet thought, getting slowly to his feet. *What're they gonna do to me now?* There was nowhere to run, so he waited, everyone waited.

The big red doors opened and Hel strolled out onto the field flanked by two minotaurs. The remaining champions bent to one knee and placed their weapons in the dirt before them. One of the minotaurs preceded the goddess, slapped the sword from Chet's hand, and shoved him to the ground. "Stay on your knees."

Hel walked up, stopping a few strides away, a tight, grim expression on her gaunt, skull-like face. "Remove your helmet, slave."

Chet did as bid.

She looked him over, not hiding her disdain. "You have interrupted my games." She held out her hand to one of the minotaurs. He drew his sword, a short, wide blade, and handed it to her. It appeared heavy, but she held it with ease. She took a step toward Chet. "Head down, slave."

Chet looked at the blade, up at the goddess, shook his head. "No. No way. That's not right. I placed the rings. That makes me the winner."

The goddess's eyes flared and an audible gasp passed through the crowd.

The minotaur struck Chet, knocking him to the dirt.

Chet shoved back up to his knees. "*Ask them!*" he shouted, jabbing a thumb toward the Watchers. "They said it. Said I placed the rings. And according to the rules. According to *your* rules. That makes me the god-damn winner!"

Again the minotaur struck Chet down.

A murmur passed through the crowd and many began to boo.

Chet pushed himself up yet again, met and held Hel's eyes.

Her lips tightened. She hefted the sword and stepped forward.

"*WAIT!*" came a booming voice. All turned to see a great stag marching up. Veles looked to the Watchers. "What say you to this soul's claim? Can a ring-bearer be the victor?"

"No!" It was Mortem who spoke. "This is madness. He's a slave. He's insulted—"

"Silence," Veles snapped, setting unforgiving eyes on the giant.

Mortem fell back a step.

"Veles," Hel said, giving him a scathing look. "It is not your place."

Veles nodded to the Watchers. "Answer me."

"The rules are as stated and are as all the gods have agreed. The first contender to gather and drop six rings into the coffer wins the trial. Rings may be gathered by any means."

"Contender?" Veles repeated, looking at Chet. "Can a ring-bearer not also be a contender?"

"There is no precedent," the Watchers answered as one. "No ring-bearer has ever placed the rings before. The rules do not state that a ring-bearer can be a contender—"

"There!" Mortem shouted. "A slave can't—"

Veles drove his fist into Mortem's face, knocking the giant to his knees, then looked back up to the Watchers. "Please continue."

"Nor do the rules state that a ring-bearer *cannot* be a contender."

"*There!*" Veles shouted, scanning the stands. He raised an arm and the crowd quieted. "What say you?" he cried, his big voice echoing up the towering stands. "Is this soul a contender? Has he displayed the boldness and courage worthy of a champion? Does he deserve victory or death? Victory or death? Which shall it be?"

The crowd threw their thumbs skyward, pressing against the rails and balconies, shouting victory, over and over until it became a chant.

Hel watched the cheering souls; slowly, a thin smile broke across her hard face. She raised the sword, pointed it at the dark clouds above, and cried, "*Victory!*"

The crowd burst into fresh cheers and began stomping their feet. The sound thundered up the towering walls, so loud as to make the very ground shake.

Hel handed the broadsword back to the minotaur, signaled two guards waiting at the red door. There was some confusion, but a few moments later two Trow came running onto the field, followed by a young woman, a girl really, carrying a tray.

Hel leaned over to Veles. "You have played your hand well."

The great stag grinned.

"Now tell me . . . what is in it for you? What are you up to, you old dog?"

"I love the spirit of the games. That is all. My motivations are pure."

"Purely selfish," she replied.

Veles shrugged. "I am a god."

She laughed, setting her chilling eyes on Chet as the Trow unclasped the shackle from around his neck and the ring from around his wrist.

"What is your name?" Hel asked.

"Chet."

"Your full name."

"Chet Moran."

"Rise, Chet Moran. You are a free soul."

Chet hesitated. *Free?* He could hardly believe it.

"Rise, victory is yours."

Chet stood.

The young woman arrived with the tray. A reef of young spruce limbs lay atop green velvet. Hel lifted the wreath and placed it over Chet's head so that it rested upon his shoulders. He took in a deep breath and his eyes widened—the spruce was real.

The crowd began chanting his name.

"Do you feel that, Chet Moran?" Hel said. "You have awakened their spirit and for this moment at least, they are alive. Any soul that can do that deserves to be a Grand Victor."

Hel folded back the velvet, revealing a short sword of polished steel laying atop a black scabbard and belt. Next to it a leather pouch with gold stitching. She lifted the weapon; it appeared sharp, as thought meant for battle, not parade. She held it up and the crowd quieted somewhat. "Let it be known that I, Hel, queen of death, hereby decree Chet Moran to be the Grand Victor of these trials." She touched the blade to each of Chet's shoulders, then handed the sword and belt to Chet.

The crowd again cheered.

Hel picked up the pouch and hung it around Chet's neck. It was heavy. She clasped him on each shoulder, pulled him close, spoke in his ear. "If we but had more spirit like yours, the netherworld would sing as earth." Her breath smelled of wet leaves in the fall.

And there, in her glow, it felt almost like sunlight, almost as though he were alive again.

Hel turned, strolling from the ring, and Chet was surprised to find that part of him wished to follow.

Veles stepped over to Chet, looking up at the cheering crowd. "The sweet nectar of victory. Savor it," he said and followed Hel out.

The band began to play, a loud, marching beat, and one by one, the remaining champions, those who could walk, left the arena.

Mortem got slowly to his feet, clutching his face. One of his tusks was broken. He gave Chet one last dark look and followed the other champions away.

The Trow entered the field, began clearing the weapons and carnage as the spectators exited the stadium. The gods left their booths and their servants began breaking down their banners, packing furs, goblets, and other items into baskets.

The drums fell silent, replaced by the deep tolling of bells. Chet walked slowly across the field until he found Ado's body. He knelt down next to his friend and just sat there in the dirt as the stadium slowly emptied. Finally Chet removed the wreath from around his neck and placed it atop Ado's chest.

# PART FOUR

## God Slayer

## CHAPTER 44

Joshua stood behind a gravestone in the middle of the little cemetery, watching Senoy. He'd been watching the angel since before daybreak. It was well past noon now. Senoy sat hunched on the stone bench just outside the graveyard, hands clasped together in his lap, staring at the ground. He had not so much as blinked in all that time.

Joshua stepped up to the iron gate. He knew it best not to disturb the angel, but he'd not spoken to him since Chet had gone below and was anxious for some news. The boy glanced wearily about, searching the nearby woods and fields for any sign of the demons. He bit his lip and slipped out through the gate, drifting like a shadow over to the bench, taking a seat next to the angel.

Senoy had never looked well to Joshua, but the boy was shocked at just how emaciated the angel had become—his eyes sunken and his skin shriveled around his bones.

Senoy didn't stir and it took Joshua another long minute to gather the courage to speak. "Mr. Senoy? Sir?"

Not so much as an eye flutter from the angel.

"Mr. Senoy? Are you okay?"

Still, no response.

Joshua reached for the angel, stopped, his hand hovering above the angel's arm. He'd never dared touch Senoy before. Didn't know if he should or even could. A moan came from far down the hill, deep within the trees. The boy tensed, then quickly tapped the angel on his shoulder, surprised to find he could indeed touch him.

Senoy blinked, sat slowly up, his eyes—stern and dangerous—coming to rest on Joshua.

Joshua recoiled. "I'm mighty sorry, Mr. Senoy. Just checking on you."

"*Joshua,*" the angel said, his voice soft like the wind.

Joshua waited for the angel to say more, but when the angel's eyes began to drift again he spoke up. "Mr. Senoy, I was wondering. Have you heard anything about Chet? Y'know, one of them feelings you sometimes get?"

Senoy nodded listlessly. "I have sensed him. When he holds the knife." Senoy's words rolled slowly out, like a man in a trance.

"So did he find it?" Joshua asked, trying to contain his excitement. "The magic key?"

Senoy shook his head. "No. Not of yet."

"Oh," Joshua said, unable to hide his disappointment. "But he's getting close?"

Senoy's eyes drifted up the hill, toward Lamia's house. "I was a fool, Joshua." Senoy's voice turned sullen. "Such a fool."

Joshua knew where this was headed. "Don't say that, Mr. Senoy."

"My arrogance cost me everything."

"She tricked you, Mr. Senoy. That's all."

"So, now, here we sit . . . trapped beneath my shroud."

Joshua had heard many versions of this tale from the angel over the long years. The shroud hid the island from Heaven's light, from all the other angels, so that they couldn't find them, and wouldn't be able to cross through even if they did. But it also meant that Senoy couldn't pass through, even to leave, and that Joshua couldn't go home to his mother in Heaven.

"It was meant to be *her* prison," Senoy said. "Lamia. So that I might play with her . . . just a little . . . without Gabriel knowing. She was so interesting. But it was not her prison that I built. No." Bitterness edged into his voice. "It was my own."

Joshua shook his head. Hearing Senoy talk like this always made him sad.

The angel held up his shriveled hand. "An angel's spirit cannot last without Heaven's light. I fear my time is running short."

This wasn't something Joshua had heard before and it scared him. What would happen if the angel passed on? How would he ever get home to his mother? "But once you get that key back, you'll be okay? Won't you? We can go on home then?"

Senoy blinked, looked at Joshua as though just seeing him. "Yes . . . the key will bring down the wall, Joshua. Set us free. And then the angels can descend and carry you to God's kingdom to be with your mother once more." The angel's eyes grew distant and his words slurred. "Lamia . . . she was just so . . . *interesting.*"

Joshua watched the sun beam through the late afternoon clouds, wondered if Heaven was up there somewhere. "*Mama,*" he whispered. "*I wanna come home.*"

## CHAPTER 45

A man approached Chet from behind.

Chet stood, hand on his sword.

The man made the slightest of bows. "My name's Martin," he said. He appeared to be Indian or maybe Pakistani, and he stood rigidly, almost at attention, arms pressed tightly against his sides. A small man, narrow through the face, shoulders, and hips. He wore sandals and a knee-length, embroidered silk shirt over a colorful sarong. "I'm Veles's steward. He sent me to bring you."

"Bring me where?"

"To him. He'd speak with you."

"About what?"

"I don't know."

"Is Ana there? At the caravan?"

"Who?"

"Ana? The woman I was with."

"Sorry, but I've no idea who she might be."

"She went into the arena with me."

Martin shook his head.

"Seet's there?"

"Yes. Seet is there."

"Good," Chet said sharply, buckling the sword belt around his waist. "Let's go."

The man nodded and led Chet toward the red doors.

A group of Trow women watched them approach. One of them, the old woman who'd doled out the ka coins, stepped in their way. She touched Chet on the forearm—a light touch, the way a mother touches her child. "You blessed by gods," she said and smiled; all the Trow smiled at him. Chet didn't know what to say to that, just nodded and kept going.

They left the field, marching down a long hall lined with iron doors. Four armed guards, dressed in Veles's colors, waited near the end of the hall. Chet recognized two of them: the heavyset man with the bulbous nose and the kid he'd first met back in Styga.

"These men here are your escorts," Martin said.

"Yeah," the kid said with a smirk. "Y'know, in case you didn't want to come along."

Martin scowled at him.

The older, heavyset guard greeted Chet with a warm grin. "The gods have sure smiled on you, son."

"Yeah," the younger guard put in. "You're a damn hero."

"Have you seen Ana?" Chet asked. "The woman I was with."

The guards glanced at each other but neither answered.

"The young Puerto Rican woman with short hair?"

"We know who you're talking about," the older guard said. "Well, just—"

"Seet's got her," the younger guard said. "It's not been real easy for her. Y'know how he is."

Chet's mouth tightened and he pushed past, heading quickly down the hall. Chet wasn't sure where he stood, what rights his newfound status would afford, only knew he had to get Ana away from Seet.

He came out onto a wide avenue; a lively crowd of souls moved up and down the cobblestone street. It was day, as day went in netherworlds, thick rust-colored clouds drifting low across the city. The black stonework was wet from the light mist, and the buildings, walls, and statues were all draped in colorful banners.

The guards caught up with him.

"Which way?" Chet asked.

The younger guard pointed down the hill and Chet headed on, walking purposefully through the crowd. Souls stopped at the sight of him; many just stared; others called out to him, called him by name. Several even touched him, their faces full of awe as though he were some sort of prophet, or a rock star. But Chet hardly noticed—he couldn't stop thinking about Ana, couldn't get away from the image of Seet yanking her away on a rope, the look of pain on her face. And the more he thought about Seet the faster he walked until he was all but stomping down the street.

"Not sure what you got in mind, Chet," the older guard said. "But if it's that girl you're after, you're going to want to take it down a notch."

"Yeah," the younger guard added. "Rub Veles the wrong way and he'll have you back in chains."

"Just remember he's a god," Martin put in. "If you wish to make an offer, you must be respectful."

Chet stopped. "An offer? What do you mean?"

"To buy the girl," Martin replied. "What else would I mean?"

"I can do that? Buy her?"

"You can try," Martin said. "Why, you've just won a god's ransom." He tapped the pouch around Chet's neck.

Chet hadn't even bothered to look inside. He loosened the string and peered in, found six shiny copper rings and several white coins. He pulled one of the white coins out. "What's this?"

"Those would be ka coins," Martin said. "Minted by Lord Horkos himself. They're white on account of their purity. It's tradition to give twelve to the victor . . . to heal any wounds sustained during combat."

Chet put the coin away and started walking again, continuing along the winding street, toward the caravans spread out in the courtyards and grounds below. Chet halted. There, in the yards, along the ramparts and earthworks, sprouting from every balcony and planter were brilliant white flowers, filling the air with their sweet scent. He looked to Martin.

"It's a magnificent sight," Martin said. "Is it not?"

"Yeah," Chet said.

"It's asphodel . . . real, living asphodel. They come from Asphodel Meadows, and bloom only when the gods arrive."

Chet marched through the wagons and past rows of merchants. Booths offered weapons, cigarettes, clothing, silk flowers, musical instruments, jewelry, and various other wares; a few offered games and gambling as well as the dark oily-looking drink called Lethe. Drums and pipes played. Souls with animal masks danced about poles and wicker men, laughing and singing. The atmosphere felt like a county fair, so different from back in Styga. And here too, the souls stop to watch him, nodding at him, some even bowing or touching him. A few gave him gifts—necklaces of asphodel and beads, or little figurines made from knots of hair.

Chet saw Veles's banner ahead.

"His wagon's this way," Martin said and Chet fell in line with the steward.

They entered a ring of cage wagons containing various animals. A horse lay on the ground between the wagons, unmoving. It looked to be the mate to the one Chet had tried to steal. And there, kneeling with one hand on the horse, was Veles. "It is *cursed*," the god growled.

Martin extended an arm, halting Chet.

"No, it is not cursed, just beyond your meager talents to heal," someone said and Chet recognized the voice. A large bird cage sat on the ground near Veles. Yevabog reclined upon a purple pillow within, weaving a small doll out of silk—the silk coming from her own abdomen. She appeared in good health.

"No," Veles snapped. "I can do this."

"Then do," Yevabog replied. "I would—" She spotted Chet and a wry grin slowly spread across her face. "Seems you have a guest, Veles."

The great stag turned, setting his golden eyes upon Chet. "Chet Moran . . . champion and Grand Victor. So good of you to come." He stood up and smiled, but there was nothing about that smile Chet cared for.

"Chet, look upon my animals." He gestured toward the cages. "The most magnificent in all the nether regions. Sadly, I am missing my favorite steed." He narrowed his eyes at Chet. "Since *someone* ran him into a wall."

"You mean to say he ran himself into a wall," Yevabog put in.

Veles glared at her. "And it is too bad he did not knock out your spirit when he did." The god returned his attention to Chet. "Chet, I consider myself a fair-handed god. Why, I even saved you. A man who *stole* from me."

Chet didn't answer.

"See this pathetic creature before you?" He gestured to the nag. "She is . . . how best to put it . . . unraveling, yes. She needs copper. Has anyone yet explained to you why copper holds such value here in the nether regions?"

Chet shook his head.

"It is fundamental to spells, curses, and alchemy, but most importantly . . . it binds ka. It seems I am out of copper."

"What he means to say," Yevabog put in, "is he squandered all his copper creating Kwan. And we see where that has got him."

Veles frowned. "What I mean to say, Chet, is it would be much easier for me to forgive certain *offenses* on your part if, perhaps, you were to make an offering . . . some noble gesture toward healing this beast before you and my crafting of a new horse. You could think of it as payment for my lost steed. What say you?"

"How much?" Chet asked.

Veles smiled. "Three copper rings."

Yevabog laughed. "It was a crude soul-shift, not a Horkos horse. If you are going to rob him, just do it and stop pretending otherwise."

Veles looked pained. "Fine, two copper rings then."

"No," Chet said.

Martin let out a gasp and everyone looked at Chet with wide eyes, even Yevabog.

"What?" Veles asked, his voice low, dangerous.

"Not unless the girl is part of the deal."

"Girl?"

"He means the woman who arrived with him, my Lord," Martin quickly put in.

Chet opened the pouch, and pulled out five copper rings.

Now it was Veles's eyes that widened.

"Two for the horse, three for Ana. Is it enough?"

Yevabog coughed. "It is too much, Chet. You could buy a hundred slaves with that."

"It is a very fair offer," Veles said, reaching for the rings.

Chet held them back. "I need passage for Ana and me to Lethe. And my property. I must have my property returned."

"Property?"

"My knife. It's special to me, and Seet has it."

"Yes. Yes, of course. Your property and passage. You and your slave will be my guests." Veles took the rings.

"You are a thief, Veles," Yevabog said.

"And you are an annoying insect. You two there." Veles beckoned over two servants. "Take her. Put her somewhere where I do not have to hear her incessant chirping."

The servants carried Yevabog away and Veles returned his attention to Chet. "You are a most curious soul, Chet Moran." He studied Chet for a moment longer, then called to Martin. "Fetch him this slave and any property that he lost that you can find. Also, some new garments."

"Yes, my Lord," Martin said and bowed.

"And," Veles said, "when you have found his servant woman, return them both to me. We have matters to discuss."

The man bowed again and led Chet away.

## CHAPTER 46

H ere," Martin said, sitting his hand on a cart. He pulled back a tarp, revealing a pile of clothes. "Choose whatever you'd like."

"Later," Chet said, looking for the golem. He spotted Pricilla's head towering above the wagons and started away.

Martin grabbed his arm, pulled him to a stop. "You will wait here," he ordered. "I'll fetch the slave girl."

Chet looked at the man's hand on his arm, then set hard eyes on him. Martin released him and Chet resumed, the thin man trailing him.

"It's best if you wait here," Martin said.

"Best for who?" Chet replied without slowing. He rounded a row of wagons and saw they'd already hooked up the slaves. He spotted her right away, chained on the outside row near the golem, her skin, like his, still streaked with the grimy red paint. "Ana."

She didn't look up at first.

"Ana," he called, putting a hand on her forearm.

She flinched, shrank back, her eyes wide, terrified.

"Hey, Ana," he said softly. "It's okay. It's me."

"Chet?"

"Yeah, time to—" He saw the wounds. No one had bothered to give her any clothes and all down her back, her buttocks and thighs, dozens of deep lash marks. "Oh, good god . . . *Ana.*"

She managed a weak smile. "Chet. You made it? You're free? Tell me you're free."

Chet found himself unable to answer, his rage welling up, threatening to overwhelm him. He snatched hold of the locking pin, yanking it back and forth, trying to rip her chain from the post with his bare hands.

"Chet, no," she said, horrified.

"Get away!" came a cry. Chet spun and saw Seet walking rapidly toward him, snapping his whip.

Martin stepped forward, putting out a hand to Seet. "Hold on. Veles has given—"

Chet charged past Martin, rushing the goblin man. Seet caught sight of Chet's face and stumbled back. Chet drove into him, smashing a knee into Seet's stomach, an elbow into his face, knocking him backward, slamming him to the ground. He tore the whip from the goblin man's hand and began thrashing the creature.

Seet snarled, fighting to ward off the blows.

"*Stop!*" Martin cried.

Chet didn't. Over and over he brought the lash down with all his rage behind it, ripping into Seet's upraised arms, his face, stomach, so intent on flaying the skin from the creature, he didn't even hear the drum of boots as the guards ran up.

Something hard caught Chet against the side of the head and he found himself on the ground with five spears pointed at his face.

"*Stop!*" Martin cried. "By order of Veles. Stop!"

The guards didn't drive their spears through Chet, but they kept their blades on him, their eyes daring him to try something.

"Are you done?" Martin asked Chet.

Chet sat up, glaring at Seet. "Will be as soon as that son of a bitch gives me back my knife."

The goblin man lay on his back, holding his face, blood streaming through his fingers.

"Do you have his knife?" Martin asked Seet.

"Fuck you," Seet spat.

"You must return it," Martin said. "By order of Veles."

"I cannot return what I do not have."

"Where is it?"

Seet sat up, glaring at Chet. "Gone."

Martin sighed. "Where is it, Seet?"

"Lost it."

"Fucking liar," Chet spat, getting to his feet.

The guards moved between them.

"Search him," Martin ordered.

The guards looked at Martin surprised.

"You heard me."

The guards shrugged, did as bid, searching Seet's cloak, his satchel.

"No knife," one of them said.

The goblin man wiped the blood from his nose, gave Chet that weird parody of a grin of his.

"What's your name?" Martin asked one of the guards, a reasonable-looking man.

"Thomas."

"Thomas, I want you to go search Seet's cabin."

Thomas looked dubiously at Seet.

"Look here," Martin said. "Veles has ordered that Seet give back this man's knife. You find any knives, you're to bring them to me. Is that understood?"

The guard nodded.

"Well, what're you waiting for?"

The guard left.

"If it's here," Martin said to Chet, "we'll find it."

One of the guards reached to help the goblin man up. Seet knocked his hand away, snatching his lash from the dirt and getting to his feet. The creature spat on the ground at Chet's feet and started away.

"This isn't over," Chet called.

Seet glanced back, let out a low hiss. "No . . . it is *not*, horsekiller." Then he headed away, up the line.

"Here," Martin called to the guards. "Would one of you remove this woman's collar?"

A guard pulled a ring of keys from his belt, stepped over to Ana, and unlatched her collar.

Chet came and took her arm to steady her.

The guard nodded after the goblin man. "Better keep your eyes open. Seet, he don't forget a score."

"Yeah, neither do I," Chet said.

Ana took a step and grimaced, her ankle turning inward.

"Here, Ana," Chet said. "Hold up a sec." He dug two of the white coins out of his pouch, handed them to her. "Ka coins. Remember?"

"Ah, magic jelly beans." She took them and placed them in her mouth, chewing slowly.

"Come," Martin said.

Chet pulled Ana's arm around his shoulder, helping her along as they followed Martin back into camp.

By the time they arrived at the clothing cart, Ana's skin had already begun to heal, the gashes closing up, her limp all but gone.

Chet dug through the pile and found a pair of jeans, combat boots, a flannel shirt, and a ragged leather jacket. Ana ended up in a T-shirt, corduroy jacket, boots, and a pair of ill-fitting jeans.

A whistle blew.

"Come," Martin said. "The caravan is heading out for Lethe."

"*Lethe,*" Ana repeated, wistfully, little more than a whisper.

## CHAPTER 47

The path was slick and the wagon—laden with muskets—sank into the mud, threatening to become stuck. Gavin hopped down and took hold of the bridle, guiding the horses around the deeper puddles.

Carlos eyed the back of Gavin's head. *Should put a bullet through him right now. Through the both of them. Tell the Colonel they were eaten by bears or some bullshit like that.* Only Carlos felt that returning without the two men the Colonel sent along just might complicate things and he didn't need things complicated, not right now, not with everything at stake. He drifted toward the back of the line, next to Hugo.

"I don't like them," Hugo said, nodding toward Gavin. "They think they're better than us."

"Yeah, like to pretend their hands aren't dirty. Wonder where their Colonel would be without us? My guess is still hiding out in some cave, just another marauder preaching his nonsense to a handful of fanatics."

"Want us to take care of those two?" Hugo asked.

"Yeah . . . as a matter a fact I do. Just not yet."

Jimmy, the lead man, halted, raised a hand. Carlos trotted forward. Jimmy pointed far down the valley to a cluster of mud huts and caves along a wide, dry riverbed.

Carlos pulled a spyglass from his jacket and took a look. "More than I expected."

"They're mostly unoccupied," Jimmy said. "Not many Edda left these days. And you see that?" He pointed to a structure built of white stones perched on a rise above the city. "That's Veles's temple. They put on their show just below. That hill there, behind the temple, that's what I was telling you about."

Carlos studied the terrain. "Yeah . . . see what you mean. We could slip the troops up behind the temple as soon as it gets dark."

Jimmy nodded. "Veles puts on a real show, boss. Fireworks, dancing, music, drums. Perfect cover. We just wait for the fireworks."

Carlos put away the scope. "Sure, open up on them with twenty muskets. Won't be a man left standing." Only he knew it wasn't quite that simple. Giving the chance, Veles would set the Colonel's whole army to fire. The key would be taking the god by surprise. "That's Lethe road down there, right?"

"It is," Jimmy said. "Three Stones is just over the rise. Best to stick to the canyons till we get around the village."

"Three Stones, that'll be a good place to meet the Colonel," Carlos said. "We can see both roads from there." He waved a rider forward. "Brent, take word to the Colonel. Tell him to meet us at Three Stones. Let him know we got twenty muskets waiting for him. That should light up his face."

Carlos watched the rider disappear up the canyon trail. *Fireworks,* he mused. It'd been a long time since he'd seen a fireworks show. He was willing to wager that this grand finale was going to be one to remember.

## CHAPTER 48

There came a loud blast, followed by a bright flash, then a cloud of smoke drifted back toward Chet and Ana. Chet flinched at the sound, feeling for the poor souls tied in the line. The massive golem started forward and the carts and those on foot fell in, all heading out of the gates and back down the mountain path.

Chet and Ana walked along behind Veles's large wagon. Ana was no longer limping, the ka having done its work. Soon the clouds began to clear, revealing mountain peaks pushing upward, grinding into those pushing down from the rocky lands above them, leaving Chet with the feeling he might fall up at any moment. He got his first clear look at Mother Eye and saw she wasn't an eye at all, but a ruddy glowing orb, with a handful of smaller orbs floating around her. Eventually the road widened, leveled out, and they began to move along at a steady pace.

"Chet," someone called. Martin walked up to them. "There you are. Come. Veles desires your company."

"Well, I for one couldn't give a shit," Ana said.

Martin gave her a stern look. "Be careful. You've seen what happens to those who insult him. Never forget . . . he's a *god*."

They boarded, climbing a ladder to the platform atop the wagon. Here the great stag lounged among plush pelts and silk pillows, smoking a long curved pipe while surveying the road ahead. Yevabog sat next to him in her cage, still weaving her silk doll—a little white-haired girl with a disturbingly real face. Chet clutched the railing, steadying himself as the cart rocked along the trail. Yevabog saw him and her eyes lit up, a mischievous smile pushing up the corners of her small mouth.

"My Lord," Martin said, bowing. "I bring you, Chet Moran."

Veles turned. "Ah, my Grand Victor."

Martin nudged Chet. "Bow."

Chet didn't.

Veles looked Ana up and down. "And this is the slave you paid such a bounty for? Are you sure this is the one you wish? I have better stock."

Ana let out a sound, something between a gasp and a growl.

"This is Ana. She's not my slave. She's nobody's slave."

Veles shrugged. "If you wish to free her, that is your business. Now, please sit."

They took a seat upon the pillows next to Yevabog's cage.

Yevabog reached through the bars and touched Chet, almost a caress, her eyes reaching deep into his. She seemed genuinely pleased to see him.

"Why's she in a cage?" Chet asked.

"Do you know, Chet Moran, that it is not wise to go around questioning the will of gods?"

"I tend to learn everything the hard way."

A wry smile touched Veles's mouth. "Yevabog is in a cage to keep her from sucking souls. Yours, my servants . . . even my own. She is a devious creature. One you should never turn your back on."

"Bah," Yevabog said. "That is an egregious exaggeration, Chet. He is still sore because I burned one of his temples to the ground."

"Two," Veles said.

"See . . . still he holds a grudge . . . three thousand years later."

"She is more demon than God," Veles said to Chet. "And it is not good to have a demon lurking about one's camp. It makes everyone nervous."

"Demon? God?" Yevabog said. "Tell me the difference. They all want your soul."

"There is a difference. A god, a true god, gives man meaning to their existence . . . they give something back."

"Plenty of demons trade favors," she said. "For blood, for a piece of your soul, sometimes even for a good game of dominos. They are just more honest about it."

"It is not a cage I should keep you in, but a hole. One deep in the ground so none should have to bear your chatter."

Yevabog laughed. "You my, darling, would dearly miss my chatter."

Veles waved her away as though shooing a fly. "Enough of your nonsense. It is from Chet Moran that I wish to hear. Tell me, Chet, what manner of soul dares to steal a horse from a god, defeats all the gods' best champions, and challenges Queen Hel herself? Who are you, Chet Moran?"

Chet shrugged.

"Come now, I would hear your tale."

"You are asking the wrong question," Yevabog said. "Ask him who his grandmother is."

The curiosity on Veles's face deepened. "Ah . . . that sounds intriguing. Tell me then, Chet, who is this grandmother of yours?"

"Lamia."

"Lamia?" The god's brow tightened as he pondered the name. "Not the lilith?"

Yevabog nodded. "The very one."

"You have lilith blood?" Veles's face clouded. "That is not possible . . . she would have to be—" He looked at Chet again. "Are you saying Lamia still prowls among the living?"

"It is the truth," Yevabog said. "I have tasted his blood. There is no mistaking her bloodline."

"Chet, you *are* full of surprises." Veles sounded excited; he leaned forward, his face eager. "Go on, Chet. Tell me. Tell me how this came to be."

Chet did, told him what he knew of his history, of how Lamia killed him. Then he spoke of Senoy, of how he was trapped there with her, but said nothing of the key, the knife, or his quest to find Gavin.

Veles listened intently, nodding here and there. Once Chet had finished, Veles stared out toward the mountains, his face in deep concentration as he puffed on his pipe. Finally he spoke. "Do you think it is possible, Yevabog, that Lamia has trapped Senoy somehow?"

"I do. Not at first, but the more I considered the more it seemed feasible."

"It would have been the angel's duty to slay her," Veles said. "To bring her here, to the nether regions. Like all the others."

281

"Yes, but the fact that he did not, that they are still together . . . it makes one speculate that maybe she tricked him somehow, or perhaps wove her spell around him."

"Are you suggesting Lamia could seduce an angel?"

"I am."

"Not Senoy. No, he is one of Gabriel's most stalwart soldiers. His heart . . . dead as stone."

"If anyone could seduce stone, it would be Lamia," Yevabog said. "Think about it. She and her ancient magic are older than the angels. She is a blood weaver. If she stole so much as a drop of Senoy's blood—*angel blood*—think what she could do."

Veles smiled, the face of a man who'd just heard a good dirty joke. "I could not concoct a better end for Senoy than to be trapped by the very creature he was sent to kill." He laughed. "I can only hope that she is feeding on him even now. That he is suffering." Veles's eyes grew distant, as though savoring the thought; eventually he let out a great sigh. "It gives me heart to know that at least one of us still roams earth. Too many have perished upon the angels' swords, too many have been driven below—the earthly spirits and gods, the ancient folk, the monsters and beasts, any that do not fit into their grand design."

"And it is not enough that we were driven from Mother Earth," Yevabog added. "From our dear moon and stars, now, now we are being driven from the very belly of death herself."

"What do you mean?"

"You know what I mean. The Green Coats, this new breed of godless souls. Ever since Lord Nergal left Styga, they have taken over. Taken over the docks, the stockades, and now they are burning the temples, driving away all the ancients."

Veles face grew somber. "Is there no word on what happened to Nergal?"

"Just rumors that he went north to parley with Kali. None have heard from him since."

Veles's frown deepened.

"They will not stop," Yevabog said. "Never. Not until we are all gone . . . all forgotten."

"Such fools," Veles replied, his tone turning acid. "What do they think will happen once we are gone? Those souls that do escape the demons will have to hide in caves. The nether region will truly become a place of death."

"They burned my temple, my husbands . . . my *loves*," Yevabog said, absently caressing her doll. "Our time is coming to a close."

"Nonsense," Veles said, shaking his head. "There will never be a world without gods."

"They have their gods."

"Bah, their Jesuses, Buddhas, Muhammads, they are aloof, distant. Why, they do not even show themselves. How can you worship a god you cannot see?" He shook his head, stood, began to pace. "It is time to remind these godless souls what a real god is. Time to become a beacon in this hereafter of death, a light in the darkness." He raised a fist and the air crackled; lightning flashed in the air directly above them. Many of the souls walking nearby moved quickly away.

Yevabog clapped—a flat, lackluster pattering. "Oh, fireworks, that should bring them to you in droves." Yevabog looked around at the line of dingy wagons, carts, and dreary souls, shook her head. "We were gods, now look at us . . . selling seekings and blessings, peddling wares, putting on little animal shows, and milking pilgrims on their way to oblivion."

Veles frowned. "Why must you always be so bleak? What happened to the blood god I used to know? The wild spirit that torched any who encroached upon her clans?"

Yevabog's eyes fell to her doll. "Life, even that of a god, is not meant to go on forever."

"With that spirit, we will all be dirt soon." Veles dropped into his chair and sat staring out at the caravan, a miserable look on his face. They all rode in silence, after a long while, Chet felt Veles's eyes on him.

"Yevabog," Veles said. "Lamia's blood truly runs in Chet's vein. You tasted it, yes?"

"I did. Why? What are you up to?"

"Chet, I am in need of a new champion. A courageous soul. One worthy of the honor."

"Honor," Yevabog scoffed. "That is a death wish. You have lost more champions—"

"Quiet, you," Veles barked. "There is no glory without risk. Chet, you have shown great courage both in and out of the arena. I see in you the makings of a great champion, maybe even the greatest."

Chet couldn't think of a much worse fate than returning to the arena.

"Can you not see?" Yevabog said. "He does not share your thirst for glory."

"He does not understand yet what I am offering. Martin, my chest."

Martin bowed, slipped through the curtains and into the cabin.

"Chet, did you wonder how the champions were so strong, fast, agile? Those champions, they were common souls once, but the gods, they gorged them on ka, shaped, conjured, and crafted them into extraordinary warriors."

Martin returned with a small brass box, bowing as he held it before Veles.

The box had no latch, no lock, no opening that Chet could see. Veles took it, danced his fingers along the top, and a thin blue line of light slid around the box, revealing a lid. Veles opened it, removed a roll of blue velvet, and unfolded it, uncovering four silver stars, each star about the size of a silver dollar. "God-blood. My blood."

*God-blood*. Chet thought of Ado, how the man had lost everything trying to attain one of these stars.

Veles pluck one out, held it up. "Poison to a common soul. But Chet, you are *no* common soul. Lamia's blood runs in your veins. You, you could partake. A half-god feeding on god-blood . . . the power you would wield. You would be undefeatable in the arena."

"He is not a half-god," Yevabog said. "Merely a soul with lilith blood, and having lilith blood does not make one a lilith. There is no telling what that coin may do to him."

"Here then, let us find out." Veles pinched one of the spikes off the star, held it out to Chet.

Chet just stared at it.

"Go on," Veles said. "A pinch will not harm you. Not with me here to help you. Try it."

Chet opened his hand and the god placed it in his palm. It wasn't much larger than a fingernail, yet the weight of it surprised Chet.

"Imagine the warrior I could shape you into. Victory would be ours."

"That would be cheating," Yevabog said.

"Cheating? They all cheat," Veles countered. "Only some cheat better than others. Hel uses sorcery. There is no other way her champion could win year after year."

"Crafting ka *is* sorcery. Her sorcery is just better than yours."

"Well, her man did not win this year, *did* he?" Veles retorted. "No, a slave won. My slave, so I believe that makes me the winner."

Yevabog chuckled. "You are a dreamer."

Veles shrugged. "All is a dream. One day, when the god of all gods wakes up, we will all just disappear." His set a hand on Chet's shoulder. "Go on, take a bite. Taste what it is like to be a god."

"Do not, Chet. It will give him too much power over you."

"By the moon, you do not know when to keep your mouth shut." Veles snatched up a fur and tossed it over Yevabog's cage. "Go on, Chet, try it."

Chet shook his head. "No, I'm not seeking glory . . . I just need to find someone." He tried to hand the silver spike back to Veles.

It wasn't anger, but disappointment that Chet saw on the great stag's face. "There is no need to decide now," the god said. "Hold on to it. When you are thinking more clearly, take a bite. Once you have had a taste of what it feels like to be a god, you will return."

Chet thought Veles sounded like a pusher, but kept the spike anyway, tucking it into his jacket pocket.

# CHAPTER 49

Carlos and the Colonel hunched behind a cluster of boulders set high on a ledge overlooking the valley below. Carlos set the spyglass to his eye and watched as Veles's caravan ramble its way up Lethe road toward the little village. "They don't have a clue," he said, handing the spyglass over to the Colonel. "See there, don't even have any scouts out. If they'd heard about Horkos, they'd be riding full guard."

The Colonel studied the wagons, then put the spyglass down. "I'm inclined to agree."

"They'll be sitting below the temple. With the fireworks and drums, they're making it easy for us."

"Uh-huh," the Colonel said. "I'll just need to get as close to Veles as I can before anyone starts shooting."

"Well, I've been thinking. I don't know if you should take such a risk. If we lost you now, right when we're getting such momentum, it could derail everything. I think we should find someone else to carry the God Slayer."

"Hard to ask a man to do something I wouldn't do myself."

"Hugo is more than willing. He was once one of Veles's slaves. He's just itching to take him down."

"I think there's a better man for the job. I'm talking about Gavin."

"Gavin?" Carlos tugged his mustache. "That man's got a screw loose."

"That may be, but in a pinch there's no one I'd rather have at my side."

"He gave me trouble yesterday. Could've blown the whole deal."

"Gavin's not real keen on us dealing with demons. Have to say I agree with him on that point."

*But it's sure not stopping you, is it?* Carlos thought, fighting the urge to call the man out on it right here and now, ask him just where his revolution would be without the God Slayer. "Well, one way or another he needs to learn to follow orders."

The Colonel laughed. "You let me know how that goes."

Carlos felt himself heating up. "He's your man, Colonel. But I won't have him riding with me again."

The Colonel sighed. "I hear you loud and clear. Gavin's not an easy man to deal with on any account. Like so many down here, he's fighting his own inner devils. Sure full of venom for these gods though. Don't think you'll find a soul who hates 'em more. I found him during a raid. He was one of Lord Nergal's slaves. He was so battered and broken, I almost left him behind. He's been with me ever since and I'll tell you again, never had a better man at my side. He'll go toe to toe with anyone, anything— demon, beast, or soul. You take a good look at those guns he carries. He took 'em from a soulwarden after he'd cut the damn thing's head off."

"That so."

"It is."

The two men watched Veles's caravan move up the valley, neither speaking for a long spell. Finally the Colonel broke the silence. "Back in the war . . . before a battle, I'd usually get a feeling in my gut. Good or bad. That feeling, it never failed to be on the money. Well, what I'm leading up to is . . . I got a good feeling about this. Not just about Veles, but all of it."

Carlos grunted.

"Do you ever think about the good we can do once they're gone?" the Colonel asked. "Once the gods are out of the way and souls are free of their subjugation and meddling? The progress we can make? We'll be able to organize. Start up manufacturing. I understand that on earth above they got devices that run themselves on electricity now. Carriages that don't need horses. You've seen 'em, right?"

"Yeah, they got all sorts of inventions. Some that even fly through the sky."

"So I've heard," the Colonel continued. "Well, with all the resources down here, I don't see why we can't have the same. Why we can't make this a half-decent place to exist."

Carlos thought about that, what it'd be like to have phones, radios, cars, even planes in purgatory. What a man like himself, a man with vision, could do with a division of tanks and a small air force. "That sounds real good. Trouble is getting these sad sacks motivated. Half of them is suicides to begin with and all they're looking for is a way out of this hell. The rest of them is too miserable to give much of a shit."

"They need purpose, that's all," the Colonel said. "Everyone needs purpose. Same as with the living. Think about all the souls down here toiling away their days. Why? Why do they build, sell, trade, mine with such ardor? It's not for food, we know that. It's because doing something gives 'em purpose, if for no other reason than just the ritual of it. They're striving for a reason to exist."

"Or maybe they just want some coin so they can buy a bottle of Lethe or a smoke of bone-spice."

Colonel smiled. "I want to give 'em a *real* purpose."

"You've done that. Killing gods. Never seen souls look so alive."

The Colonel's face grew pensive. "I've always thought there were two types of fanatics: those who spend their lives building something and those who tear down what others have built. I've done too much tearing down . . . in the states war and now this ugly business. But after these gods are gone, I'm hoping to be the kind of man who builds something, hoping to lead others along the same path. Think about it. All of us working together to make this a decent place to be." He patted Carlos's shoulder. "We can give them the purpose they seek, Carlos, just like these false gods. Only we'll be doing it for the benefit of all, not just a few."

"You're beginning to sound a bit like a communist," Carlos said.

"A communist?"

"It's a political movement from after your time. People working together toward the common good of the state."

"That sounds right good to me."

Carlos smiled and could see the Colonel mistook it for camaraderie. *Colonel,* Carlos thought. *Men are always going to need someone to kneel down to, someone to tell them what to do, and I intend to be that person.*

# CHAPTER 50

Martin approached. "My Lord."

Veles opened his golden eyes.

"The temple."

The great stag sat up, peered forward into the dusty haze. Dusk approached and the sky was shifting toward maroon. In the distance, Chet could make out around two hundred figures standing on either side of the road. Beyond them was a structure built from the surrounding white stone.

The land had turned arid and the long trek had left the caravan covered in a fine gray dust. It was in their hair, on their clothes and skin, making them all appear ghostly.

Veles scanned the figures as they approached, his face drawn. "Every year there are fewer. How long before I am greeted only by the wind?"

Farther down the road, past the temple, Chet could make out mud huts and caves cut into the low ledge along a wide, dry riverbed.

Veles stood, steadying himself on the rail as the wagon rumbled up the rocky road. He raised a hand outward and the figures cheered. They were a short, stocky people, solid through the shoulders and neck, with shaggy, reddish hair, protrusive jaws, and ponderous brows. Most were nude, covered only in swirling body paint, the same forest green as Veles's fur.

"They look like Neanderthals," Ana said. "Like little Neanderthals."

"They are the first people," Yevabog said. "The Edda. They were using stone tools while men were still in trees. They never had much heart for war, though, and thus fell beneath the swords of mankind. They considered me a demon, but they worshipped their beloved Veles. He tried to save them, but in the end, war, slavery, and interbreeding spelled their doom. Now their ghosts, the few that remain, sift the sands along the riverbed for copper."

The great stag's fingers danced, the golden corona hovering behind his magnificent antlers glowed, and the air around him sparkled.

The Edda responded with awed cheers; many began to cluck their tongues and spin in place. Drums started and those carrying baskets tossed handfuls of ash into the air.

"Look at Veles," Yevabog said, her voice laced with scorn. "Look at him playing to them, like a little dog dancing for a treat. He has several temples in the river realms, several clans and tribes. Spends his days traveling from one to another, pandering his little animal circus, his little fireworks show. Do you want to know why?"

Chet shrugged.

"Because without them he would end up just like *me*," she said bitterly. "*Forgotten.*"

When Veles's wagon reached the end of the row of Edda, he spun away with a dramatic flourish, leaving the platform through the curtain to his cabin.

Yevabog sighed. "I guess the show is over for now."

The caravan continued up the road to a barren field of stone just below the temple, where it circled and stopped. The Edda marched on to the temple. Martin hopped down from the wagon and accompanied their procession. When they reached the temple they set two large cauldrons ablaze, then entered.

Chet and Ana watched from the platform as souls jumped from wagons and carts and set about erecting tents and booths. It wasn't long before Martin returned.

"Lord Veles," Martin called. "All's prepared. They await you in the temple."

The curtain pulled back and Veles stepped out in a long flowing turquoise robe, holly and bright red berries hanging from his antlers. "How are the offerings?"

Martin looked pained. "A bit thin, Lord."

Veles nodded, his lips tight. "Very well. I am sure they gave all they could. Now I must give all I can."

"Be sure to dance well for them," Yevabog said.

Veles glared at her. "Why is she still here? Put her with the other animals and curiosities. Put her next to Piggy."

"Yes, Lord," Martin said as Veles marched away through the curtains.

Martin quickly waved two servants over. They lifted Yevabog's cage and carried her down the steps.

Martin looked at Chet and Ana. "I believe Veles is done with you for now. You're free to leave."

"That's mighty gracious of him," Ana said, not hiding her smirk. They followed after the servants as they carried Yevabog through the wagons. They came to the line of cages and set her down between a hairless goat and piglike creature. One of them scampered off only to return a moment later with a sign, a crude painting of a monster spider with bloody dripping fangs. He propped it in front of Yevabog's cage. Chet thought Yevabog couldn't have looked more miserable.

"Chet," Yevabog said. "Do me a favor. Take that pretty sword of yours and stick it through Veles's eyes. Would you do that for me? Please."

"He might treat you a bit better if you weren't so hard on him."

"And where would the fun be in that?" Yevabog grinned.

Chet shook his head.

"Yes, I know," Yevabog said. "I have become a bitter and resentful old grouse."

Two Edda women walked slowly past, both staring at Yevabog as though she might spit poison at them. Yevabog bared her teeth and hissed. The women scurried on. Yevabog let out a long, pained sigh. "I would prefer Veles just burn me to ash than this."

"I think he might know that," Ana said.

"Yes, and I should be beyond caring." Her tone turned morose. "Yet I am not. I keep reminding myself that oblivion awaits. It will all be over soon."

Ana nodded. "Yeah, I get that."

"C'mon," Chet said, not liking where the conversation was heading. He gave Ana a tug. "Let's have a look around."

They wandered through as the colorful tents went up. Only a few vendors were setting up, mostly clothes and tools. They came upon a man selling the dark drinks. His sign read ELIXER OF LETHE.

"How about a drink?" the man asked. "Two for one."

Both Ana and Chet gave the bottle a curious look.

"Ah, you guys are still wet, aren't cha? Nothing to it really. Makes you forget for a little while. Y'know, that you're dead and all."

"Oh," Ana said, sounding more than a little interested.

"Here, take a seat, have a taste on me. It'll at least *look* like someone's buying."

They sat down and the man slid two small dirty glasses over, pulled a cork, and started to pour.

Chet held up his hand. "No thanks."

"You sure?"

"Yep."

"Just a pinch," Ana said.

He poured her about a teaspoon worth.

She held the glass up, staring at the dark liquid.

"Yeah," the man said. "The Edda, they aren't big on the drink. The only coin I make here is selling to pilgrims and carneys."

Ana raised the glass to her lips but stopped, her eyes suddenly big and focused on something behind Chet.

Chet spun and caught sight of Seet walking along a row of carts. The creature hadn't noticed them.

"Motherfucker," Chet said and hopped up, starting after him.

Ana grabbed him. "Chet, what're you doing?"

"Just want to see where he's going."

She narrowed her eyes at him.

"Really," he said.

They followed at a distance. Seet looked worn out, head down as he trudged along. He walked up to a tall wagon sitting on the outskirts of the caravan. Several doors ran along the side. Seet tugged a key from his satchel, stepped up on a short stair, unlocked one, and crawled in.

Chet caught a glimpse inside before the goblin man pulled the door shut. It was just a sleeping compartment, not much bigger than a coffin.

"Think your knife's in there?"

"One way to find out." Chet started forward.

Ana grabbed him. "Chet, have you lost your mind? Look around. There're too many people."

Chet could see she was right. He took a deep breath. "Okay, you can let go. Not gonna do anything stupid." He grinned. "At least not right now."

## CHAPTER 51

Drums.

Gavin pressed his back against the temple wall, removed his hat, and peered down at the amphitheater below. It was dark now and torches sputtered around the perimeter, illuminating the rows of Edda filling the lower seats. Many sat cross-legged on the ground, holding small horned figures made of bones and hair, painted green and with gold stones for eyes—smaller versions dangled from necklaces and bracelets. Much of Veles's caravan had turned out as well, servants, vendors, pilgrims, and guards. Gavin was pleased to see that the guards appeared at ease, sitting about smoking and chatting—some even had their feet propped up. Gavin knew his only chance to take Veles lay in surprise, that if the god got wind of them, he would ignite them all in flames.

Carlos, along with a handful of his Defenders, slid up behind Gavin, spreading out along a low wall. They were armed with muskets and Gavin was glad to see they had the sense to keep their heads down. The Colonel and his Rangers waited farther back, just below a nearby ridge. The plan was to move forward the moment Veles's little firework show began.

A giant stag, nearly thirty feet tall and made from shards of bones, stood in the center of the amphitheater. Hundreds of smaller stag figures, also woven from shards of bone, were stuffed inside the giant. A chair, more of a throne, sat atop a stack of cut stone, facing the effigy, its back to Gavin. Gavin marked his best approach, hoping to take the god from behind. He clutched the spear, wondering what it would feel like to bring down a god. Would it take away his pain? Make him forget the screams of his own children? *Maybe,* he thought, *for a while. It just*—Gavin tensed as a tall kid with red hair entered the amphitheater. *It's him. The kid . . . the one from my vision.*

# CHAPTER 52

T hey're starting," Ana said.

"You wanna watch?" Chet asked.

She shrugged. "Why not?"

They headed toward the drums and entered a natural amphitheater carved from the stone ledge below the temple. The Edda filled most of the seats. Yevabog's cage had been moved and placed like a trophy next to a throne. A pig and goat sat in cages just behind her. Chet caught sight of her face. She did not appear happy with the arrangement.

Chet nudged Ana and they headed over, taking a seat next to her.

"You got the best seat in the house," Chet said.

Yevabog gave him a dismal look. "Yes, Veles spares me no consideration."

The drums ceased, and everyone fell quiet. Veles entered through a stone arch, stopped, and surveyed the gathering. He appraised the giant bone stag, then began to stroll around the arena, speaking to the Edda in their own language—a peculiar combination of hand gestures, clucking, and grunts, touching those that reached out to him. The Edda followed his every move, captivated by his slightest gesture. And Chet saw it, on their faces, in their eyes, not just devotion, but love. They began to chant his name.

"They adore him," Chet said.

Yevabog let out a long, pained sigh. "Yes. It is most annoying." She sighed again, more a sound of giving up. "You are looking upon a god that is one with his people. Even in ancient times, Veles was always out among his clans, traveling from temple to temple, spreading his name, growing his congregation. I rarely did such things, too lazy, too proud. Ha, and that is why he still has disciples, while I have none." She shook her head. "Never share that I spoke thus of him, but Veles, in his day, fought hard to keep disease, pestilence, and all the dark spirits at bay. His people thrived. He always gave back more than he took, and that was what made him a great god." She was quiet a minute, then a coy smile slipped up on her face. "And that is why I burned his temples. For even then, I was a spiteful, jealous creature."

Chet laughed, couldn't help himself.

"I should not tell you this," Yevabog said. "But he fed me god-blood, to heal me. Back at Styga. I cannot say I would have done the same for him."

Veles climbed the steps to his throne and stood with his hands on his hips, surveying the gathering. Slowly he raised his arms, closed his eyes, and bowed his head as though in deep thought. His fingers did their dance, his golden corona glowed, and all the torches around the amphitheater flared, sending up a host of sparks. The sparks sprouted wings, fluttered around the giant bone stag like flaming butterflies.

The Edda oohed and awed.

The butterflies swirled about the giant figure and everywhere they touched, a small blue flame lit, until the entire giant was ablaze.

Veles opened his eyes and the drums started back up.

One by one the Edda stood and entered the ring, stomping to the beat. They clasped each other's hips and began to circle the burning stag, dancing and chanting Veles's name. The pace picked up, and some of them broke away—leaping, spinning, and hooting.

A loud howl came from behind Chet and to his surprise Veles hopped down into the ring with the Edda, spinning and leaping about right alongside them. He let loose howl after howl, laughing—an exuberant, hearty sound that echoed into the night, that seemed to chase away all the bad things that might be hiding out there.

The Edda laughed too and Chet found a grin on his own face, found his feet drumming out the beat, found that part of him wanted to join in, to dance and howl and forget all else.

The tempo picked up and some of the souls, the ones that had come with the caravan, did join in, the Edda welcoming them with lively hoots and big grins.

"You feel it, do you not?" Yevabog asked. "Veles's spirit."

"Yeah." Chet nodded, he did, all around him, almost a thing he could touch. He inhaled deeply; it was sweet, like the air when winter turns to spring. He caught Ana smiling, nodding her head, and drumming her feet. She looked happy.

"See," Yevabog said, "their energy . . . it weaves together. The gods and souls. It is a real force and with enough believers, the gods could make the underworld like earth above. There was a time, long since lost, when the ancient gods created entire gardens and forests full of flowers and animals such as the Elysium Fields and Asphodel Meadows. Such wonders to behold. But as our worshippers faded, so did our power. Now our crumbling statues and temples are all that remain of those ancient days of glory."

The tempo slowed and the Edda moved at a more plodding pace. Veles spun away from the circle, bounded up the stones to his throne, and took his place. He appeared bigger somehow, full of zeal. His golden eyes sparkled as he watched his people dance. The Edda too, seemed more vital, their flesh taking on an almost lifelike sheen as though for this moment, real blood flowed in their veins. As Chet watched them circle the burning giant, he felt he was catching a glimpse into a different time, a long ago earth, felt he understood on some level this nourishing, healing relationship between gods, souls, and earth.

Ana stood. "C'mon, Chet. How 'bout it?"

"Huh?"

"Let's dance."

Chet looked at her shocked. "Really?"

"Why not?"

Chet hesitated.

"Go," Yevabog said. "Might be your last chance to have a taste of life."

Chet followed Ana down, but didn't join in, just stood on the edge of the circle, nodding and tapping his toes to the drums. He watched Ana move, a slow, groovy sort of dance, swaying to the rhythm. She smiled at him, a warm sweet smile, and something about that smile reminded him of Trish, of happy times. *It's Veles's magic,* he thought, but let the spell take him, let his memories drift back to Trish, the smell of her hair, the taste of her lips.

Chet caught sight of Seet and blinked as though slapped awake. He'd forgotten about the goblin man, about the knife, all of it, and felt a wave of anger at himself for letting Veles's spell distract him from his purpose. He glanced around, realizing that most of the caravan was here at the show, that there couldn't be a better time to break into Seet's little cabin.

Ana was adrift in the rhythm, dancing with her eyes closed. Chet slipped out of the arena and moved rapidly through the camp, sticking to the shadows. He found almost no guards, only a few souls wandering here and there. He came to the wagon with Seet's sleeping compartment. One of the doors was open and in the fluttering torchlight he could see a man lying inside. He appeared to be sleeping, a bottle of Lethe clutched to his chest.

Chet slipped up to Seet's door. He tried the handle, but it was locked. He slipped out his sword, glanced around, saw no one, and wedged the blade into the lock, giving it a quick, hard tug. The latch pulled out of the plank with a loud screech.

"Whut . . . whut?" the man mumbled, half-raised his head, then plopped back down.

Chet pulled the door open and crawled in. The compartment smelled of mud and sour rags. He tossed the bedroll, then rifled through a bundle of clothes beneath the bunk. Nothing. He found a sack, emptied it—just some tools. Then his hand hit something solid—a chest. He pulled it out, shook it, something clanked within. *That's it. Gotta be.* He sat it on the bed and set his sword blade atop the small lock and popped it off with one hard thrust. He opened the lid and dumped out the contents. There was a knife all right, along with a pair of brass knuckles and a handful of coins. Only it wasn't his knife.

"This what you want?"

Chet started, tried to stand, knocked his head against the low roof, and fell back down again.

The goblin man stood blocking the door, Senoy's knife in his hand. He pointed the deadly blade at Chet. "You think me stupid, horsekiller? Think I do not know you were following me? You are—"

302

There was a loud pop behind the creature, a streak of light followed by an explosion, and the sky lit up. Seet glanced sideways and Chet threw the chest, the knife, the brass knuckles, catching Seet in the neck and face, causing him to stumble back. Chet followed with a hard driving kick to the creature's stomach, sending him to the ground.

Chet rolled out of the tight compartment, bringing his sword up and around, intent on Seet's neck. Seet met the blow with the angel knife, cleaving the blade off near the hilt and sending Chet off balance. The goblin man struck out in a flash of white gold, catching Chet across the forearm then down, slicing deep into Chet's knee. Chet let out a cry, tried to leap back, but his knee went out and he slammed hard into the wagon wheel.

Fireworks lit up the sky. Chet could hear the crowd oohing and aahing. The glow glistened off Seet's scaly hide, revealing his horrible parody of a smile.

Chet clung to the wheel, trying to keep on his feet. He thrust his sword out, trying to ward the creature away.

Seet looked at the cloven blade, snorted, then pressed in, leaving Chet nowhere to go. The creature rolled the knife back and forth in front of Chet's face, then struck out, slashing the blade across Chet's cheek.

Chet gritted his teeth against the pain.

"*That is for Styga,*" Seet hissed and slashed again, this time catching Chet across the other cheek.

"Fuck!" Chet cried.

The goblin man's eyes gleamed. "That is for—"

Rapid popping erupted, something—many somethings—whistled past them in the air, planks and boards splintered all around, and suddenly the night was full of screams.

Seet flinched as splinters rained down and Chet drove into him, knocking the creature off his feet and landing atop him. Seet thrust his knife into Chet's ribs. Chet felt the blade burn deep into his chest, then tear out his back. He locked his arm around Seet's forearm, trapping the goblin man and the angel blade. He shoved his broken sword into the soft underside of Seet's neck, jabbing, slashing, tearing open the creature's throat.

Seet let out a weak gurgle, then fell limp.

## CHAPTER 53

Ana lay on her back watching the fireworks explode. There, then, that very moment, she wasn't in purgatory, wasn't even dead, and neither was her child. She was six years old, it was New Year's Eve, and the world was a good place to be.

There came a sudden rapid session of loud blasts. *The grand finale,* Ana thought and felt disappointed that the show was almost over.

Then the screams came.

Ana sat bolt upright.

There was carnage everywhere. Souls, mostly the guards, lay writhing on the ground, riddled with gaping wounds.

A shout from the dark came from somewhere behind Veles.

Another blast.

Heads exploded, torsos ripped open, and more souls crumbled.

Something smacked into Ana's shoulder, hard, knocking her down. She cried out against a wave of searing pain. *Those are bullets,* she thought, as shards of stone cracked and ricocheted around her. She stayed low behind the stones.

Veles let out a roar, his face a mask of fury. He thrust his hands skyward, and the air above him crackled.

A third volley of fire slammed into the god, tore his throne to splinters, and knocked him to the ground. Veles lay upon his back, his clothes ripped and smoldering. He sat up, shaking his head. He appeared dazed, but Ana saw no actual wounds, no torn flesh or blood.

A man carrying a spear charged out from the dark, his eyes cold, dead, his face grim. He didn't yell, or shout, just ran directly for Veles as the god was getting to his feet. The man swept the spear across the back of Veles's hocks, cutting completely through the god's legs. Veles toppled backward to the ground, his eyes blazing with rage and confusion. He raised his hands skyward, his fingers dancing, the clouds overhead crackling. The man struck again, whipping the spear around, taking off one of Veles's hands at the wrist, the other at the elbow. Veles's eyes widened with shock and before he could even cry out, the man whipped the spear around once more, slashing the gold blade across the side of the god's face, cutting away most of his jaw and snout.

A loud yell went up and a wave of men streamed into the arena. Wild-eyed men, with red scarves tied around their necks, some carrying muskets, most with swords, spears and axes. They drove into the crowd, cutting down any who stood in their way.

A small group of Veles's guards rushed forward and Ana scrambled behind the stonework in an effort to escape the vicious fighting.

A man, one of the attackers, fell in front of her, his head split open. Ana snatched up his sword, started to crawl away, stopped, tore off the man's red scarf, tying it around her own neck. She stood and ran from the arena.

Ana slid into the shadows of a wagon, trying to catch her breath as she searched for Chet. Flames sprouted up here and there as wagons burned. Souls from both sides dashed past. Screams and the clang of arms came from all around her. *Dammit, Chet, where did you get off too?* Then it struck her. *Seet.*

# CHAPTER 54

Chet opened his pouch, snatched out three ka coins, then chewed and swallowed them as fast as he could. The wagon above him burned and armed men with red scarves rushed past, heading into camp, killing any they met. Chet closed his eyes, tried to ignore the screams, the growing flames, tried to concentrate on his wounds, knew he wasn't going anywhere until his knee healed.

A loud snap came from above him and the wagon sagged, raining down sparks and embers. One of the wheels cracked and the whole flaming heap tilted precariously.

"Shit!" Chet cried, rolling out from beneath the blazing wagon. The wound, the one across his chest, tore open, and it felt like someone was twisting him in half. He let out a yell and just lay there, out in the open, panting, waiting for the pain to subside.

More men were coming.

Chet held still, even though his shirt was burning, just lay there playing dead, ignoring the flames until the souls had passed. He sat up, slapping out the embers. The pain in his knee and chest was finally starting to recede and Chet was hopeful that he might be able to stand. He clenched his teeth and forced himself up onto one knee.

More footsteps.

Chet turned, saw a figure silhouetted against the flames, sword in hand and wearing a red scarf. Chet snatched out his knife, the angel knife.

"Chet?"

"Ana?"

"Oh, thank God." She rushed up, slipped an arm beneath his, and helped him to his feet. "We need to get out of—" Shouts, more men heading their way from out in the dark. Chet and Ana headed off, Ana supporting Chet as he hobbled along as fast as he could.

Souls dashed in all directions, but Chet noticed that the Edda were all going the same way—up a short rise and into a cluster of boulders. Chet pointed after them. "That way."

They headed up the slope and Chet soon found he could put more and more weight on his knee, until finally he was walking on his own.

They topped the rise and Chet glanced back. The amphitheater lay just below and he could see bodies everywhere. He caught sight of Yevabog's cage, lying on its side. He was trying to see if she was still inside, when a figure walked past her cage—a tall man in a fitted long coat and knee-high boots carrying a spear.

"*Gavin*," Chet whispered.

Ana tugged him. "C'mon. We need to go."

The man stopped and looked up, as though he sensed Chet was there—those dead eyes searching the hillside.

A horse topped the rise in front of Chet. A man wearing a green jacket sat in the saddle, carrying a torch in one hand and a musket in the other. He spotted Ana, then Chet. His eyes grew wide. "*Hey! It's him!*" he shouted, pointing the musket at Chet. "Don't you move."

Chet dove forward.

The musket went off; dirt and rock exploded next to Chet's head.

Chet slashed the angel blade across the horse's leg, cutting the animal down at the knee. The horse shrieked and toppled, throwing the rider. The man had no sooner hit the dirt than Ana hacked into his neck with her sword. He screamed and Ana hacked again, silencing him.

"They're over here!" someone cried. More men on horseback, carrying muskets and torches, were riding up the slope. Chet locked eyes with the lead man. It was Carlos.

"*Go!*" Chet yelled, pushing Ana. They dashed over the rise, Chet running as fast as he could to keep up with her. The rocky dirt crumpled beneath Chet's feet and he stumbled into Ana, knocking her over, sending them both sliding down a steep incline.

They landed among a cluster of boulders in a dark ravine. Chet could see the horsemen far above searching for them.

"They're down there!" someone shouted and several muskets went off. The dirt kicked up around Chet and Ana and they fled.

## CHAPTER 55

Gavin propped the god spear against the boulder, looked down at his gut. A sword hilt protruded from his stomach, the blade sticking out his back. Normally he would've wrapped both hands around it and tugged it out. But he had only one hand remaining, the other gone at the elbow. The fighting, there at the end, had been fierce. A group of zealots had rallied, made a final run to save their god.

Gavin set the blade point against the boulder and pressed back, pushing the pommel outward. He wrapped his remaining hand around the hilt, and tugged, gritting his teeth as he twisted it free. He let out a grunt, tossed the sword, and slid down, taking a seat against the stone.

He watched the shadows of the dead flutter in the dwindling blaze of the burning bones, saw Carlos heading toward Veles. Veles lay on his back in the dirt, surrounded by Carlos's men, his great antlers broken, his hands and hooves gone, what remained of his arms and legs bound. Carlos walked up and stood over the god, the flames underlighting his smug smile. "Should I bow? Would that please you?" Carlos asked, then spat in the god's face.

Veles stared up at him, his mouth a jagged wound, his eyes wet with bloody tears.

Carlos nodded to his men and they shoved a sack over Veles's head, tying it tight around his neck with a cord of rope. "You like fire. Like burning souls. Well, where you're headed you're going to know what it is to burn." Carlos kicked the god twice, hard in the head.

Gavin fumbled beneath his long coat and tugged out his satchel. Sat it on his lap and untied it with his remaining hand. Several ka coins spilled out. He plucked up three, shoved them in his mouth, and chewed.

He scooped up the remaining coins, dropping them back into his satchel, then leaned against the stone and waited for the ka to do its magic. Ka coins were as important to him as his bullets and he always tried to have a good supply on hand, even eating them mid-battle when he had to, fighting while his wounds healed. He'd determined that fighting in purgatory wasn't always about how strong and fast you were, but about how much pain you could endure. How well you could fight with your gut sliced open, your leg broken, or half your face missing. Gavin had long since lost count of how many wounds he'd suffered. Only knew that if he'd been a living man, he'd died at least a hundred deaths by now.

The warmth seeped down into Gavin's arms, his legs, and wrapped itself around his wounds. He closed his eyes as a wave of relief washed over him. He'd come to enjoy the itchy crawl as his flesh wormed itself back together. Slowly his arm and hand returned to flesh, his deep wounds healed. But as usual, they didn't heal completely. Always with a slight scar, a reminder—his flesh was riddled with them.

Gavin pushed up onto his feet with the spear, grunting against the pain. He didn't have time to wait for his wounds to fully heal; there were things he needed to attend to. He left the amphitheater and headed into camp, stepping over bodies and through the smoke of smoldering wagons, the smell of burning ka not too unlike that of flesh. The screams were dying out, replaced with the moans and groans of the wounded.

Gavin found himself searching faces. "*The boy's not here,*" he said under his breath. "*You know it.*" He scanned the hilltop, the rise where he'd thought he'd seen the kid, and decided he'd either run off or was lying dead somewhere.

Gavin spotted what he was looking for: a tall wagon bearing Veles's banner. He walked to it, stopping as something ran toward him out of the smoke. It was a tiger, its eyes terrified. Gavin watched it run past and disappear into the night, then climbed up into the wagon.

He found two men pillaging the god's cabin. The men spun around, swords on guard, looking ready for a fight.

"Get out," Gavin said flatly.

The men got a better look at who they were dealing with, and decided to leave.

Gavin rifled through the cabinets, closets, and chests, ignoring the furs and jewelry until he found what he was seeking. He tugged a small brass box out of a woven basket and sat it on the floor. It was locked; not only that, it had no latch or keyhole. Chet drew one of his guns, jabbed his thumbnail into a wide flat screw in the handle, and gave it a twist. The handle flipped loose, revealing a red copper key hidden within the recess. Gavin took the key and touched it to the box. A thin line of blue light ran round the box and the lid popped open. Gavin quickly placed the key back in his revolver, and the revolver back in his holster. He glanced over his shoulder, then flipped up the lid. He pushed aside several copper rings and pulled out something heavy wrapped in blue velvet. He unrolled the velvet, letting four silver stars fall into his hand.

Gavin sucked in a quick breath. *"Four,"* he whispered. *"Four of them!"* He'd attained a small piece of god-blood long ago, about the size of a dime. It had served him well; he had rationed it over several years. He now held four complete stars. He could hardly believe it.

He pinched off a flake, barely larger than a nail clipping, and held it up. He knew the risk of taking god-blood without a god to craft it, had seen a man rupture after taking a bite not much larger than what he now held between his fingers. He placed the sliver in his mouth, and closed his eyes.

It hit him fast, hard, pressure building from his core, swelling and throbbing outward. He let out a groan, clenched his eyes shut, gritted his teeth, and doubled over, clutching his stomach, fighting to contain it. And then, just when he thought his guts and bones would tear from his flesh, it subsided, the throbbing turning into a pulse, like a heartbeat. He leaned back against the wall, let out a long breath, let the warmth, the vitality pump through him. He smiled; it was like when he was young, alive and full of vigor, like a shot of whiskey with cocaine, a feeling he could take on the world.

"Gavin?" someone called. "That you?"

Gavin slipped the stars inside his coat, and stood. The world blurred, then came into focus, sharp focus—no detail escaped his notice. He could see and hear with startling clarity.

"Here," Gavin said.

The Colonel pushed through the curtains, saw Gavin, and a big grin let up his face. "Gavin! Gavin! You did it!" The Colonel stepped forward, clutched Gavin's shoulders, and shook him. "By heaven above you did it!"

"There's copper," Gavin said, nodding to the chest.

"Copper? How can you worry about such things at a time like this? You've just taken Veles. You've taken a *god*. Think, Gavin. How many souls can ever say such a thing? You've got to learn to celebrate these moments. You don't get many like this."

Gavin hefted the spear, handed it to the Colonel. The Colonel took it, admiring the gold blade. "Ah, the God Slayer. Such a gift. Such . . . a . . . gift."

"And not without a price," Gavin said.

The Colonel's face sobered. "Don't start, Gavin. We're in it now. There's no going back."

Shouts came from outside. The Colonel walked out onto the platform; Gavin followed.

Carlos and his Defenders rode up below—seven of them on horseback, a small cart behind one of the horses, Veles in the bed, bound and half-covered beneath a tarp.

Carlos gave the Colonel a salute, a big grin on his face. "We've done it!" he called.

The Colonel saluted back. "We most certainly have."

"Have to get a move on," Carlos said. "The fuse is lit. Too many got away into the canyons. Word's going to spread real fast."

The Colonel nodded and the men rode away.

"Feel that?" the Colonel asked Gavin. "Revolution. It's in the air."

Davy and Billy

Lamia in her youth

Yevabog

The Red Lady

Veles

Hel

Lord Kashaol

Lord Beelbeth

# PART FIVE

Lethe

Thunder rumbled in the distance. A drop of rain slapped against Ana's cheek. Black clouds rolled overhead, damping what little light there was. She couldn't believe it would soon be dark again, that they'd spent the night and most of the day walking through this gorge, this endless maze of cliffs, boulders, and passages, all leading in different directions, doing their damnedest not to fall into holes and bottomless chasms, and still getting nowhere.

"And you're sure it was your grandfather?" she asked Chet.

"It was him."

"But he was with *them*? With those raiders . . . with Carlos?"

Chet didn't answer.

"Doesn't that concern you? I mean, do you really think . . ." She was trying to find the right way to put it. "Chet, are you sure you *want* to find him now?"

"I have to."

"What's that?" Ana said. Whispers, almost hissing, drifted down out of the dark pits and caves around them, causing her flesh to prickle. "This can't go on forever," she said. "Right?" Chet bit his lip; she could see his frustration. She thought neither one of them wanted to state the obvious, that this was purgatory and for all they knew these canyons *could* go on forever. Or that maybe they were wandering around in huge looping circles, or worse, they could be headed for Hell itself.

Ana scanned the towering black cliffs. They seemed cut from obsidian or some other glassy rock, slick with razor-sharp edges and impossible to climb. They'd tried twice and both times ended with one or both of them falling.

"Hey," Ana said. "Look. Tracks!" This time, they weren't their own. Their path intersected a much larger trail, the dirt along the trail kicked up by dozens of horse hooves.

"They have a wagon, too. See there." She pointed to two grooves atop the tracks. "You think it's them? Some of Carlos's crew?"

"Doesn't much matter," Chet said. "Just so long as they lead us out of here."

They fell in with the tracks and for the first time in hours, Ana began to feel a little hope, then a few more rain drops hit her—big raindrops. A minute later the rain started, quickly turning into a downpour. Water began to flow beneath their feet, the trail turning into a small brook.

"Christ," Chet said.

"What now?"

"The tracks."

The water was washing away the tracks.

"Damn," Ana said. "Let's just hope this rain lets up, or we'll be swimming out of here."

A long shriek rolled down the canyon, like claws on a chalkboard. It seemed to go on forever, making Ana's teeth hurt.

Chet's face was grim. "We can beat this," he said, picking up the pace. They moved along as fast as they dared, but the sky grew darker, the rain fell harder, splashing down the steep stone. The canyon fell into darkness and soon they could barely even see the trail. Ana thought she caught movement, shapes there and then not, in the flashes of lightning.

"Look out!" Chet shouted as lightning revealed a fissure dropping away before them. Ana tried to halt, but her foot skidded out from beneath her. Chet caught her before she fell, pulling her back from the fissure.

"We can't keep going!" Ana shouted. "Not in this."

Chet shook his head. "We have to."

"Chet, we can't see a thing." The water was almost to their knees now. "There!" she yelled, pointing to a nearby ledge about twenty feet off the canyon floor.

Chet nodded reluctantly and followed her as she climbed up the rocky slope. They found a small cave beneath the ledge. It was dry and out of the wind. Ana crawled in, collapsing on her back, and let out a long gasp. Chet entered and sat next to her, his back against a stone. A screech echoed down the canyon. It was the same sound they had heard earlier, but much closer. Chet pulled out his knife, keeping watch on the entrance.

Thunder rumbled over as the rain drummed down. Ana closed her eyes and tried to pretend she was a little girl back in San Juan, listening to a thunderstorm from her bed. Chet placed a hand on her shoulder and she clutched it. A small gesture, but right then, right there, it meant everything to her.

Slowly, she drifted off to sleep.

## CHAPTER 57

Senoy watched Lamia walk out onto the porch. In the dim moonlight, the ghost of her former beauty still lingered, the Lamia he'd fallen in love with, the Lamia of before—before the great tragedy, before Gavin shot her, before time wore her down.

She closed her eyes, basking in the moon's pale glow.

He crept closer, staying to the shadows, studying her like a connoisseur before his most beloved painting—the grace of her long neck, her fine bones. He craved to touch her, to stroke her flesh, hold her hand, felt his heart fit to burst. *How much of my love, this overpowering longing is true,* he wondered, *and how much is her bewitchment? Do I care? If a spell makes me feel such, then I prefer to stay under it always. The world is but a glamour anyway, all smoke and mirrors.*

He stepped closer.

"I know you're there, my angel," she said. "I hear your heartbeat."

He smiled at that, knowing his heart no longer beat, that it was as dead as his flesh, that if not for his will and the power of his celestial spirit he would be nothing but a pile of rotting bones.

She opened her eyes, peered down upon him. And if his heart *had* been alive, it would've thrummed. "Lamia, my love."

"Is my guardian watching over me?" Her voice was lyrical to his ears. He knew it was all part of her magic and still it did nothing to spoil the sweetness.

He stepped out from the shadows and she couldn't hide her shock. "Senoy . . . why, you're withering away."

He grimaced, wondered how many more ways he would have to pay for his folly. Lamia had known, even all those years ago, the power of the key Heaven had bestowed upon him. She'd teased and beguiled him with promises of what she could do if he allowed her to use it. Had vowed she could unlock a spell to mix their blood, turning his celestial spirit to flesh. He'd scoffed until she'd reminded him that she was an ancient blood weaver. Had she not used her blood on God's own beloved humans, twisting them into her vessels of immortality? "Why not dare?" she'd asked. He *had* dared and she *had* done it—a thing impossible. He closed his eyes, recalling the feeling of warm blood pumping through his flesh, the rush of those minutes, those precious minutes of life that he had had before Gavin shoved the knife into his chest, before Gavin had killed his flesh, trapping him within his own corpse for all these years.

"Come," she said, walking over to the porch swing. "Sit with me." It had been so long since she'd allowed him near, he was sure he'd not heard right. She beckoned him again and he clearly saw she was motivated by pity, not by any desire to share his company. He wouldn't quibble, wouldn't allow what was left of his pride to stand in the way of any invitation.

He walked up the steps, carefully stepping over the bells. She patted the seat next to her and he sat down, mindful not to bump her, knowing how much she hated his touch.

"I hear you've sent Chet away on a fool's errand."

"You have eyes and ears everywhere."

"Why do you do this to yourself?"

"Don't leave me, Lamia," he said, hating the plaintive tone of his own voice, hating himself for breaking his own promise to never again play the heartsick fool.

She looked at him then, not as an equal, certainly not as a lover, but as something sad and pitiful.

"The boy will return," Senoy said. "Just give him time."

"You are a shameless, wicked creature, Senoy. Betraying Chet's trust, using him for your own means."

Senoy shook his head, ever amazed at Lamia's blindness to her own nature. She truly didn't see the suffering she wrought on her own children.

"We will have the key again," he said. "I will be set free. Think of the things we can do."

She sighed and the sound was like a hammer, for it spoke that she truly believed his fate sealed, that he would never be able to leave this island, much less follow her. "Senoy, we both know you're grasping at straws."

"I am grasping at anything I can."

"When did you last sense the key?"

"Not so long ago. Only a glimpse, but it was Gavin. I am sure."

She eyed him skeptically. "Sometimes we see what we want to see."

"No, it was Gavin. I always feel him when he uses the key. Only a flutter, but there is no mistaking his black heart."

She brightened. "Then there *is* hope." He saw desire in her eyes, but knew it was not for him, but for the key and its power.

"Yes," he said. "There *is* hope. But only if you stay. The key . . . it will do me little good without you." There was little need to say this, she knew only her blood, her sorcery could bring his flesh to life once more, but Senoy *needed* to say it.

She didn't respond and he knew he shouldn't press, but he did, he always did. "You will stay and wait with me?" And of all his folly, it was this twist that hurt him most, that the shroud could not hold her, not her or her demons. It was cast for divine spirits only. Why even Joshua could leave if he but knew and could get past the demons. Lamia had remained on the island all these years only to await the return of her bloodline. She had that now.

"I will stay."

"Yes?"

She nodded. "For as long as I can."

He looked into her face and her eyes dropped, the way they always did when she lied to him. He knew she loathed this place of tragedy and black memories, that it was killing her just as it was killing him. His fear was that in her haste, her desperation to flee, she wouldn't wait until the child was old enough to take, but feed on her, growing just strong enough to leave, to take the child elsewhere to raise, jeopardizing everything.

"It is too dangerous," he said.

Again she made no response and he knew he needed to stop before he went too far. "It is not safe to venture from this sanctuary. Not without me to shield you," he said, his tone forceful. "The angels will find you. You know this. I know you know this." He saw it on her face then, the coldness returning. Why must he always do this? It was why they'd stopped talking; she'd grown tired of his pleas and threats. And here he was at her again, trying to scare her.

"This is no sanctuary," she said. "This is a prison. This is death. I'd rather risk Gabriel and his wolves than spend another day here."

Senoy looked out toward the ocean, wondering if she had any idea how deep her words cut him. He had no desire to live in a cell either, but he would rather live in a cell with her, than to be free without her. His eyes fell on her hand; it rested between them on the swing. *So close.* And despite her words, her manner, the desire to touch her overwhelmed him.

He touched her—tracing a single finger along the top of her hand.

She recoiled. He caught the revulsion on her face and felt as though he'd been struck.

"I am sorry," he said. "It is not easy to be so close."

She stood. "Don't apologize. It's just that your flesh . . . it . . . it's as though being touched by death."

"I know . . . all too well, for it is I who must live within this carcass."

"If only—" she didn't finish.

"Yes, if only." *A thousand if-onlys,* he thought. *If only Gavin hadn't shown up when he did. Hadn't brought ruin to all our dreams. My flesh would, this very minute, be pumping with warm blood—her blood, my blood, mingled together. We would be as brother and sister, as lovers, as one, sharing a thousand mortal lives together. If only. Oh, if only.*

"Let us not dwell on the past," she said. "Let us instead put our hopes on Chet. I'll be strong again soon and once we have the key, we can finish what we started."

And to hear someone else say it, he could see just how ludicrous such hopes sounded. *Yes, if Chet finds the key, finds the needle in the haystack. If he survives the trials of the nether regions, if the demons do not hunt him down, if Gavin does not kill him. If he makes it back before Lamia leaves me, before I waste away and become just another shadow among the shadows. So many ifs.*

The children gathered on the hill, their little glowing eyes on Lamia—their faces, like his, so full of yearning for her. And he saw in them how pitiful he must appear. He, who was once a great hunter of gods and monsters, he, the angel that Gabriel had called his sword of might, reduced to begging just to be allowed to sit next to this lilith, this ungodly creature that he was sent to cast down.

The children called to her and she smiled at them, encouraging them. "They love me," she said, and beamed. And they too, these lost souls, could leave the island if they wished. Only they would never, not without their mother; they would follow her to Hell itself.

Senoy sighed. *I should have killed her. How did it ever come to this? How did I ever fall so far?* "I gave up God's light for you, gave up everything."

Her smiled fell away.

It was the worst thing he could say, he knew it, but he said it anyway, said it because there always came some satisfaction in seeing the sting. Because the sting meant that on some level, she still cared. But he saw no sting, no sorrow, no regret, nothing.

"Lamia, this flesh you bound me to, this flesh that once ran with both our blood, is dying, truly dying. You must understand that when I put up the shroud, I blocked out God's light as well, and without it my spirit is starving, becoming too weak to carry this carcass much longer."

She was staring away, out at her children, as though she didn't even hear him.

"There is no release for me, Lamia. Not even in death. Can you not see that without your hand, I cannot escape these rotting bones? I will be trapped forever, Lamia. Trapped within this prison within a prison, unable to ascend or even descend. Does that not mean anything to you?"

She turned away.

"I do not have much longer, so please, I beg . . . yes, I am begging you . . . don't leave me, Lamia. Please give Chet a little more time."

She gave him a small, sad smile and left the porch, left him with all her children.

He heard snickering from the oak trees. Davy and Billy stepped out and the children scattered, ran back down the hill and into the woods.

"She's gonna leave you," Billy said. "Leave you to die . . . *alone.*"

## CHAPTER 58

I think that's the worst of it," Isabel said, pushing the cart onto the firmer trail. Her boots, the hem of her cloak, all their cloaks, were caked with mud.

Mary knew it wasn't going to be easy—the canyon trail never was—but she hadn't expected such a downpour as came the previous day. But even though the rain had slowed them down, she still felt she'd made the right call.

"There," Isabel called, pointing to a bit of high ground well out of the mud. "Looks to be a good spot for a rest."

The sisters rolled the carts over and stopped, finding dry ground to sit on. Mary watched the women tend to the infants, reassuring those who needed it, calming any who were crying.

A little girl reached for Mary, looking up at her with trusting eyes. A stab of guilt caught Mary by surprise and for a moment, it wasn't this little girl she saw before her, but her own infant daughter. *They killed my babies,* she thought. *As sure as cutting their throats . . . and all because no one dared care for them.* While she'd sat in a cell accused by the Salem Governor's Council of witchcraft, all three, the oldest being only six, had succumbed to starvation and exposure that brutal winter. *They'd warned me, told me to take my tools of Satan and leave. But did I? No. I was too proud to bend to the will of fanatics. And the price of my pride was my daughters' lives. So then, who, who is to blame?* Mary picked the little girl up, cradled her, and when the girl hugged her back, the pain, the guilt, began to fade once more.

The Red Lady sat up suddenly, sniffing the air. She glanced skyward and Mary followed her gaze. There, high in the clouds, was a trail of green smoke.

"You think that's coming from Osiris's Mother?" Isabel asked.

"I do," the Red Lady said and stamped her great paw, the fur rising along her back.

"What is it?" Isabel asked. "Demons? Is it demons?"

Mary set the child back in the cart and drew her sword.

# CHAPTER 59

"There's another one," Ana said.

The hoofprints had all washed away, but the wagon wheels had left deep ruts and they'd spotted a trace here and there and followed them off the wider trail, down a narrow side ravine. The trail here was washed clean, just black sand and stones and they soon lost any signs of the tracks, but the ledges appeared to be getting lower, flatter, so they continued. About an hour later the clouds lifted and a dim amber glow lit up the canyon. The land began to dry out, the rocks shifting toward a rusty red color.

Chet scanned the cliffs. "We might be able to climb out here. Have a look around."

Ana nodded. "Worth a try."

They scaled a series of ledges until they found themselves on a plateau composed of large jagged rocks and boulders. Veins of crimson crystal glittered across the red stones. They topped a ledge and a valley spread out below. Enormous towering stone pillars jutted upward across a valley pocked with craters and fissures spewing steam.

"You see that?" Ana said, pointing toward a thin cloud of green smoke drifting into the sky. "Think we should take a look?"

Chet nodded and they wove their way through a forest of standing stones as they tried to get a better view. They came out upon another ledge and halted.

"Wow, now that's something," Ana said.

Far below them a giant iron statue of a two-headed woman stood among crumbling ruins. Six breasts sat atop her bulging belly and green smoke poured from her mouth and eyes.

Chet spotted movement below her—a wagon, horses, and men wearing green jackets.

"It's them," Ana said.

Chet scooted up to take a closer look, rounded a boulder, and froze.

A creature, draped in a dirty crimson cloak, sat astride a huge stallion. The creature's face was long and goatlike with horns curling back over its head. It stared down into the valley below. The stallion, a stringy, skeletal beast with a mouthful of jagged broken teeth, jerked its head around in their direction. It stomped and bellowed, sending a blast of smoke and sparks from its nose and mouth.

Chet slid back behind the boulder, pulling Ana down, hoping the creature hadn't heard or seen them. They crouched, waiting for the beast to leave, but it didn't. Instead it began to pace back and forth along the ledge, leaving them nowhere to go.

Chet slid out his knife and prayed he wouldn't need to use it.

## CHAPTER 60

Two demons on horseback trotted into the ruins. They nodded to Carlos, then spread out, circling the giant iron statue, peering into the crumbling buildings, searching the hilltops and ledges. They met back where they started and one of them waved its spear toward the canyon pass. Figures on horseback moved out from the shadows, kicking up a red cloud of dust as they rode toward them.

Carlos exchanged a glance with Hugo.

"You ready?" Hugo asked.

Carlos took a last drag on his cigarette and flicked it into the dirt. "As much as I'll ever be." He'd never met Lord Kashaol, never knew anyone who had even seen one of the fallen angels before. They were said to be powerful and dangerous beings, beings that had fought against God himself. He swallowed hard and sat up tall in the saddle, determined not to appear cowed.

"You ever worry that once the Red Lady is gone, one of these demon lords might try and take over?" Hugo asked.

"What, demons, ruling openly in the river realms?" Carlos snorted. "The One Gods would never stand for that. To my understanding there's some sort of pact in place, y'know between all those One Gods, the Hindus, Christians, Buddhists, and such, that none of them should rule the river realms. If that's so, imagine if one of Lucifer's lords tried that shit. Why Kali herself would probably come marching in and crush them. See, that's the beauty of our situation. Lord Kashaol needs us as much as we need him, maybe even more so. If he wants souls, then he's going to have to work with us."

Carlos counted seven figures: six on horseback, another at the reins of a black wagon. He realized these were the lord's escort and was surprised to see such a small guard, especially in these territories. As they drew near Carlos saw the guard wore ragged, mismatched armor. They looked more like common bandits than elite guards. He spotted no insignia, no banners. This troubled him. He'd not expected the black and gold of Lucifer's regiments, but these were low-caste demons, little more than twisted souls. Carlos had heard that Hell wasn't one unified kingdom, but many, much like medieval Europe, all vying for Lucifer's favor. He had no clear idea of Kashaol's standing, but judging by his ragtag guards, it didn't appear to be much.

The procession entered the ruins, the guard spreading out, their anxious eyes peering in all directions. Gar rode in and gave Carlos a knowing smile. They halted and Gar dismounted, scurrying over to a hunched figure atop a cadaverous horse. The horse had long, skeletal legs—not a warhorse, but a creature built to run.

A dark purple shroud ringed with golden tassels and embroidered with intricate patterns enveloped the figure. But even though the shroud was made of rich material, it was frayed and tattered, turning brown with age. Moreover, demons coveted their gold and copper and this creature wore none, only a few necklaces of beads and bones and faded blue flowers whose pointed petals writhed like tentacles. Carlos began to wonder just what rank this demon lord actually held.

Gar took the reins as the figure slid from the horse. Gar gestured toward Carlos and whispered a few words. The figure shuffled over, the hem of its shroud dragging along in the dirt. It stopped a few steps away and pushed back its hood, revealing a pitted bronze helmet with a faceplate covering all of its face but its mouth and bony chin. Its pallid flesh was covered in veins and bruise-colored spots. It shed the shroud, Gar catching it as it slid from its shoulders.

Carlos made a nod, almost a bow. He'd heard God robbed the fallen angels of their beauty and grace, but it was hard for him to accept that the twisted creature before him had ever strolled the halls of Heaven.

The lord cocked its head left and right, as though listening for something. "Where is she?" it rasped, its voice sounding as tortured as its body.

"She?" Carlos asked, then understood. "The Red Lady?"

The lord nodded, its tongue darting out between jagged broken teeth, licking its black, shriveled lips.

"Last word she was in Styga gathering children. That was about two days ago. She should be on the caravan road to Lethe about now. At least a day's ride from here. I would've heard, otherwise."

The demon grunted and scanned the cliffs. Carlos noted a sentinel on a distant ledge. The sentinel raised and lowered its spear. This seemed to appease the lord and he returned his attention to Carlos. "I take great risk entering the river realms," Lord Kashaol said. "But it is important that I meet the man in whose hands I am placing my fate." He faced Carlos, tracing a bony finger down his own ominous faceplate. Spikes began to sprout from the top and sides of the demon's helmet, forming into a great jagged star, then splintering off into smaller barbs that floated around them. "What sort of man are you, Carlos?"

Carlos's thick brows knotted together. He had no idea how to answer such a question.

There were three small cones set atop the helmet, and an eye formed within each, staring at him, into him. "Are you a man who knows what he wants? Are you bound by sentiment or do you write your own dogma? Do you kneel with martyrs or carp with the philistines? Do you bear the weight of a thousand crosses? Are you a sadist, a murdering bastard? Who are you, Carlos?" The creature leaned in on him and Carlos met his own reflection in the tarnished faceplate. His eyes locked on themselves, took on a life of their own, glaring, boring into him. Carlos saw himself first as a boy, struggling not to cry as Sister Phyllis smacked his knuckles with her sharp ruler over and over until they bled. But the tears had come, big, sobbing tears, and the class had laughed at him, not out loud, but snickering behind their hands. Then as a young private in the army, Sergeant Johnson, that beast of a man, singling him out over and over again to make an example of, forcing him to stand at attention all night in his boots and skivvies while the other men made their little jokes, their little digs. Then prison, Pedro, big fat Pedro, and his gang, taking turns at him, the taste of Vaseline in his mouth. But he'd killed Pedro. Because enough was enough, and he'd decided then and there, regardless of the cost, he'd never, *never*, again *take it*—not from nuns, cops, or prison fuckheads. And when Pedro's gang came for him, cut his throat and left him to bleed out in his cell, he'd thought of Pedro, of the man's brains splattered all over that barbell, and smiled, actually smiled. Carlos saw that smile, that face, in the reflection—beastly and manic as the blood pumped out from between his fingers—and just when he thought he could bear it no longer, his eyes, the ones in the reflection, closed, releasing him.

Carlos fell back a step, blinking and rubbing his eyes. They burned as though he'd been staring into the sun. He noticed a small smile on the demon's mouth; the creature appeared to be enjoying his discomfort.

The three eyes on Lord Kashaol's helmet closed. "You have something for me?"

"What . . . ?" For a moment Carlos forgot why he'd even come here. "Oh . . . yeah," he said weakly, struggling to regain his composure, trying to push away the image of his own death. "Yeah, I do." Carlos waved and Jimmy and Hugo walked the small wagon forward, pulled the latch, and dropped the gate. Carlos flipped the tarp back, revealing Veles's trussed, mutilated body.

Lord Kashaol stepped over, peering down at the bound god.

Carlos tugged the sack from Veles's head.

Veles blinked, saw Lord Kashaol, and his eyes widened, the mutilated corners of his mouth quivering.

Lord Kashaol smiled. "Two gods in two days." He reached out, pinching Veles on the muzzle. "How does it feel, Veles, to know none will ever hear your voice again?" He returned his attention to Carlos. "Tell me, how did the battle go? Did you suffer many losses? Is your army still intact?"

"It was a rout. Took them completely by surprise. Veles fell before he even knew what was going on."

Lord Kashaol nodded, appearing pleased.

Encouraged, Carlos continued. "With Lord Horkos and Veles out of the way, Styga and Lethe are all but ours. The other gods are spread out and too damn arrogant to work together. It won't take much to bring them down. Even Queen Hel herself can't hold out on her own. Once I'm in control of the port cities, well, then there'll be no more games. Those who escape Hell will have nowhere to hide. We'll be bringing you the damned in cartloads." Carlos stroked his mustache. "We just got that one last problem."

"The good Red Lady.

"Come," Lord Kashaol said. "I have something to show you." He walked Carlos over to the black wagon, and nodded to Gar. Gar hopped into the bed and lifted the lid off a long crate, revealing a device somewhere between a small cannon and a blunderbuss—a short, flared barrel mounted to a bone stock and fitted with a dragon-shaped firing mechanism.

"Would you look at that," Carlos said, unable to resist sliding his hand along the black ore; it felt smooth as glass, not a pit or crack. "Divine, simply divine."

"Yes, divine. Forged in Hellfire by the great sorcerer Jaraol. Once a smith for Heaven above. We fought together, Jaraol and I . . . in the great war against *God*. And now, again, we find ourselves joined in our cause. As he too has had his share of being kicked by Lucifer's lords."

Carlos glanced up. It was the first hint he'd heard that Lord Kashaol might not be in Lucifer's good graces.

Lord Kashaol withdrew a fist-sized ball of cloth from his cloak and sat it down next to the blunderbuss. Carlos realized it was shot for the weapon—shards tightly bound in oiled rags.

"The gold here," Lord Kashaol continued, indicating the shot, "and that which is upon the spear—they come from Heaven itself. It fell with the angels . . . their swords and spears. They are coveted among the lords and extremely difficult to come by. I have gone to extraordinary lengths to secure these. But it was Jaraol's alchemy, his sorcery that devised an ore from which they could be shot. And . . . I will show you something more." The demon slid back his cloak, revealing a large revolver made of the same black ore as the canon. He pulled it free of its holster. "The bullets in this gun are tipped with the same gold."

Carlos looked on amazed. "You're kidding?"

"Once I secure more of God's gold, Jaraol has promised to forge another. Perhaps, such a gun for you one day."

Carlos couldn't take his eyes from the weapon. *A god-killing gun,* he marveled. *Why, that would almost make a sport out of slaying those cocksuckers.*

"All is coming to fruition," the lord said and smiled. He stroked the gun with long, bent fingers, caressed it like some beloved pet. "Bringing in Veles will win over more to my cause. Soon I will take back all that was stolen from me . . . all, and then some." His voice became almost a growl.

The demon slid the gun back in his belt and pushed his visor up. Carlos was surprised to find no red glowing orbs of hate and fire, but instead, deeply soulful eyes beaming with intelligence. But they were also sorrowful eyes, the eyes of a being who'd lost everything. "Carlos, I have traded in every favor to make these weapons, spent all I have, my rings, my own heavenly sword, even stolen from Lucifer himself. If I fail, my fate will be far worse than that of Horkos and Veles. So I will not play games with you. I will not insult you with talk of loyalty and fealty, of lofty ideas. Because I see in your heart that you are a man who serves only himself, and that is just the creed of soul I am seeking. Because a man such as you sees that our goals can only be attained together and there is no stronger alliance than that of necessity." He paused a moment, scanning the cliffs. "I have no army, thus it would be too great a risk for me to try and take down a monster as powerful as the Red Lady, even with these weapons. But more than that, we both know it is crucial that my hand not be exposed, lest I bring down the wrath of Lucifer and the One Gods. But *you* are a soul. You have no such restraints, and you *do* have an army. A proven force. Carlos, if you can fulfill your part, can fell the Red Lady, then all the port cities will be yours. You could become an emperor. Think of that. And so long as the souls flow my way, I will keep you well stocked with the weapons you need to protect your kingdom.

As my own kingdom grows, so will my influence among Lucifer's court. An ally in Lucifer's court is not a bad thing to have. The old gods grow weak. Who is to say, but one day, with my aid, you might conquer the Elysium Fields themselves."

Carlos found himself nodding. *How easy it is to become swept up in such sweet talk,* he thought. Yet, he had to admit he felt a closer kinship to this demon than the Colonel. No pretense, no need to hide behind idealistic rhetoric. He looked at the blunderbuss again. *I could build my own kingdom, my own empire. Once the Colonel is out of the way, who is to stop me? Think of that . . . from a flesh trader to an emperor. And why not?*

## CHAPTER 61

Chet peered slowly around the boulder. The demon still sat upon the stallion, its back to them, watching the figures below. A second group had joined the first and they appeared to be exchanging items. As Chet watched, the parties split apart, each leaving the ruins by opposite gates. One of the groups, the one that appeared to be creatures, or demons, headed toward the cliffs—toward *them*.

Chet shifted, trying to get a better look, when a rock slid beneath his foot with a clack. The horse snorted and the demon creature turned around. Chet withdrew, pressed his back up against the stone, praying the demon hadn't seen him. Ana tugged her sword out, her face tense.

The horse snorted, its hoofbeats moving in their direction. Chet could hear the demon sniffing, closer and closer, and clutched his knife, ready to spring.

The horse trotted into view on Ana's side of the boulder. The rider spotted Ana, yanked out its sword, and let loose a piercing screech that echoed all down the valley. Dozens of howls came in answer from below.

The giant horse snapped at Ana and she stumbled back, falling on the rocks. The beast tromped after her and Chet dashed around the boulder, coming up on the horse from behind, raking his knife across its hind legs just below the hock. The angel blade did its work, wholly severing both of the horse's back legs. The steed let out a shrill cry as it collapsed to the stones, tossing its rider from the saddle.

Chet leapt after the rider. The demon tried to bring its sword around, but Chet hacked into its arm, slicing the limb off just below the shoulder. The demon howled and Chet howled back, driving the blade upward, catching the demon beneath the chin, hacking and slashing as though half-mad, cutting the demon's head from its neck. The head bounced and rolled away.

"Look out!" Ana cried, just as something bit into Chet's arm, yanking him onto his back. Chet found himself face-to-face with the stallion. The monster snarled and shook its head back and forth, thrashing Chet against the rocks. Ana struck, bringing her sword down across the thing's snout. It shrieked, letting loose of Chet and turning on her. Ana dashed back behind the bolder as the beast clawed and kicked up the dirt, snapping at the air, trying to come after her despite its severed legs.

Chet stumbled away, trying to get clear of the snarling monster.

Howls came from up and down the valley, growing closer.

"C'mon! C'mon!" Ana shouted, helping Chet to his feet.

Chet could hear approaching hooves, but couldn't tell from which direction.

"This way!" Ana cried.

"No, they're coming from—" Two horses crested the rise. "Shit!" Chet yelled. They turned to flee when four more horses rode up, blocking their escape.

The demons circled, lances ready.

"Well, c'mon!" Chet shouted, knife out before him. "C'mon, you ugly motherfuckers!"

Two more riders appeared, followed by a black wagon. One of the riders, a bent creature draped in a purple shroud, pushed back its hood, revealing a tarnished faceplate. It surveyed the scene and cocked its head, sniffing at the air. Its attention fell on Chet and Chet felt the mark heating up in his palm.

"Not a good place for a damned soul to be," the creature said, speaking to Chet. "Were you aware that demons stalk these hills? That they can smell the damned?"

"I'm not going to Hell," Chet stated with absolute conviction. At that moment he wasn't thinking of Trish, the baby, he was thinking of the sermons Pastor Thomas used to give on the torments of Hellfire, of having one's flesh burned off one's bones over and over for all eternity. "I'll cut you down. Cut every one of you down." Chet held the knife up so they could see the strange glint of the blade.

The creature with the faceplate smiled. "Such pluck, such stoutheartedness. If I but had a hundred souls such as you . . . why, I could conquer a kingdom." It sighed. "Heaven is full of sheep. Hell is full of those who actually shaped the world. Men who carved out their own paths, the courageous, the bold, they are the ones that end up damned. It pains me to say this, but you, my brave soul, you will not win this day. Your fate is—"

A bell tinkled, a delicate sound like a wind chime. All heads turned to a large boulder set into the rise. There, watching them with calm green eyes, sat the Red Lady, the light breeze ruffling her long red hair. She spoke, her voice deep, yet feminine, that of a mature woman. "You are very loud, and smell very bad."

The demons seemed as statues, unable to move, staring at her with mouths agape. Their mounts snorted and began to back away. The Red Lady cocked her head, regarding them like something fun to play with.

"Take her!" the lead demon commanded, its voice suddenly reedy and weak. It fumbled beneath its cloak, yanking out a large black revolver, but before it could even sight the gun, the Red Lady leapt upon the demons nearest her with a loud roar.

The demons tried to bring their weapons to bear, but she tore into them, all claws and teeth, knocking one horse into the other. Demons and horses shrieked as she ripped them apart, thrashing them against the wagon, smashing it into splinters.

The remaining demons broke and ran, scattering in all directions, all except the one with the revolver. It leveled the big gun and fired. A deafening explosion thundered down the valley and a large hole opened up on the Red Lady's chest, knocking her backward.

She looked at the wound, at the blood—appeared confused.

"It ends this day!" the demon screamed, and pulled the trigger again.

The Red Lady brought her wings down in front of her like a shield.

The gun boomed four more times. Fur and feathers flew with each blast until there was only the sound of the hammer clicking on spent chambers.

"Die, die you whore of Ra!" the demon hissed, but when the smoke cleared the Red Lady still stood. One wing appeared to be broken and blood ran from her chest, yet her eyes were more alive than ever and locked on the demon.

"*Monster!*" the demon cried, its lips quivering. It drove its heels into its mount and the horse sprang forward. The Red Lady snarled and leapt for them, but stumbled, falling short, something obviously wrong. The horse dashed past, flying down the rocky slope.

The Red Lady let loose another roar, the echoes chasing the demons as they raced away. She took two shaking steps, then collapsed.

## CHAPTER 62

Trish twisted loose another nail, then about an hour later, another, until all the nails were gone from one side of the slat. She stuck her fingers into her mouth, sucking away the blood, then pried the board free with a loud creak. Trish froze, listening. No one came. She hid the nails, then peered out of the window.

It was about a six-foot drop, just far enough to worry her. She would need to remove at least one more slat to slide out. She hoped she'd be able to use one plank to pry loose the other. She looked at the board, at the nail sticking out the end, and realized it could make a decent weapon if it came to that. *And the demons? Just how am I gonna get past the demons?* She thought she might have an answer, that she could just tear some of the bells loose from the string and carry them along with her. *But will the bells really scare them away?* She shuddered, knowing there was only one way to find out. *Sometimes people leap from burning buildings, don't they? When there are no other choices.*

Footsteps came her way; she quickly set the board back into place, drew the curtain, and slid into bed.

The key hit the lock and the door swung inward. Lamia walked in. She glanced at the untouched tray of food on the foot of the bed. "My, dear, you haven't eaten?" She picked up the plate of vegetables and sat down on the bed next to Trish. She jabbed the fork into a chunk of broccoli. "Here, now. Have a bite."

Trish stared at the far wall.

"You're only hurting the baby," Lamia said, her tone growing terse. "I cannot allow you to hurt our baby. Now eat."

Trish continued to stare past her.

Lamia plucked a long pin from her own hair and before Trish could even raise an arm, jabbed it into the side of her neck.

"Oww, Jesus!" Trish yelled, pushing away from Lamia. She rolled off the bed, intent on the door, only the door suddenly appeared far away. Her legs grew weak, her hand hit the wall, and she slid to the floor. Everything became blurry.

Lamia's face was before her, twisting, distorting into something primal and wicked, a toothless hag, then a succulent beauty, then scales and horns and yellowy serpent eyes—all of them, then none of them. Trish let out a cry and recoiled.

"You think you're the first to play games with me? I've prowled this earth since before the dawn of men. A thousand maidens have danced for me. I'm a goddess . . . *your* goddess. You *will* obey me. Now open your mouth, child."

And Trish found herself powerless to do anything else.

Lamia shoved a clump of broccoli into Trish's mouth. "Eat."

Trish did, dutifully chewing her food, chewing twenty times just as her grandmother used to tell her to. She swallowed and when another bite was presented, she ate that one as well. It was as though she were a passenger in her own body now, sitting in the backseat and watching someone else drive.

"Eat," Lamia commanded, presenting more food, and again Trish chewed and swallowed. This continued until the plate was clean.

"There," Lamia said, her tone now soft, gentle. "That's a good girl. Now, come . . . back to bed." Trish crawled over to the bed and Lamia helped her up and onto the mattress.

Trish lay staring at the ceiling, unable to move.

Lamia climbed onto the bed, straddling her, and set her ear against Trish's stomach. She slid a hand beneath Trish's gown, gently caressing her swollen belly. "*Not much longer, my little dear,*" Lamia whispered. "*Not much longer.*"

Trish tried to push her away, tried to shout, tried to scream, but could only stare upward as tears ran down her cheeks.

# CHAPTER 63

The demon groaned, clawing at the dirt, trying to drag its broken body away. Chet walked up behind it and jabbed his knife into the back of its head, over and over, until it stopped moving. He stood and surveyed the broken bodies of the downed demons and horses, satisfied that they were all dead now or at least no longer a threat.

Ana sat next to the Red Lady, pressing her scarf against the sphinx's wound, trying to stifle the flow of blood. The Red Lady lay on her side, staring at the blood as though it couldn't be hers.

Someone was yelling, a muffled wailing sound, the cries coming from the smashed wagon beside the sphinx. Chet found Veles's mutilated body under some boards. He tore the gag from the god's mouth, then cut the bonds from what remained of his arms and legs and helped him to sit up. Veles's hands were gone and his mouth was little more than a jagged raw wound, hard for Chet to look at. The god tried to speak, but what came out was more of a garbled sputter.

A woman shouted and Chet turned to find Mary—the woman from the docks—running up the slope, sword in hand, her cape fluttering out behind her. She spotted the Red Lady and rushed to her.

"Oh, dear Mother Eye," Mary gasped, sliding down to one knee. "Sekhmet, you're bleeding. But *how?*" Mary yanked her satchel around, digging through it. She pulled out four ka coins, shoved them into the sphinx's mouth. "She needs more!" Mary looked to Chet and Ana, her eyes desperate, the jewel in her forehead glowing. "We need ka. Quick, give me what you have!"

Chet put away his knife, digging out a several of the white coins from his satchel and handing them over.

Mary fed these to the sphinx and demanded more.

Chet gave her a few more.

"Stop playing games!" she snapped. "Give me all you have."

Chet handed her the satchel and Mary emptied it upon the ground, snatching up more coins and feeding them to the sphinx.

A loud wail caused Mary to glance up. She saw Veles and her brows furrowed. "Veles? What *is* going on?" Before anyone could answer she scooped up several coins, handed them to Chet. "Here, take these to him."

Chet hesitated; they were the last of his coins.

"Quick!" Mary yelled.

Chet fed them to Veles.

Blood still pumped from the Red lady.

"We don't have enough," Mary said, the panic growing in her voice.

Chet's hand went to his jacket pocket, pulled out the silver spike of god-blood.

Mary's eyes fixed on the spike. "How?" Without waiting for an answer, she snatched it, started to give it to the Red Lady, when Veles let out a garbled wail, his eyes also fixed on the spike.

Mary hesitated, clearly weighing what to do; finally she snapped the spike in half, giving one piece to the Red Lady, handing the other to Chet. Chet fed it to Veles.

"It's helping," Mary said, her voice full of relief. "By the Wyrd, it is."

Indeed, the Red Lady's wounds began to heal, the blood slowing to a trickle.

"Now let's pray it's enough to stop the bleeding." Mary looked at Chet, the gem in her forehead slowly losing its glow. "It's Chet? Right?"

Chet nodded.

"Sorry I was cross," Mary said. "The Red Lady's not like them, not like the gods. She's divine, but still mortal. Her heart pumps live blood."

Chet noticed then, that despite Veles's great wounds, there was very little blood. And it was different, with a silver glint to it.

Mary looked at the empty satchel in Chet's hands. "We'll repay you as soon as we can. You have my word."

Chet shook his head. "I'd be swimming in the river right now if it wasn't for you."

Mary gave him a small smile, then looked at the blood on her hands. "She's never been injured like this. Never been injured at all that I can recall."

"More," came a sputtering voice. It was Veles. His mouth had healed somewhat, at least enough for him to speak. The ghostly apparitions of his hands and hooves slowly appeared. "Bring me more," he spat, his eyes full of fire. "Bring me—"

"We've given you all we have," Mary interrupted. "Now calm yourself. Focus on healing."

Veles's face showed he didn't care to be spoken to this way.

Two more women came running up the slope. Chet recognized one of them as Isabel, the young woman with the fiery temper. Their faces grew grim upon sight of the Red Lady and they rushed to her.

"What's happened?" Isabel asked. "Oh, Lord, is she dying?"

"No," Mary said, her voice resolute. "She is *not* dying. Now, do either of you have any ka?"

Isabel shook her head, but the other woman fished four coins from her pack. Mary fed them to the Red Lady, then began to examine the large wound on the sphinx's chest. "It looks like a bullet wound."

"The demon shot her," Ana said.

"But she's been shot before," Isabel said. "Never made a scratch. I don't understand."

"Here, help me," Mary said tersely. "Hold up her wing."

Isabel held the wing while Mary examined it. She let out a relieved sigh. "These only hit feathers, not flesh. We need worry only about the bullet in her chest." She dug into her satchel and retrieved a small knife. "Okay, Sekhmet. You will feel this." Mary gently probed the wound. "Ah, there it is. It's not too deep." She pried out the bullet and wiped away the blood. "I've never seen one like this before." She held it up for the Red Lady to see. "Have you?"

The Red Lady shook her head.

"Here," Veles sputtered, sounding like a man without teeth. "Let me." He held out his hand. It was solid now, but thin and frail. Mary sat the bullet in his palm and he examined it, not appearing pleased by what he saw. "This is new sorcery." He tasted the tip. "Heaven gold."

"From one of the Fallen?" Isabel asked.

"Yes. When the angels were cast down, their weapons fell with them. But great sorcery has been at play to melt this down and forge it so." Veles grunted. "And even then, it should not have injured her. She is the Red Lady, the Eye of Ra, guardian of gods. There was a time when all on earth feared her tread. Man, angel, and demon alike." He shook his head. "I fear there might be some truth to Yevabog's words. That we are not what we once were and these demons . . . they sense it."

"And you?" Mary asked. "How did you end up here? Like this?"

"Raiders and Green Coats," he snarled. "Armed with muskets and a spear, a demon blade. They ambushed my caravan during celebration . . . slaughtering everyone they could."

"They possess a demon blade?" Mary asked.

"I rode here with a sack upon my head," Veles said. "My ears clogged with blood. Still I overheard enough to understand that they are in league with these demons. The muskets, the demon blade, they all came from Hell."

Mary scanned the dead demons. "I see no markings, no insignia."

"I heard the name Lord Kashaol spoken," Veles said. "Have you heard of him?"

Mary and the Red Lady both shook their heads.

"Could be some low lord," Mary said. "There are so many."

"But is he acting alone?" Veles asked. "It is hard to imagine Lucifer would have a hand in this. He would not be so clumsy."

"I thought there was some sort of pact in place," Isabel said. "Between the ancients and Lucifer."

Veles snorted. "Such things mean little now. When the angels first fell and were weak, the ancient gods, the true underworld gods like Hel, they drew lines in the dirt. Killed any demons who dared cross them. Now the gods rarely leave their temples. The Red Lady is the only one truly keeping the demons at bay."

"Demons and souls fighting together against the gods." Mary shook her head. "Can these souls not see they're being played? If they think themselves miserable now, how do they think they will fare with demons for overlords?"

"No," Isabel said, horrified. "Demons can't rule over the river realms. The One Gods will never stand for that."

"That is true," Veles said. "The One Gods would stop them from ruling, but they would not stop them from killing every last one of us. We are nothing more than a nuisance to them. One they would just as soon disappear."

"Let us go and find these godless men," the Red Lady said, her words full of venom. "Hunt them down, every one, and send their ba to Mother Eye."

"Neither of you will be doing much of anything," Mary said. "Not until you heal. You need god-blood."

"Lethe," Veles said. "We go to Lethe. Lord Horkos will have god-blood. It is time for the gods to set aside our petty squabbles and purge the realm of this rabble."

# CHAPTER 64

Mary halted, waiting for the others. Ana stopped next to her, glanced back, watching Chet and the two sisters assist Veles up the slope. The Red Lady hobbled along behind them, her wing wrapped in a sling made from Mary's cape; she refused to allow anyone to help her.

"Her blood is up," Mary said. "She's determined to make Lethe as soon as possible. But all will come to nothing if she kills herself trying."

They topped the rise and there, far below, were nine carts being pulled along by forty or so women armed with swords and spears, their black robes fluttering in the strong wind. Several of the women ran up to meet Mary as she made her way down the slope. They were full of questions and concern upon seeing the Red Lady. Mary told them what had happened.

Infants and toddlers sat or stood in the carts. Ana guessed there to be at least a hundred all told, many of them crying. Mary walked around, lifting them out of the carts, cradling them. The gem in her forehead glowed a soft green as she spoke to them in a soothing voice, quieting them one by one.

Once Veles and the Red Lady caught up, they began to move out, the procession making its way along the valley, the wheels rattling over the black stones and dirt.

Mary lifted a crying infant out and handed it to Ana.

Ana cradled the child.

"Do you not recognize her?"

Ana looked again, realized she did. "Is it—?"

Mary nodded. It was one of the children Ana had brought across the ferry—the little girl. Ana began singing a soft hymn, one her mother used to sing to her. The child looked into Ana's eyes and stopped crying, as did several of the other children nearby.

"You have a gift," Mary said.

Ana tried not to think about how close this sweet-faced child came to drowning in that dark, awful river. And a horrible thought struck her. *Is my baby, my little boy, is he here . . . somewhere?* "Mary, why are these children here?"

"What do you mean?"

"I mean how did they end up in purgatory? They're innocents. They couldn't have done anything wrong. Why would God turn his back on them?"

"If by God, you mean the Christ god, then they aren't his to do anything with."

"I don't get it."

"What I've come to understand is that a god cannot just take a soul, nor can a demon for that matter. A soul must give itself over . . . to Jesus, to Buddha, Muhammad, Odin, and so on, to Satan even. A soul's will is what makes it a soul. That is why the gods battle so fiercely for a soul's devotion. Once a soul gives itself over, only then does that god have power over it. Does that make sense?"

"I guess so," Ana said, but it didn't, not really, not to her.

"By believing in Christ, they give their souls to Christ, to his rules, his dogma. If in the end he judges them unfit, then he can damn them, or just deny them Heaven's kingdom, let them drift into purgatory. The irony is, if all those souls burning in Hellfire had never believed in Christ in the first place, then they'd never have ended up in Hell."

Ana walked in silence for a while, trying to wrap her head around all that. "So the children, how do they fit in? They're too young to give their souls to anyone. Right? Too young to make such a choice?"

"That's exactly it. Those not baptized or claimed through similar rituals, they belong to no god. With none to claim them, they are lost, left behind."

"But they never had a chance."

"No, they didn't."

Ana's baby had been baptized. Juan had insisted, even against her protest, and now she found herself thanking God he did. Tears sprang to her eyes at the mere thought of her little boy lost down here, crying for her. She hugged the little girl tightly to her bosom.

Mary was watching her. "You have a child? Had a child?"

Ana nodded.

"Purgatory is full of children in need of a mother."

Ana thought that to be a strange sentiment. "Do they grow? I mean grow up down here? Or do they stay like this?"

Mary looked at her sadly. "They never grow up. Never understand what has happened to them."

Ana nodded.

"But, they do bond. They want what any child wants . . . to be held, to be talked to, to be loved."

"What's going to become of these children?"

"That will be up to the river."

"The river?"

"You will soon see."

What's going on?" Hugo asked. "What do you see?"

"Nothing," Carlos replied, scanning the hills with his telescope. They could see for miles from their perch atop the plateau.

"Those were gunshots back there, and that shriek. Don't know how you couldn't have heard that."

"I heard it."

"Over there," Hugo said.

Carlos lowered the glass, squinted in the direction Hugo was pointing. "Where?"

"There. See? Near that cluster of rocks. There's a bunch of them."

Carlos saw several dark specks far down the valley among a maze of large boulders. He put the spyglass back to his eye. "Oh . . . shit, it's them, the sisters and their little brats. What the hell are they doing out—holy fuck, he's with them."

"Who, who's with them?"

"The kid, the one with the red hair. I think that's him anyway." Carlos handed the telescope over. "Here, look."

"Yeah, that's him all right, and that's *her*."

"Her?"

"The Red Lady. She's there. She's right *fucking* there. Looks like there's something wrong with her."

Carlos snatched the glass back, catching only a brief look at the sphinx before she disappeared behind the rocks. She was limping, and her wing was wrapped in some sort of sling.

"Did you see her?"

Carlos nodded.

"She looks pretty bad, huh?" Hugo said.

"Yeah, like maybe someone shot her up with some gold-tipped bullets."

"You think?"

"I do."

"I wonder how Kashaol fared."

"Well," Carlos said, "judging by the fact that she's still here, I'd say not too well."

"Man, I bet he wished he'd had the cannon. Might've stood a chance then."

"This sure wasn't in the plan," Carlos said, wondering what they'd do if Lord Kashaol wasn't in the picture anymore. Then it struck him that now that they had the cannon, had all those rifles, maybe having one less lord to answer too might not be such a bad thing. *Things just got a little more interesting.*

"Hey, maybe we should go after them?" Hugo said. "I mean if she's hurt, y'know. Might be our best chance."

"We've got six men."

"I know, but we've also got that cannon."

"We do, don't we?"

Hugo nodded.

"I'd feel better with a troop of rifles backing me up. How about you?"

Hugo thought for a minute. "Yes, I guess I would."

"That road leads to one place." Carlos put the scope away and grinned. "What d'you say we go round up the Colonel and set up a little welcoming party for our friends in Lethe?"

Hugo grinned back.

## CHAPTER 66

A sound, like a car door.

Trish opened her eyes, sat up clutching her head. She was dizzy, but at least she could move on her own accord again. She slid off the bed and over to the window, pulling the drape back, saw movement outside through the slats.

Voices.

*That's not Lamia.*

She swayed, almost fainted, steadied herself, then grabbed the board, the one she'd loosened, tugged it free for a better look.

A heavyset woman in her early sixties, dressed in a mint green polyester dress suit, stood next to a white Chevy Impala. She was talking to someone in the passenger seat. The far door swung open and a young man—maybe in his late teens, a big kid, looked like a ballplayer—climbed out of the sedan holding a yellow Tupperware container.

The woman retrieved several pamphlets from the car as the boy came around. She gave him a smile, straightened his tie, and wiped dandruff off his navy blue suit jacket. Trish guessed by their nice clothes they were either on their way to, or maybe from, church. One thing she was sure of, if she ever intended to get out of here now was her chance.

Trish shoved the board beneath the second slat, tugged upward trying to pry it loose. The nails creaked and for a moment it looked as though it might pull free, then the slat, the one she was holding, snapped, causing her to crash into the wall.

She picked herself up, started to try again, when she saw Lamia walking down the path toward the lady and boy. The lady greeted Lamia with a large smile and began talking. Trish couldn't make out the words, but could see by the way she waved her hands that she was very passionate about her message.

Lamia smiled back, but her body language was all nos and when the lady tried to hand her a pamphlet, Lamia refused.

Trish shoved the board beneath the slat again, tugged, but there wasn't enough leverage. She put her full weight into it. The board slid out, throwing Trish into the wall again. A sharp pain shot down her arm and she let out a cry. She grabbed the board, tried to tug it free; it didn't budge.

The lady, looking crestfallen, was heading back to her car now.

"No!" Trish cried. "No!" She banged the window. "Hey!" she screamed. *"Hey, help me!"*

Lamia glanced her way, her face tense, but the lady appeared not to hear anything. The boy walked around and got back in the car, still holding the Tupperware container.

*"No! Don't you leave me!"* Trish cried and slammed the slat into the window, shattering the glass.

They all looked her way.

*"Help!"* Trish screamed. *"Help me!"*

The woman stared at Trish, her face puzzled, and didn't see the knife as Lamia pulled it from her sleeve. Lamia slashed the blade across the side of the lady's neck. The pamphlets flew skyward, fluttering down as she fell atop the hood, clutching her neck, trying to stem the flow of blood gushing through her fingers.

Trish could see the boy's face, how big his eyes were. He fumbled for the door handle and all but fell out. He made it to his feet, appearing unsure whether to help the lady or flee. Then he saw the two boys come out from behind the oak tree.

*"Run!"* Trish screamed. *"Get out of here!"*

The demons gave the boy their smile, the one with a hundred teeth, and leapt upon him. One sank its maw into the boy's crotch. As the boy doubled over, the other tore into his neck, ripping his throat open.

Trish turned away, sliding down to the floor. She pressed her face into her hands and began to cry. A sudden sharp pain jabbed at her abdomen; she clutched her stomach. A few minutes later there came another jab, then another. It was the baby, she knew it, it was coming. "Oh, God," she said. "Oh, dear God."

## CHAPTER 67

Gavin spotted the riders approaching the camp, coming on at a fast trot.

"They're back," the Colonel said, his voice ripe with relief.

Carlos rode in, hopped down from the saddle, his face alive with excitement. "We got it!" he called. "And she's a beaut."

Hugo followed in with the wagon, along with the rest of the Defenders looking dusty and trail-beaten.

A large group of Green Coats had arrived in camp from Styga while Carlos was away. Carlos's face lit up when he saw them. "We got it!" he called, waving them over.

"Here, have a look, Colonel," Carlos said, leading them all to the back of the wagon. He dropped the latch and unwrapped the long bundle sitting in the bed, revealing the weapon.

The Colonel ran his hand along the black barrel, hefted one end, and sat it back down. "Damn that's heavy. Can one person fire that thing?"

"I think so."

"What's it shoot?"

"This." Carlos withdrew the shot from his jacket, sat it on the bed next to the cannon. "Shrapnel made from the same stuff as that spear. You can image what it'd do to the Red Lady."

Judging by the Colonel's face, he could.

"There's more."

"Yeah?"

"Yeah. The Red Lady, she's almost to Lethe."

"What? How'd she—"

"She took the canyon trail."

"That's odd. I thought—"

"There's plenty odd. Listen to this. She's hurt bad. We're pretty sure she got in a dustup with Lord Kashaol."

The Colonel appeared to be having trouble taking this all in.

"This is our chance," Carlos continued, talking fast, his voice full of excitement. "We set up an ambush in Lethe. Take her *now*. Take her while she's hurt. Never gonna get a better chance."

"Whoa, hold on. You're saying she had a fight with Kashaol?"

"Pretty sure."

"Is Kashaol dead? What happened to Veles then?"

Carlos shrugged. "No telling. We didn't see the fight, didn't see Veles either. But get this: we did see that redheaded kid, that Chet. Makes me think he's in on it, y'know. That he somehow led her to the demon. I mean . . . you have to ask yourself how it is he keeps showing up every time there's trouble."

*The kid still lives,* Gavin thought, surprised to find it mattered.

"And you want to go set up an ambush in Lethe of all places?" the Colonel asked.

Carlos nodded. "I do. Here's why. If Veles is with them, then we know the shape he's in. I'm just going to assume that kid's been feeding them information on us. That he's trying to rally these gods against us. But the one thing I believe they still don't know is that Lord Horkos is dead. I think they're headed there in hopes of getting his help. So where do you think they'd least expect us?"

"Lethe," the Colonel said.

"That's right."

"But you're guessing."

"I'm gambling, and based on what we know, sure looks like a good bet to me."

The Colonel stared at the ground. Gavin could see him chewing it over. After a minute he looked back up at Carlos. "What exactly did you have in mind?"

Carlos stuck both thumbs into that oversize scorpion belt buckle of his and smiled. "With the babies and the Red Lady limping like she is, they're moving slow. That gives us time if we act quick. We bring as many men and muskets as we can ride with, doubling them up on the horses. Can't be much of a guard left in Lethe. They'll be headed for the temple, so we just slip in quietly and wait for them there."

The Colonel thought on it for a minute, then nodded. "Well, being half-crazy has got us this far." He grinned. "Looks like we're heading to Lethe."

# CHAPTER 68

Trish felt the contraction building, her abdomen clenching, cramping. She took quick shallow breaths, gritting her teeth and clutching her stomach as the pain rolled over her.

The door opened and Lamia stepped in, the blood of the churchwoman splashed across her white dress. She came to Trish's side, only concern on her face. "It's time," Lamia said, speaking in a gentle, soothing voice. She helped Trish up onto the bed, then left. Trish could hear the quick click of the old woman's shoes as she hurried down the hall.

Another contraction rolled over Trish, then another. She clawed at the bedsheets as the pain racked her body, each contraction worse than the previous. *God,* she thought, *is it really supposed to be this bad?*

When she opened her eyes, Lamia was there with her black box of roots and potions along with a small basket of some freshly pulled leafy plant. She sat the basket on the nightstand, left again, and returned with rags and a pot of steaming water.

Several milder contractions hit Trish in quick succession, then it felt as though her entire stomach were twisting into a knot and not letting go. She let out a cry that turned into a scream.

"Sit up, child," Lamia said, trying to get Trish into a sitting position.

"No!" Trish yelled, the slightest movement only making the pain worse.

"Trish," Lamia said in a soft, motherly tone. "It'll make things easier. Now please. Sit up."

365

With Lamia's help, Trish managed to work herself into a sitting position against the headboard, but found little relief through the next wave of contractions.

Lamia dipped a handful of the leaves into the steaming water and swabbed them across Trish's forehead, neck, stomach, and breasts, leaving the warm, wet leaves atop her chest. They smelled of mint and black licorice, but somehow were soothing. When the next wave of contractions came, the pain was there, but distant, and Trish found herself able to focus, to push.

"She's on her way," Lamia said, her voice full of excitement. "You're doing well, child."

Again, the contractions came in waves, each crashing atop the previous, stronger and stronger until Trish felt sure her hips would snap.

"I see her!" Lamia cried. "Now, push. Push, child. Push!"

Trish did, clawing at the sheets as she strained, grunting, yelling through her teeth. All at once the pressure dissipated; it was as though a huge weight had been lifted off her belly. She heard a cry, opened her eyes, and through a blur of tears saw her, saw her little girl.

Lamia cut the birth cord, then took the warm leaves and washed the child. "You did well," she said, handing the child to Trish, propping her against Trish's breast, helping the baby to latch on.

The baby began to suckle and for that moment Trish forgot about Lamia, about demons, about the churchwoman lying dead in the driveway. It was just her and her child. Trish began to cry. "My baby. My sweet little baby."

# CHAPTER 69

A low fog crept up from the river as Mother Eye slowly dimmed and the shadows claimed the rugged terrain. Clouds rumbled overhead, but so far the night had been dry. From his vantage point atop the cliff, Carlos watched a lone guard lighting torches along Lethe's eastward gate.

"They're back," the Colonel said.

Carlos put away his scope and stood as two of his men scurried up the rocky trail, returning from Lethe. In their ragged cloaks they looked like any other pilgrims on their way to the river.

"Well?" Carlos asked.

"Not much of anything's going on," one of them said, pushing back his hood. "Just the usual parade of sad sacks, most half out of their wits on the drink."

"Yeah," the other added. "That place always reminded me of a tomb and right now it's deader than usual. Most of the guards left with Lord Horkos and we all know where they ended up."

Carlos nodded. "Any sign anyone knows about Horkos? About the attack?"

"They don't have a clue. No extra guards or sentries anywhere and the few we talked with sounded ticked off they got left behind."

Carlos nodded. "Good, just what I was hoping to hear."

"We're ready then?" the Colonel said.

"I guess so," Carlos replied, sucking in a deep breath. "We should start sending the men in."

The Colonel corralled the group, close to thirty altogether.

"All right," the Colonel said, addressing the men in a low voice. "Looks like everything's going to plan. No more than three to a group. Keep your weapons out of sight, blend in, spread out, enter through different gates. If you're not sure where Temple Lethe is, find someone who does. Once in, we'll need about half of you up on the balcony. Wait for Carlos's signal." He patted the big gun in Carlos's hand and grinned. "And believe me, you won't miss it."

The men began drifting down toward the city in small groups, each leaving several minutes apart.

A rider approached from the canyon road and several of the men drew their swords. They hadn't lit any torches, so it was hard to tell who it was until he was right up on them.

"It's me, Hugo," a voice called and Hugo appeared out of the gloom. He dismounted and a man took his horse away, hitching it up with the other mounts. "They're a good two hours down the trail," Hugo said. "And get this, Veles *is* with them."

Carlos exchanged a look with the Colonel.

"That's gonna complicate things," the Colonel said.

"Maybe not," Hugo said. "The Red Lady and Veles, neither one of them looked very well. The Red Lady is moving even slower than before. Veles is so bad off they're pushing him along in one of their carts."

"So, something *did* happen with Kashaol," the Colonel said.

"Give half my ba to have seen it," Hugo said.

"Well, time to finish this business," the Colonel said, his eyes all but gleaming.

"It sure is," Carlos said. "It sure as hell is."

## CHAPTER 70

Carlos crossed a short bridge and walked into Temple Lethe. It sat on a small island along the edge of the river. He found a spot within the shadows near the main entrance. It gave him a clear view of the arched passageway. The passageway led to another short bridge—the only way in or out of the pools—so he knew they'd have to pass right before him.

He'd wrapped the heavy weapon in rags to make it look like a bedroll, and now gently set one end on the marble floor, being extra careful, as the weapon wasn't just heavy, but also packed with the shot and black powder. It was a flintlock, so he didn't think a hard knock should set it off, but he preferred not to take any chances.

Carlos leaned against the wall, lit up a cigarette, and let his eyes drift about the large chamber. A towering statue of a veiled woman carrying a child stood at the center of the rotunda. The veil covered her face but you could still read her features, see that she was resolute in her purpose. Twin waterfalls gently cascaded down a series of marble ledges on either side of the statue. The sound of falling water reverberated off the white marble walls and up into the dome above.

Souls of every sort lay or sat in heaps upon the steps before the statue. Dozens more lolled about in clusters on the floor, stairs, window ledges, all along the mezzanine and second-floor balconies, spilling out into the courtyards beyond. Souls wandered through staring at the statue, up at the faded paintings in the dome, or out through the tall, narrow windows on the river just below. These were lost souls, missing arms and legs, chunks of their faces, hobbling along, their flesh moldering, turning dark gray and going to rot, souls that had long ago given up. Most of them appeared drunk on Lethe, clutching bottles of the black stuff to their chests, wandering about as though at a wake, whispering and weeping.

Carlos's men continued to drift in, several of them carrying bottles, shuffling along, playing the part, blending in. They placed themselves to best advantage along the windows and balconies. Guns and swords poked out here and there from beneath their cloaks, but Carlos realized it didn't matter—no one was paying attention. He'd seen only one patrol since they'd entered the city, and that was a couple of bored-looking sentries back near the city center.

A handful of souls shuffled past. They stumbled down the stairs, out the arched walkway, heading through the short corridor toward the pools. Carlos shifted his position, lining himself up with the corridor. He only had one shot and intended to make it a good one. A moment later the Colonel entered carrying the spear. He'd insisted and this time Carlos hadn't argued, feeling the Colonel's usefulness was about up anyway.

The Colonel had smeared the spear tip with mud to hide its golden gleam. He knelt in front of the statue, and in his dirty robe, he looked like any other dispirited pilgrim on his way to oblivion.

Hugo wandered in and took a seat next to Carlos. *"We're all here,"* he whispered.

Carlos nodded and marked each man, counted twelve guns along the windows, and the rest up on the balcony. *Going to be like shooting fish in a barrel,* he thought, then caught sight of Gavin staring at him with cold, dead eyes. Carlos leaned over toward Hugo. "Don't look, but the Colonel's man, Gavin, he's up on the balcony. Be a real shame if in all the confusion a stray bullet just happened to catch him in the back of his ugly head, wouldn't it?"

"Sure would," Hugo said, "Probably won't be needing those guns anymore either. I mean, if he was to get his head blown off, that is."

"Probably not. I think they'd look real nice sitting in your holsters."

"Me too," Hugo said. A moment later he stood and headed up the stairs. Carlos glanced back up at Gavin and gave him a smile.

CHAPTER 71

Ana crested the rise and there, below, torches outlined the ghostly shape of a city. There was just enough light to see the city was far smaller than Styga.

Mary called a halt to allow the Red Lady to catch up. She'd tried to get the sphinx to stop for the night, but the Red Lady insisted they soldier on. Veles had become so weak they'd finally had to make room in one of the carts for him and now many of them carried infants, including Chet.

The baby in Ana's arms was awake, fascinated by the procession of torchbearers snaking out along the river path below, stringing out so far as to look like stars twinkling in the night. Ana noticed that the line all headed one way—into the city. She saw very few leaving. Chet and Mary stood watching the marching lights with Ana. "Are they all seeking oblivion?" Ana asked, though she knew they were, knew they were souls like her, come to put an end to this retched existence.

"They've all heard of the river's promise," Mary said. "Traveling leagues from all realms just so they can enter here, at Temple Lethe. They believe that by paying tribute at the temple or by confessing their wrongs, their regrets here, the river will ensure their safe journey into oblivion."

"And you . . . do you believe that?"

"Some say the river sends them away into nothingness forever . . . oblivion . . . it is what so many seek. Others believe the river cleanses the soul of all past memories and guides it back to earth to be reborn. I'm not sure how that is different."

"But what do you believe?"

Mary looked at her. "I believe Lethe smiles on the children. Beyond that, I don't know."

Ana nodded, then noticed a faint fiery glow far in the distance from the way they'd come. It pulsed like a heartbeat and there was something ominous about that pulse; it seemed a hungry thing. "Is that Hell back there?"

Mary nodded. "We have Hell on our southern border, Jahannam east of Mother Eye, Naraka pressing in from the north. All seizing what they can. It is hard to understand, with all the vast underworld, why they are so intent on squeezing out the old gods. Veles says it's because the five rivers meet here. I feel it's because the One Gods and their devils are never satisfied with what they have. Once I saw Kali marching across the northern plains as though they were her own, tall as a ship mast, flaming swords in her six hands, the heads of a hundred demons around her neck . . . all singing her song of death. It is a scene I hope never to witness again." She shuddered. "But if the ancients lose the great Sekhmet, the Eye of Ra, their protector, then there is little in the way of such as Kali."

"Sekhmet, that's . . . the Red Lady?"

"Yes. She has many names. Long ago, Ra and the other ancient ones combined their powers and created her to guard their realms, but as they fade, so I fear does the Red Lady's might."

The Red Lady crested the hill. She appeared weak, but resolute.

"You made it," Mary said. "All but killed yourself doing it, but you made it."

A weak smile poked at the corners of the sphinx's mouth, but there was no humor in her eyes, only fire. She didn't stop, just continued down the trail.

Mary let out a sigh and followed. "The ka doesn't bind the same as godblood. With time she will heal, but not if she keeps pushing."

They made their way to the river road, falling in line with the pilgrims as they approached a large gate.

A guard leaned upon the wall, staring mindlessly out into the darkness.

The Red Lady cleared her throat and the guard glanced up, all but dropping her spear upon seeing the sphinx. She made a slight bow, stopped. "Hey . . . are you okay? Oh, gracious, what's happened?" She looked to Mary. "What happened to her?"

"Demons," Mary said. "Now, tell us quick, where's Lord Horkos?"

"He's away. Gone to the Gathering."

"Horkos was not at the Gathering," Veles said, pushing himself up out of the cart.

The guard appeared confused. "He must've been. He left several days ago."

Veles met Mary's eyes. "This does not bode well."

"Has there been any sign of trouble?" Mary asked the guard.

"Trouble? Here? No, of course not. Why? What's happened?"

"We're not sure. Look, keep an eye out for any armed men."

"I don't understand."

"It doesn't matter. You see anything suspicious, you ring the alarm. Understand?"

The guard nodded.

"Okay," Mary said, speaking directly to Veles. "Let's go to the temple. Find one of the priests. They might be able to aid you and the Red Lady."

Veles nodded and they headed into the city.

Ana found Lethe to be very different than Styga, quiet, solemn, with no real sign of commerce. The dim lanterns gave off just enough light to guide them down the maze of narrow, winding cobblestone streets. They passed rows of windowless buildings, most of which were carved directly into the white stone of the surrounding rock. Ana caught movement in the shadows, among the piles of trash. She heard murmuring and realized the piles weren't trash, but souls, clustered together in the alleys and along the gutters.

They came upon one of the drinking establishments. Ana wasn't sure if you would call it a bar or saloon or what; the sign simply had a picture of a black drink. Several dozen souls lay about the front, most against the wall, a few lying right out in the street. A woman came stumbling out of the door, nude, missing an arm, her eyes blank as she stared skyward, smiling.

"Why don't they just drown themselves and get it over with?" Chet asked.

"I think," Mary said, "that even in this life within death, there is a part of them that can't let go. The drink makes it easier, taking their memories away in small pieces. The sad thing is . . . many lose too much of themselves to the black water, and forget why they even came here. They end up wandering out into the canyons to be eaten or just fading away in one of the alleys or nearby caves."

Ana smelled the river, inhaled the moist air, felt a sense of calm steal over her. The children smelled it too. They quieted. It was as though they knew, or at least sensed, what this place was.

They passed a terrace that overlooked the river below. A small fountain stood at its center surrounded by white, polished standing stones. Piles of clothes, weapons, coins, lay around the fountain. Even as they passed, a soul was stripping down, folding his clothes and stacking them atop the others.

"There," Veles said, not hiding his contempt. "That is why Horkos has such wealth. He's convinced these fools that leaving him all they possess will please the river gods."

"Sounds about like every other church I've ever heard of," Ana said.

The street leveled off, running along the river. Torches lit up the fog, illuminating the surrounding statues, arches, and terraces.

"Temple Lethe," Mary said.

A domed structure loomed out of the gloom ahead of them. It sat on an island of white stone; a single bridge led over to an arched entrance. A handful of souls meandered across the bridge, and many more leaned over its railing, staring down into the dark water. As they neared, Ana noticed several pools around the temple. The pools were composed of rings of steps leading into the depths. Souls sat on the steps, some wading into the pools, others adrift, drinking in the water as they floated out into the river.

Ana watched a woman sink beneath the water with a blissful smile upon her face. Ana understood everything about that smile. *It'll all be over soon,* she thought. *Never have to hear my son screaming . . . not ever again.*

The woman disappeared. No arms took her, no tormented faces; she just sank slowly away, that peaceful smile never leaving her face.

"It's not at all like Styx then?" Ana asked

"Oh, no," Mary answered. "Though Styx too offers an end. Only the soul is purified first. Or at least that is what they say."

Veles nodded. "It's true, after about a century of torment, Styx releases what she claims."

Ana shuddered.

They rolled the carts and children across the bridge, entered the rotunda. Souls lay everywhere, the voices of the children bringing many out of their stupor, staring at the infants with dazed confused faces.

The sisters began unloading the infants, carrying them down the steps, through the short archway, and out into the courtyard between the pools.

The Red Lady stooped, entered the chamber. She looked up at the statue, swaying, as though she might collapse at any moment.

"Sekhmet," Mary said. "Come, time for a rest." She put a hand on the sphinx's shoulder and led her down the steps into the corridor leading to the pools. Veles, aided by two sisters, followed, as did Chet and Ana—none noticing the man with the thick handlebar mustache hiding within the shadows.

# CHAPTER 72

Ana walked to the edge of the pool—the pool being a series of submerged steps leading out into the currents of the river—and watched as Isabel handed one of the infants to Mary. Mary, one step at a time, waded into the calm water until she was chest deep, then gently lowered the infant into the river.

Ana was surprised that the child didn't thrash and cry out, but instead appeared calm. Mary cradled it and whispered into its ear, the gem set in her head glowing a soft green. The child smiled. Mary placed a kiss upon its head and let it go. The infant slowly sank away, its face showing no alarm, no fear, but serenity, the face of a child falling asleep.

The sisters worked in silence, handing the infants one by one down the steps to Mary. She repeated the ritual with each one, taking her time, cradling and kissing each child as though they were her own, before setting them adrift.

The scene was almost more than Ana could bear. *But what else is there for them?* she wondered, trying to imagine what it must be like for them, lost, confused. *An eternity of being alone.* She shuddered and told herself that it *was* a mercy. What she saw on each face was peace, as though the river were the arms of the mothers and fathers these innocent souls most desired.

Ana stepped into the water. She still held the child, clutching it to her bosom as though she'd never let it go. *I'm dead,* she reminded herself and took another step, and another; the water felt warm, comforting. *We're all dead*. She was up to her waist now, staring into the river. The river made no judgment; all were welcome. She'd wanting nothing but this since the fire, an end, a true end, yet here, upon the brink, she hesitated. *Why?*

Someone was beside her. It was Mary; she seemed to read her thoughts. "There's no return. Never another chance to make it right."

*Make it right?* Ana thought. *My son is dead . . . because of me. How can I ever make that right?*

The child reached for the water, patting it, making small splashes. Ana knew it was time for both of them. Fighting back tears she held the child out to Mary.

Mary shook her head. "It's you she trusts. You should be the one to give her to Lethe."

Ana looked into the child's eyes, nodded. She took another step down and she was up to her chest, the water feeling like a warm blanket wrapping itself around her and the child. The infant let out a small cooing sound. Ana hesitated. *There's nothing here for her, nothing. Not for her, not for me. It is time, little one . . . time for us to go.*

She released the child, letting her slip beneath the water. The child held on to her hand, looking up into Ana's eyes, her little face peaceful. She gave Ana a tiny smile, a smile that said more than words ever could, then let go, just slipped away, disappearing into the gentle currents, her smile never wavering.

Ana found herself smiling and this confused her. What right did she have to smile, to feel good about anything? But she did and she knew why: because no matter how hard her mind worked to twist things, to punish her, her heart knew what she'd done. She'd saved this child from untold misery, possibly even an eternity of torment.

Ana closed her own eyes, preparing herself for that last step.

"Forgive yourself first," Mary said.

"No," Ana replied. "I can't."

"You can. One child at a time."

"What?"

"There are more innocents out there. They need you."

"But there're so many."

"There will never be an end to suffering. You do what you can, *only* what you can. Peace comes from knowing you helped those that you could."

Ana glanced back at the bank, at the empty carts. *How many more are waiting for someone to care?* And she thought then of her own child. *What if he'd ended up down here? Crying for me. Waiting for all eternity for me?* The thought brought tears to her eyes. *Would I want someone to take him to Lethe? Of course.* She took a step back, then another. *"Maybe,"* she said, whispering to the water. *"Maybe after a few more children, a dozen, maybe a hundred, a thousand . . . maybe then I'll have earned the right to leave it all behind."* But she thought maybe she'd already started down that road, because for the first time since the fire, she didn't feel consumed with self-loathing.

Mary was there, arms open. Ana stepped to her and was enfolded in her embrace. Ana began to sob.

"You're not alone, child," Mary said. "Yours is a road we all travel."

## CHAPTER 73

*Could he really be a Moran?* Gavin peered down upon Chet from the second-story window. *Sure looks like a Moran. Who is he then? My grandson? No, couldn't be. 'Cause that would mean Lamia lived . . . and that bitch is dead.* He scanned the courtyard, searching for a way to get to the boy. The infants were all gone to the river and the last two women left the pools. One of them, the young woman with short hair, went to Chet. They embraced, holding back as the others followed the Red Lady toward the temple.

Gavin glanced down to the chamber floor and spotted Carlos smothering the torch nearest the corridor, then slipping into position next to the archway. The long corridor made the perfect trap; there was no other way off the island, nowhere to run or hide.

The Colonel slid up to the opposite side of the archway, spear in hand, ready. The others too, the Colonel's men and Carlos's Defenders, all withdrew their weapons and began moving up. A few souls began to notice, their faces confused.

The Red Lady staggered along looking haggard and exhausted. *Christ,* Gavin thought, drawing his own guns. *We could probably take her with just the spear.*

Gavin lost sight of Veles and the Lady as they, along with the sisters, entered the corridor. A moment later the echoes of their footsteps preceded them into the chamber, louder and louder as they approached, then the cast of the Red Lady's large shadow upon the three wide steps. Veles, leading the way, walked up the steps and into the chamber. He was talking over his shoulder, so he didn't see Carlos standing with the demon weapon pointed at them, a nasty smile upon his face.

"Boo," Carlos said, giving them just enough time to see him, to register what was about to befall them, then pulled the trigger.

There came a flash as the flint struck the pan, followed by an enormous explosion. The blast kicked Carlos to the ground, the shot tearing into the Red Lady, into Veles and the sisters, knocking them back down the short steps into a heap of torn flesh and screams.

# CHAPTER 74

The concussion thundered from the chamber, echoing down the river, followed by musket fire, smoke, screams, and shouting. Chet and Ana instinctively ducked down.

*It's happening again,* Chet thought, horrified. *How can it be happening again?* The gunfire all seemed to be coming from the temple. He glanced about seeking escape, but they were on an island. He started for the bank, intent on swimming for the shore, stopped, looking at the dark waters, realizing he had no idea if the river would claim them if they tried to cross. He decided their best chance lay with the boulders clustered about the base of the temple. "C'mon!" he cried, yanking Ana to her feet. They dashed for the rocks.

There was more musket fire, random blasts. Smoke billowed out of the archway and several of the sisters—about twenty of them—came stumbling out. Chet spotted Mary, her leg injured, being helped along by a women.

Several pops from above; men shooting from the windows. Flesh and limbs exploded, women dropping, falling onto the ground and into the pools. Others scattered, seeking cover. The women helping Mary was hit and collapsed. Mary fell to one knee.

"Hell!" Chet cried, dashing out. He grabbed Mary, dragging her back behind the rocks. Shards of stone exploded around them.

"We can't stay here!" Ana shouted.

Chet spotted several windows and balconies along the low wall that led around to the towers on the back side of the temple. He saw no raiders positioned there. Chet put an arm around Mary. "We have to get over to the wall. Can you do it?" Mary's leg was torn open below the knee, the pain visible on her face, but she nodded. Ana took Mary's other arm and they hefted her to her feet.

"One," Chet counted, "two, *three*." The three of them dashed for the stoneworks, a few musket balls kicking up dirt around them as they ran. They dove, tumbling, ending up behind a row of large cut stones at the base of the wall. They headed down the wall until they were just below a balcony. Chet climbed up the first stone and reached back to take Mary's hand.

"Look out!" Mary cried.

A blast went off just above Chet.

Ana let out a cry and fell to the ground.

A man stood on the balcony, reloading his musket.

"*Motherfucker!*" Chet cried, his rage setting him to fire. He scrambled up another stone, then caught hold of the bottom railing of the balcony, pulling himself up and over just as the man finished reloading. The man swung the barrel up, but Chet drove into him, the two men crashing into the dark room beyond. The musket went off right next to Chet's head. The blast was deafening.

Chet landed two hard blows to the man's face, then tore the musket from his grasp. He brought the stock down on the man's head, slamming it three times with all his strength, crushing the man's skull.

Smoke and dust filled the dark, murky room. Chet coughed, his ears ringing. Someone else was in the room with him, he felt them. He turned, knowing who it was even before he saw the tall figure in the doorway.

Gavin stood staring at him, two large revolvers pointed at Chet.

Their eyes locked.

"Who are you?" Gavin asked, his face cold stone.

"I'm your grandson."

The man didn't flinch, as though expecting Chet to say just that. He nodded. "What's your mother's name?"

"Cynthia."

And there, for a second, the stone facade of the man's face cracked. Chet saw pain, deep pain.

Suddenly, a gunshot blasted through the doorway. Gavin's upper shoulder tore open, the slug knocking him several steps into the room. The attacker, one of the Defenders, pulled his sword and rushed in to finish the business. Gavin brought up his good arm and fired once, the bullet taking the top of the man's head off. The man's momentum carried him forward, colliding with Gavin, and the two landed in a tangle.

Gavin shoved the body off him, but before he could stand, Chet was there, angel knife in hand. Chet swung hard, the blade catching Gavin in the throat, a perfect strike. Gavin's head flew from his neck, landing against the wall, his body collapsing in a heap.

Screams and shouts came from outside.

*Ana!* Chet thought and dashed back to the balcony.

They were *gone*.

"*Ana!*" he shouted. "ANA!"

Cries and the clang of arms came from the arch: somehow a handful of sisters were putting up resistance. Chet scanned the rocks, but found no sign of Ana or Mary. "*ANA!*" he cried again, starting back down the balcony. He stopped. "No," he snarled. "The key. Get the fucking key."

Chet dashed back into the room, slid down beside Gavin's body, and began digging through his grandfather's coat pockets.

A clamor came from the hall; several souls ran past, their faces confused and terrified.

"You better hurry," someone said behind Chet. Chet jerked around, knife ready. No one was there.

"They're gonna be here any sec, then you're gonna be screwed." It was Gavin's head, his grandfather's head, talking to him.

Chet ignored him, returning to the man's coat.

"It's not there," Gavin's head said.

"Shut up," Chet said, continuing his search, digging through any pockets he could find, the coat, vest, pants. He found nothing. He unlatched the satchel, dumping out the contents. Plenty of coin and bullets, even several of the silver god-blood stars. But Chet hardly noticed; he was looking for one thing.

Shouting, men's voices, echoed up the hall.

"Where's the key?" Chet snapped.

Gavin grinned at him.

Chet slid over, pointed the blade right at Gavin's eye. "Where is it?"

Gavin didn't even blink.

"I said where is it? Where's the key?"

"Thought you told me to shut up?"

Chet sliced Gavin's ear off.

Gavin hardly flinched. "You think I'd be stupid enough to have it on me?"

"You got one more chance before I drive this knife into your skull!" Chet growled.

Gavin laughed, actually laughed. "You do and you'll never find the key. That's for damn sure."

"Where is it?" Chet demanded, hating the desperation in his own voice.

"I'm telling you it isn't here. But you get us out of here, and sure enough, I'll take you to the key."

*It's a trick.* Chet knew it; he also knew the man had him.

"You're running out of time," Gavin said, his voice cool, calm, making Chet want to smash him in the face.

The shouting was growing louder, coming down the hall.

"Okay," Chet snarled. "Hell, okay."

"Good. Now, you better get my guns and quick."

Chet shoved his knife back into his belt and snatched up one of the big revolvers off the floor.

Boots clumping—sounded like several men heading right for them.

"Down," Gavin hissed. "In the corner. Take the shadows. They'll be looking at the bodies."

Chet crouched into the corner. A second later two men barged into the room—one with a sword, the second a musket—and indeed, all eyes went to Gavin's decapitated body.

Chet fired, the recoil almost blowing the gun from his hand. He missed both men and had a second to wonder how he could've missed when they were only four feet away. Then the man with the musket fired, the slug catching Chet in the chest, slamming him into the wall. The other man rushed him.

Chet fired again, catching the forward man in the face, blowing off most of his head. Chet was astounded at the amount of carnage the gun made. The remaining man spun round for the door. Chet got off another shot but missed, hitting the top of the doorway. The man ran down the hall yelling.

"You shoot worse than a drunk on dope," Gavin said. "You sure you're a Moran?"

"Fuck you," Chet snapped. He tried to stand, but collapsed, the pain in his chest overpowering.

"Ignore the pain," Gavin said. "You gotta move."

Chet gritted his teeth, forcing himself to his knees.

"Fetch yourself a few ka coins."

Chet, clutching his chest, crawled over to where he'd emptied out the satchel, scooped up three coins, and shoved them into his mouth.

"Grab the gun belts and the bandolier. You're gonna have to shoot your way out of here."

Chet fumbled with the gun belt, the pain making him clumsily. He winced, clutched the wound again. His whole chest felt as though on fire.

"Stop dicking around, move."

Chet grimaced as he worked through the pain, gathering up the gun belt, bandolier, and other revolver, shoving them into the satchel.

"The ka coins," Gavin said. "The way you shoot you'll be needing plenty of those."

Chet raked the coins, along with everything else he'd dumped out, back into the satchel.

"Now put on my coat and hat. Disguise yourself. C'mon, kid, think."

Chet yanked off the coat, slipped it on, shoved the flat-brim hat down low onto his head. He then grabbed his grandfather by the hair, slung the satchel over his shoulder, and pushed to one knee. He sucked in a breath against the pain, stood up, and stumbled to the door—the big revolver in one hand, his grandfather's head in the other.

The hall ran both ways, but Chet couldn't see far due to the gun smoke and gloom.

"Head right," Gavin said.

No sooner did Chet step into the hall than he heard men coming.

"Move, kid."

Chet took off, running as fast as the pain in his chest would allow.

"That's him!" someone shouted and a shot rang out, the slug smacking the wall just in front of Chet.

"Shoot, boy," Gavin cried. "Let 'em know you got bite."

Chet shot blindly back into the smoke. It didn't stop them, but it certainly slowed them down.

He shoved past a few dazed souls as several more shots came his way. One of the slugs caught a woman in the side of the neck and she fell directly in front of Chet, forcing him to leap over her.

The hall curved slightly. Chet hit a few steps then headed down a long straightaway and felt the ka kicking in, felt the pain subsiding.

"The lanterns," Gavin cried. "Snatch 'em and throw 'em."

Lanterns hung about every fifty feet along the narrow hall, giving just enough illumination to see the ground in front of him. Chet snagged the next one he passed, hurled it behind him, the lantern shattering, the oil exploding into a ball of fire and black smoke.

Cursing and more musket fire came from behind, sending shards of stone bouncing off Chet's neck and cheek.

"There," Gavin said. "Take the steps down."

The hall split ahead, two sets of stairs, one leading up, the other down. Chet took the stairs down and found himself in a long cavernous tunnel with damp, dripping walls, the floor spotted with pools and puddles.

Another shot rang out behind him. Chet shot back, stopping the men in their tracks. He pulled the trigger again and the gun clicked on an empty chamber.

"Run, kid. Just run."

Chet did, knocking out every lantern he passed, throwing the tunnel into darkness behind him. Slowly, the sound of pursuit fell farther and farther behind. Chet hit a flight of stairs heading upward, then another, coming out into a large dark chamber. Four halls led out of the chamber.

"Which one?" Chet asked.

"Be still. Feel the air."

Chet froze and closed his eyes, at first feeling nothing, then a slight breeze from his right. He opened his eyes and dashed out by the right hall, the smell of night air growing as he ran.

The hall ended at an iron gate, an alley leading into the city just beyond. He grabbed the latch and yanked. It didn't budge, the latch held in place by an iron lock.

"Fuck," Chet growled, giving it several more hard yanks.

"They're coming," Gavin said.

Chet heard them too, not far behind. He glanced around, but saw no other way out.

"Load your guns, kid. You're gonna have to make a stand."

"No," Chet said. "There's another way." And this time it was Chet who sounded cool and calm. He shoved the gun under one arm and slid out Senoy's knife. He set the blade against the bolt, pressed down with a sawing motion. The blade cut right through, not as easily as flesh, but it did the job. The lock fell away.

"Well," Gavin said. "Good to see you got some sense."

Chet yanked open the gate and ran into the night.

# PART SIX

Gavin Moran

Chet gasped. The wound in his chest, though mostly healed now, still burned and throbbed. He stopped, bracing himself against a large boulder, and glanced back down the road. The lights of Lethe were now far behind them.

"Keep moving," Gavin said. Chet had bound his grandfather's head to the satchel so he could have both hands free, high up on the strap against his shoulder to give Gavin a good vantage point. "You need to keep moving."

Chet continued to stare at the city. It was Ana he was thinking of, her troubled eyes that there at the end had appeared to have finally found some solace. He tried telling himself there was nothing he could do for her, not now. But, what if there was? "I left someone back there."

"All your friends are dead or in the river. You go back and they'll catch you. That's a cold, hard fact."

*He's right,* Chet thought. *The river, it was right there behind her. Where else could she have gone? And it was what she wanted. Right?* Chet stood up, facing the city. *Maybe? Maybe not. I can tell myself whatever I want, but I know the truth. The truth is Ana is dead. I'm dead, Gavin is dead, Mary and all those infants back there, they're all dead, but Trish and my baby, they're alive. And if I want them to stay alive, I need to keep moving.* He took one long last look at the city, sucked in a deep breath, and headed away, pressing on as fast as he dared in the darkness. *Ana, God, I hope you find some peace.*

"Load your guns."

"I already did."

"Both guns. Where we're headed you're gonna want every chamber ready."

Chet thought about putting a bullet through his grandfather's head; instead he pulled the second revolver out, reloading it as he walked.

"We don't want to be caught out on the open road come daylight."

"I know, you already said that."

"The cutoff will take us a bit out of our way, but it's a road less traveled. Plenty of caves and cover. You can rest up a bit there."

Gavin had told Chet the key was hidden in some tomb on the outskirts of Styga, stashed away with a few other treasures he'd gathered over the years. Chet wasn't buying it. Senoy had made it clear the man wasn't to be trusted. Chet felt sure the key had to be somewhere among the man's belongings, that he'd just missed it somehow. He intended to find out one way or another once they were out of immediate danger.

A rumble echoed up behind them.

"Riders," Gavin said. "At least three. Get down."

Chet scrambled off the trail, sliding into the shadow of a large rock. A moment later three horses galloped past.

"Sure in a hurry," Gavin said. "Look to be Carlos's men."

It was hard to see much in the dark, but Chet thought Gavin was right. He stood and resumed his march. They left the trail shortly thereafter, heading down into a rocky ravine.

"I gotta stop," Chet said. "Just for a bit."

"All right. How about up there, beneath that ledge. Give us the drop on anyone wanting to sneak up on us."

Chet climbed the short knoll, found a cave, and crawled into it, collapsing on the sandy floor. He lay there, eyes closed, every bone and sinew in his body aching. The wind picked up outside, kicking the dirt around. A low howl whistled down the ravine and Chet hoped it was just the wind. His mind drifted to Trish and he was horrified to find that it was becoming more and more difficult to see her, that the longer he stayed here, in this purgatory, the more his time on earth seemed like a dream.

"Chet," Gavin said, a note in his voice that caused Chet to open his eyes. "Tell me about Cynthia, your mother. How did she . . . I mean . . . I thought she was dead. I thought they were all dead. What happened?"

Chet sat up, glaring at Gavin. "You murdered them. That's what happened. Tried to kill them all and now you're gonna pretend to give a shit?"

Gavin winced. "It's not like that. That's not what—"

"Look, asshole. I'm not here to ease your conscience or whatever it is you're after. I just need the key. If you can't give me the key then you can just go to Hell."

Gavin's eyes dropped to the dirt. After a long moment he spoke. "The key. What's the key to you?"

"I need it. Need it to save my wife, my daughter."

"*Daughter?* You have a daughter?" Then in a whisper. "*I have a great-granddaughter?*" His face hardened. "Save 'em from *what?*"

Chet didn't answerer.

"Talk to me, Chet. If you want the key, you're gonna have to talk to me. How's the key gonna help save your daughter?"

"I need the key to cross back."

"Cross back? You mean to earth above?"

"Yeah, 'cause you fucked up," Chet said. "You left Lamia alive. Now, if I can't get—"

"Lamia?" Gavin looked dumbstruck. "Chet, wait, nothing's making sense. Lamia is still alive? Still on earth above?"

"Yeah, she is. And she's got my Trish."

Gavin looked as though his whole world had been turned upside down. "Lamia?" he spat. "Goddamn the day I ever laid eyes on that witch. Tell me, Chet, what makes you think the key can take you back?"

Chet laughed, a vicious sound. "What kind of game are you playing? Y'know, Senoy warned me about you. Told me you'd be full of lies and tricks."

"Who's Senoy?"

"Stop playing dumb," Chet snapped. "I know what happened. He told me. Told me you stole the key from him. That you sold the souls of your own children."

Gavin clenched his eyes closed as though trying to shut out the world.

"Look," Chet said. "I'm not on some quest of vengeance. I don't give a good goddamn about you. I just want to save my wife. So here, I tell you what, you just get me to the key, and I swear I'll give you plenty of ka coin and let you go your way. How's that sound?"

"Senoy," Gavin said. "You're talking about the man with pitch black skin, with a gold ring about his head?' He eyed Chet. "Yeah, you are. So this Senoy, he sent you down here after me, right? To get the key?"

Chet didn't answer.

"Chet, Senoy . . . he's playing you."

"Yeah, funny you should say that, because Senoy said—"

"*Chet, dammit!*" Gavin shouted. "*I don't care what lies Senoy told you!*" He lowered his voice. "I'm not looking for sympathy or forgiveness, just a chance to set a few things to right. And . . . and . . . hell, to save my great-granddaughter. Now if you wanna save her too, then you need to listen to me. You need to hear the truth. Because your wife and your daughter, they're gonna die the worst kind of death if you don't." Gavin locked eyes with Chet, waited. After a moment Chet sucked in a breath. "Go on, I'm listening."

"I shot 'em. That's true. So let's just get that out of the way. I shot Lamia. I shot both of my boys. What you need to know now is *why* I shot 'em.

"I first laid eyes on Lamia on the border of Hungary. This was back in the war. My patrol wandered into a refugee camp and there she was about to be burned alive. Our eyes met and she had me, right then and there. I was under her spell. I freed her, threatening to shoot anyone who stood in my way. There was this old man, he begged me to leave her, said she was a witch, that she drank the blood of children. Christ-o-mighty, not a day don't go by without me wishing I'd listened to that man.

"Brought her home with me, to Moran Island. We had the boys, then Cynthia. I can't say I was a good man. I could blame the war, what it did to me, blame Lamia, but I think for the most part I was just drawn to trouble and if ever a soul deserved to be damned, it was mine. But when it came to my children, especially that little girl of mine, I did right. I *always* did right.

"Then came that night. That godforsaken night." Gavin paused, his eyes far away. "I heard her, y'know, as I pulled up in the drive, heard her from all the way out by the road. My daughter screaming. Chilled me to the bone. She was calling for me, calling 'Daddy,' over and over. I've never run so fast. Thought a bear or maybe a rabid dog had done got in the house. That's how bad them screams were. Pulled my pistol and rushed in. What I seen . . . well, nothing could've prepared me for that.

"They were in the den, a red quilt spread out on the floor. Lamia lay there, sweaty, naked, her face and hands covered in blood, her eyes closed, looking exhausted. A man I'd never seen before laid next to her, his skin slick and oily, black as pitch, a thin gold band sitting atop his head. He had blood smeared down his face, neck, and chest. Then I saw my boys, only they weren't my boys, their skin was covered in scales, and their eyes were just pits. They had something pinned down between 'em."

Gavin paused, his eyes wet. He cleared his throat. "It was Cynthia, my sweet little girl. Pale and still. I thought she was dead. All these years . . . I thought she was dead." He cleared his throat again, continued, his voice thick with emotion. "The knife, the one you have, it lay there beside her. You could see where they'd cut her, high on the inside of both her thighs. They'd marked her, using the blood to draw symbols on her flesh.

"Don't know how long I stood there. I remember I couldn't move, couldn't even breathe. One of my boys saw me, let out this ungodly howl, and I swear my mind just walked away. I shot him, shot him in the chest, then his brother, Davy. Lamia sat up and I shot her too, twice. Then that strange man, he opened his eyes and what I saw wasn't human. He tried to sit up, tried to speak, but he was in a state, hardly able to move. I put my last two bullets into his chest and still he stared at me with them eyes. My wife and my boys, the three of them fled, running from the room and out the back of the house . . . left me staring at that creature. I snatched up the knife, the one beside my poor Cynthia, the one you now possess, and I drove it into his heart. Killed him dead. Only, seems I didn't."

Gavin paused again, his face troubled. "I got my rifle and a lantern and went after Lamia. Things get a bit blurry after that, almost as though I wasn't even there, like part of me had already died. She was bleeding pretty bad and I tracked her down to the creek, down near the boy's play fort. She was there on her knees, scrawling something in the dirt with a red key—a square shape, full of strange symbols. I shot her in the head and just stood staring at the strange marks she'd made in the ground while her lifeblood pumped out of her.

"I heard 'em, my boys. They were in the fort. I couldn't bear to set eyes on 'em again. I was afraid I might get weak. So I set it on fire. Burned 'em. Burn my own sons to death." Gavin closed his eyes as though trying to block out a vision. "After that . . . all I wanted was an end, an end to the pain. I stuck the barrel of my rifle up under my chin and pulled the trigger."

He was quiet; the wind outside picked up. He opened his eyes. "Only, as I'm sure you now well know, one doesn't escape one's sins so easily. A lesson so many down here learn just a little too late. I found myself staring down at my body as the flames from my boy's playhouse licked the sky. I noticed an eerie sound emanating from where the key lay. I stooped and picked it up and when I did, that square, the one Lamia had drawn, it opened like a door upon the blackest blackness I'd ever seen.

"I heard howls coming from the swamp. The moon and the stars disappeared and I felt a fear like I'd never known. Felt sure Satan was coming for me. Coming to collect. I crawled away through that door. Crawled away from one nightmare and into another. Since that night all I've been trying to do is forget . . . until now, until you showed up."

Chet studied the man's face, listening to the distant thunder as he tried to see past the hard lines, searching for something to tell him if this man was telling the truth. "You should know," Chet said, "my mother died, she killed herself."

Gavin's mouth tightened and Chet saw pain, true pain, in the man's eyes. *Whatever he's up to,* Chet thought, *he cared for my mother. That much is real.*

"Lamia's demons," Chet said. "They drove her crazy. Drove her to do it."

"Chet, the revolver. Pick it up."

"What?"

"The gun. The one in my tote sack."

Chet frowned, looked at the satchel.

"Go on, pull it out."

Chet did, looking it over.

"Set your thumbnail into the screw there. Give it a twist."

Chet did, prying until it loosened up, then spun it out. The handle fell away and there in the cavity, a key, a red copper key.

"I'm not your enemy, Chet. I got no other way to prove it other than what's there in your hand. I want . . . what you want . . . to save your daughter and kill Lamia. That is all I want. Before you leave me here, think about that. Because if there's any chance at saving your daughter, it'll be a lot better if we work together."

# CHAPTER 76

**C**arlos rode into camp, the burnt bones of Veles's wagons casting long shadows in Mother Eye's first light.

"We made good time," the Colonel said.

Carlos nodded, glancing back at the riders and wagons trailing behind them, checking on the Red Lady. He found he couldn't stop looking at her, not because he feared she might attack or try to escape, there was no chance of that, not after what the shrapnel did to her, but for the simple fact that he still couldn't believe they'd taken her.

She lay in the back of a wagon, bound in chains, a steel pail clamped round her head, covering her face. The Colonel had done a brutal job on her, taking no chances, hacking off her wings and paws. There'd been a lot of blood and Carlos hadn't seen her moving or even breathing since, felt pretty sure she was gone. Veles lay next to her, and a few of the sisters, those bearing the mark of the damned, were in the wagon behind them. They'd taken the wagons from Horkos's own stockyard, along with more horses; could've taken anything they wanted. The little resistance they'd met from Horkos's guard had crumbled once they'd opened up on them with the muskets.

"Isn't that your friend?" the Colonel asked. "One of Kashaol's men?"

A hooded figure stood next to a black horse, waiting for them.

"Gar," Carlos called, unable to hide his surprise. "Hell, didn't think we'd be seeing you again. How about Lord Kashaol, how'd he fare?"

Gar didn't appear to hear him at first, staring at the Red Lady in disbelief; finally he spoke. "You *did* it. By Lord Lucifer, you *did* it."

"Yeah, we did," Carlos said. "Now you have to tell me, is Lord Kashaol still with us?"

"You knew then . . . about the attack?"

"Sure, we heard all the racket, then when we found Veles again . . . not hard to put two and two together."

Gar's eyes still hadn't left the Red Lady. "Lord Kashaol is still with us."

"Well, that's damn good to hear," Carlos said, and found he meant it, was glad to hear he still had an ally in Hell. He caught sight of the Colonel's face, saw the man didn't share his sentiment, and hoped he had the good sense not to say anything stupid.

Gar finally looked at them. "Lord Kashaol will be very pleased. He'd feared all was lost. Bring the bounty and meet us at Osiris's Mother in two days' time." And that's all he said, mounting up and riding away.

## CHAPTER 77

Chet sat upon the ledge watching Mother Eye slowly come to life, watching her copper glow light up the low-lying clouds and reveal the desolate landscape below. He caught a sound, faint, a moan, thought it was just the wind. The moans turned to wails and cries. It took him a moment to realize the sounds were coming from above and he noticed a cloud unlike any he'd seen before, crimson and rolling across the sky, almost boiling. He saw them then, the wispy shapes of men and women, tumbling, churning together, forming and unforming, a hundred, a thousand, a hundred thousand—such woe, such utter sorrow upon their faces. It rolled away, the moans fading, leaving him chilled to his core. He shuddered, wondered if these were the lost souls, the unfettered ba, wondered if Ana was up there. Ado? Johnny? Wondered if he was foolish to trust Gavin, if he too would soon find himself among their number, and if Trish and his daughter's last chance would be forever lost. He looked at the mark on his palm. *"Damned if I do, damned if I don't,"* he whispered, managed a grim smile at that, then headed back into the cave.

Gavin watched him as he gathered up the revolvers and satchel. Chet met and held his eyes. "You're coming with me," Chet said. "For now."

"Okay, that'll work."

Chet tied him to the satchel strap, slid it up over his shoulder, and crawled back out, stood staring down the ravine.

"Which way?"

"Toward the black stones."

Chet moved down the trail, the walls of the ravine growing steeper as he went, eventually leading into the canyon, with its slick, glassy walls of obsidian. The day rolled slowly along, Chet's long stride eating up the miles.

Gavin led them down one trail after another, always seeming to know the way. After trekking the better part of the day, Chet once again found himself hopelessly lost within the maze of sheer cliffs and towering boulders.

"How'd you do that?" Chet asked.

"What?"

"Remember which way to go?"

"I don't always. See them marks up there, at the rim of the canyon?"

"Yeah."

"Those are wind marks. The wind blows strongest on the through paths; that's where you'll find the deepest marks. If there're no marks, then the trail probably leads into a box canyon or dead end. The wind blows away from Mother Eye. Mother Eye is stationary, as are her moons, so as long as you note the direction of the wind and shadows, you shouldn't get lost. Make sense?"

"I think so."

"It's not foolproof, but it'll at least keep you from going in circles. To get to Styga we need to head downwind and stick to the main vein of the canyon, so just pay attention to the deepest wind marks."

Chet did pay attention and after a bit found he could predict, with some degree of accuracy, which path to take.

"Stop," Gavin said. "Into the shadows."

Chet slid behind a stone. "What is it?"

"Up on the crest, toward Mother Eye."

Chet caught sight of a mounted figure on a distant ledge.

"Might be a demon," Gavin said. "That's certainly a demon horse."

The figure disappeared back behind the cliff.

"Demons shouldn't be so far in," Gavin said. "Something's going on. Let's go."

Chet spotted another about a mile farther along. "Hey, look—"

"I know," Gavin said. "Don't let on you see them."

"Them?"

"They've been following us for the past half mile or so. I was hoping they'd let us be, but I don't think they're gonna. Keep an eye out for a spot to hole up in case you have to make a stand. High ground. A cave, or ledge. If you make it hard enough, then they just might ride on."

A gunshot rang out and the stone next to Chet's head shattered.

"Shit!" Chet cried, ducking down, trying to figure out which direction the shot came from.

"Get up!" Gavin cried. "Move!"

Chet stood and ran down the trail, spotted a drift of crumbly lava leading up to a ledge, and scrambled up. He slipped twice on loose stone, almost fell, but then topped a small rise and to his surprise came upon steps.

Another shot. It came from behind them.

Chet dashed up the steps; they led into the mouth of a small cave. The entrance was square, with a few crude figures chiseled into the obsidian on either side. A gunshot punched Chet in the upper arm and spun him, almost knocking him from the ledge. He dove over a pile of stones and into the cave, flattening himself behind the rocks as he snarled against the pain.

Several more shots hit the ceiling of the cave, sending shards of rock against Chet's back.

"There're at least four of 'em," Gavin said. "They're gonna start moving up on you unless you give 'em some lead."

Chet clutched his arm, the bullet had caught him up near the shoulder. He could still move it, but the pain was unbearable.

"Move!" Gavin shouted. "Shoot back, now!"

"Fuck, okay!" Chet cried, snatching out the revolver. He peered down through the rocks, spotted one of the demons moving up, and fired twice. No idea if he hit anything, but things quieted down.

"Okay," Gavin said. "Now get two ka coins."

Chet put the revolver down and reached for the satchel.

"Quick, kid. You wanna get out of this you need to move."

Chet pulled out two coins and shoved them into his mouth.

"Good, now, take your time, aim. The point is to actually hit something."

Chet snatched the revolver back up and inched forward, slowly lifting his head to peer down the ravine. Several blasts came from below, bullets slapping into the stones in front of him. "Shit!" Chet cried, ducking back down.

"Give me ka, Chet."

"What? No way."

"There's too many. At least six. More might be coming. You wanna get out of this with your hide then you're gonna have to give me some ka."

More shots rang out, closer now.

"They're moving up," Gavin said. "They're gonna have the high ground soon and then it's over. Now stop screwing around."

A shot hit the dirt beside Chet. He rolled away, spotted a demon on the ledge just across the ravine, and fired three shots back, then the trigger clicked on spent shells. He had no idea if he'd hit the demon or not, but Gavin was right, once they gained the high ground, he'd be easy pickings. Chet slid farther back into the shadows of the small cave, snatched the ammo belt out of the satchel, and started to reload.

"Chet, those are demons. They'll take both of us to Hell. Do you have any idea what that means?"

Chet met Gavin's eyes.

"I'm your blood," Gavin said.

"Dammit," Chet growled. He plucked out three coins, shoved them into Gavin's mouth, reloading the guns while Gavin chewed.

"More. Quick."

Chet gave him four more; already he could see the ghostly outline of Gavin's body on the dirt. Chet scooted back up, keeping to the shadows, peering down, waiting for a clear shot. He could hear them creeping up the embankment.

"Chet, here."

Chet glanced back, saw Gavin leaning against the back of the cave in front of a round relief set in the wall. He was nude, his flesh pale but solid. "Here." Gavin waved him over. Chet could see he was still gaining substance. "The key, quick."

"The key?"

Gavin laid his hand on the relief. It was as tall as he was, with crude runes circling its edge. "The key, *now*."

Chet had the key tied to his belt and stuck down in his pocket. He tugged it out and handed it to Gavin.

Gavin touched the key to the carved circle, tracing its outline, and the runes began to glow.

"What're you doing?"

"I think it's a door," Gavin said. The key finished the circle and there came a loud pop, the sound of cracking stone. The circle dislodged itself from the wall, falling inward, revealing an opening.

Gavin got to unsteady feet and slipped through.

Chet snatched up the satchel and followed to find himself in an immense chamber. Light spilled in from above, revealing a massive statue, some one-eyed beast, its broken form laying half-buried in rubble. Gavin was making his way down toward an opening at the base. Chet hurried along to catch him.

Gavin stopped before the opening. "More ka. Two more should do it."

Chet dug out two coins, handed them to Gavin. He realized that the ka had done its work on him as well, his arm now back in working order. Gavin was walking strong, his tall frame fleshed out into hard, wiry muscle.

Gavin tugged a few of the larger rocks from the opening, giving him enough room to crawl out. Chet followed. They came out upon a narrow ledge that led them back into the canyon.

"Down," Gavin whispered.

Chet ducked. Three demons were crawling along the ledge well ahead of them. The demons were closing in on the cave. Chet understood they'd managed to circle around behind them.

Gavin held out his hand. "Gun."

Chet handed him one of the revolvers and one of the ammo belts. Gavin draped the belt across his shoulder.

"They're carrying muskets," Gavin said in a hushed tone. "They gotta reload after each shot. The key is to draw their fire then attack while they're reloading."

Chet nodded.

"These look to be lower-caste demons, that means they're alive. Flesh and blood. They can be killed." Gavin finished checking the load and snapped his gun shut. "You're gonna run to that stone, gonna draw their fire. Once they shoot, I'm gonna attack. When I stop to reload, you keep their heads down. Got it?"

Chet nodded.

Gavin gave him a small smile. "Time to go to war."

Chet sucked in a deep breath, stood, and ran for the stone. The three demons let out a whoop and fired at him. The whole ravine echoed with howls. *God, how many are there?* Chet dove behind the bolder. Bullets flew from all directions, kicking up the dirt and stones. Then there came a pause, just as Gavin had said, as they reloaded.

Gavin stood then, came out from behind the rocks; he walked slow and steady right for the demons, like he was just out for a stroll. He raised his arm, calmly aimed, and fired. The first demon's head exploded. He fired again, taking down the second one as it struggled to reload. The third gave up on reloading and ran. Gavin blew out the back of its head.

"Holy shit," Chet said.

Two shots rang out from the ledge directly across from Gavin, one of the slugs catching Gavin in the side, knocking him into the ledge. Gavin pushed back to his feet, set eyes on the two demons. They had nowhere to hide. He fired, catching one in the gut, the other in the face.

A shot rang out below, a bullet punching into Gavin's gut.

Chet spotted at least four more demons taking cover.

Gavin staggered, then started downward, heading right for them. One poked its head out to fire, but Gavin fired first, catching it in the shoulder, knocking it backward. The demon screamed and Gavin fired again, this time catching it in the throat, almost taking its head off.

Gavin dropped to one knee, snapped open his gun, dumped the shells, and started plugging in fresh loads, his fingers flying over the weapon.

The demons stood to fire and Chet came out shooting, making them duck. He paced his shots, buying Gavin time to reload. The demons turned fire on Chet. "Steady," Chet growled between clenched teeth, trying to heed Gavin's example, trying to set aside his fear and focus on his aim. He caught one of them in the shoulder, then something hot thumped against his chest, knocking him backward and to the ground.

Chet let out a grunt, rolled behind a rock, clutching his chest as the pain overwhelmed him. "Up," he growled at himself, determined not to leave Gavin out in the open. He sat up, tried to raise his gun, but Gavin was already firing: three shots, and three demons fell. The last demon leapt up and ran. Gavin fired twice, the first shot missing, the second catching the demon in the lower back, sending it tumbling into the dirt.

Things quieted down after that, no more gunshots, just the moans of the wounded and dying.

Chet forced himself up onto his knees, tried to stand. *God, how does that man keep fighting with two bullet holes in him?* He pulled out another ka coin, shoved it in his mouth, made it to his feet, chewing as he stumbled his way down the hill.

He found his grandfather standing over one of the demons. Gavin was nude, covered in mud, two gaping wounds in his torso, his feet shredded by the jagged lava rocks, yet his only concern seemed to be the creature lying before him. "These are true demons. See their armor, their weapons . . . those belong to a lord of means. A lord in good standing with Lucifer. You never see their likes in these parts."

"Here," Chet said, handing Gavin two coins.

Gavin took them, handing one back. "Should conserve these. I think there's gonna be more trouble ahead." He spotted the wound in Chet's chest. "You done pretty good, kid."

Chet shook his head. "I'm still kicking."

"That's the goal."

The demons were of various shapes and sizes. Gavin walked over to one that appeared almost human, stripped it of its pants and boots, and tugged them on. He held the key out to Chet. "This is yours now."

Chet nodded, took it.

"Think I could have my coat and hat back?"

"What? Oh, yeah, sure." Chet stuck his gun in his belt, slid the long coat off. When he went to hand it over he found Gavin holding his revolver on him.

"Should never let your guard down on a man you can't trust," Gavin said.

Chet's mouth went dry.

A mischievous grin crawled across Gavin's face. "I'm gonna take it that means you trust me." The grin turned to a smile, a warm genuine smile. He spun the gun around, handle out. "Here, hold this for me while I put my coat on. If you don't mind, that is."

"Fuck you," Chet said, taking the gun, but he was smiling too. He didn't know if the man before him was the murdering bastard Senoy painted him to be or not; what he did know was at this moment he was sharing a genuine smile with his grandfather after killing more than a dozen demons together, and it felt good, damn good.

## CHAPTER 78

They walked along at a rapid clip, two lean men who could easily be mistaken for brothers, their long legs eating up the trail. Mother Eye was just starting to wane, her amber glow glittering off the sheer obsidian cliffs.

Gavin slowed, glanced behind, then forward. "Not much cover along this next stretch, so keep a keen eye out." Chet nodded as they entered the narrow passage, the towering cliffs hemming them in on either side.

"Gavin, the door. The one back at the cave. How'd you know how to open it?"

"I didn't. The key did. It's never failed to open any door or lock. I've found by running the thing around doors, or just touching locks, the key finds its own way. Though it did me little good when I was enslaved by Nergal, on account that I was bound by a rope through my ribs, here," he touched his chest. "There was nothing to unlock."

"Through your bones?"

"Yeah. That was when I met the Colonel. When he raided the camp and set the slaves free. I still had the key though, had it hid inside my own flesh the whole time, shoved up into my arm here." He pushed up his sleeve, revealing a scar on the underside of his arm.

"The key has certainly come in handy over the years, allowing me to get into places no other soul ever could . . . even into the temples of the gods. Had it all this time with no idea it could take me back across. Not sure I would've even if I did. I believe, in the right hands, it can *make* doors as well. Lamia created one when she was trying to escape, the one I crossed over through. But as you know, she's some kind of witch creature. After thinking about what you told me, I think Lamia must've stolen it from that demon, Senoy. That it's some sort of talisman, somehow channeling their sorcery."

"Senoy said he's an angel."

Gavin grunted.

"Veles and Yevabog seem to think so as well."

"Angel. Demon. What's the difference? These demon lords, the Fallen, they were all angels once. What does that tell you?"

"Senoy said if he can just get the key back he can stop Lamia . . . save Trish. You think there's any truth to that?"

"Chet, all I know about this Senoy is that he had your mother's blood running down his face. That both him and Lamia did. They were drinking my little girl's soul. Makes them no different than any of these other gods to me. They're all vampires and soulsuckers. So you need to just keep that in mind."

Chet fell quiet, wondering where it all left him. Who could he trust? He knew so little about this man he was walking with. "Is that why you hunt them? The gods. Is it some sort of vengeance thing for you?"

"Maybe once. In the beginning. At least I think that's what I was after . . . searching for something to set my rage, my hate on. Killing seemed to serve that purpose. Took me a while to realize that it was myself I really hated. So, of late, I've mostly been working on that . . . on killing myself. Not sure why it's taking so long. Maybe at the end of it all I'm just a coward. What I hope is that somehow . . . I was meant to hang on. To be here when you came along . . . to help you."

They walked in silence for a while.

"It's not like it seems," Gavin said. "Nothing ever is."

Chet wasn't sure what he was talking about.

"The killing. It started out good. The Colonel lost his way, that's all. Got tangled up with that jackass, Carlos . . . and those demons. In the beginning he did a lot of good. Raiding gods, freeing slaves, hunting down flesh traders and soul hunters." Gavin laughed. "It's kinda funny when you think on it. I mean the man just wants to make purgatory a kinder, more civilized place for us souls. Imagine that, purgatory, a swell place to live. Bring your wife, bring the whole family. Stay for eternity."

Chet shook his head. It was all too much; he wanted a little time to sort things out.

"Chet, your mother. You said she died. What was her life like?"

"I hardly knew her. She died when I was only—"

Gavin held up his hand, silencing Chet. "Someone's coming."

They pressed up against the stone, peering back up the long corridor from where they'd come.

Chet heard it then, tromping, heading their way.

A moment later a host of figures marched out of the distant haze, and behind them, creatures on horseback.

"Shit," Gavin said. "Looks like an entire regiment. Why, they're even carrying banners. Oh, you gotta be kidding . . . that's a *demon lord*."

Chet caught sight of a tall figure on horseback in the lead. The figure was engulfed in a flaming aura. A chill, a crippling terror spread through Chet. Was this the *Burning Man* Billy and Davy had taunted him with? Was this devil going to drag him to Hell after all, after all he'd been through?

Gavin slapped Chet on the shoulder. "We need to move."

Chet took one last fearful glance at the demon and followed Gavin as he sprinted away.

# CHAPTER 79

*Y*ou *need a name, little one,"* Trish whispered to the baby as she suckled at her breast. *"How about Amy? After my grandma."*

The curtains were drawn back and sunlight filtered through the slats. Jerome had come in a few days ago and fixed the broken pane, hammering a square of plywood in its place. The door stood open and Trish could hear a scratchy phonograph playing upstairs—an old jazzy tune. A tray sat next to her with tangerine peels and grape stems. She'd meant to only eat a few of the fruits, but they were so sweet and juicy she'd ended up eating them all and wondered at the witchcraft used to grow them, especially this time of year.

Lamia's voice drifted through the house as she sang along to the record. She sounded vibrant, happy. Trish tried not to hear her, tried to pretend there was no one else in the world but her and her daughter. She combed her fingers through the baby's soft hair, noticed a bit of grime on the child's stomach, just below her navel. She tried to wipe it away only to realize it wasn't grime, or a stain, but a marking—a strange scribble. She found another below it and looked for more, saw two marks high on the inside of Amy's leg and let out a gasp. These weren't marks, but wounds, tiny punctures. "Oh, dear God."

Trish slid out of bed and carried Amy over to the window. Jerome was loading up the station wagon—the one she and Chet had stolen—with a few old suitcases, a trunk, and several baskets of Lamia's plants.

It was obvious to Trish that Lamia meant to take the child and leave. But when, to where? Did Lamia plan to take her along as well? Or just to kill her? One way or another, Trish felt sure she wouldn't be around long.

Trish had watched Chet hotwire the station wagon, felt confident she knew which wires to touch together to get it running. She just needed to get herself and Amy out there. Trish turned around and started. Lamia was standing in the doorway looking at the platter of fruit.

"I'm glad to see you're eating," Lamia said and smiled. "Fresh fruit will do both mother and child good." The old woman appeared healthy, almost radiant. She walked over and peered out upon the station wagon. "Have you ever been to Brazil?"

Trish didn't answer.

"I've read about the jungles down there . . . the people who live in them. I believe there's a place for me there." Her eyes went to the child. Trish saw longing, but not that of a mother, something else—almost a hunger. Lamia reached for the baby and Trish pulled back.

A dark look flashed across Lamia's face.

"I don't want you touching her," Trish said.

Lamia cocked her head.

"The marks. These." Trish pointed to the tiny wounds. "What did you do to her?"

Lamia shrugged. "It's where I drink." And the way she said it, as though nothing could be more natural, sent a chill straight to Trish's heart.

# CHAPTER 80

Gavin came upon a narrow ravine splitting off from the main corridor and stopped. He walked in several yards and came back out shaking his head. "Dead end." He slapped the slick black stone, searching the tops of the towering obsidian cliffs, then looked at Chet. "We can't climb out of here, and there's no hiding. That's a demon lord heading our way. If he gets much closer he'll smell us if he hasn't already. This canyon will take us to Osiris's Mother . . . maybe two more miles. Plenty of paths there. We just have to beat 'em there."

"Make a door," Chet said. "Just make another one of them doors with the key."

"I can't. Don't know how."

"But . . . back in the cave."

"That door was already there."

They continued down the canyon at a steady run. After about two miles Gavin halted.

"Almost there," Gavin said, but Chet could tell by his face something was wrong.

"What now?" Chet asked, trying to catch his breath.

"Hear that? Sounds like men ahead . . . or maybe more demons."

"Ahead. Oh, that's just perfect." Chet could see the towering cliffs opening up: the canyon was at an end. He glanced back, saw no sign of the demons, but knew they couldn't be far behind.

The two men pressed forward, rounding the bend and peering over a massive shard of obsidian.

Chet saw the towering iron statue, realized he was back where he'd first seen the demons, then he saw the soldiers. "It's *them*. Your friends." Wagons, horses, and soldiers wearing red scarves and green coats were spread out among the ruins—at least two hundred marauders, maybe more.

"They're not my friends," Gavin said. "Those men there, the ones in green, they want me dead. So understand me when I say this, Chet. They are *not* my friends. We're gonna have to try and get past 'em without being seen."

Chet wondered how they were gonna do that. The canyon corridor emptied directly into the ruins with nothing but sheer cliffs on either side. Once they stepped out from the bend, they'd be right out in the open. He could see plains beyond—mountains, clusters of boulders, monoliths, a thousand places to get lost in—but they might as well have been on the moon, because the only way to get to them was through the marauders.

Sounds echoed down the corridor behind them. *There's no way out of this,* Chet thought. He could see Gavin felt the same, his face sullen, grave.

"I got an idea," Gavin said, pulling Chet back around the bend. "Here, hand me your knife."

"My knife. What?"

"Quick. We don't have much time."

Chet slipped it out and handed it to Gavin. Gavin pointed to the rubble behind Chet. "We can use that brick there."

Chet looked about, didn't see a brick, but felt his gun leave his holster. He spun back around, and Gavin drove an elbow into his chest, knocking him to the ground. The man fell on him, pinning him beneath his knees, pressing Chet's face down in the dirt. He set the knife to Chet's neck. "I don't wanna cut your head off, but if you struggle I sure as hell will."

"Gavin, what . . . *why?*" But Chet already knew, already guessed. He'd been played, been played the whole time. Senoy was right. "You're a bastard. A fucking bastard!"

"Yup, that I am," Gavin said. He yanked the rope from the satchel, tied it around Chet, binding his arms to his side. That done, he cut off Chet's sleeve and wrapped it tightly around Chet's mouth. There came a moment of searing pain, first on his right wrist, then his left. Chet cried out against the gag, realizing the man had just cut off his hands. He struggled, but Gavin held him, stripped him of his gun belt, then took the key back.

Gavin stood, sliding the satchel over his shoulder, then yanked Chet to his feet, gave him a shove toward the camp, half-carrying, half-dragging him along. "Sorry about this. Really am. I was pulling for you. I just can't go to Hell. Not for you, not for nobody."

Heads turned, one by one, all staring at the tall man and the kid he was dragging along.

Chet spotted Carlos, his dark eyes on Gavin, his thick brows cinched together. Carlos summoned several armed men, four of them, all carrying muskets. They stood waiting as Gavin drew near.

"That's far enough," Carlos said. "You care to tell me where you've been?"

"No, I don't."

Carlos's mouth tightened. "This isn't a game. You got about two seconds—"

"Gavin!" someone shouted, a man wearing a Confederate officer's jacket.

Gavin kicked the knees out from behind Chet, knocking him to the dirt. "Brought you something, Colonel."

The Colonel walked up to Gavin, slapped him on the arm. "Damn good to see you. Thought we'd lost you for good this time." His eyes fell on Chet. "Well, I'll be. That's him, ain't it?" He turned to Carlos. "That's him, right?"

Carlos nodded.

"Well how'd you like them beans?" He let out a laugh. "Told you Gavin's your man. How'd you ever catch the son of a bitch?"

"Saw him fleeing the ambush," Gavin said. "Back at the temple. Carlos's right, he's not what he seems. A witch, a hoodoo man maybe, not sure. Just know he's slippery. I tracked him all the way into the canyons. He knows a few tricks, did some funny business, some sorcery. About got the best of me."

The Colonel gave Chet a wary look.

"Hasn't given me any more trouble," Gavin said. "Not since I cut his hands off."

Carlos didn't appear to be buying any of it, but the Colonel nodded. "Don't wanna be taking any chances with a spookman. Why don't you put him with the others. We got 'em tied up over there, in the circus wagons."

Gavin nodded, hefting Chet to his feet.

"Hold up," Carlos said. "The kid had a knife on him. A special kinda knife, might even be a demon blade. You happen to find it?"

Gavin ignored him, pushing Chet forward.

Carlos stepped in the way. "Hey, I asked you a question."

Gavin let out a sigh, one that sounded like he was running short on patience. "I didn't find a knife."

"How about I take a peek in that bag of yours then."

"If I didn't know better, I'd think you were calling me out."

"You can think what you like, but I'm going to have a look in that bag."

Gavin's hand dropped to the handle of his revolver, a small, dangerous smile touching his lips.

"Whoa!" the Colonel called. "Whoa, now. Everybody hold up. Christ, what the hell is wrong with you two? Can we just take things down a notch?"

"Hey, boss," one of the men said. "Looks like we got company."

Carlos, the Colonel, all of them looked toward the pass, to where a line of figures came marching around the bend.

## CHAPTER 81

Carlos stared at the approaching horde, at their banners, their weapons and armor, trying to make sense of what he was seeing. *Those are demons. Yes, certainly demons. But that's not Lord Kashaol. It can't be.* Whoever they were, Carlos couldn't believe they could be so brazen—demons, an entire regiment, here, in the middle of the river realms.

"What are they doing here?" the Colonel asked, not hiding his irritation. "Carlos, I thought I'd made it clear we were to meet Kashaol in the canyon, away from the men. Goddamnit, the last thing I need is the men to see me dealing with—"

"That's not Lord Kashaol, Colonel."

"What? What did you say?"

"I said I don't know who that is."

The Colonel squinted at the approaching troops. "Ah, Christ, what's going on?"

Carlos wished he knew. He did know that they were at a serious tactical disadvantage, that these appeared to be real demons, possibly an elite regiment, well armored and well armed—he saw plenty of muskets among the spears and swords.

The Colonel spun about, snapping out orders. Men began gathering arms and forming up into ranks along the edge of the ruins. Carlos could hear the alarm in their voices, feel the tension.

A single rider spurred forward, rode up to Carlos and the Colonel.

"Hail, Carlos." It was Gar, a mischievous grin on his face.

"Where's Lord Kashaol?" Carlos asked.

Gar's grin widened. "That worm is where he belongs . . . cooking in the pits."

It took Carlos a moment to get the gist of that, found himself at a loss for words.

Gar turned, swept his hand toward the horde. "This is Lord Beelbeth. He's traveled far to see you. I have informed him what a steadfast and dependable servant you have been. He is looking forward to having you in his service. Now come and meet your new lord."

*Servant?* Carlos thought, the word catching him like a fist to the stomach. *Servant?* He looked again at the horde, at the hungry red eyes, and couldn't suppress the chill running up his spine.

## CHAPTER 82

Three of Carlos's Defenders escorted Gavin and Chet over to two large wagons sitting end to end—cage wagons, the ones Veles used to house his animals. Iron bars lined three sides of the wagons, the back being planks. Chet saw the crumbled form of the Red Lady as they passed the first one. She lay on her side in a pool of her own blood. Great gaping wounds covered her body, raw gashes where they'd hacked off her wings and paws. Her face was covered in a mask constructed of a steel pail wrapped in wire and chains. He saw no signs of life.

They halted before the adjoining wagon.

"Open it up, Bill," the Defender said, addressing one of the two guards standing watch. "We got one more."

Bill wasn't paying them any attention, staring instead at the horde of demons, his mouth ajar.

"Hey," the Defender said, nudging Bill. "Open the damn door."

"What's going on?" Bill asked. "What are all them demons doing here?"

"Hell if I know. Now open the door. We have to get back and quick."

Bill fumbled a ring of keys from his pocket and opened the door, his eyes hardly leaving the demons. "I don't like it," he said. "Not one bit."

"Yeah, well I'm not so keen on it either," the Defender said as he reached for Chet.

"No," Gavin said. "I'll take care of it."

"Suit yourself," the man said.

Gavin pushed Chet up the steps and into the wagon.

Veles lay bound to the bars at the far end, his body riddled with wounds, his hands cleft from his wrist, his face wrapped in blood-soaked sackcloth, one eye glaring out at Gavin. Lying beside Veles was Yevabog, all six of her arms hacked away. She glanced up at Chet and the sadness on her face deepened. Mary sat next to Yevabog, bound and gagged, her leg obviously broken, but at least they hadn't cut off her hands or otherwise mutilated her. Chet didn't know whether to be glad to see her or not. She'd survived the battle, but for what? He saw no fight left in her or any of them. They were all going to Hell and they knew it.

Gavin shoved Chet down between Mary and Yevabog and glanced over his shoulder at the guards. The guards' attention remained fixed on the demon horde. Gavin yanked Mary's gag down, shoved three ka coins into her mouth, then pulled the gag back into place. He did the same to Chet. He slid out the knife and snipped both their bonds, then pushed something into Mary's hands. "God-blood," Gavin whispered to both of them. "You know what to do."

Gavin shoved one of the revolvers into Chet's belt, laid the knife against the wall behind him. "Chet, when the fireworks start, look for me. I'll have two horses. Remember, nothing matters now, but getting out of here and saving your daughter. Got it?"

Chet was too stunned to even nod. By the time he did, Gavin had left the wagon, pushing the door shut and locking it.

The Defenders were gone; only the two guards remained.

"It's locked up," Gavin said.

Bill tore his eyes away from the horde just long enough to see that the door was indeed closed and locked.

"I'd find some good cover if I was you," Gavin said.

"What? What d'you mean?"

"I mean, I hear there's a fight a-brewing and I don't think it's a real good idea to be standing right out in the open when it starts. Did you see all the muskets them boys is carrying?"

The two guards exchanged anxious looks.

"Shit," Gavin continued. "I don't know about you two, but I didn't sign up for no demon fighting. Least not an entire army of them anyhow. Matter of fact, I'm starting to think it might not be such a bad idea to get the heck out of Dodge altogether."

"You thinking about leaving?"

Gavin shrugged and headed away.

"What d' we do?" Bill asked the other guard.

"I didn't sign up for this sorta shit either."

"We can't just leave."

Apparently the man felt otherwise and headed away, disappearing into the ruins, and a moment later, Bill followed suit.

As soon as they left Mary pushed one of the silver stars into Yevabog's mouth, then slid over and started working to free Veles from the chains and sackcloth around his head, neck, and mouth.

The god-blood's effect was immediate on Yevabog. The ghostly forms of her arms bloomed, shimmering as they took form and solidified. Chet's own hands formed as well. He grabbed for the knife but his hands were still numb and it slid through his grasp. He tried again, slower, got a grip, and scooted over to where Mary was struggling with the chain about Veles's mouth. Chet pressed the blade against the metal, a gentle sawing motion. The knife cut right through and the chain fell away.

Mary pushed a star into Veles's mangled mouth, crumbling the star in order to get it down the god's mutilated throat.

Veles's eyes blazed to life.

Chet's hands regained their feeling and grip. He took the knife to the lock and had the door open in a few seconds. He hopped down, stepping over to the second wagon, the one housing the Red Lady, grabbed hold of the lock.

"What are you doing?" someone called.

Chet turned, saw a Defender walking rapidly toward him with a musket aimed at his head.

# CHAPTER 83

The Colonel and Carlos followed Gar toward the line of demons.

"Look at the bastards," the Colonel growled. "A whole slew of 'em, parading in here like they own the goddamn place." The man's blood was up; it was in his voice and on his face. Carlos knew it took a lot to set him off, but also knew that once you did, he didn't tend to back down and that's what had him worried. "I thought they couldn't come here," the Colonel continued. "Not like this, not a whole army of 'em."

"They can't. It's forbidden."

"Well, someone sure as shit forgot to tell this ugly cur."

"Listen to me, Colonel," Carlos said. "We don't know what's going on yet. You're going to have to keep yourself in check. You hear me? This is not the time or place for a confrontation."

"They shouldn't be here. That's all I know."

"But they are here. And in case you haven't noticed, they got us out-manned and outgunned."

The Colonel spat. "Son of a whore. Sure like to know how this happened."

"Just let me do the talking. You have to promise me you'll let me do the talking."

The Colonel didn't answer, just kept stomping forward.

Gar halted before the line. The forward ranks parted and a figure on a massive war steed sauntered forward escorted by six guards. The

427

guards were huge brutes, as tall as the steed, looking as though they could easily tear a soul asunder with just their bare hands. They glared at Carlos and the Colonel as flame drizzled from their snouts, sizzling as it hit the sand.

Carlos waited for the lord to dismount, but he remained seated, looking down upon them from his steed. Unlike Lord Kashaol, this figure was tall and straight, an androgynous face with high, prominent cheekbones, pale skin, and pink lips and eyes. Two great horns curved out from a jagged triangular headpiece. But what was most odd was that the creature's head and hands were not attached to its body, but floated in place as though by unseen bones. The lord was dressed for battle, wearing serrated armor plate atop chain mail—the mail looking more like the scales of some giant lizard than metal, and the plate craggy as though grown from the ground.

"Lord Beelbeth," Gar said. "These are the souls of which I spoke." He gestured to each man in turn. "Carlos. And this one here, the Colonel . . . the leader of the troops."

Lord Beelbeth stared at them, obviously waiting for something.

"Excuse their manners, my Lord." Gar turned toward the men. "It is customary to bow when introduced to his Lordship."

Carlos felt a sinking feeling, a growing certainty that this creature wasn't here seeking an alliance, but only to stake its claim. Carlos made a slight bow; the Colonel did not.

The demons continued to spread out, encircling the ruins. Carlos could see he'd miscalculated their number; there were even more than he'd first thought.

"What's all this about?" the Colonel asked.

"You will not address the Lord unless spoken to," Gar hissed.

Lord Beelbeth raised a hand. "We will not bother with formalities today, Gar." The demon lord's voice was loud and deep, crackling like a worn out horn. "I am here to welcome these men into my service." He managed a ghost of a smile. "I smell your fear, gentlemen, but I assure you it is unwarranted. Nothing has changed . . . only now you serve me, instead of the traitor Kashaol."

"Serve?" the Colonel said. "We don't *serve* anyone. We're free men. That's what this whole campaign's been about."

The demon's smile faded. "These are my lands now." He spoke with a tone of absolute authority, the vaporous aura of flame atop his head flaring when he spoke, sending small sparks fluttering skyward. "Any who wish to remain . . . serve me."

"What?" the Colonel said, shaking his head. "No, that's not how this is gonna go."

Lord Beelbeth's eyes flared; Carlos actually felt their heat and grabbed the Colonel, tugged him aside, pressing into the man's face. "*Stop it!*" he hissed. "He's about to turn us both into ash. Now stop it."

The Colonel glared at Carlos, then the demon lord, then turned and headed back toward the ruins.

*Ah, shit,* Carlos thought, desperately wanting time to consider his options, needing to find out what his options even were. "Forgive the Colonel's outburst, but . . . I hope you understand that this is all a bit of a turn. I mean . . . things were different with Lord Kashaol. The deal was supposed to—"

"Bring her to me."

"What?"

"The Red Lady. I would see her. Bring her here . . . to my feet."

Carlos nodded. That would certainly buy him some time, a chance to flee if need be. "Okay . . . yeah, sure . . . I'll have the men pull her round." The demons, all their eyes, those burning eyes were on him. "Please excuse me." Carlos bowed, then bowed again as he back away. He turned, double-timing it to catch up with the Colonel.

"Did you hear what he said?" the Colonel asked. "Serve him? Well I for one will die before bending a knee to that bastard. Let me tell you."

Carlos nodded along, thought, *Yeah, that just might do the trick.* Thinking how the Colonel had about worn out his usefulness anyhow. He wondered if there was a way he could play this to his advantage, actually turn the Colonel over, make a show of it. Claim he was planning to attack or some such.

They walked back into the ruins, passing through the ranks of men, questions coming from every direction. The men wanted to know what was going on, what the plan was; their nervous, fearful eyes locked on the ever-spreading line of demons.

"Dammit, Carlos," the Colonel spat. "I knew these demons would lead to trouble. Goddamn knew it."

"Is that so?" Carlos shot back. "Strange, I don't recall having to twist—" Carlos spotted Gavin leading two horses away from the line. "Well, look there. It appears your most stalwart soldier is running away." And despite the demons at his door, Carlos found himself taking the deepest satisfaction in pointing this out. "Why, I believe he's deserting you, Colonel."

The Colonel halted in his tracks but his eyes weren't on Gavin: they were on the man lying on the ground in front of the wagons, his head a smoldering mass. The wagon was empty, the door open.

Veles walked around the side of the wagon, staring at them, the golden corona hovering behind his great antlers so bright they had to shield their eyes. He wore a smile, a most terrible smile.

"No!" Carlos cried, fumbling for his revolver. "Oh, no!"

Veles rubbed his fingers together and the Colonel let out a horrific scream as his head burst into flames. Carlos's head began to heat up, to smolder, then burn. He let out his own scream, turned, and fled.

## CHAPTER 84

Chet cut through the last chain and yanked the pail from the Red Lady's face. Her lids were half-open on lifeless eyes. He felt certain she was dead, but as men all around them began to go up in flames, as their shouting and screaming grew, the faintest glow came into her eyes.

Mary leapt up next to Chet. She held one of the stars for the Red Lady to see. "Sekhmet, it's god-blood, take it." The sphinx made no response. Mary pressed the star into the sphinx's mouth.

The Red Lady began to chew.

Mary pushed in another star. "That's all I have."

The Red Lady let out a groan and Chet felt a wave, like a blast of air, pulse outward from her body and push through him. He started backing away, when another pulse came, so strong as to distort the air and knock both him and Mary against the bars. He grabbed Mary and together they leapt from the wagon.

The ghostly outlines of the sphinx's wings and large paws bloomed. She let out a low howl as they gained weight and substance. Fur and feathers sprouted and the large wounds riddling her body closed, disappearing.

The screaming continued as Veles stomped toward the line of men, his arms extended, fingers twirling, setting any who stood before him to flame. He was met by sporadic musket fire, but the rounds only bounced off his fur and the blue aura surrounding him.

Chet caught sight of Yevabog; she'd obtained two knives, and was darting here and there among the souls, cutting them down as she scuttled past, her eyes full of fever. She looked almost gleeful in her fury.

The men began to break and run.

There came a terrific cry, a sound that rang around the ruins and bit into Chet's very bones. It came from the mouth of the canyon, followed by horns and bells. Howls and shouts roared up and down the line of demons and the horde charged, the ground rumbling beneath their boots and hooves as they headed toward the ruins. At their helm was a tall figure upon a powerful warhorse, its purple cape flapping in the wind. The creature pulled a great sword from its sheath, raised it above its head, and set its sights on Veles. Chet caught the golden glint of the blade, knew it was Heaven forged like his knife.

The Red Lady rolled into a sitting position, hunched over in the narrow confines of the wagon, her wings pressed tightly about her. She snarled and shoved to her feet, thrusting her wings upward, bursting through the planks and busting from the wagon. Mary and Chet ducked down as planks and splinters flew through the air.

And there she stood, the great Red Lady, surveying the fleeing men, the ruins, and finally the attacking horde. They were almost to the walls. The sphinx raised up tall upon her hind legs, her wings spread wide, her great mane gusting like a flame in a gale. Her eyes landed on the warlord and she let out a roar, a roar that shook the very ground.

The mass of demons faltered, toppling and falling over one another as they stumbled and staggered to a halt, all fixed upon the fearsome sphinx towering before them—her emerald eyes ablaze.

And there came a moment, as the Red Lady locked eyes with the warlord across the scattered ruins, when all seemed frozen, when the very air felt ready to ignite.

## CHAPTER 85

Carlos stumbled along, struggling to reach Veles's master wagon, his head smoldering, the smoke and pain blinding him as he fought against the tide of fleeing soldiers.

He found the wagon unguarded and unmanned. He climbed the steps, collapsing into Veles's chamber. He saw the god-slaying spear, but that wasn't what he was after, crawling instead over to a chest, yanking it open. He pulled the blunderbuss out from the velvet, dug about until he found the powder and shot. They'd managed to gather enough of the shrapnel from the first blast to create a second shot. Though not as large, he felt sure it would be all he needed to kill Veles. He stuffed the cannon, loaded the shot, and stumbled back down the steps.

The flames were out on his head, but still the burning persisted, his flesh continuing to broil and blister as he searched for Veles. *"Fuck!"* he screamed, trying not to succumb to the pain. He heard a roar, couldn't tell from where as his ears were full of crackling cinders. He stepped over burning husks, dodged screaming men—souls fully engulfed in flame— and guessed he must be heading in the right direction.

Another roar, this one he couldn't miss. He turned, saw the Red Lady far down by the wagons, standing up on her hind legs. She leapt forward, charging out toward the edge of the ruins, toward the demons.

He took a step after her, collapsed, and realized he was too far gone to ever catch her. *No,* he thought, *it's not her I want. It's not Veles. It's him. It's that little fucker . . . that Chet.* And now, sitting there, slowly burning to death, it was all clear, so painfully clear. The boy, just like Gavin had said, was some sort of magic man—a god, a demon. Who knew? What he did know was that each time the kid showed up things went bad. *He fucked this up. He's fucked everything up.*

Carlos pushed himself back up to his feet, stumbled down the alley, heading back to the last place he'd seen the boy, back to the animal wagons.

## CHAPTER 86

The Red Lady charged through the ruins, trampling any souls unfortunate enough to be in her path. She roared and sprang, a magnificent leap of over fifty yards, coming down like a meteor, smashing into the forward line of demons.

Chet watched, captivated as the sphinx tore into the demons, smashing, stomping, slashing. The feathers of her wings were like sword blades as she spun, cutting them down by the dozens, her tail like a whip, carving out great swaths, sending limbs and bodies flying through the air. Their weapons were useless against her, the blades and musket fire bouncing off her feathers and hide.

Over all the chaos, a voice rang out. *"KILL HER!"* It was the one atop the great steed, the demon lord. Its voice cut Chet to the bone. *"KILL HER!"* it shrieked, compelling its soldiers onward. The huge demons closest to it lumbered forward, bearing great axes and mallets. The Red Lady spun on them, slashing, all teeth and claws, and when she did, the demon lord attacked, riding up fast from behind.

*"Look out!"* Chet screamed even though she was too far to hear. Something warned her though, for at the last moment she spun, but not fast enough.

The demon lord swung its great sword. The angel blade caught her wing, slicing through it, cutting the limb off just above her shoulder.

She snarled and snapped her tail, knocking the lord from its steed. The steed, a fearsome beast in its own right and nearly as large as the Red Lady, leapt upon the sphinx. The Red Lady caught the horse's head between her huge paws, tugging it down, twisting and tearing its neck from its torso. She pushed past the floundering body and rushed the lord, catching him with a mighty swipe of her paw just as he was getting to his feet, flipping him through the air.

The demon lord crashed into a wall at the edge of the ruins, knocking the wall over and sending stones tumbling in all directions.

"Chet, now. Let's go!" It was Gavin, coming up from behind the wagons, leading two horses.

The Red Lady charged the lord with a roar, leaping high and coming down upon him with her full might, thrashing and tearing. The ruins blocked his view, but Chet saw parts of the demon lord go sailing through the air.

Gavin grabbed Chet. "C'mon!"

Chet set eyes on Gavin. "You're a bastard."

Gavin appeared taken back, then understanding came to his face. "Chet, I had to bring you in that way. Nothing else would've worked. Here." He handed Chet one of his revolvers. "You can shoot me if you want, or we can go save that little girl of yours."

Chet looked at the big gun, thought about it, truly thought about putting a bullet in the man's head, but he didn't because he knew that Gavin was right, knew they'd both be on their way to Hell right now if he hadn't brought him in the way he did.

"*Fuckers!*" came a throat-tearing shriek.

Gavin and Chet turned to see a man, a man whose head was little more than a blackened cinder, stumbling toward them. Chet didn't recognize him, but he did recognize the big brass scorpion belt buckle. "Carlos!"

Carlos brought the blunderbuss to bear, pointing it right at Chet.

"*Down!*" Gavin cried, diving into Chet, knocking him from his feet.

There came a concussive blast as the cannon went off. Chet felt heat tear into his legs and back as he hit the ground. He rolled up, squinting through the smoke. Carlos was on his butt, staring at them. "*Die, you fuckers! Die!*"

Chet still had the revolver clutched in his hand, pointed it at the man's head, and fired twice. Both shots found their mark, blowing the top of Carlos's head off.

"See that, Gavin?" Chet shouted. "Now that's shooting like a Moran!"
Gavin didn't answer.

"Gavin?" Chet's grandfather lay on his back, clutching the side of his
head. The shrapnel had shredded Gavin's chest and shoulder, taken off an
entire arm, had torn the man wide open. Gavin had caught the bulk of the
shot, and Chet understood then and there that he'd done it to save him.

"Oh, Jesus, Gavin." Chet scooted over to the man, reached for him,
hesitated, seeing the wound, the huge gash running along the side of his
head. The bone was smashed and small tendrils of silvery smoke seeped
from the injury.

"No!" Chet cried, grasping the wound in his hands, trying to hold his
grandfather's skull together, trying to stem the escaping ba. He glanced
over to where his satchel lay on the ground several feet away, wanting to
grab it, to get some ka, but not daring let go of the wound, not even for a
second.

Gavin clutched his hand. "Chet, listen. Senoy wants one thing . . . your
daughter's blood . . . they both do. Remember that." More and more of the
tendrils of smoke slithered through Chet's fingers. Gavin's speech slowed,
his words becoming slurred. "Don't . . . don't give him a chance to play
you. Just kill him . . . straightaway. Swear it." He clutched Chet's shirt,
tugged him close. "Swear it."

"Yeah. I swear it."

Gavin nodded. "And when you do . . . while he is dying, speak my
name to him . . . let it be the last goddamn thing he hears." Gavin slid his
hand into the inside pocket of his coat, pulled out the key, and handed it to
Chet. "Go. Go save your daughter, Chet."

The smoke billowed out around Chet's hand, drifting upward, joining
the others as the dead and dying passed, a cloud of unfettered souls lost to
the wind.

Chet clutched the key, felt a hand on his shoulder. "I am sorry, Chet."
It was Yevabog. "Your grandfather, he turned out to be a good soul." She
was staring at the key.

Chet slipped the key away out of sight, set a hand on Gavin's chest.
"Yeah . . . I believe he was a good soul. I truly do."

## CHAPTER 87

I s that him?" Veles asked, gazing upon Gavin's body.

Yevabog nodded. "He's the one that saved us."

"I know this one," Veles said. "It was he that cut me down at the Edda gathering. He was a brave and fearsome warrior, for one must be truly stout of heart to attack a god."

"His name's Gavin Moran," Chet said. "He's my grandfather."

Veles looked up at the drifting clouds. "Sometimes death's end is hard to find. Maybe his story is not over yet."

Mary walked up carrying a spear, the God Slayer, the very one that had cut Veles down. She tossed it onto the ground, on top of the blunderbuss and the demon lord's sword.

"Where is Sekhmet?" Veles asked.

"She's gone into the canyon," Mary replied. "She's hunting them down, every one of them. We will not be seeing her again until the last demon is slain."

Chet scanned the ruins; bodies lay everywhere, the smell of burning ka thick in the air. All was quiet now, the screams and moans silenced. Veles had seen to it, killing every man and demon left behind, sparing none, not even the wounded.

"Mary," Chet said, "do you know what happened to Ana? Back at the temple? Did you see her?"

A shadow crossed Mary's face; she slowly shook her head. "I'm not sure. The last I saw of her, she was running for the river. Then the men were upon me." She started to say something more, then just shook her head again.

Chet nodded.

The great stag picked up the blunderbuss. "This will go to the bottom of the river. Then I ride to Hel, Duat, and Hades to gather the ancients. It is time for the gods to wake up, time to remind the netherworld what happens when we are angered." Veles tossed the blunderbuss into the back of a wagon, then picked up the demon sword, holding it high. "It is time to go to war."

# CHAPTER 88

Chet searched through the twisted remains of the demons until he found what he was seeking: a bandolier of bullets that matched the caliber of his revolvers. He'd taken his grandfather's long coat and now slung his arm through the bandolier, wearing it across his chest in the same fashion as desperadoes from the old West. He then rifled through the pockets of the dead souls, taking any ka coins he found until he had gathered several dozen. He took no shame in this; if there was one thing Gavin had taught him, it was to be prepared. He was on his way back to Moran Island, to Trish, and he intended to do whatever necessary to ensure he made it.

Chet trudged back to the wagons, where he'd tied his horse and found Yevabog waiting for him.

"I thought you were going with Veles?"

"I would like to see that key."

"What key?"

"Chet, you know you can trust me."

"I'm not real big on trusting anyone these days. Especially a god."

She smiled at him. "You have learned much then."

A leather cord hung about Chet's neck; he tugged it up from out of his shirt. The key dangled from its end. Yevabog reached up and ran one finger slowly along its length. "It is real," she said in awe. "You intend to try and cross back. Yes?"

"I have to."

She nodded. "What a thing it would be to see the moon again," she said absently.

"Cross with me."

She tore her eyes away from the key, looked at him. He thought he caught a touch of fear on her face. "Put it away," she said, urgently. "Put it away and let no one know you have it."

He slipped it back under his shirt.

She took a quick glanced about, spoke softly. "Keep it well hidden. It is a true key between worlds. Gods, demons, souls, all would go to any length to attain it . . . to have a chance to escape purgatory and return to the world of the living."

"And you wouldn't?"

She let out a sigh. "It is why I came to you. To go with you . . . to even take the key from you if I had to." She smiled coyly at him. "But now, with nothing in my way . . . I am unsure. No, I am *scared*. Yes . . . of what I might find. A world with no place for the likes of me." She shook her head. "And I fear them. The angels. They have no mercy for my kind. And mankind too, they would see me as a monster now. I would never be able to rest without fear." She seemed to be contemplating her own words. "Even so, I must admit . . . the temptation is great. It just might be worth being burned at the stake to have the chance to walk among the trees again, to smell the sweet spice of life."

"Still got your mind set on Lethe then?"

She was quiet a moment. "No . . . no I do not." She sounded like this surprised her. "Not anymore, not after seeing the Red Lady in all her glory. By the moon was she ever magnificent." Yevabog tapped the knives she now wore in a belt draped across her chest. "It felt good to kill those who deserve death . . . a final death. It reminded me of what it is to be a god." There was a spark in her eyes now. "I will go with Veles . . . try and rally the gods. Perhaps I will eventually seek out a few new husbands and begin anew. Who knows, maybe one day mankind will wake up and turn their backs on these One Gods. Then there just might be a place on earth again for one such as I." She laughed, then her face grew serious. "Chet, I would warn you though. Purgatory does not give up her dead easily. What you are attempting to do . . . even with that key . . . it will be dangerous . . . perhaps impossible."

"I have to try. There's no other choice. Not for me."

"The key gives you many choices. It can even open the gates of Elysium. Chet, after what you have seen, would you walk away from eternal paradise?"

"I wasn't real good at keeping promises when I was alive. But, just before I died, I made one last one. And I intend to keep it. I don't care the cost."

"You do not understand." She clasped his hand and a vision bloomed, golden fields beneath a honey-colored sky, a warm breeze fluttering through trees full of songbirds, and in the distance, the laughter of men, women, and children, their voices calling to him, filling his heart with joy. She released him and he gasped, shutting his eyes, trying to hold on to the vision. "*Elysium?*" he whispered.

"Yes, and it awaits you if you choose it."

"How?"

"Elysium Fields lie on the border of purgatory. Its gates are barred to all but those deemed worthy by the ancients. Chet, you hold the key."

He pressed the key against his chest.

"It is a journey," she said. "But not impossible. I would be glad to guide you."

He met and held her eye, then shook his head.

"How can you walk away from paradise?"

"Because . . . it *isn't* . . . it could never be, not so long as Trish or my daughter could end up lost in purgatory or somewhere worse."

A sly smile spread across Yevabog's face. "Ah, Chet, you have indeed learned much. Too many Heaven-borne souls find out too late that eternal bliss comes at a price. Their scriptures and verses never illuminate just how one can be in joyous rapture while their mothers, fathers, children burn for all eternity."

She sighed. "The river will let none return. Should you try to return by boat or ferry, her hands will reach up and drag you down. There are many gods and souls alike whose bones rest upon the river bottom that can attest to this. You must use the bridge."

Chet recalled the dilapidated structure hanging above the river. "The one in Styga, near the ferry?"

She nodded. "Once, there was just the river and the river let none return. But the first gods built several great bridges and for a while the world of the living and the dead lived side by side. It was a golden age and the netherworlds were a place of magic and splendor. It was the One Gods that closed the gates. Locked them shut. Even an angel's blade cannot cut through those doors." She touched Chet's chest. "But . . . that key you hold, it comes from Heaven itself. It *will* open the doors." She was silent for a moment, appeared deep in thought. "Beyond that I do not know, nor can I predict. I do know that there are many forces aligned to stop souls from leaving, that Mother Eye herself might burn you to a cinder."

Chet shrugged. "As I said, I don't have any other choices."

"Sometimes our destiny is not our own."

"I need to be going," Chet said, untying the horse.

"Chet, listen to your grandfather. Senoy *is* a monster. If you are to have any chance at all it will be to strike quick and fast. Use the knife he gave you. It is from the wars in Heaven and is meant for the divine. Show him no mercy. As for Lamia, she has survived since the earth's beginnings. I can only hope the Fates are on your side." She stood up on her hindmost hands, kissed her fingers, then touched them to Chet's lips. "My blessings might not be what they once were, but I send them with you just the same."

Chet smiled at her, pulled himself up into the saddle, and rode away.

# PART SEVEN

The Lilith

It's just your hand," Dirk said, enjoying the look of horror on the man's face. Dirk tried to remember how many years he'd worked at Tubby's Carwash dealing with guys just like this, guys sporting the same nose-up-their-ass haircuts, telling him he'd missed this spot or that on their overpriced foreign sports cars. *Well, death has a way of evening things up,* he thought as the man dropped to one knee and began begging to keep his hand. Dirk liked that, liked it when they begged. *Things are sure running smoother with those witches out of my hair,* he thought. Carlos had promised that they wouldn't be coming back, none of them, had even gone so far as to say that the Red Lady's time was coming to an end. Dirk tried to imagine how things would be without them sticking their noses in everything. *We'll do whatever the hell we feel like. Make our own damn rules, our own damn laws.* Carlos had promised they'd all be lords and kings soon. Dirk smiled. *Imagine that, me, a former mop hand at Tubby's . . . a king.*

The man pushed his wristwatch into Dirk's hand.

"No," Dirk said. "I told you, it's a piece of junk. Look, I'm not going to say it again: you want to keep your stupid hand, then start swimming."

The man finally seemed to get it and stood up, walking slowly over to where Big John Thomson waited with the cleaver. There came a flash of the blade and the man's hand fell into the basket with all the others. The man let out a cry and stumbled away clutching his wrist.

"Fun's just beginning," Dirk called after him. Dirk caught the ferryman glaring at him and gave him a crisp salute. The ferryman grimaced and looked away. Dirk smirked. *Thick bastards still think this is their show.*

Dirk looked at the cheap watch, at the time. *It's noon somewhere,* he thought. *Sun's probably out, people sitting down to a good meal.* He sighed. *God, to see the sun again, to taste . . . to taste anything.* He heard a cry, a child, and cringed. *Hell, why do these souls have to keep bringing these miserable brats across? So fucking tired of dealing with them.*

It was a woman—usually was—a homely-looking lady who appeared to be in her late thirties. Of course Dirk knew that didn't mean a lot, she could easily be in her nineties. She clutched the infant tightly to her breast as she came forward, arms about it as though she could somehow shelter it from death itself.

"Here, lady," Dirk said, reaching for the baby. "Let me make things easier for you."

She pulled the infant back. "No. I'll carry her. I don't mind."

He let out a sigh. *Really, really getting tired of this.* "Lady, here's the deal, it'll cost you two pounds of flesh. That's your hand and the kid's arm. You going to pay that?"

She stepped back horrified.

"That's what I thought. So just give over the little tyke right now."

The lady shook her head. "No. No, I won't."

Dirk punched the woman, hitting her square in the face and knocking her to the dock. The lady landed hard, and the child began to wail.

Dirk nudged one of the guards. "Give me your club." The guard handed it to Dirk and he stepped to the woman, looming over her. She looked up at him, horrified, and he wondered why he was putting up with any of this nonsense. Wasn't he the one making the rules now? "Y'know, lady, I think I've been too nice for too long. I think it's time to put things in order."

She tried to get away, scuttling backward while still clutching the baby. Dirk chuckled, couldn't help it. She just looked so pathetic, half out of her wits with fear and doing that one-armed crab crawl. He swung, aiming for the baby, but the woman twisted, trying to protect the child, and he caught the woman on her shoulder, knocking her over. And still—she held on to the child.

Dirk considered himself a pretty good hitter back in high school. Now might be a good time to show these guards how to handle a club, how to knock one out of the park. He pulled back, sights on the woman's head—

"Leave her alone, asshole!" someone called in a loud, stern voice.

Dirk stopped, stopped because there was something in that voice that sounded like real trouble. He turned, saw a man standing on the stairs wearing a long coat, the sort of coat Wyatt Earp might've worn. It took Dirk a moment to realize he knew this man. "Well I'll be damned." It was the redheaded kid, the one Carlos was looking for. And for a moment Dirk wondered if the kid had an older brother, because the figure standing before him appeared older, harder, his face weathered, his eyes severe, the eyes of a man who'd seen more than his fair share of bad.

The guards and souls all fell quiet, all watching the kid as he walked down the steps, his boots clumping on the stones. He stopped a few feet away and set eyes on Dirk. "Let her by," he said, his voice cool and calm.

Dirk snorted. "You have to be kidding." Dirk thought about taking the bat to the kid, but there was something in the kid's eyes he found unnerving; he seemed just a little too sure of himself. *What're you up to?* Dirk glanced behind the kid, up on the stoneworks, but saw no sign of the sisters, or anyone else who might be backing him up. "All right, boys. I want you to break his arms and his legs. Then we'll see how well he can swim."

The guards started forward and the kid withdrew a gun from his satchel. No fancy play, no slick moves, just calmly, almost casually tugging out the biggest fucking revolver Dirk had ever seen. The kid leveled it at his guards, his hand sure and steady. The guards stopped.

Dirk was liking this whole thing less and less. "All right, you little twat," Dirk barked. "Here's the deal. You turn around right now and we'll let—"

The kid shifted the gun on Dirk and fired. The slug punched Dirk in the gut, knocking him off his feet and onto his rear—the blast echoing up and down the river.

"*AH, FUCK!*" Dirk screamed, clutching the giant hole now in his stomach. "Ah, Jesus. Jesus Christ!" The pain doubled him over. "*Kill him!*" he shouted. "*Kill the fucking son of a whore!*"

The guards didn't move.

"Throw your weapons in the river," the kid said in that same infuriating cool, calm voice.

The guards hesitated, glancing back and forth at each other.

Chet pointed the gun at the closest man's head. "I won't ask again." He was looking for a reason to shoot them; they all saw it plain as paint on his face.

The guards complied, tossing their clubs, swords, spears, and knives into the river.

"Carlos, the Colonel, most of the rangers," the kid said. "They're all dead. Veles burned them up. Veles and the Red Lady . . . they're real pissed off and on their way here to clean shit like you out of the gutters. To put it in their words, they're coming to remind souls why they should be afraid of the gods. My suggestion would be to get as far away from here as you can get before they arrive. That sound like good advice?"

The guards all nodded.

"And you just might wanna tell your friends as well. Because anyone found wearing a green coat or hanging around these ferries is gonna be made an example of."

The guards nodded again.

"Good. Now get."

The guards left in a hurry, heading up the stone steps and disappearing down the road.

The kid walked up to Dirk.

Dirk tried to push to his feet, but the pain wouldn't let him, started to crawl away, found only the river.

The kid pressed the barrel against Dirk's forehead. "I'm giving you a choice. You can swim or eat the next bullet out of this gun."

"Wha . . . what?" Dirk said, struggling to get the words out. "But . . . I can't swim."

The kid kicked him, drove his boot into Dirk's side, knocking him backward. Dirk found himself half hanging over the ledge, looking down into the black river. He heard a cackle, glanced up to see the ferryman laughing at him.

The kid placed his boot against his side.

"For the love of Jesus!" Dirk cried. "*No!*"

The kid kicked him over.

Dirk hit the water, sank down deep into the cold, dark current. He heard them, the wails, the moans, growing louder and louder. He clawed at the water, fighting for the surface. A hand caught hold of his ankle, then his wrist. Then they were all over him, sinking their long nails into his flesh, his mouth, his eyes, pulling him down, deeper and deeper.

## CHAPTER 90

Chet stood before the doors of the bridge, towering doors made of iron and wood, true wood, not bone, doors made for giants. He walked up the short flight of steps and laid a hand on one. The wood, petrified by age and the elements, felt hard as stone. He gave the door a shove. It did not budge.

There was no knob, no handle, only a gilded key plate. Chet glanced back toward the cobblestone street where several fresh souls wandered aimlessly with dazed, lost looks upon their faces. He fished the key from around his neck and slid it into the slot. The fit was perfect. He turned the key and there came a deep grinding, like huge gears turning.

Chet stepped back, waiting. When nothing else happened he pressed against the door. It didn't budge. He pushed harder, putting all his weight behind it. It was like pushing against a gale, but the door slowly ground inward. He withdrew the key and stepped in, the door falling shut behind him with a resounding thud, showering him with dirt and debris from the rafters above.

Crumbling arches and columns disappeared into the gloom ahead, giving Chet the impression of an endless nave of some long-abandoned cathedral. Mother Eye's amber glow shifted in through the tall, narrow windows lining the walls and down from several collapsed portions of the vaulted roof.

Chet couldn't keep Yevabog's words out, her warnings of forces aligned against him and Mother Eye setting him to flame. He swallowed hard and started forward, up the slight incline, stepping over and around the fallen chunks of stone and broken tile, avoiding the portions of the walkway that appeared ready to give way to the river below. He stopped once, peering down through a hole in the path, saw only the fog swirling beneath him, wondered what would happen to him when he crossed, if the river would change him back to pure spirit?

He pressed on and Mother Eye did not burn him, no thunder or lightning, no wall of fire; angels did not come down and smite him. The only sound was the low moan of the river below and he felt oddly peaceful, as though he were the only soul left in existence. The bridge began to slope downward and Chet allowed himself his first breath of relief. Shortly thereafter he saw the doors just ahead.

He did not need the key to leave. When he pulled the doors inward, they simply opened. He stepped out onto the far shore and they fell shut behind him.

He laid his hands on his chest, then his face. "I'm whole," he said. "Solid." He touched the knife, the key, relieved that all had crossed with him.

Faces, dozens of curious faces turned toward him, the long parade of ghostly souls slowing, stopping, staring at him in confusion and wonder. The questions started. "What's going on? Where are we? Which way should we go?" and on and on. Chet paid no heed, marching down the steps, wading into the throng of souls. They had no substance and he moved through them as though they were smoke. Many reached for him, tried to touch him, but could not. Some ran from him, others followed him, peppering him with questions. He kept the river on his left, following its bank and keeping a keen eye out for the shadowy jellyfish creatures as he walked through a world of gray. He saw a few infants here and there, tried not to look at them, tried not to think what would happen to them.

After about an hour he came to the first trail leading up into the cliffs above. He started up, then stopped. *No,* he thought, *doesn't feel right.* He continued on, passing two more such trails. At the third he headed up, feeling sure it was the way; it was as though his bones were calling to him.

He climbed the steep trail until the river was lost in the mist far below. Onward he went, ever upward, one cavern leading into another, each progressively smaller than the last, meeting fewer and fewer souls until at last he was alone.

He heard a voice, turned to see a woman wearing a simple knee-length dress, her hair in disarray, walking toward him. He recognized her from his journey down.

"Have you seen my baby?" she asked, her eyes desperate.

"What's your child look like?"

"A little girl . . . her hair is—" She seemed to be trying to remember. "Blond . . . no, auburn . . . maybe." She became distressed, her lips quivering. "It's hard to remember."

"Yeah. I've seen her." Chet peered deep into her eyes. "She's waiting for you. Follow the trail down until you come to the river. Search for her along the river trail. You'll find her there."

The woman's face lit up. "Oh, bless you! Bless you!" she said, scurrying away, heading down the trail.

Chet hoped she would find a child, one of the lost ones, that maybe the two would bond and keep each other company. He watched until she was gone from sight, then continued upward.

The trail branched off repeatedly, and at each junction he would stand still with his eyes closed until he felt them, his bones, like a soft current tugging at him.

As he marched through the seemingly endless caverns he tried to formulate a plan, a strategy for dealing with Senoy. He would use the knife, as Yevabog had said, that much was clear. He'd seen what the blade could do against gods and demons alike. He just needed the right opportunity and one way or another he intended to make one. *"I'm coming to get you, Trish,"* he whispered. *"And nothing, not man, angel, or demon, is gonna stop me."*

The caves narrowed until they weren't much more than consecutive tunnels, the only light coming from the small pools of gray mist. Soon he was crawling, trying to make his way along in total darkness. He slipped out the knife, relying on its faint glow to see by. The tunnel ended in a shaft. He clawed his way upward, using the knife as a pick to help pull himself up.

At last he came into a small cavern and saw them, just like Joshua had said he would—his bones, shimmering above him.

## CHAPTER 91

Senoy leaned against the oak tree, neither asleep, nor awake, neither dead, nor alive, merely holding on, trying not to fade. A feeling came to him in the form of a voice, one that only he could hear. He let out a gasp, stood upright. *"The key,"* he whispered. *"Oh, sweet above. The key."* He closed his eyes, concentrating. It was him, the boy, Chet. He had it. Senoy was certain.

The angel stumbled down to the graveyard, so weak now that even walking was an effort. He reached out, above the gate of the cemetery, until his hand struck something solid. There came a slight glimmer, the ghostly outline of a wall as the shroud lit up momentarily, then faded. He pressed an ear against the barrier, listening, hoping for another sign that the boy had the key. He stayed like that until his shadow grew long.

"You okay there, Mr. Senoy?"

Senoy opened his eyes and looked over at Joshua, who was watching him from behind a gravestone. Senoy let out a sigh. "As good as one can be under such circumstances." He pushed away from the wall, all but collapsing onto the stone bench next to the graveyard.

Joshua glanced furtively about, then ventured out from the graves and took a seat next to Senoy.

"Joshua, I believe our friend Chet has found the key."

Joshua's face lit up. "Why, Mr. Senoy, that's wonderful news. Ain't you happy about that?"

"I am. Just so very tired, that is all."

"I'm sorry you ain't feeling so good."

Senoy could see the child was deeply concerned for him. Senoy had never cared much for humankind. It was hard for him to reconcile why God would favor these flawed creatures, these tailless monkeys, over the angels. But he found he couldn't help but like this boy. *Why then had I lied to him? Told him he was trapped within the shroud, when the spell only kept the divine at bay. Why had I not escorted him past the demons, walked him down to the bridge so that he might escape?* Senoy studied the boy's large, compassionate eyes. *Because . . . because he brought me comfort.* And that was all there was to it. He'd kept this child from Heaven for almost half a century for a little comforting. *I should feel shame. Yes. So why do I not?*

"Well, when Chet get's here with that magic key of yours, I'm sure Miss Lamia can fix you up like you said."

Senoy nodded, thinking of her sorcery with blood and the key and its ability to unlock spells. It would take time. Lamia needed to heal first, ration the baby's blood. He felt sure she would keep the mother alive, for a year at least—the baby feeding off the mother, Lamia feeding off the baby. Then when Lamia was ready, she'd take the child, drive out its soul. There'd be no hurry, because once he had the key, he'd no longer have to fear her leaving him, as she lusted for its power the way he lusted for her.

And the boy, Chet, he was damned. One way or another Hell awaited him. Lamia's demons would most surely see to his end. Senoy found he cared little, his mind turning to how wonderful that rush of warm blood had felt coursing through his veins all those long years ago. *The world will be our playground, Lamia. Two immortals sharing a thousand mortal lives.*

# CHAPTER 92

I made it," Chet said. "Oh, Lord. I made it." His elation only lasted a second, because he knew he wasn't home yet. He still had to rise, had to find his way up. He recalled Joshua saying that going up was the hardest part, that he had to concentrate on his bones a long time before he could rise. But Chet understood that Joshua was pure spirit. He wasn't. He was ka and he feared things wouldn't be so simple.

He set his hand against the roof of the cave. It wasn't dirt, more of a wavering glassy rock. He assumed then that he wasn't truly in the ground below the graveyard, not as one would think. He guessed he was in a place where the two worlds intersected, that he could no more dig his way up than someone could dig their way down. But Chet thought there might be another way. He tugged the key out from his shirt, started to draw a circle, the way that Gavin had shown him, but he needn't, for when he touched the key to the ceiling a square shape lit up beneath his bones. The door was already there.

He kissed the key, hoping for the best, and touched it to the glowing mark in the square's center.

The square became translucent.

"Stars," Chet cried. "Oh, God, stars!" Chet quickly reached up, clasping dirt and roots and pulled himself upward. He got one elbow up, then the other, caught hold of a gravestone, and hauled himself into the world of the living.

# CHAPTER 93

Chet lay on his back, clutching the key to his chest, staring at the moon and stars as though they were the most wonderful things he'd ever seen. He inhaled deeply, smelling the marsh, the dirt, the leaves, and for a moment forgot everything else. *Heaven,* he thought. *Earth* is *heaven.*

"*Chet,*" someone whispered.

Chet sat up. It was Joshua, the boy's face full of joy. He put his finger to his lips. "*Gotta keep quiet, Mr. Chet,*" he said in a hushed voice. "*We don't want them demons to hear.*"

"Is she still alive? Is Trish still alive?"

"Yes," came another voice. Senoy stood just outside the iron gate, his eyes brimming with tears, his face in disbelief. He too spoke softly. "Chet, by Heaven above you have come back. You have done it. You have saved us all." He stepped closer and his hand hit something unseen. There came a momentary glow revealing a ghostly barrier ringing the cemetery. Senoy stepped back and the glow faded. "Quick, Chet, the key," Senoy demanded. "Bring it to me." It was then that Chet realized that the angel couldn't cross into the graveyard.

"Where is she? The baby? Did she—"

"Yes. Yes," Senoy said, with growing impatience. "The baby is fine. They are all in the house. Now bring me the key, my knife, and let us go free them." Senoy glanced anxiously about, eyeing the shadows. "Chet, we do not have much time."

Chet stood, slipped his hand into the satchel, as though searching for the key, instead grabbing the hilt of the knife. He walked slowly over toward the gate. "How do we kill Lamia?"

"Do not worry, Chet. I will take care of her. I just need—"

"I think they're having a party without *us*," came a guttural voice.

"Sure looks that way," came another.

Billy and Davy stepped from the shadows, their boyish guises gone, their scorched skin covered in thorny scales, their faces hungry.

Senoy snapped about, his face stricken. He raised his hand above his head. "I give you fair warning. Leave now or I shall smite you both."

The symbol in Senoy's hand began to glow, but the two demons continued forward.

"*Back,*" Senoy hissed through his teeth. Chet could see the strain on his face as the soft blue light intensified, drifting toward the demons.

The demons halted, shielding their eyes, but Chet saw no sign of fear.

Senoy's hand began to tremble, causing the light to flicker. The glow dimmed.

Billy laughed. "I got a feeling your smiting days is done, angel man."

Senoy backed up until he was pressed against the barrier, setting it aglow. "Chet," Senoy snarled, keeping close watch on the demons. "Give me the knife. Now, before all is lost."

Chet slid the blade from its sheath.

The demons followed the ever-diminishing ring of light, closer and closer.

"Give . . . me . . . the *knife,*" Senoy demanded, his voice shaky.

"How did you become flesh?" Chet asked.

"*Give* me the knife."

"Did you drink her blood? My mother?" Chet caught it then, beneath the strain, just a flash, but it was there on the angel's face—the undeniable look of a man caught in a lie.

"Chet, now is not the time. I will explain all. Just give me the knife."

"I would like to hear it now."

"Chet," Senoy gasped, his hand shaking as though bearing a great weight, the light flickering. "Please, *please*—"

Chet drove the knife through the ghostly barrier, plunging it deep into one of the angel's eyes, two quick, hard jabs. Senoy screamed, stumbled away, clutching his face.

The light died and the demons' eyes blazed in the darkness. They howled and leapt for Senoy, knocking him to the ground, tearing into him, snarling and snapping, all teeth and claws. Senoy wailed as they ripped into his groin, tore open his stomach. But the angel wasn't done. He let out a powerful yell, a battle cry, and there came a concussive blast of light from his very core. It kicked both the demons backward, slamming them into the wall surrounding the graveyard, lighting up the field. Chet ducked back, but the blast didn't pass through the wall.

For a long moment nobody moved; slowly Chet raised his head.

The two demons lay motionless in the grass, their skin and scales smoldering. Senoy lay near the bench, his hands clutching his own chest, quivering as smoke drifted from his nose, mouth, and ears, up from all the great wounds riddling his body. He let out a weak moan. Chet leapt to his feet and slipped over the iron railing, striding quickly to Senoy with the knife ready.

The angel stared upward at the stars with his remaining eye. Chet dropped down beside him, pressing the knife against Senoy's neck.

"*No!*" Joshua cried. "Don't do it, Mr. Chet. *Please!* He's gonna save me. Gonna take me home to my mama."

Senoy's eye found Chet, his brows furrowed, and he tried to raise a hand, but it fell back to his chest. "I am an angel of God. An *angel* of God."

"You are a devil."

The words seemed to pain Senoy even more than his great wounds. His lips trembled. "You will never escape the wrath of the Lord."

"I'm already damned . . . *remember*?" Chet hissed, slicing the blade across Senoy's neck. But the angel's flesh was unlike any other, and Chet had to saw back and forth with great force until finally, Senoy's head rolled from his body.

Chet heard a low growl. He stood quickly and saw the bigger demon, Billy, standing between him and the graves. Davy, the smaller one, still lay in the grass, quivering. Billy raised a hand, his fingers sprouting jagged claws. The claws began to smolder, sizzle, glowing red hot. He smiled. "You got to the count of ten, Chet, to find a good hiding place. Better get running."

Chet didn't run: he locked eyes with the demon and started forward, one step, another and then another. Billy's smile faded, replaced by a low snarl. Chet charged, bringing the blade around in a wide arch, making his target, the demon's neck, obvious, just as Ado had shown him. The creature took the bait, leaping forward to meet the strike with its sizzling claws, committing wholly for the knife. Chet reversed at the last instant, bringing the blade down low, coming up under the demon as it shot past, the blade ripping into its stomach.

Billy spun round ready to come again, but hesitated, his brows cinched in confusion. He looked down at his belly, at the huge gash, at his own shriveled black guts as they spilled out onto the grass. Billy clutched his stomach, glanced over to his sibling as though Davy could somehow help him. Chet rushed in and the creature stumbled back, fell. Chet dropped upon the demon, slamming the knife into the creature's neck before it could so much as put up a hand—two quick hacks and the demon's head rolled away, hissing, its eyes two tiny pits of rage.

Davy stared at his brother's severed head, his eyes wide with horror.

Chet stood and came for him.

"No," Davy bawled, trying for his feet. He fell to his hands and knees, looking back over his shoulder terrified as he crawled, clawing at the grass, trying to get away. Chet's long stride quickly closed the gap.

"Stay away from me!" Davy shrieked. *"Stay away!"*

Chet drove his boot into the demon's rear, sending it facefirst into the dirt, stomped down hard on its back, pinning the monster, slicing and hacking until its head too rolled from its shoulders.

The only sound then was Joshua sobbing.

Chet looked up at the house, saw there were lights on upstairs. Lamia was there, he knew it, could feel her—knew she'd be waiting for him.

Chet dug one of the revolvers out of the satchel and started up the hill.

CHAPTER 94

Chet walked around the station wagon, knife in one hand, one of the revolvers in the other. He took a quick peek through the windshield, saw that the car was packed and ready to go. He glanced up at the second-floor windows. Candlelight flickered through the slits in the curtains, but all was dark below. He crept up the walkway, realizing he had no real plan other than getting in, finding Trish and the baby, then doing whatever he had to, to get them out.

He stopped before the steps, before the string of bells, wondering if he could cross in his current form, or if he would need the key? He slowly extended a foot over the bells. There came no sound and he met no resistance. *Am I truly flesh?*

He crossed over the bells and up onto the porch, over to the door. It was unlocked. He pushed the door inward and stepped inside.

The long hall was dark, the only light coming from the top of the stairs. Music drifted down—the crackling warble of an old phonograph—some bluesy tune.

Chet started for the stairs, then stopped, noticing a dim glow escaping from beneath the bottom of a door at the end of the first-floor hall. He crept toward it, peering into each room as he passed, trying to discern the shapes and shadows within.

Someone began singing along with the phonograph. It was Lamia, from upstairs, her song drifting down, echoing all through the house.

463

Chet was struck by how beautiful her voice was and for a moment, just an instant, he felt a tug, a longing for her. "*NO!*" a voice inside him shouted. It was Gavin's voice, like a slap to the head.

He forced himself forward and thought he heard a sob, pressed his ear to the door—another sob. "Trish," he gasped. He shoved the revolver back into the satchel and tried the knob. It was locked. The crying stopped. Chet slid the key from his pocket, touched it to the key plate, and there came a "click."

He opened the door, knife ready.

Trish sat on the bed in her nightgown. She looked pale and wan, with dark circles under her eyes. Slowly her expression changed from one of fear and apprehension, to confusion, then disbelief. "Chet?" she said, barely able to utter the words.

Chet nodded, putting away the key, moving quickly to her.

They embraced.

"Chet," she whispered. "Oh, my God, Chet . . . how?" She pushed him back, searching his face, then grabbed his hand in hers. He saw her flinch. "Chet . . . you're so *cold*." She pressed her hand to his cheek. "God, what's wrong?"

"Another time. We have to get you out of here." He pulled her up from the bed and started away. She didn't follow.

"I saw your body," Trish said. "You were dead. Chet . . . I don't understand."

"I died." He looked deeply into her eyes. "But I came back . . . that's all you need to know right now. I came back . . . for *you* . . . for our *child*." He extended his hand.

She stared at him a moment longer, then took his hand, following him from the room.

They moved quickly down the hall, heading for the front door. Lamia could still be heard singing on the floor above. Trish grabbed him, pointed to a closed door. "*She's in here,*" Trish whispered. "*Our little girl.*"

The door wasn't locked, and they walked in.

Dried flowers hung in bundles along the wall and a spinning night lamp projected stars across the walls and ceilings. A crib stood in the corner, draped beneath a canopy of white lace. Trish ran to it, throwing back the lace and lifting up a child with dark curly hair.

She brought it to Chet, smiled at him. "Isn't she beautiful?"

He nodded. "She is." Her eyes were open and looking at him. "She looks like her mother."

Trish beamed.

"What's her name?"

"Amy. It was my grandma's name."

Chet wanted to cradle her, to crush her to his chest, embrace both of them, to bask in their warmth, their love. This was his family, his flesh and blood, everything he'd fought so hard for. "We need to hurry," Chet said, putting an arm about Trish and leading her from the room.

The record still played, but Lamia was no longer singing. Chet switched the knife to his left hand and tugged one of the revolvers back out from the satchel with his right, as they moved quickly to the front door. They pushed out onto the porch, Chet keeping a close watch on the stairs behind them.

Trish let out a sharp cry and Chet spun around.

Lamia stood there on the porch, staring at them.

# CHAPTER 95

Stay the hell away, damn you!" Trish cried and whirled away from Lamia, intent on the far side of the porch, saw the figure, the towering shadow behind Chet. "*Look out!*" she cried as Jerome grabbed Chet from behind, snatching him up off the ground in a crushing bear hug, pinning Chet's arms to his side.

The gun went off, blasting a hole into the porch. Chet let out a yell, more of a growl, thrashed and kicked, but the big gardener didn't so much as flinch.

"*Run!*" Chet shouted.

Fingers, hard as roots, locked on Trish's arm, twisting her around, prying the child from her grasp. Trish fought to hold on but was helpless against the might of this woman, this creature.

The baby wailed.

"*Let her go!*" Trish screamed, trying to pull her back.

Lamia shoved Trish, sent her flying down the porch steps. Trish's foot caught between the planks as she fell. Something popped in her knee and pain shot up her leg. She let out a cry, clutching her knee.

Lamia cuddled the baby, touched her lip with one finger, cooing to her. "There, there now. You're okay. Mother has you."

The baby stopped crying as she always did when Lamia held her.

"Mama," came a voice, then many voices, the children; hundreds of them were coming up the hill.

Lamia walked up to Chet. "Chet, my lovely child. You left me. Why did you leave me?" Her silver eyes were pulsing.

Chet's face cinched into a snarl. "Fuck y—" He never finished, the anger, the rage, slipping away, replaced by . . . *what?* Trish wondered. *Love? Longing?* He looked like the children, the ones now gathering about the yard, staring at Lamia as one would their dearest love.

"I missed you," Lamia purred.

Chet nodded absently, his eyes never leaving hers—a man in a dream.

"Where's the key, Chet? My lovely sweet child." She traced a finger down his neck, his arm, slipping the revolver from his hand, tossing it out into the yard. She then took the knife, clutching it like a long-lost treasure. She nodded to Jerome and he sat Chet down, keeping one big hand on his shoulder.

"Chet, the key?"

Chet reached into his coat and pulled out a key tied to a leather cord, handed it to Lamia.

"Mama," the children called in their low drone. They were at the steps, pressing as near to the line of bells as they dared. One of them bumped the string; there came a light tinkle and they all fell back.

*The bells,* Trish thought. *The bells!* She snatched up the strings. The bells rang and the children fell farther back, their hands clasped to their ears. Trish tugged at the tattered strands, pulling them apart. The old yarn tore easily, snapping between her fingers.

"What are you doing?" Lamia shouted. "Stop that!"

The string fell apart, the barrier severed. The children's faces lit up and they pressed forward, rushing up the steps and onto the porch, giggling, laughing as they swarmed about Lamia, hundreds of them, all trying to touch her, their wispy fingers trailing along her hair, dress, arms, mouth, and eyes.

"*Get away,*" Lamia hissed. "*All of you.*" Her face twisted into something horrible, something cruel and wicked. "*Away from me!*"

## CHAPTER 96

Chet blinked. For a moment he wasn't sure who or where he was. He saw Trish on the steps and it came back to him in a flash. He spun, tearing free from Jerome's grasp, dropping and rolling across the porch. Jerome lumbered after him but was no match for Chet's speed. Chet shoved his hand into his satchel, found Gavin's other big gun, yanked it out, and fired. The slug tore a massive hole in the gardener's chest, sending him crashing backward over a chair. Chet was up and at the man, jabbing the revolver against the side of his head and firing again, blowing the top of Jerome's head off.

Chet turned the gun on Lamia, looking for a clear shot. She clutched the baby, glaring at him through the swarm of ghosts, then her eyes changed, turning into pools of affection, of tenderness and devotion, all inviting him in. "Chet, I love you."

"No," Chet said, but the gun grew heavy, and his arm began to droop.

More and more of the children swarmed around Lamia, creating a swirling shroud. She wavered and blinked, slashing at them with Senoy's knife. And each time she did, each stroke of her arm, Chet saw her not as the mother of all his longings, but as something dark, something sinister—he saw the lilith, her pulsing silver eyes with black slits slicing down their middles.

Someone was shouting. A woman. *"Shoot her, Chet!"*

Chet knew that voice. *"Trish,"* he whispered, tearing his eyes from Lamia, and when he looked upon Trish, on this woman he'd been through so much with, had suffered so much for, he remembered what true love felt like.

469

He raised the gun, stepped forward, and jammed it into Lamia's chest. He pulled the trigger twice.

The blast knocked Lamia into the wall. She shrieked, a horrible inhuman sound. Chet grabbed for his child as Amy began to slide from her grasp. The lilith's eyes flashed, blazing white hot. She yanked the baby back, slashing at Chet with the knife. Chet jumped back, hit one of the chairs, tripped, and fell.

Lamia spun away, stumbling into the house, clutching the baby to her chest. Chet raised the revolver and started to fire again, but didn't, fearful he might hit Amy. He leapt up after Lamia, but she slammed the door shut before he could reach her. He grabbed the knob, found it locked, and began kicking the door. On the fourth kick the door flew open.

Lamia was nowhere to be seen.

Chet entered the dark house. There was a trail of blood along the floor, leading up the stairs. He followed, reloading the gun as he went.

The children too, moved up the stairs, blowing past him like a light breeze. The blood led to a closed door at the far end of the hall, but he didn't need the blood to tell him where Lamia was; the children flowed through the closed door, physical barriers meaning nothing to them.

He heard a wail, then a baby's cry. He grabbed the knob, twisted, putting his shoulder into the door. The door wasn't locked and flew inward. Chet stumbled to a halt.

The only light in the room came from the hall, but it was enough to see that Lamia was dead, her eyes now black, unmoving, staring up at the ceiling. She lay in the center of a large pool of blood, the knife on the floor next to her and the key clutched to her chest. The baby, his child, sat cradled in the crook of Lamia's arm, wailing.

He could see where Lamia had hastily tried to draw a circle around her and the baby with her own blood. There were even a few arcane symbols scribbled along the edges. He shuddered to think how close she must've come to creating a door, to escaping to who knew where with the child, the key, and the knife.

Amy's cries grew and Chet stepped into the circle, keeping the gun on Lamia as he plucked up his child. He could see the massive hole the slugs had made in Lamia's chest, felt sure she was gone, but Chet had spent too much time in purgatory to be satisfied with that. He slid the blood-soaked key from her dead fingers, shoved it back in his pocket, then picked up the knife and deftly cut Lamia's head from her neck, her hands from her wrist, her feet from her legs.

He watched her for another minute before putting the gun and knife away, then stood, clutching the baby close to his chest, and left the room, heading back downstairs.

Trish had managed to pull herself to the door and when she saw Chet and the baby she let out a cry, began to weep. Chet knelt down next to her, handing her their child. She cradled it to her breast, clutching it as though she would never let it go again. After a minute of just hugging the child, she reached out to Chet, pulled him close, and they held each other, the baby between them. A feeling of utter fulfillment swept over him, of happiness beyond anything he'd ever known, and he clung to it, wanting to be sure to carry it with him always. *Always,* he thought.

Chet noticed a few of the children circling them, watching them with curious faces as though they too wished to join them. Chet wondered if these poor famished souls had ever known what it is to have a family. His own pale hand caught his eye, distracting him. *I'm flesh,* he thought. He'd not been able to see past all the obstacles, the key, Senoy, Lamia, to even consider what might happen if he made it this far. *Can I leave this place? Go with them? What would happen?*

More and more children surrounded them, all staring at Trish, a few of the bolder ones trailing their ghostly hands along her shoulders.

"Mama," one of them called, and the others began to pick it up. "Mama," they said, a chorus of moans, all looking at Trish. For a moment, Chet thought they must be mistaking Trish as their mother, or possibly wanting her to *be* their mother, then a chill swept him. *Oh, Christ,* he thought, *they aren't reaching for Trish.*

Trish stared at Chet in horror, then down upon the baby as she slowly lowered her to her lap. The little girl looked up at them with pulsing silver eyes.

Trish shook her head. "No," she uttered weakly.

Chet slipped the knife from the satchel. "*Set her down,*" he whispered.

Trish looked at the blade. "Chet? What—"

"Trish, put her down. *Now.*"

"No."

"That's not Amy," Chet said. "Trish, listen to me."

The child's eyes found the knife and a long hiss escaped her throat. Chet grabbed for her.

She kicked out from Trish's arms, tumbling onto the porch. She rolled onto all fours and scrambled away, moving quicker than should've been possible.

Chet was up and after her, tugging out the pistol.

"*No!*" Trish screamed. "*NO!*"

The infant sprang down the stairs, skittering along crablike on her hands and feet, her limbs twisting and bending in impossible ways. She glared at Chet with bulging, pulsing eyes, her lips peeled back into a toothless snarl, hissing like some misshapen spider from Chet's darkest nightmare.

Chet fired just as the baby reached the end of the walkway. The infant darted into the bushes leaving Chet unsure if he'd hit her or not.

"*STOP!*" Trish cried, the angst in her voice cutting Chet to the bone. He didn't slow down, chasing the baby into the bushes. He found no trace of her, but quickly realized he need not worry about losing her. The children flew past him, all following an infant toward the gravestones. Chet saw that she was crawling, that he'd hit her after all.

He ran up behind her.

She stopped, turned, looking up at him with those pulsing silver eyes. "Chet, I love y—"

Chet fired, the slug catching her in the chest, knocking her to the grass, almost tearing her in half. He let out a moan, as though it had been him that was hit, then walked up, his teeth clenched so tight his jaw ached. He held up the knife.

Her face softened, her limbs returned to form, and she reached for him with her tiny hands. "Daddy," she said, her voice now that of a little girl. "Please don't hurt me, Daddy."

He clutched the knife tighter and tighter, thought of Gavin, of a man forced to shoot his own two boys, could think of no torture worse. Gavin's voice came to him. "*It's not your daughter. Finish her. Do it now. Or hell will have no end for you.*"

"*God!*" Chet cried, his hands shaking. "Oh, God." He dropped to one knee and slashed the blade across the child's neck, severing her head from her body.

Lamia's eyes glared at him blazing with hatred, then slowly fell shut.

Chet turned away and began to sob.

## CHAPTER 97

Trish sat on the porch, watching as Chet shuffled along the walkway and up the steps. He walked over and knelt down beside her.

She searched his face for some sign of a miracle, some trace of hope, but found only grief and pain. She turned from him, began to sob again, felt his hand on her arm and pulled away. *"Don't,"* she whispered.

He let go, collapsing against the wall. "I'm sorry, Trish. So sorry."

She hardly heard him.

She wasn't sure how long they sat there, him staring at the moon, her at the blood slowly drying on her hands, but when he called her name again, she realized that the moon was gone, that she could see a hint of daybreak on the horizon.

"We need to get you away from here," he said. "I'm not sure how long I have."

When she didn't answer, didn't do anything more than stare blankly at the marsh, Chet put an arm under hers and lifted her up onto her good leg.

Trish had long since given up on the idea that this might all be a dream, a nightmare that she would awake from, but of late she'd begun to hope maybe she was insane, all of this some hallucination. "This isn't real, is it? I mean . . . it can't be."

"I don't know what's real anymore," Chet said, his face grim. He carried her down the steps, down the walkway to the station wagon, helping her into the passenger seat. He got the engine going and they drove away from the house.

Trish saw them as they passed the graveyard, the children, gathered around something in the grass. *It's not her,* she told herself. *Whatever is over there, it's not my baby.*

Chet stopped at the bridge, seemed unsure, but they crossed with no problems. A couple of miles farther, she spotted a porch light glowing in the early morning mist. It belonged to a small unpainted house, not much more than a shack. A thin trail of smoke drifted from the chimney.

Chet parked, helped her out, and walked her up on the porch. He knocked lightly upon the door.

She could hear talking inside and a moment later the door opened a crack and an old man with dark, deeply wrinkled skin and a head of burly white hair peeked out. "What 'cha want?"

"Just need a little help, sir," Chet said. "Hoping you could call someone for us."

The man looked them over, his eyes lingering on the blood staining Trish's nightgown. "Yeah, might be a good idea if I called someone. Y'all can wait on the porch." He closed the door.

Chet started to take Trish to an old bench when the door opened again. An old woman stood there. "You two get yourselves in here. Shouldn't be out in the chill like this."

"Thank you, ma'am," Chet said.

She led them to a couch while the old man dialed the phone, staring at Chet the whole time. *Like he's a ghost,* Trish thought, and she looked at Chet too, here in the light, at his pale skin, colorless lips. He looked hard and grim, like a cadaver.

The old man asked for an ambulance and the police. Trish wondered how long it would be before her father got word of her whereabouts.

"Stop your staring," the old woman said to the old man and he shot her a look, pulled her into the kitchen. Trish could still hear them. "Can't you see?" the old man said. "That man, he ain't right."

"I can see," the old woman said. "He's just lost, that's all."

"Trish," Chet said, "I have to go now. I have a promise to keep." And when she didn't reply he added, "I have to go back for her. For our daughter."

Trish searched his face. "What?"

"She's back there . . . with the other children. I need to go find her . . . see to it she's not alone."

Trish let out a small cry, covered her mouth with her hand. The thought of her little girl, like one of those ghosts, those poor tormented little children. "Yes, Chet. Go get her. Please." She clutched his hand. "And bring her here. Bring her to me. *Please.*"

He was silent a minute, his face pained. He slowly shook his head. "I can't do that, Trish. Just . . . well, there's just no way."

"Yes, you can. You have to."

The pain on his face deepened, a man who'd lost the world. "Trish, I love you. I'm sorry . . . so sorry." He stood, but she wouldn't let go of his hand.

"Chet . . ." She tried to find something else to say, but there was nothing. He was dead; so was her daughter.

"Listen to me," he said, speaking softly into her ear. "Lamia is gone. We stopped her. No more children are gonna have to suffer from her wickedness. Our sacrifices, our daughter's sacrifices, they mean something. Do you understand that?"

Trish thought she did and slowly nodded her head.

"Always, always remember that," he said. "Now, there's something you have to do for me, for your daughter. You have to move on, have to make the best of your life, because . . . because, life is precious . . . a precious fragile gift and you'll never understand just how precious until it's gone. So you have to live to your fullest, for me, for Amy. Have to put this nightmare behind you. Promise me."

Trish couldn't promise, couldn't see how she'd even ever be able to smile again.

"Promise me . . . *please.*"

Trish sucked in a deep, shaky breath and nodded.

Chet kissed her atop her head and stepped away. Trish still clutched his hand.

"Goodbye, Trish. I'll love you always." He pulled loose and walked to the door, opened it.

"Chet!" she called.

He stopped, looked back at her.

"I love you too," she said.

He smiled then, a real smile, and for one second, through the blur of her tears, he looked alive, like the boy she'd fallen in love with.

"Take good care of her," she said, the tears flowing freely now. "Okay? Take good care of our baby."

He nodded. "I will."

He left then, gently closing the door.

## CHAPTER 98

Chet stood on a ledge above the River Styx. He held a broom he'd taken from the barn, a head hung upon one end. It was that of his daughter, only it wasn't—it was Lamia. He'd wrapped it in rags so he wouldn't have to see her, see the long black tongue and glaring eyes. The key had opened the way back down, allowing Chet's physical form to descend, allowing him to bring Lamia's head along. The children had followed him, or her rather, all of them. It had been a long journey, several days at least, maybe weeks, hard for him to say as time felt meaningless in the ghostly Erebus, but the children had stayed with Lamia the whole way. Chet felt they would go anywhere she went, even to Hell. But he wasn't headed for Hell.

Chet carried one of the children—an infant girl—in the crook of his arm. She didn't really have substance, but clung to him just the same. Her eyes were like her mother's. He smiled at her, and when he did, she smiled back—every time.

A sack also hung from the broomstick. He propped the broom against a boulder, set his daughter down, and untied the sack. Three heads fell out—Davy, Billy, and Senoy. They were flesh, like him. He'd had to use the key to bring them down this far. Billy and Davy glared at him while Senoy stared sadly out at the dark misty river.

Chet picked up Billy and Davy, held them out over the bank. They gnashed and snarled at him, but when the current began to churn, when hundreds of tormented faces and mangled hands clawed at the surface below, they fell quiet.

007

9

9

7

Chet tossed them into the current. They hit the water, sizzling like hot coals, steam bubbling around them as they sank. The hands grabbed them then, tearing at them. Chet could see their eyes, those gleaming dots of fire as they were pulled deeper and deeper into the depths, could actually hear their screams of rage from far below.

Chet picked up Senoy.

"Chet, please. I understand I am culpable, that I cannot deny my crimes against you, my sins against God. But I, like you, was under her spell. You *must* see that. At least extend me the mercy of Lethe. Chet, I am begging."

Chet raised Senoy's head until they were eye to eye. "There's something I'd like you to take with you, to carry always. It's a name—*Gavin Moran.*"

Senoy flinched.

Chet threw the angel's head out into the river. Watched the current tumble it along until the hands caught it, gouging its eye sockets and tearing out its tongue, tugging it deep down beneath the black water.

Chet lifted his daughter, Amy, stood there cradling her ghostly form for a long time, the two of them just watching that slow-moving river roll by. There was no longer any sense of urgency. *Death's forever,* Chet thought, and allowed himself to look at the land, to really soak it in. *Purgatory is a majestic and solemn place,* he thought. *Terrible and wonderful. A good place for a soul to find himself.* "And," he said softly, looking at Amy, "maybe . . . one day, to find some kind of peace."

He picked up the broom and the children began to gather back around. He tried to count them, to even guess at their number, two hundred at least. But more now as Chet had picked up every child they'd found along the way, handing over those who couldn't walk to the older children, telling them to carry them along.

He continued down the path. When the other souls saw him—a dead man leading a host of children along with a head upon a broom—they stepped aside, watching in wonderment and awe. When the inevitable questions came, Chet simply told them to follow.

Chet came to the docks and waited. He didn't have to wait long. The barge rolled up out of the mist. The ferryman spotted Chet, the children, and a small smile snuck across his face.

## CHAPTER 99

They crossed, the children becoming flesh as they passed through the river fog, and for a moment all that mattered to Chet was that he could hold, truly hold his daughter, crushing her to his chest.

The embankment appeared out of the mist ahead and the ferryman rang the bell three times. The landing was empty, no sign of any souls, the baskets and crates, all gone.

The barge bumped up against the dock and Chet led the children off, both him and the ferryman helping those too small, or unable to walk, onto the landing. Once they were finished, Chet picked Amy back up, cradling her as he surveyed the children, wondering what his next step would be.

Three figures came down the stones steps toward them—hard to make out in the fog. Chet's hand dropped to his gun.

"You won't be needing that," the ferryman said.

Chet saw they were women, that they were dressed in black robes. The lead woman had a jewel set in her forehead. She saw the children and smiled at Chet.

"We've driven them away," Mary said. "The Green Coats. At least from the docks. The sisters are gathering here in Styga, coming from all over. The Red Lady will be here soon as well."

Chet heard more footsteps approaching, saw two more robed women striding quickly toward the landing. "Chet?" one of them called.

Chet squinted. "Ana?"

She pushed back her hood and he saw it was her. She embraced him. Chet's daughter made a cooing sound and Ana stepped back, looking at the infant, at all the children in amazement.

"Chet, what's going on?"

"It's a long story. Ana, I thought you were—"

"In the river."

He nodded.

"Oblivion can wait," she said. "There are things I need to do."

"The children?" he asked.

"Yes, the children. Life's more than flesh and blood. It's how you live. In a way, purgatory is a blessing, a second chance. I don't intend to throw that away." She watched the children. "I've found a purpose." Her smile made her look alive. "Chet, what about you? You could join us."

"Maybe . . . one day," he said, combing his fingers through his daughter's unruly dark hair. "But there's somewhere Amy and I need to go first." He looked to Mary. "Mary, which road leads to the Elysium Fields?"

# EPILOGUE

Joshua watched the sun slowly rise above the marsh. For more years than he could count, he'd wanted to take a walk down that way. He looked again at the headless bodies of Billy and Davy lying in the leaves, their shriveling remains smoldering in the daylight. *Are they gone?* he wondered. *Truly gone?*

He stepped cautiously from the graveyard, keeping a watchful eye on the bodies, stopping when he came to that of the angel. "Senoy?" he called, sure there'd be no answer because Chet had taken the angel's head with him, using the key to create an opening into the below. The fact that Chet was able to take Senoy from the island left Joshua wondering if the key had possibly opened the shroud. The boy searched the clouds for any sign of an angel.

"Mama, can you hear me?" He stood listening for a long spell, but when there came no reply he headed off along the drive. Joshua came to the marsh and took a seat on an old stump, watching the fiddler crabs scuttling about in the pluff mud. He studied the sky, waiting for the angels, sitting there until the sun began to slide toward the horizon. No angels came.

A rabbit hopped up to the stump and began to feed on a sprig of grass.

"How you do, Mr. Rabbit?"

The rabbit didn't answer.

"Starting to worry, y'know, that maybe them angels can't see me after all. That maybe that old shroud is still up. What'd you think?"

The rabbit hopped away and Joshua let out a long sigh. He watched the clouds awhile longer, then something struck him odd. *Senoy . . . why . . . he wasn't able to enter the graveyard.* Joshua hadn't known that. He realized now that he'd never seen the angel even try before. But there, at the end, Senoy *had* tried and the shroud had lit up, keeping the angel out. *Then how come it didn't keep me out?* Joshua was pondering this when another thought struck him. *Or in?* He jumped up, looking toward the woods in the direction of the bridge. He bit at his lip and began walking rapidly down the sandy road, excitement and apprehension mounting with each step. He passed through the woods. They were full of shadows, but he saw no fireflies. When he came to the bridge, he stopped.

"Mama? Are you there?" He searched the sky. Nothing. Senoy had told him they were trapped on the island, but he'd never said what would happen if he tried to leave. *And if that shroud* is *still there?* Joshua wondered. *What then? Would a wall of fire spring up . . . a bottomless blackness? What?*

He stepped up to the bridge, slid one foot onto it. Nothing happened.

He kept going, one cautious step after another, his hands groping the air before him. When he reached the far side he stopped again, staring at the straw dolls tied to the posts. "Mama, if you can hear me, please ask Jesus to let me cross on out of here."

He stepped off the bridge. No fire, no shimmering walls blocked his path.

"*Am I free?*" he whispered. "Mama, am I free?" He took off at a run, not looking back, not once, not daring to. Sure if he did, something would come after him.

He continued down the road, not slowing, until he came to a trail. The path was overgrown with bushes and vines, but he knew the way, following it until he came out upon a shack.

The roof had falling in and weeds grown up through the floorboards, but his mother's old rocking chair still sat on the porch. He stared at that chair, thinking of his mother sitting their shelling peas, smiling at him and his brother while they played in the yard.

"*Joshua,*" a voice called, sounding like the wind.

He turned, saw a light coming toward him from out of the trees. A woman walked out of the glow.

"Mama?" Joshua called.

She smiled, extending her arms to him.

Joshua began to tremble. "*Mama!*" He ran to her, ran into her arms.

She picked him up and hugged him tight. She smelled of honey and sunshine.

"Are you ready to come home?" she asked.

He nodded, wiping at his eyes.

She set him down, took his hand, and together they walked into the light.

# ACKNOWLEDGMENTS

When I started writing this novel I never stopped to consider the logistical challenges of my idea. I, like so many creatives, don't have time for such silliness. I needed to plunge in, chase my muse before she slipped away. I did not realize until later that in order to make my particular vision of purgatory believable, I would need not only to invent an entire history, a system of government, a political/social structure for both souls and gods, tie it into all religions, add some kind of monetary system, define magics and spells and powers, but also to invent a physiology for the dead, figure out if souls eat, drink, and if so, what. Can the dead die? If so, how? And, as with most mysteries, answering one question often leads to ten more. But the real question was what details needed spelling out, and which ones could simply be left in the background to keep from bogging down the story, and here is where Rebecca Lucash, my editor, stepped in.

However you end up feeling about this tale, you can be assured it is far better because of her stewardship, her attention to detail and logic, her intuitions of story and character. And for that, I would like to thank her. And if you happen to run into her, you should thank her too. Thank you, Rebecca.

Two other people were instrumental in this process: Robert Brom and Erika Hoel. And, if I were in charge of giving out medals, I'd see to it that they both received a very large, very shiny one for giving up several days of their lives reading an early draft of this novel, and for taking the time to give me much-needed input on where I was going wrong and ideas on how to make things better. Thank you, Robert and Erika.

And, as always, a much-deserved thank-you to Julie Kane-Ritsch for her friendship, enthusiasm, diligence, and for being such a smart dresser. Thank you, Julie.

# LOST GODS

ALSO BY BROM

*Krampus*

*The Child Thief*

*The Devil's Rose*

*The Plucker*

HARPER Voyager
*An Imprint of* HarperCollins*Publishers*